A CRUCIBLE
OF SOULS

A
CRUCIBLE OF
SOULS

Sorcery Ascendant Sequence
Book One

MITCHELL HOGAN

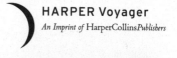

HARPER Voyager
An Imprint of HarperCollins*Publishers*

A CRUCIBLE OF SOULS. Copyright © 2015 by Mitchell Hogan. All rights reserved. Printed in the United States of America. No part of this book may be used or reproduced in any manner whatsoever without written permission except in the case of brief quotations embodied in critical articles and reviews. For information address HarperCollins Publishers, 195 Broadway, New York, NY 10007.

HarperCollins books may be purchased for educational, business, or sales promotional use. For information please e-mail the Special Markets Department at SPsales@harpercollins.com.

A previous trade paperback edition of this book was published in 2014 by the author.

Designed by Katy Riegel

Maps designed by Maxime Plasse

Library of Congress Cataloging-in-Publication Data has been applied for.

ISBN 978-0-06-240724-5

15 16 17 18 19 OV/RRD 10 9 8 7 6 5 4 3 2 1

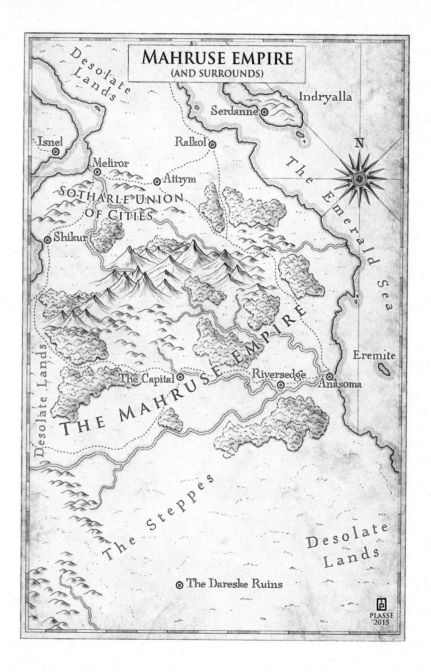

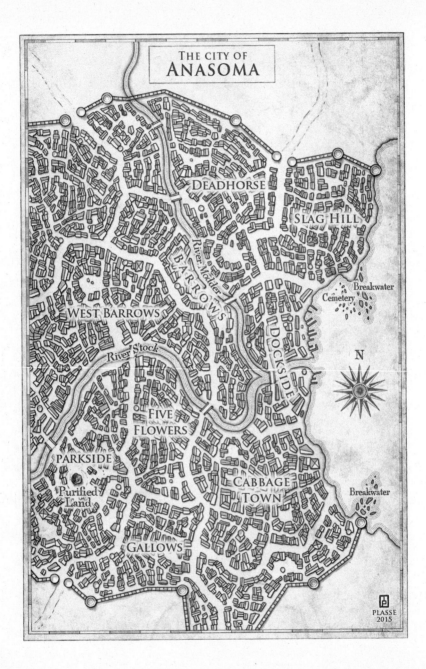

THE CITY OF
ANASOMA

DEADHORSE

SLAG HILL

River Medder

BARROWS

WEST BARROWS

Cemetery

Breakwater

River Stock

DOCKSIDE

N

FIVE
FLOWERS

PARKSIDE

Purified
Land

CABBAGE
TOWN

Breakwater

GALLOWS

PLASSE
2015

PROLOGUE

A trickle of blood oozed down the cold steel of Aldrich's sword. Drops splattered onto dry leaves, staining them red. He pressed his back against the old tree's gnarled trunk, rough bark scratching his skin through his shirt. Thirty yards away lay the still-warm corpse of the man he'd put down, one arm outstretched, reaching for a knife discarded in the undergrowth. There was a smell of wrongness about the body, and something odd about its appearance; it looked . . . denser, somehow.

Eyes closed and barely breathing, Aldrich waited, listening. All was silent.

A faint breeze blew over him, carrying the scent of apple blossoms from a nearby orchard and the cool dampness of an approaching storm. Leaves rustled in the wind.

He ducked his head around the tree trunk, saw no one else had followed the man he'd killed, and breathed a sigh of relief. Either stupid or overconfident, and he didn't think they were stupid. He wiped his sword clean on the man's cloak, keeping an eye on the forest, then sheathed the blade and hurried off to where he'd left his wife and child.

ALDRICH SAW THEM before they noticed him. He whistled softly and Iselle turned and gave him a relieved wave. They rushed to greet him.

"They're still coming," Iselle said, "and my crafting won't last much longer. If it rains, it's done for."

Nerissa clung to her arm, body slumped in fatigue. She rested her head on her mother's stomach, and Iselle reached down to stroke her hair.

It pained Aldrich to see they weren't bearing up well under the strain, not having his advantages. But he'd had to push them hard the last few days. Dust from the road covered their boots and leggings, and hollow eyes peered out from grime-covered faces. Three days on foot'll do that to you.

Iselle sighed and peered down the road toward a lichen-covered stone bridge, which crossed a narrow river; the light was already fading. She leaned on Nerissa's shoulder, causing the child to mumble in protest, and then relented when she realized what she'd done.

"Patience," Aldrich said, taking a sniff of the wind coming from behind them, noting the scent of sweat and unwashed bodies. He knew Iselle and Nerissa wouldn't be able to detect it. He also knew much would be resolved before the storm hit.

The day had started badly and gone to worse with shocking speed. If only he hadn't insisted on staying at an inn overnight, for their sakes. A mistake, because their horses had been stolen while they slept. Yes, he'd wanted shelter and rest for his family, but not at the cost of their lives.

Releasing Nerissa, Iselle cupped her hands and whispered a few words that were carried away on the breeze. Moments later, a small shape emerged from the trees, flying erratically. Landing in Iselle's cupped palms, paper wings protruding over the sides, the dark green dragonfly looked creased and worn, as if it had flown long and hard without rest. It never ceased to amaze Aldrich just what sorcery Iselle could perform merely by scribing tiny runes on the surface of a sheet of paper.

Aldrich beckoned Iselle and Nerissa to follow him, and they obeyed, though their limbs were already stiffening in the cool night air. As they reached the center of the bridge, he placed one hand on the hilt of his sword, loosening it in the scabbard.

"Head on into the forest. Keep moving. I'll join you later."

"Why? What are you going to—?" Iselle asked.

A knot tightened in Aldrich's gut. He feared she already knew and dreaded what he planned. He'd never doubted his abilities, but he'd often wondered how he would fare in the face of impossible odds.

"They're too close. We can't outrun them." He could have on his own, but Iselle and Nerissa lacked the stamina he'd built up from years of training. "You know I have to do this; I have to try and stop them. You know what'll happen if they get their hands on the trinkets. Try to make it through the forest. You should be able to avoid any search with your crafting." He gestured at her dragonfly.

"No! We should stay together. My crafting can keep them at a distance, and we can lose them. We can!"

Aldrich shook his head. It was time to make a stand. Delaying their pursuers would give his wife and daughter a chance at escape, and at least he would be doing something other than running. For a while at least, the hunted would strike back.

He pushed Iselle and Nerissa ahead of him. "Go now! I can hold them, perhaps kill them all, but you need to hurry."

Tears welled in Iselle's eyes. She wiped at them with the back of her hand.

"Don't you . . ." she croaked, breath coming in harsh gasps. "Come back to me . . . to us."

"I will. I promise." Aldrich placed a long kiss on the top of Nerissa's head, then pulled Iselle close into a fierce embrace, tasting the salt of her tears on her lips. Reluctantly, he broke away.

Iselle took Nerissa by the hand. "May the ancestors be with you," she said.

"And you. Go quickly."

He watched them cross the bridge, hastening along the road toward the forest. As they reached the trees, Iselle paused and glanced back. She reached inside her pocket and drew something out, throwing it into the air. It fluttered, hovering above her. She waved her hand, and the paper dragonfly flew back to the bridge, landing in a tree close to the river.

Removing his cloak, Aldrich flung it behind him, where it would not get in the way. Drawing his sword, he sat cross-legged in the middle of the bridge, facing back the way they'd come. Pommel and guard worn and chipped but blade still strong, the sword had seen him through many a confrontation and not a few battles. Etched along the first third of the blade from the guard were crafted runes. Without them, the sword was merely exceptional; with them, it was powerful—*more* than exceptional. Closing his eyes, he opened himself to the night, calming himself and clearing his mind.

Time passed. The moon broke through the clouds. Back along the dirt road, a shadow moved, then another.

Aldrich opened his eyes. Forty yards away stood a strongly built man dressed in dark gray, cloak and hair rippling in the wind. Like the first man he'd put down, this one looked solid, denser than normal.

"Greetings," called the stranger. "I see the two ladies have gone ahead without you. Never mind. I'm sure they're not far. We can catch up with them later."

A shadow detached itself from a tree beside the road and solidified into another denser-man, moving in behind the first.

Five at most. If there's more . . . Aldrich brushed the thought away. It didn't bear thinking about.

A woman joined the two men before the bridge. More shapes left the concealment of the trees. The group grew to thirteen, spreading themselves in a half circle around their leader. Still more remained hidden in the forest, flitting shadows, the scrape of leather, and the clink of metal betraying their presence.

Taking a deep breath, Aldrich achieved a state of calm within himself, and the nightscape became clearer, its details sharper. For all his life, he had followed the Way of the Sword, and the one thing he dreaded was to die having failed. His masters always said, if you were resolute and your spirit strong, you could not fail. Correct in theory, but sometimes reality had a way of pitching you on your ass and making a fool of you.

You will not fail, if you accept death. Aldrich had never feared death . . . only not being good enough.

Adjusting his stance, he moved into an upper attitude guard. Taking another deep breath, he released it through his nose and became one with his spirit.

"There's no need to fight," said the leader. "You are but one man against all of us. You will lose. The light from the moon is hardly enough to see by—at most you may kill one or two of us, and for what? Why throw your life away for nothing?"

As he spoke, his followers shifted, drawing their swords, ready to cross the bridge at his signal.

He has no idea, Aldrich thought. *Too little light. They should have guessed by now from the chase we led them on. For this mistake, they'll pay dearly.*

"Perhaps you're the ones throwing your lives away," Aldrich said, raising his voice to carry to them all. "I can't let you pass. I'm sworn to guard them with my life. If I die here, then so be it. I'm sure all of you would like to see another sunrise, but if you continue on this path, some of you won't get the chance. If I were you, I'd turn tail and flee."

The leader smiled, baring his teeth. "Kill him," he said to the darkness, and his followers flowed around him onto the bridge.

Aldrich leaped across the intervening space in a heartbeat, faster than any normal man could move. His blade blurred in the night, shifting fluidly. He beat through the guard of a stocky man and sliced open his throat, moving on to the next before the others had time to react.

The leader cursed in a harsh tongue Aldrich couldn't understand, but he gathered they realized what they faced now.

Spinning first to the left, then to the right, he cut one man's arm to the bone, then drove his sword through another's guard into his chest, yanking it out before more closed in. As he'd planned, the width of the bridge restricted his opponents to coming at him no more than three at a time.

Stupid. No time for thrusts. Keep cutting. Blade a glittering whirlwind, he held the next three men off for a moment, searching for weaknesses in their style.

There.

Aldrich stepped in. Sparks flew as swords clashed. His opponent stepped back, as if to withdraw, then sprang in with his sword. Aldrich twisted, avoiding the blade. He expanded forward, flowing like water, and his attack found flesh. A heartbeat later, two more were down. He cut left and right without giving the denser-men a chance to take the initiative, trying to drive them together so they would hamper each other.

A sharp pain and spurt of warm wetness warned him of a cut along the ribs.

They were good, but he knew his spirit was stronger . . .

He danced forward fluidly, adopting the lower left attitude as the next denser-man attacked. Blade swooping up to clash against a sword, he parried to the right. His return stroke from above buried itself deep between a shoulder and the neck, and another body dropped lifeless onto the bridge.

Steel sliced deeply into Aldrich's thigh. He gasped at the burning agony and clutched at the wound to stem the flow of blood, but in that instant, they came at him again. His sword was a dead weight in his grip, and a blade passed his feeble attempt at a parry, carving his shoulder open to the bone. Ignoring the searing pain, he beat the weapon away as another blade nicked his scalp.

He struck out vainly before his whirling sword cut across a face. Throwing himself at them with no more thought for defense, he split an arm open, wrist to elbow, then drove his sword tip through the jaw of another.

A thrust from the side plunged deep into his stomach. There was an icy, biting coldness, and numbness spread from the wound. Weakness rose in him.

Aldrich slumped to one knee and dropped his sword. Every breath sent shards of glass lancing through his lungs. He placed a hand on the ground to steady himself, then looked into the eyes of the approaching leader.

Forgive me. I have failed you both.

Steel flashed—

ISELLE STUMBLED, SOBS racking her body. Only the need to keep Nerissa safe stopped her grief from overwhelming her. Tears trailed down her face and dripped from her chin unchecked.

"Mama, what's wrong?"

Nerissa's voice sounded faint. Iselle's awareness was divided: half on their plight, and half looking through her dragonfly's eyes. She brought her focus back for a few moments. "Nothing, darling. It's . . . nothing. Keep going."

Sending her senses back to her crafting, she once more surveyed the bridge, where their pursuers congregated. A broad-shouldered swarthy man with a nose like a hawk's beak, who looked to be the leader, prodded Aldrich's body with his toe. Iselle suppressed a moan.

The man shook his head at the bodies heaped around the swordsman—his final attempt to save his family. Ten dead or wounded.

"Touched by the ancestors," the man said. "What ill luck."

His remaining followers gathered around Aldrich's corpse steaming in the cool night air. He reached for the sword, but his hand stopped short, and he hissed, obviously feeling the virulence of the force Iselle had imbued the blade with. He slid his boot under it and lifted his foot. The sword sailed over the side of the bridge into the water with a splash, where it sank into the cold depths.

"Come. We still have to catch the woman and child."

At his words, Iselle snatched back her awareness and sent her dragonfly a number of commands. It bunched its folded legs and launched itself into the air. Circling the bridge once to gather information through its crafted eyes, it took in the crimson auras of the men, then flew toward the forest, passing the two sent on ahead.

Knowing there wasn't much time, Iselle tried to hurry Nerissa, but her daughter no longer had much strength. The forest path hindered their steps with its roughness. Roots snaking from nearby trees seemed to spring up in the dim light to tangle their feet. Iselle lifted Nerissa, cradling her, moving farther into the forest.

There was barely any moonlight to see by, and the last thing they needed was a twisted ankle. They entered a clearing, where a fire pit ringed with river stones lay off to one side. She paused for a moment to catch her breath, pushing Aldrich's death to the back of her mind. She tried to work out where the path started on the other side. She shuddered and swallowed, suppressing sobs. After a few moments, she drew herself up.

"Nerissa, come closer; we have a problem. Stay near me, for the time being. I'll tell you what you need to do soon."

"Yes, Mama."

As they turned to run again, Iselle stopped. Two dark figures stood between them and the path on the other side of the clearing. They did not move, clearly satisfied she would not try to escape. She knew that to flee blindly into the forest now would be of no use; their pursuers would capture them with ease. Acting calmer than she felt, she removed her cloak and wrapped it around Nerissa, warding her from the night's chill.

She was too young to be caught up in this.

Iselle knelt and looked into her daughter's eyes, stroking her cheek with a thumb.

"When the bad men come, I'll distract them. Then you have to run as fast as you can. Can you do that for me, Nerissa?"

She removed her rings from her fingers, one glinting silver in the moonlight, the carved bone of the other dull and looking of no worth. She threaded both onto a chain from around her neck, which she placed over Nerissa's head, tucking the rings beneath her clothes. "Hold on to these. Whatever happens, you must keep them safe."

"Yes, Mama. I can run," Nerissa said. "But I'm so tired . . ."

"Don't worry, little one. When the time comes, I'm sure you will be able to run like the wind. Stay close, and remember what I've told you.

Run as fast as you can when you think they're not looking. Follow the path, and do not stop, even if I'm not with you. I'll catch up later."

Iselle reached into her shirt and removed a sheet of paper. Jet black, its surface was covered in patterns of tiny silver runes that ran along straight lines. Every master sorcerer who passed the tests knew this crafting. It was one of the last trials that had to be undertaken: the making of a finality. With nimble fingers and practiced deftness, Iselle began folding, all the while murmuring under her breath.

More men emerged from between trees, entering the clearing and moving to surround her and Nerissa. Iselle looked around frantically for an escape, then stopped as the broad-shouldered man pushed past two others and took a few paces toward her.

"What have we here?" he said. "Perhaps you are lost and in need of some assistance? My brethren and I would be only too glad to help."

Iselle's mouth was dry. "No, thank you," she replied, still folding.

"A pity."

His use of *brethren* revealed to her far more than she wanted to believe. These weren't just hired flunkies, and they might even have sorcerous powers of their own. Her crafting would require much more energy than she'd first thought and might take too much from her once it was released.

Breath catching in her throat, Iselle forced herself to speak. "All right, all right, you've got us. Take the rings. But let us go."

She lifted a palm, on which sat a small paper box. Silver runes glittered on the surface.

The man eyed the box warily. "Perhaps we *could* come to an arrangement . . . I'll accept the rings. Give them to me."

"Take them . . . and may the ancestors damn you for eternity!"

She threw the box high into the air, where it hovered above her head and spun, runes sparkling in the moonlight.

The crafting gyrated faster and faster, its movement creating an eerie keening sound that rose in volume. A sharp crackling noise filled the clearing, and tongues of fire danced around the box.

At a gesture from the man, his men charged toward Iselle with naked blades, howling in alarm.

They were too late.

Iselle shrieked, raising her hands above her head. A mounting gale whipped her hair in every direction. Lightning flashed from her hands and shot into the box. She felt herself failing, strength leaching from her under the immense strain until she had no more to give.

She collapsed, looking up at Nerissa trembling and cowering in fear. *Run*, she thought in despair, seeing her daughter standing there, staring wide-eyed at her.

Run!

THE GALE STOPPED suddenly, as if it never was. With a thunderous crack, the box burst apart. Nerissa gasped in horror as silver lightning ripped through the clearing, arcing from one man to the next, blistering skin and turning veins black. A shock wave rolled across the ground, throwing up clouds of dirt in its wake, knocking the men from their feet. They made terrible sounds—screams and roars—and they twisted and jumped as the lightning forked into them. Smoke billowed from skin and clothes.

All movement ceased. Misshapen mounds smoldered on the ground. Swords remained gripped in the blackened hands of burnt corpses.

The breeze from the approaching storm blew the dwindling smoke from the bodies toward the river. A sob squeezed through Nerissa's lips, and her chest felt so tight she could hardly breathe. She bent over and gently touched her mother's shoulder. She didn't stir.

"Oh no! Oh no! Oh no! Please wake up! Please . . ."

With a crackle, Mama's body shifted and rolled over on the ground, scorched grass crumbling beneath her.

Nerissa looked around at the gruesome scene. Moonlight and shadows turned the clearing into a nightmare. Stifling another sob, she put one hand to her mouth and bit down hard on her knuckles, drawing blood in an effort not to scream.

She reached out with her other hand and touched her mother's body. It was hot—far too hot—and she knew she was alone. Tears streamed from her eyes. She heard her mother's voice in her head: *Run as fast as you can!* But she was so tired; she was afraid her legs wouldn't work properly.

At the thought of resting among the corpses, terror flooded through Nerissa, filling her with strength. She fled into the forest, diving into a briar close to the edge of the clearing, heedless of the thorns scratching and poking at her exposed skin. She wriggled low in the dirt, making herself as small as possible. For long moments, she lay there, scarcely breathing, not believing what she'd seen. Not *wanting* to believe her mother was gone—and would never come back.

Movement at the corner of her eye startled her, and her heart thumped in her chest.

Monsters.

Suppressing a cry of fear, she worked herself farther into the dirt.

Drawn by the smell of meat, a pack of wolves warily circled the clearing at the tree line. The largest wolf edged toward a corpse. One paw after another, it crept forward, barely stirring the ashes with each step. As it leaned closer, nose scarcely touching the remains, a charred hand latched onto its throat.

Nerissa whimpered.

Snapping and snarling, the wolf strove to break away, but the hand wouldn't let go. Another hand reached up and traced a symbol on its fur, and it stopped struggling. The symbol reminded Nerissa of the runes Mama used on her craftings.

The rest of the wolves stared as the blackened body shifted, lifting its head to rest against the one it had captured.

On the ground, the hand sketched another symbol. Cold air pressed down on Nerissa and hummed. The wolf's fur shriveled, skin tightening, molding to its bones. The man inhaled, and then, covering the beast's mouth with his own, he breathed out, and the wolf's body expanded back to normal shape. The corpse's blackened skin cracked, flaking off in sections onto the earth and revealing a grayish crust underneath. The skin on one arm sloughed off entirely, leaving bones, which dropped to the ground and shattered into fragments.

Whimpers from the wolves echoed in the dark night. The strange new wolf shuddered and howled. It stumbled to the left, then sank to the ground. After a few moments, tongue lolling, it staggered to its feet and stood, trembling.

As the wolf loped down the trail toward the bridge, the others of its pack started to rip into the dead men. Nerissa covered her ears and sobbed into the dirt. Her mother's voice whispered in her ear: *Run as fast as you can. Run like the wind . . .*

Nerissa scrambled to the back of the brambles and out the other side. And she ran. Ran as if all the evil spirits of the ancestors were going to eat her and crack her bones.

CHAPTER 1

Gliding sideways across the hard-packed earth, Caldan shifted his wooden sword to a middle guard position. Beads of sweat trickled down his back, and he was breathing hard after the last exchange. He tried to ignore the pain in his shoulder where he knew a bruise would appear by the night's end. He squinted to cut the glare of the sun, keeping his eyes on Amara.

Her grin, which had appeared when she broke through his guard, grew broader. Her stance indicated she was ready, sword held high, body still. Caldan's sore shoulder would not prompt her to relax her attacks on him.

Quite the opposite.

She's too good, he thought. All his training the last few weeks, and he hadn't improved.

"Again," he said, moving his guard to a low position, then springing at her. He made a rapid series of cuts, which she easily parried as he tried to force down her blade.

She effortlessly blocked his sword and battered it aside. Penetrating his guard yet again, she slammed her blunted tip into his chest. Grunting, he clutched at his ribs where she had marked him and dropped to one knee, hand touching the ground to steady himself. He drew a slow, shallow breath, which was all he could do above the pain.

Master Krige stepped toward them, black robes flapping in the breeze. He laid a hand on Caldan's shoulder and slapped him gently, open palmed, against the side of his head. Caldan bowed before the Master of Blades, listening.

"You must always move *in* the pattern; every movement must be within the pattern."

"I'm sorry," Caldan managed to gasp out. "I guess I'm not in the right state of mind for this today."

A firmer slap rocked his head to the side.

"Well, I hope you are in the correct state of mind in your first real fight—otherwise you will be dead." Master Krige looked at Amara, leaning on her sword and still grinning. Sweat from the exertion trickled down her face and soaked her practice shirt.

"Enough for today," Krige said, waving a hand to dismiss her.

She mockingly saluted Caldan as she walked to the weapons rack and replaced her sword.

Krige sat cross-legged on the ground, expression unreadable. "What did you do wrong? Or more important, what did she do right?"

"I . . . I'm not sure," Caldan said. "I was trying to force her down so she couldn't attack, yet her sword came straight through mine, and she hit me. I can't explain it."

"Your mind was not in it. You were trying to defeat her at the start, trying to push her sword down so she could not rise. You were not achieving the spirit of the attack. You must tread with the body, with the spirit, and with the sword. You must achieve the spirit of not allowing her to attack. Since you did not do this, you did not cling to her enough, and she cut you. Remember this well, for you must strike with all things in harmony to win, not just with your hands."

"I still don't understand what you mean by spirit."

"One day you will. Amara doesn't fully understand either, but she is very close. Meditate on it tonight."

Caldan nodded. "She is good, though."

"Yes. You could certainly use more practice if you want to defeat her."

Scowling, Caldan stood. "Is that all for today, Master?"

"Yes. Think about what I said tomorrow, whenever your bruises pain you." There was laughter in Krige's voice. "Harmony. Spirit and body together. Go now. I am weary of young would-be swordsmen tripping over their own feet."

Caldan gave a slight, painful bow and shuffled gingerly to the water barrel. As he did, a hot flush ran through his body and he trembled. As with the other times this had happened in the last few weeks, it dissipated quickly to be replaced by a chill. His head began to ache.

Removing his sweaty, dirt-stained shirt, he cupped his hands and splashed cold water over his body, then scooped another handful over his face. The headache lessened, and he bent over the barrel to drink. As he did so, a hand grasped the back of his neck and dunked his head under the surface. For a moment Caldan struggled against the force holding him down, until it relented and he jerked his head above the surface.

Taking a breath and squinting water out of his eyes, Caldan came face-to-face with a smirking Jemma.

"Anything interesting down there?" she asked, releasing her hold and folding her arms across her chest. She leaned back against the wall.

Caldan took another breath, suddenly conscious of how pretty she looked. Sunlight brightened her face and emphasized her dark eyes; her folded arms tightened her tunic, accentuating her curves . . . He looked away, heat suffusing his face. *Stop it,* he told himself. *She only wants to be your friend.*

Then why did he have the feeling that she stared at him whenever he turned his back? Aware of his bare chest and Jemma's frank appraisal, he pulled his shirt on, not wanting to take the time to dry himself off first.

Jemma looked at the barrel and picked at a splinter with a fingernail. There was a faint glow in her cheeks.

"Thanks for the dunking," Caldan said. "I needed one after that workout."

"Looks like you managed to get hit a few times. What happened?"

"Nothing. Just a lack of concentration."

Jemma snorted. "Since when have you ever lacked concentration? You're one of the most single-minded and stubborn people I know!" She brushed his arm with her hand. "Is there anything wrong? Something you haven't told me?"

Caldan shook his head. "No. It's probably the pressure the masters keep piling onto me. I just need a hot soak in the baths, a good meal, and some wine to relax and take my mind off things for a while."

"And good company, I hope," she added.

"Dominion tonight? I reserved a board for a few hours; even managed to get one of the more secluded ones. I was going to practice a few things on my own, but if you'd like a game . . ."

"Sounds good. I'll see you after dinner, then."

Caldan watched as she sauntered off. Why did life have to be so complicated? Her brother, Marlon, would scorn him even more if he thought they were seeing each other. Marlon cared for nothing but himself and how people saw his family.

Scratching his head, Caldan despaired at the state of his shirt. He would have to find a clean one before the evening. Which wouldn't be a problem for most of the other students, but for him it was something of a dilemma.

For while he wasn't as bad off as some of the poorer families in the city, he would never be considered as fortunate as the students—and definitely not one of their equals. His meager possessions were testament to this. And yet, as he walked to his room, he realized it was also the first time he'd cared enough about Jemma's opinion to try to make a good impression.

"CALDAN? ARE YOU there?"

Caldan peered around the door of his wardrobe and saw Brother Maksim, one of the initiate monks at the Monastery of the Seven

Paths. Maksim shielded his eyes from the glare of the sun, which shone through the only window of the small room and reflected off the polished floor. His eyes roamed over the sheets of paper scattered on the cot. As he inspected Caldan's room, a shape wobbled in his direction toward the edge of the windowsill, a lion created from many precise folds of a dark brown paper. Tiny black runes dotted the animal, whose steps faltered, then stopped. Maksim frowned at the crafting.

"Yes, Brother," Caldan replied. "What can I do for you? Sorry about the mess; I was just looking for something." He gestured to the pile of clothes on the floor.

Maksim glanced at the discarded clothes, then the paper lion, before returning his gaze to Caldan. "The masters would like to see you tomorrow, before the evening meal. Please make yourself presentable, and remember, you are here on their sufferance, so behave."

The younger monks liked to point out his position at every opportunity, and Caldan bristled at his tone.

"You might not consider me part of your order, Brother, but I've been here a damn sight longer than you or any of the other initiates, and most of the junior brothers. A word of advice: Don't think of me as an outsider. The masters certainly don't."

The monk hesitated, weight shifting from foot to foot. "The masters have not been in a good mood these last few days. Perhaps they want to discuss your place here once you come of age in a few months, but I cannot say."

Caldan read the thinly veiled hint in Maksim's words. On a few occasions, the masters and he had argued over what he could and couldn't do as a ward of the monastery and not one of the initiates. Maybe they'd come to a decision about his future.

"Perhaps. We'll just have to see, won't we? Thank you, Brother. Is there anything else?" he said, bowing.

Maksim shook his head, turned, and left.

Caldan considered the pile of clothes on the floor and sighed. Bending over to pick them up, he decided that whatever the masters wanted, it must be important; he was never called to a meeting with them if they didn't consider the matter significant.

Stuffing the clothes into the bottom of the wardrobe, he moved to the basin on the table and washed his hands and face with tepid water. He dried off with a towel and ran his hands over his shaven scalp. It was stubbly and needed shaving again. A regular annoyance. He'd started following the monks' convention and shaving his head because he thought it showed them how grateful he was for their assistance, but now many of their habits rubbed against the grain. He wondered what they had decided regarding his place here. He was easily the best at most of the practical arts, like Dominion and crafting, and no matter how many stupid tasks they gave him, he never complained. He never asked why the master's courtyard needed to be swept three times a day; he just did it. His skills were progressing rapidly—a few of the masters had already hinted they would be pleased to continue his instruction after he came of age, if he was willing.

Lost in thought, he became dimly aware of a wisp of smoke rising from his paper lion. A flame erupted from the surface, rapidly spreading until the animal was engulfed.

"By the ancestors!" he cursed, waving the smoke away while fumbling with the latch and pushing the window open. He grimaced at the smoldering pile of ash. The fifth one that'd burned out within as many days. He was missing something.

But what? He swept the remains out the window.

A bell sounded four times, indicating the hour. Hurrying out the door, he hastened to meet Jemma, rubbing at the ash staining his hands.

SPARKS WERE FLYING, but the noise of the spitting fire went largely unnoticed by Caldan. Firelight danced around the room, twisting shapes and distorting perspectives. Yasmin had tagged along with Jemma, and she knelt by the fire, poking at the burning wood in the grate. As Dominion wasn't one of Yasmin's strengths, the game between Jemma and Caldan held little of her attention. With her fair hair and pale skin, she was one side of a coin, and Jemma was the other.

Head tilted to the side and brow creased in concentration, Jemma remained focused on the game board. It was of far better quality than the ones Caldan normally played on. It was big, too, four paces to a side and the top of the third tier out of reach unless you stood on a stool. Most of the pieces were of carved obsidian, but there were also a few in either clear, rose, or smoky quartz in the shapes of mythical creatures and stylized humans.

After his last two moves had staggered her, leaving her plans in ruins, she'd wandered around the board to examine the game from all angles, forehead furrowed. She obviously had no idea what tactic she could employ to get out of the bind she was in, and must have been aware her position was extremely fragile.

She doesn't realize she's already lost.

Hoping to be gracious, Caldan offered them refreshments, a platter bearing an assortment of sliced fruits along with a bottle of wine. Not used to having one person to entertain, let alone two, he was unsure whether he should concentrate on the game or on the women. He found himself hovering too close to either Jemma or Yasmin on occasion, making small talk as best he could, and at other times completely ignoring them while he analyzed the game.

Jemma picked up a piece of pear and frowned at him. "Curse you! Why do you have to be so good at this?"

Caldan smiled deprecatingly and spread his hands. "Hard work and no small talent."

Jemma muttered something under her breath. She chewed on a fingernail, then the pear, and glanced distractedly at Yasmin. She took a step closer to the side of the board for a better angle. She had only one extra move left, while Caldan still had five. He'd decided before this game to handicap himself by not using any of his, although she didn't know that.

Yasmin helped herself to some dried figs. "Looks to me like he has a hold on you. In the game, I mean."

Jemma wrinkled her nose. "Next time, you can stay in your room and study on your own, for all I care."

Yasmin sniggered. "Don't get nasty because you've been outplayed.

You've never won against Caldan, and that doesn't look like it's changing anytime soon. Besides, I'm glad I came. Someone has to keep an eye on you two to make sure no rumors start. A young man and woman alone in a room for a few hours . . . Who knows what people would think? You should be more careful of how often you're seen together."

"There is nothing wrong with playing Dominion," Jemma said.

"Hmmm," Yasmin said. "But you have to agree, you two being together at night might get people's tongues wagging. Marlon, for one, would be quite upset if he heard about anything untoward."

"People will think what they want to, no matter the evidence. Isn't that right, Caldan? There's nothing going on between us."

His face grew hot and he turned away from them, making a show of studying the board. "Er . . . yes."

"See. Nothing to worry about."

"Let's hope Marlon thinks the same," Yasmin said.

"Well, he only has to ask me if he wants to know the truth." Jemma glanced at her fingers and wiped them on her pants.

Out of the corner of his eye, Caldan saw her turn to him.

"I haven't worked out a way to escape your clever little ambush. I guess you've won."

"Yes, sorry," he said.

Yasmin rolled her eyes at Jemma.

"It was a fine trap, though," Caldan said, "for the spur of the moment. I'll have to remember it for another time. If you'd seen my strategy a few moves earlier, it would've been much closer."

Jemma nodded. "Some of the masters have said you might surpass them one day; not as gifted as the famous student Kelhak, but certainly exceptional."

"No one could be as good as Kelhak," Caldan said, shaking his head. "Sometimes I think he's only a myth."

Yasmin munched on a fig, licked her lips, and shifted in her chair, maneuvering closer to the bottle of wine. "What's in this, Caldan? I could use a good drink after watching you two battle it out. The monotony was getting positively dreary."

"Yasmin," Jemma said, "you know how you get after one glass of wine. We wouldn't want Caldan to think you're a drunkard, would we?"

"Oh, one sip can't hurt. Besides, that night I think I ate something which made me sick."

Jemma stepped over to the table and scooped up the bottle before Yasmin could reach it. Breaking the seal, she took a quick swallow, eyes closing in obvious delight as the taste hit her tongue.

"My, my, Caldan. Where did you get this? You mustn't waste your good wine on us; we're not worth it."

Yasmin reached for the wine. "Speak for yourself. I, for one, fail to see why we shouldn't drink good wine when it's being offered for free."

Caldan looked down and smoothed a crease in his shirt. "It was a gift from another friend. I couldn't even handle half the bottle. Better to share than to waste."

Jemma hesitated, then stepped over to him and looked him in the eye. "Another 'friend' who had a problem and needed someone to help them?"

"Yes. It was something small. For some things, the city guards are . . . restricted. Sometimes a different approach is needed to solve a problem."

Jemma let out an exasperated sigh and glanced at Yasmin, who sat there, eyebrows raised.

"How long have you been doing this?" Jemma asked. "And what problem can't the city guard deal with?"

"Like I said—little things. People have problems, that's all. The guards need proof before they can act."

"What, and you don't?"

"No, it's not like that. Some things I can see better, that's all. I'm more observant than them. I see patterns a few steps ahead. It's what I'm good at. Sometimes I have to act before the guards can be alerted, but mostly I can find a solution to a problem, and the guards do the rest."

"So you *work* for the guards?"

"No . . . not exactly. People ask me to do things when they haven't got enough proof to go to the guards, and they give me whatever they can for my crafting services. Silver ducats, food, wine—whatever they can spare. Although some families don't have much, so I try not to take anything from them."

Jemma walked to the game board and picked up a rose quartz piece carved in the shape of a strange furred creature with wings. She ran her fingers over the details, not speaking for a few moments. "Even if it's not against the emperor's laws, you could still get into trouble with the monastery for undercutting the Sorcerers' Guild. This island is still part of the Mahruse Empire."

Yasmin remained silent for a few moments, then spoke. "Perhaps our friend here needs something to spice his life up. Or perhaps he is a man of noble nature, helping the less fortunate and all that. Do you see yourself as a good person, Caldan?"

"I just want to help. It can be tough for some people outside the monastery. Most students with their fat purses stuffed full of ducats from their families don't realize how hard it can be to live in the real world."

Jemma placed the piece back on the board and smiled. "Enough of this profound talk. Pass the wine, Yas. I'm parched, and my brain needs relaxing after such a difficult game."

Yasmin handed the bottle to Caldan instead. "Caldan should have some first. He earned it, after all."

Jemma wrinkled her nose at her friend and laughed. "All right, the winner of the game should get something for his trouble, I guess. Pass it over here when you've finished, though."

Caldan took the bottle, wiped the opening with his sleeve, and took a sip. It was good. He wondered if Yasmin would keep quiet about what she'd heard, as she was Jemma's friend and not his. If she wanted some reason to hurt him, she could easily do it now.

Stop it, he told himself. *She couldn't care less about what happens to you.* The warmth of the fire, and the wine he had consumed, helped him relax. He was enjoying the evening so far and was content to exchange small talk with Jemma and Yasmin as the night wore on.

The logs burned to coals in the grate, and the silences between conversations grew. Eventually Yasmin yawned, and Jemma flashed her a smile. They both stood.

Jemma leaned over Caldan as he slouched in his chair, one leg swinging, eyes half-closed.

"We have to leave now. We have a crafting class in the morning and don't want to perform less than our best, what with the end-of-year places still being decided. Don't finish the rest of the wine by yourself, okay?" She moved on toward the door, saying, "Good night."

Yasmin waved over her shoulder as they went out the door. Traces of their perfume left lingering in the air were gradually lost in the scent of the smoldering fire. Struggling out of his cozy chair, Caldan placed a few sticks on the coals and stirred them to life.

Without warning, an agonizing pain ran through his legs. He staggered, clutching at a wall to steady himself. Then as suddenly as it had appeared it was gone. Caldan sucked in a breath through clenched teeth and slowly straightened. This wasn't the first time: he'd experienced similar pangs a few times over the last month. Perhaps a growth spurt? He wasn't sure.

He wandered over to the board and started laying the pieces in their velvet-lined holders. After a few moments, he realized his actions were reverent, as if the carved game pieces contained some meaning. As he put the last one away, leaving the box open for the next players, he paused. Once again he was conscious that although his mood lightened considerably while the girls were around, it had descended back into despondency now that he was by himself. Jemma and her attempts to befriend him served only to highlight the times he was alone.

But she does *want to be friends, so maybe I don't have to be alone.*

With this surge of hope, he headed for the door, tracing the edge of the board with his fingers. Sighing, he hesitated before a smoky quartz piece. He rested his hand on its head. It resembled a thin man clothed in feathers, clutching something in his right fist. He was named the Wayfarer. Nobody knew what he represented, whether he was based on an ancient hero or villain, or what he was supposed to have clenched in his fist. The piece was unpredictable on the board, its properties varying from one colored square to the next, depending on where it was positioned. Lately, it had started featuring in many of the strategies he had been employing in his games, surprising many; because of its volatility, it was often not utilized. The Wayfarer had become his favorite now, its instability adding an additional element of difficulty he used to keep games interesting.

Caldan gave the room a final glance to check that all was in its proper place. Satisfied, he closed the door and made his way toward his room, oil lamps lighting the corridors. Some sleep would be a good idea before his morning duties and the crafting lesson, followed by his meeting with the masters.

CHAPTER 2

Caldan walked up the final flight of stairs and along the corridor that led to the crafting chambers. Dim light from dusty whale-oil lamps lit the way. Crafted sorcerous globes would have provided a constant light source, but they were expensive, and the monks frowned on excess.

Stone statues decorated the passage. Many mimicked or looked to be related to various pieces from Dominion. Despite their familiarity, these weird creatures and misshapen humans unnerved him each time he saw them, and he quickened his pace.

He stopped before a large door banded in gray metal. Its surface was overlaid with runes and wards, a few of which he recognized, though their style was old and obscure. The door swung open on screeching hinges.

Numerous dark wooden tables and chairs, all laden with crafting materials and books, gave the impression of clutter. Shelves on one wall held wooden and stone carvings and a number of mechanical devices, whose functions were unknown to him. The other three walls sported chalkboards covered with writing and diagrams.

Most of the students were lounging in chairs, while a few were working at different tables. Although they had studied together for a few years, he gave each barely a nod as they noticed him—those who bothered to acknowledge his presence at all. A few of the girls were admiring a gold bracelet studded with gemstones Mariska was showing off, probably a gift from her wealthy parents. It could have been crafted, and gemstones were of interest to him, so he made an effort to join them, only to have two girls shift their weight and close the gap he was aiming for when they saw him coming. He should have known they'd never change. He'd learned early on not to try to join the wealthy students' conversations, both because they made it all too obvious they weren't interested in him . . . and because what they talked about was of no interest.

He walked to the desk at the back and sat down. One or two of the students had their noses buried in open books, trying to memorize what they could before their final exams, which were due to start soon. Luckily, as a ward of the monastery and not a student, Caldan didn't have to sit any of the exams—for which he was eternally grateful.

The door opened to admit Master Kilia, the craftmaster, a wrinkled, thin nun no taller than Caldan's chest. As always, she wore crumpled dark brown clothing, her gray hair tied in a bun secured with enameled metal pins. Limping across the room to the large padded chair at the front, she settled into it, taking her time to make herself comfortable before looking up. Piercing green eyes surveyed them all, and the few students who were trying to look attentive couldn't hold her gaze for long. With a grunt, she looked away and eyed the mess.

"Everyone will have to take their work back with them when they leave today," Kilia said. "I don't want anything left over, or it will go straight into the refuse pit."

Groans of dismay met her announcement. Most of the students had been crafting in stone, clay, and metal, and some of their works were heavy.

"And don't complain to me about needing help. If you'd followed my advice and worked in lighter materials, such as wood, there wouldn't be a problem."

"We aren't all able to craft using parchment, like Caldan," Eben said. "Some of us more normal students need to work with harder materials. Our wooden craftings don't last long, and paper is worse."

It never ceased to amaze Caldan. For what seemed like the thousandth time, one of the students was giving voice to their ridiculous objections. *Stop worrying about what other people can do and concentrate on your own talents,* Caldan wanted to tell them. If they spent less time complaining and more studying, they wouldn't find crafting so hard.

"I'm sure you have a talent for something as well," Kilia responded. "It's just hidden from us." Her statement elicited a few sniggers, but they died down at her stern glare.

"Everyone has strengths and weaknesses to their crafting. Remember that," she continued. "A few have a talent that buffers the forces more effectively, like Caldan's. Others are able to create harmonious works that last much longer. Everyone is different."

Another student spoke up—Tamara, a young girl. "Not everyone needs to craft something so quickly that the materials need to be light enough to carry around. The days where speed was necessary for battles and self-defense are over."

"They never existed in the first place!" exclaimed Owyn, a boy who had joined the monastery recently, and whose talent had already elevated him to this class.

"There are plenty of books on the sorcerers of old and how they could use offensive sorcery. Fire from the sky, shattering castle gates," retorted Tamara.

Master Kilia stood, and the room fell silent. "Old tales are just that. Some people still think sorcery can be used that way, but have any of you been able to do so? Have any of you ever *seen* one who could do so?" She paused for a response. None came.

Caldan leaned forward, eager to catch the words from the master. Stories held kernels of truth, and he believed any sorcery lost from before the Shattering could be discovered again. Sometimes he dreamed of discovering how to make trinkets, like most who had a talent for crafting did when they were young. It was all a fantasy, though, for in the thousands of years since the Shattering, no one had come close.

"Of course not," Kilia answered her own question, "since it can't be done. Oh, I'm sure many of you have tried since you found out you had a talent for crafting. Heads full of the tales your mothers told you or you read from one of the old storybooks. But it isn't possible. Crafting is for the creation of useful items. A good sorcerer is a valuable member of the community, not the army."

How could it be impossible? Caldan wondered. *We know trinkets exist, and someone had to have made them. Why not crafting for battle? Only the knowledge is lost, and what's lost can be found again.*

Another student raised his hand and spoke after receiving a nod from Kilia.

"Valuable, but boring."

"Boring, are they?" said Kilia, raising her eyebrows. "You students with your coddled lives . . . You don't understand what goes on in the rest of the world. How do you think I injured my leg?"

"We thought you got it falling down some stairs," Mikkala said to widespread laughter.

Kilia gave a wry smile. "The truth is that it happened a long time ago, when I was young and foolish—like you."

The room quieted as the students now strained to hear her every word. Caldan realized they had never heard her mention how she had come by her limp. "Back then, I was sure of myself and my skills, until I came up against something that was . . . adaptable, shall we say? My stone craftings failed, and I was injured. There was no time to craft out of stone or wood and imprint the materials with runes and unveilings. I was glad I had a few sheets of paper to fall back on."

The room fell silent. Kilia's intensity had become too much for them.

Caldan placed both elbows on the desk. "What was the thing you fought? What happened?"

She looked straight at him. "What it was is best left unsaid. As to what happened . . . I escaped from there as fast as I could." Kilia paused and shifted in her seat. "Everyone has a proficiency or predilection for how they want to use the craft. Some prefer wood or metal, and a very few, paper. As you now know, the difference is durability. The forces you access through your well require an anchor, and the anchor and the crafting need to weather the force being focused through them. To create something that lasts takes time and effort, and harder materials. On one end of the spectrum there is paper, and on the other are trinkets. The same manipulation can be made with any medium, but the strength of the material determines how long it will last. Except for certain sorcerers, who have a talent that enables them to use weaker materials for a longer period than others can." She stood, resting her weight on her good leg, and leaned on her chair for support. "Enough of me talking for today. I want you to split into four groups and discuss theories on making a trinket. At the end of the class, you can present your best theories to the rest of us."

Another round of groans echoed around the room. Owyn spoke over them. "But no one's been able to make a trinket for thousands of years!"

Kilia smiled. "Then maybe you'll be famous."

CALDAN'S KNOCK ON the door echoed down the corridor, making him flinch. He bit at one of his fingernails as he waited for a reply.

"Enter," barked a commanding voice from inside—Master Rastar, unless he missed his guess.

Steeling himself, he stepped into the doorway and saw three of the senior masters sitting around a table in the center. All of them looked as if they had been chewing iron nails. With a rustle of cloth, the masters exchanged glances and shifted in their chairs.

Caldan looked around in vain for an empty chair, but as usual there were none. The masters liked for their visitors to remain standing.

"Well, boy, don't just stand there. Come inside, for the ancestors' sake!" Master Rastar said, giving him a stern look as he closed the door. Rastar, a pale, wrinkled man with a wispy gray beard, appeared pleased that Caldan was flustered.

Caldan hesitated a moment, then, seeing the open window, decided to stand in the cool afternoon breeze. On the table were the remains of a midday meal, along with a pile of letters in brown paper envelopes sealed with wax. Next to the letters was a package half as big as a fist, tightly wrapped in oilcloth and bound with string.

Across from Rastar sat Master Delife. He was taller and thinner than Rastar, and he was clean-shaven. Farthest away sat the third master, Joesal, whom Caldan had had little to do with over the years. All three monks were bald, heads shaved according to their tenets, though Joesal's was covered with a layer of stubble.

Delife spoke. "For many years we have fostered a few talented youngsters who, for whatever reason, would normally have been unable to study at our monastery. It is our duty to offer this island what assistance we can. Some have come from poor families; others have had difficult childhoods, like yourself, and we recognize that you all need special understanding while you adjust to our life. Such a simple monastic existence may not be for everyone, but we give what we can without asking for recompense. However, as in all things, someday it must come to an end."

Delife paused to gather his thoughts, and Caldan took advantage of the break to get a word in.

"I appreciate all you've done for me, but, as you said, good things can't last forever. That's why I'm asking that, by the end of next year, a position or placement could be found for me on the mainland. Plus references from here, of course. It would take a while for you to arrange a position, which is why I wanted to mention this now. Over this next year I can study and prepare myself for a specific role. After leaving, I will send back to the monastery a portion of my earnings for the next few years as a sign of my appreciation." He looked at the three masters hopefully. It was a good idea, one he had given much thought to the last few days. They couldn't object to its fairness.

The masters looked at one another for a moment. Rastar then gave a shake of his head and Joesal dropped his gaze to the table, as if interested in the pattern of grain in the wood.

Delife drew a deep breath. "I don't think so," he said.

Caldan's thoughts ran at a furious pace. They wanted something, most likely with the approval of the Supreme Master. But Caldan's plan was advantageous to them—even if they had another idea, how would it benefit them more than his own?

Before Caldan could protest, Master Joesal raised his hand to forestall his response.

"We have been over your situation thoroughly, and as far as we can see, the monastery can no longer have you attending classes with the paying students. Some have noted your presence in the classes in letters to their families, and questions have been raised. The parents of some of the students do not want their children associating with people of lower birth. We"—he gestured to the masters at the table— "have to protect our main source of income, however distasteful. We have decided you're old enough not to need our wardship anymore. It is our heartfelt wish that, despite your desire to stay with us, there remain no ill feelings between us."

"How long do I have? I was counting on being here until the end of next year. I haven't exactly learned much that will get me work on the island. That's if . . ." His words trailed off as he realized what was coming.

"What we think is best," Delife said, "is that you travel to the mainland as soon as possible. We have already arranged some references for you." He tapped the bunch of letters with two fingers. "You shouldn't have a problem finding employment, wherever you decide to go."

"We recommend the city of Anasoma as your first port of call," Joesal said. "It is one of the founding cities of the empire, and you could do worse than starting there."

Caldan moved stiltedly to the table and leaned his weight on it. He felt the blood drain from his face, and his stomach churned.

"As soon as possible?" Caldan said. "What about my projects? What about the younger students I'm tutoring?"

"It's all been arranged," Rastar said. "Your projects you can either leave or take with you. The classes will be taken over by Bothar, who's shown some promise."

"You've got to be joking—" Caldan began, but Rastar talked over him.

"You do not exactly have many friends or . . . any family . . . to say good-bye to."

Caldan glared. "No, no family at all, as you well know."

"I didn't mean to offend you."

Delife raised both hands. "Now, now, we can all agree this conversation isn't pleasant, but there are some things you don't know, Caldan. Please, stop frowning at us and calm down. There are reasons we have come to this decision, if you would hear us out."

Eyes flicking to each master, Caldan ground his teeth and folded his arms across his chest. He breathed deeply as the masters watched him struggle to control himself. Trembling, he tried to swallow, but his throat caught. "And there isn't anything I can say to make you change your minds?"

"Hear what we have to say," Delife said. "Then you will better understand the situation we, and you, are in."

At his words, Rastar and Joesal nodded, both favoring Caldan with a grim look.

"After what you just said, I think I understand just fine."

"I think not," Rastar replied. "If there were anything we could do to have you remain with us, we would have already done it. But there's no leeway in this. Once you hear us out, I'm sure you will realize why you cannot stay at the monastery."

"You mean you'd rather I stayed?"

"Of course we would!" Delife said.

"Yes, no doubt," added Joesal.

"So what's the problem?"

"Normally," Delife said, "you would be too talented for us to lose, and we would have welcomed you, had you decided to stay with us, helping out around the monastery and assisting with the classes."

Caldan frowned. "But?"

Delife wrung his hands. "Ah, yes . . . This will be news to you, but your family was known to the monastery—one of the reasons, among many, we took you in."

"You . . . you knew my family?"

After all this time, they decide to tell me only now, then ship me off as if nothing's happened?

"Indeed. Both your parents came here often, for advice and to learn from us. And I have to admit, we learned much from them. Considering their talents, that's not so surprising." Delife glanced at Rastar, who shrugged. He paused for a moment before continuing. "We have kept some things from you while you grew up, both for your own protection and because we didn't think you would be mature enough to hear them until you were older. As it is, we have decided to tell you certain truths before sending you off. Hence this meeting."

"What do you mean when you say my parents had talents?"

Rastar shifted in his seat and cleared his throat. "Much like you, they both had an aptitude for crafting. Your mother's crafting was exceptional, especially her work with metals. And apparently, your grandmother was also skilled at crafting, and your grandfather with the Way of the Sword. It seems the talents run in the family."

"Not with me," Caldan said. "My sword work is middling."

"Ah, it's not that bad, and your crafting is far from it. You have a talent quite like your mother's. I can see parts of both of them in you."

Caldan's eyes watered and he blinked them clear. "You knew them well, then?"

"Yes. In fact, I saw them the day before the . . . accident. They stopped by to discuss a few things before heading back to their farm."

"Wait. If my mother's crafting was exceptional and my father knew the Way of the Sword, why were they farmers?"

Rastar sighed. "They were hiding."

"From what?" Surely they hadn't been on the run. Caldan's first memories were of their house on the island. But if they were . . . "Then . . . the fire . . . that means . . ."

Holding up a hand, Rastar forestalled Caldan's words. "Before you jump to conclusions, let us finish, or rather, let us start from the beginning. Your parents came to us a few years before you were born, and though they mostly kept to themselves, it was obvious they were running from someone or something. On this island, we don't get people arriving to start farming; they usually travel in the other direction to get away from this place. We are isolated and, well . . . although some grow up here and stay, many others feel there is something better out there." He waved a hand. "Anyway, I digress. Your parents seemed to be honest folk, and we welcomed them, as did the other residents they came into contact with. But still they were reticent to discuss some subjects and seemed to be always looking over their shoulders. They also took an unusual interest in people visiting the island."

"Running and hiding, and fearful that someone would come after them?"

"That is the conclusion we arrived at. And though we had come to know them over a few years, we decided, for the safety of the island and our order, that we had to know why. In the end, it wasn't difficult for them to explain to us, once we assured them any secrets would remain with the senior monks. You see, we knew they were good people, and they knew we could be trusted."

Caldan clenched his fists. "Were . . . were they killed?"

With a sympathetic look, Rastar replied, "I'm afraid so, though we do not know by whom."

"But they told you why they were hiding and who was chasing them, so you must know who did it." Caldan's eyes stung, and he gave them another rub.

Rastar shook his head. "It's not that simple. Your mother, Nerissa, told us her parents—your grandparents—had also been killed when she was young, and she had seen it happen. Since then, she had made her way as best she could and found some measure of happiness marrying your father and making a life with him. Her talent for crafting was quite remarkable, so she had no trouble finding work. But she couldn't forget what had happened to her parents. She began digging for information about them, innocent enough of itself, and a natural thing for a daughter to do. But what she found troubled her, very much. People started asking after her and why she was searching for information." Rastar spread his hands. "She didn't tell us most of what she had found, only that your grandparents were both from the empire and worked in some capacity for the emperor. Not directly, of course, but for one of the divisions in the empire."

They knew, thought Caldan. *All this time the masters have known far more about my parents than they let on.* Probably to shelter him while he was growing up, but he couldn't shake the feeling that he had been lied to, or at least that people he trusted had withheld the truth from him.

"Please, Master Rastar," Caldan said. "Do you have any idea who killed my parents?"

"We don't know," Rastar said. "All we know for certain is what we have told you—that your parents feared something they had uncovered and wanted to get away. They desired a normal life for you and for . . . your sister, may the ancestors look after her."

All three monks' eyes searched Caldan's. They looked drawn and worried, and he could read concern in their faces. His chest tightened and breath caught in his throat, as it always did at the mention of his sister, who'd died in the fire. His eyes began to burn, and he tore his gaze away from theirs.

Voice low, Joesal added, "Should we give him the, er, rings?"

"Yes," replied Delife. "Pass them to me, would you?"

Robes rustled, and a chair scraped across the floor. Caldan opened his eyes to a blurry room. He blinked a few times, and his sight cleared. Delife stood in front of him, hand outstretched. In it sat the small package that had been on the table.

"Go on," the master urged. "They are yours. Before the accident, your mother left them with us to study and keep safe."

Caldan reached out to take the package. The string felt rough against his fingers. Hesitantly he untied it, then unwrapped the oil-cloth bundle inside with trembling fingers. Two rings lay on the cloth, one silver and as wide as his small fingernail, the other of bone, slightly larger. The silver ring caught his eye first; the outside surface was covered in a knotwork pattern into which two stylized lions with onyx eyes had been worked, detailed enough that he could see tiny claws and fangs. On the inside, the band was etched with unfamiliar symbols.

He frowned, peering at the metal the ring was made of. It didn't quite have the color of silver; it was subtly different. His eyes widened, and he glanced up at Delife, who gave him a grin. *Is it real?*

"Yes," the master confirmed his unspoken question. "It's a trinket. Your family's, now yours. It was decided that, approaching your majority, you would be of sufficient maturity to be able to take possession of the trinket. As you know, they are valuable and not playthings for mischievous children."

Caldan gasped. A trinket his family owned? And it was now passed down to him, as it would have been if his family were still alive to see him come of age. His mind swam with thoughts and possibilities. How had his family come to possess something so rare? Would it provide a clue as to who they were and where they had come from?

He turned it a few times, still not believing it was his. "Thank you," he stammered. "You could have kept it, and I wouldn't have known."

"Ha! You know we wouldn't do that." Delife took the wrapping, string, and cloth from him and placed them on the table. "The bone ring looks to be a poor copy of a trinket. I fear it is worthless, most likely of sentimental value to your mother. The trinket, though . . . The origin and function of it is unknown to us, despite extensive and exhaustive examination using crafting. However, as you know from your lessons, this is not unusual. One of the symbols is a variation of the symbol we use nowadays for 'shelter,' but we are uncertain if it means the same thing. Be careful with it, Caldan. Keep it on your person at all times and preferably out of sight. Possessing trinkets has been the cause of many troubles, thefts, and deaths."

Nodding, Caldan turned the ring on his finger, feeling the details on the surface as he pushed it around and around, touching it to make sure it was real. The bone ring he slipped into his pocket. "So I shouldn't wear it?"

"Goodness, no. It's far too valuable to leave in plain sight. Hide it somewhere until you can work out a better solution. Perhaps a chain around your neck would suffice?"

Caldan nodded. "This still doesn't explain why you want me to leave the monastery for the empire."

"No," Delife said. "It doesn't. And as I said, we don't know exactly who killed your family. What we do know, however, and part of what your mother found out, is that the emperor values talented people. Once they are in his service, it is hard for them to leave, and it seems your family had some valuable talents."

"You think my mother . . . no, my grandparents were killed because they left the emperor's service?"

"It is a possibility. One of many."

Joesal cleared his throat and sat up straighter. "It is not unknown for generations of a family to remain in the emperor's service—those of unusual talent, that is. Your mother and now you have shown an aptitude for crafting. I would imagine that the empire wouldn't take lightly to losing a valuable resource. Perhaps the emperor's agents would track them down and ask them to return, and perhaps others would be interested as well. Who can say?"

Caldan pondered the master's words, nodding slowly. Though he found it hard to believe anyone would kill someone for simply refusing to work for them, he had heard of appalling incidents occurring on the mainland.

"So," he said, "you think someone might come after me as well? Should I go into hiding?"

With a sigh, Rastar rubbed the back of his neck. "It didn't help your parents, and we think it wouldn't help you, either. You have been safe here while growing up, but if anyone is keeping track of your family, then they might know you exist. A boy is no threat to anyone, but a grown man with a talent for sorcery is another story."

"So that's it?" Caldan asked. "A few weeks, maybe a month, then I have to leave?"

"We can't protect you if someone comes looking for you."

"I've been safe so far, and you hadn't even thought to tell me all this! What's changed now? I'm not . . . prepared for the mainland. There's so much I don't know, much I need to learn . . ."

Delife pushed the brown paper envelopes across the table. "What's changed? Simply that now you are old enough for the truth. And that means you'll want to leave us anyway—your own proposal is evidence of that. You'll see, eventually. We can offer you a fine set of references and a small amount of silver ducats to help you along. You know, I remember when I went off into the world as a youngster—"

"Yes, thank you, Delife," Rastar said. "I am sure Caldan will want to question you later about your travels. There is much he needs to do and think about in the next few weeks before setting out. We can discuss more at a later date, once he has mulled over what we have told him. It is a great deal to take in."

Caldan clenched his fists to stop his hands shaking. "Well, thanks so much. That's so incredibly helpful of you." He scooped up the reference letters. "I have to go. As you said, there's much I have to think about."

Delife stood and offered a hand to shake. "We wish you all the best, young man. Despite the circumstances, I know this experience will benefit you greatly."

Caldan glared at the offered hand and then softened. Maybe he was being too hard on the monks; after all, he'd known them most of his life. He might find himself back here one day and should try to leave on good terms. He bit his tongue, reached across the table, and grasped Delife's hand briefly but firmly. Then he left the room, closing the door quietly behind him.

CHAPTER 3

Caldan woke suddenly, bare chest heaving and covered in sweat. He felt like a fish out of water, gasping for air. A trickle ran from his brow into his open mouth. The salty taste helped anchor him back to reality. With heavy breaths, he heaved himself up for a moment and then fell back, lacking the strength to stay upright. He shook his head to clear the feeling of dread that remained from the nightmare.

Even after so many years, time had not faded the memories of that day. Fire and blood. Ten years since he came home to find flames consuming their house. The front door was wide open, and through the doorway he could see both his parents and sister inside, lying on the floor, motionless. Try as he might to reach them, the heat was too much; he couldn't even get close to the opening. He remembered crying, and the smoke—a metallic smell.

He doubted he'd ever forget the despair he'd felt. There was never a day when the memories didn't surface, triggered by inconsequential things: the sight of a small girl running in the street; the glowing orange coals of a low fire; the same metallic smell when potent sorcery was executed.

Late-afternoon light shone crimson through the window, giving it a strange appearance, as if the light filtered through a pall of smoke. From Caldan's position on the bed, hands clasped under his head, there wasn't much to see. Just the Dominion game piece of the Way-farer carved from smoky quartz on the window ledge. He'd purchased the carving a while ago on a whim from one of the more expensive purveyors of Dominion figures in the city. It had stood by the window gathering dust and watching him ever since.

This had been his room for the last ten years. He gloomily sur-veyed the sparse furnishings and distinct lack of personal belongings. It was somewhere he lived but definitely not a home.

He closed his eyes and thought of the first day he'd arrived at the monastery, too young, shattered by the loss of his family. The place had felt odd, so unlike his life back then. It seemed bizarre that, after becoming accustomed to it, he considered the monastery stranger and stranger, the people different from what he'd always thought of them, especially the masters.

He trembled as another hot flush ran through his body, followed by a chill, and his arm hairs stood on end. He hadn't felt well the last few days, and the flushes seemed to be getting worse.

He stood up suddenly, then dropped back onto the bed, overcome with dizziness. His body ached, and his stomach rumbled. Resting for a few moments, he wondered whether he should see a physiker, then his stomach growled hungrily. He frowned. Over the last month he'd been continually hungry and had to eat every few hours. Strangest of all, he craved green leafy vegetables, mushrooms, and cheese. He wondered if that was a result of stress as well, but with the exercise he'd been doing, the extra food looked to have gone into muscle rather than fat. A few of the monks had commented he'd put on more bulk, the blade master included. "Not too much more," he'd said with a grin, "or else we might have to start training you with a broadsword!"

Which reminded him, he needed to check whether his good shirt still fit. The gathering was tonight. After the day he'd had, he didn't feel like going anymore, but he'd given Jemma his word.

He rummaged through the pile of odds and ends at the bottom of his wardrobe, struggling to find his medicine. He pulled out a leather pouch containing the drug and herb mixture he'd bought as a remedy for his headaches and body pains.

Undoing the ties, he licked a finger and dipped it into the pouch. Rubbing the mixture onto his tongue, he grimaced at the bitter taste. A small amount to get him through the night. Too little and he might as well have not bothered, but too much and he would appear befuddled.

Still feeling unwell, he slipped on charcoal-gray pants and black leather boots with plain iron buckles. Hesitating for a moment, he pulled on a cream-colored shirt with mother-of-pearl buttons. Not normally concerned with his appearance, he nevertheless felt he needed to make a display this evening, if only to show the masters they had not upset him . . . and for Jemma's sake. The shirt was tighter than when he had tried it on a few months ago. If he kept growing like this, soon most of his clothes wouldn't fit.

He washed his face and hands. The flushes had now passed, and the medicine had calmed him nicely. As he dried off with a clean towel, the eventide bell tolled. He shook his head and let out a sigh; it was evening already and time for the gathering.

CALDAN TOOK THE stairs two at a time and paused at the top to look around at the square. To his right the beach started, and to his left there was a paved road along the water's edge.

An obsidian statue of Lady Misterin, one of the island's first settlers, stood in a fountain at the center of the square. Stylishly garbed in seaweed, in one hand she held a conch shell, spouting freshwater piped from an underground spring.

Caldan touched the water running over Lady Misterin's bare feet for luck, splashed some across his face, and continued on down the paved road.

A short time later, he paused at the top of the steps that led down into the hall where the students' social gatherings were held. Brought up in wealthy families, they were no strangers to parties and late nights of revelry, though the monks took a dim view of such things. *Too privileged to realize the opportunity they're squandering,* Caldan told himself. Most of them would learn far less than they should. He wondered why the monastery let them get away with it. But he also knew the answer: because the students brought in enough ducats for the monks to survive.

And so over the years an uneasy truce had evolved, and the students were allowed to gather and let off steam, as long as they didn't allow anything to get out of hand. And while the monks permitted them to gather, the students were made to use the rooms in the citadel, away from the monastery and close to where guards could keep an eye on them.

The hall was located in the citadel's north wing. Archways led onto a balcony, which overlooked a garden. Tapestries and paintings covered two walls, many depicting scenes from history that had made past governors of the island of Eremite famous: the finding of the ancients' caverns, the staying of the volcanic eruption, and a game of Dominion between masters. Oil lanterns suspended from the ceiling provided a warm yellow glow, and strings of seasonal flowers were pinned to the walls, giving the atmosphere a sweet fragrance. Aligned against the center of each wall were tables laden with food and refreshments, and a stage had been set up in a corner, where a quartet of musicians played a popular tune. The musicians were a luxury and must have been hired by one of the wealthier students.

Not recognizing anyone he knew well—but seeing plenty of people he didn't want to run into—Caldan stepped down the stairs and helped himself to a glass of fruit punch. He took a hefty swallow, gagged on the sweetness, and returned to the drinks table, where he added wine and took another sip. This time, it was palatable, if only just.

A pale face framed by a shock of fair hair appeared in front of him—Yasmin. Dressed up for the party, she wore a low-cut dress made from a sheer material that left little to the imagination. Caldan reddened and looked away. He thought it likely she wouldn't be able to wear that dress on the mainland under her parents' supervision.

"Caldan, how lovely to see you here tonight."

Her voice was too smooth for him, and he wondered what she was up to. "A pleasure to see you as well, Yasmin," he replied. "I . . . Have your studies been going well?" Caldan inwardly cursed himself for such a feeble question. Tonight was a celebration; the students wanted to forget about their studies and exams. But Yasmin always unnerved him for some reason. He glanced down at the fabric stretched across her breasts before catching himself and looking away. Maybe if he concentrated on the musicians . . .

"Do you think the other boys will be as bored as you are in my company?"

"No! I mean yes! I mean . . ."

Yasmin chuckled evilly at his discomfort. Caldan's face burned as he realized the trap she'd set with her cleverly designed question. Damned if he'd said no, damned if he'd said yes. He peered over her head. "Have you seen Jemma?"

"Ah, Caldan . . . the truth comes out."

Caldan looked at her sharply, trying to penetrate her smug exterior. "And what truth is that?"

"I'm not blind, as you may have noticed. And neither are most people." She sighed and touched his arm gently. "Jemma is my friend, and I know her better than most. Your thoughts are as plain as the sun."

"You're wrong. She's just a friend. You know how the students treat me, so I value any friendship highly. Anyway, what's it to you?"

"I don't want to see her hurt any more than you do. And some people would look unkindly if things progressed further. You two have been spending far too much time together, and it has been noticed." Caldan snorted, but she continued. "I have heard, as well, that you may not be with us for much longer."

Caldan stared at her in amazement. "How . . . What I do is no concern of anyone's. And what Jemma does is her business, as well." If

Yasmin knew, then the other students probably did, too . . . including Jemma. Now he needed to see her more than ever, to explain it to her.

"Unless she could get hurt, and then it's her friend's responsibility to ensure that doesn't happen."

He couldn't believe what she'd just said. She wasn't exactly being subtle. "I know you're trying to protect her, but Jemma is her own person and can make up her mind about what she wants. But—no, *because* I value her friendship, I'm not about to ruin anything by doing something that would hurt her. Especially since I'm leaving soon. What I'd like to know, though, is how you found out already."

"A friend told me." She shrugged. "Still, it's good you are leaving. For her sake." She gave him a wave of her fingers. "Bye. Try not to get into too much trouble."

He stood there seething while she weaved away through the throng. It was only as she moved out of sight that it hit him.

She's right.

Oddly, that made it somehow easier for him to relax. Flustered and uneasy as he was with crowds, he nevertheless decided to make something of the evening. He needed to take his mind off everything that had happened in the last few weeks.

Moving around a couple of students, he spied Jemma over by a wall, surrounded, as usual, by her friends. He hesitated, but she caught his eye, took a moment to excuse herself from the group, and hurried over to greet him. She was dressed in close-fitting black pants with a tight black shirt, and wore a fine silver necklace and bracelet.

She was, as always, breathtaking.

"Hello, Caldan. Would you care to dance?" She nodded toward the space in front of the musicians, where a few couples were already dancing. Surprised, Caldan could only nod his agreement.

She clasped his hand with hers and led him over to the dance floor. Several people stared at them as they passed, no doubt offended by his presence and startled by his companion. Unflattering comments were audible, no doubt pitched to be heard by those around them.

" . . . never would have guessed . . ."

" . . . don't understand why she would lower herself . . ."

Ignoring them, Caldan tried to concentrate on having a good time, although thinking about it made it hard to relax. They were about to start dancing when the music stopped.

"Great timing," Jemma said.

The musicians started tuning their instruments before beginning the next song. She took both his hands in hers and leaned in close.

"I hope your dancing skills are adequate," she whispered in his ear.

"They should suffice. I can do a few things well." He gave a short laugh. "Anyway, enough flirting, the music is about to start!"

"Oh . . . were we flirting?" she said with a smile. Before he could answer, the musicians struck the opening few chords of a lively tune, to which Caldan and Jemma struggled for a few moments with their inexperienced dancing but managed not to step on each other's toes during the first verses.

A number of songs later, Caldan realized he was having the best night of his life. A pretty girl wanted to dance with him, someone who, despite their differences, had become a firm friend.

And—maybe—more than that?

He didn't want to leave early, as he'd thought he would. Becoming breathless, they agreed to take a break and have some refreshments. As Caldan acquired two glasses of wine, Jemma excused herself to freshen up. Hot and sweaty from the dancing, Caldan told her to meet him outside, where the fresh air should cool them off.

He pushed his way through the press of bodies and out onto the balcony. The crowd was blessedly thinner there, and a cold breeze blew across his head, drying the sheen of sweat and offering relief after his exertions. He leaned on the balustrade, looked out over the moon-lit garden, and relaxed, taking a sip from his glass. A few souls were wandering among the trees and bushes—mostly couples, he noted enviously. *It must be nice not to be saddled with the complications I face,* he thought. One man stopped to pick a flower, which he placed in his companion's hair. Her soft laugh of delight reached Caldan on the wind.

Someone slammed into his back, knocking him sideways. Wine splashed onto his shirt, marking it with a red stain. Caldan cursed and turned to look into the eyes of Marlon, who smirked from ear to ear. Much like his sister, Marlon was dark, tall, and handsome. Exceptionally athletic from all his work with the sword, he moved with a languid grace that was hard to mistake for anything other than dangerous.

Unlike Jemma, though, he regarded Caldan—when he regarded him at all—with undisguised contempt.

"Looks like you've made a bit of a mess," Marlon said with a sneer. "Perhaps you should retire for the night; after all, we can't have you going around looking like a dirty commoner. Oh, I forgot! You are a dirty commoner!"

A few of his hangers-on laughed at his attempted wit. Caldan tensed as Marlon leaned in close to him and sniffed. "And what is that stench?"

More sniggers arose from the growing crowd. Students at the back asked what was going on.

"It's just as well you had this little accident, because now you can leave to change and have a wash!" He turned his head to grin at his friends.

Caldan sighed. He had hoped this wouldn't happen tonight. "Excuse me," he said and attempted to push past.

Marlon shot out a hand and grabbed his arm in a strong grip.

"Let me go," Caldan demanded.

"Not so fast," Marlon said, and used his weight to push Caldan back against the balustrade. "We don't like you and the putrid filth you come from." He leaned in close, sour breath in Caldan's face. "I've been told you've been seen hanging around with my sister, a lot more than I'd realized. She even admitted it to me earlier, as if she didn't care what people thought of her or our family's reputation. But *I* care, and when I saw you dancing with her . . . well . . . If I catch you with her again, I'll hurt you. Is that clear?"

Caldan shook his head. "Your sister likes me, and it's up to her who she sees."

Without warning, Marlon struck out at him. Still, Caldan blocked and hammered a fist into Marlon's stomach. Marlon staggered but took an uppercut swing at Caldan's groin, hitting him in the hip as he twisted.

Hands from the crowd forcibly restrained both of them.

Marlon drew himself up, still held by two other students but regaining his arrogant air. "No more playing now, you bastard. This needs to be settled somewhere else, without these idiots interfering." His tongue ran across his bottom lip. "The practice ground tonight. In an hour."

Caldan swallowed. "That's fine by me, but what weapons?"

"Your choice," Marlon said with a smile. "It will not make any difference."

He was right, Caldan realized, but he could not let this pretentious, conceited bully think he had him scared. "Wooden practice swords," he said and heard an incredulous intake of breath all around him. Marlon's blade work was without peer among the students.

"Swords it is, then," Marlon said with a puzzled but satisfied look.

Caldan nodded slowly, and the students released them.

Marlon turned without a word and strode off into the hall with his followers trailing behind. The crowd started to thin, leaving Caldan and a few students on the balcony. He peeked inside, looking for Jemma, and saw Marlon whispering fiercely to her, gripping her arm tightly. Marlon looked around and then marched Jemma away.

An older student, whom Caldan knew only by his nickname—Quill—quietly approached.

"You realize that he'll try to hurt you?" Quill said.

Caldan rubbed his eyes. "I know."

MOONLIGHT SHONE THROUGH patchy breaks in the clouds that passed over the practice ground. It looked much as it always had, hard-packed earth and stone walls, but tonight the moonlight lent the place a sinister air, which gave Caldan a chill.

Without warning, another hot flush through his body quickly dissipated that feeling. He swayed on his feet, momentarily dizzy.

He was pleased to see that his opponent and the admirers who usually followed him had not yet arrived. Caldan dropped the gear he carried next to a wall, slumped down, and leaned back to rest against the cool stone. A few deep breaths later, he felt well enough to move again.

Why he had agreed to this in the first place was beyond him. Part of him acknowledged the need he felt to fight back, to do something, at least before he was sent away. But he was certain that when this was over he would be just another peasant given a lesson by a popular student. They probably wouldn't remember this in a few months, even as a joke. Despite his own skill with a sword, he knew, as everyone else did, that he was outmatched. The ancestors were laughing at him, he was sure.

He tried to relax. Although his defeat was inevitable, he could at least make a show of it and hope he wasn't injured too badly. A slight numbness touched his skin, and another hot flush ran through him. He gathered his strength and tried to pull himself together. He began some stretching exercises.

Finally Marlon strode through one of the openings in the walls, followed, of course, by a group of friends. Behind his group hurried more students come to watch the spectacle as part of the night's entertainment.

Still weary, Caldan bent over and picked up his well-used wooden practice sword. He took a few steps forward in the moonlight to indicate his readiness.

Marlon, as usual, took his time preparing himself. He liked everything to be just so. After much preening and adjusting of his clothes, he marched toward Caldan, practice sword in hand and a huge grin spread across his face.

Idle chatter and the occasional clever remark could be heard among the students, but the conversations trailed off as the throng realized the fun was about to start.

Caldan and Marlon stopped a short distance apart, far enough that they couldn't strike at each other, but close enough to touch swords. Caldan was sweating, and Marlon was a smug study in confidence. They touched swords and Caldan strove to reach a calm state of mind, one where he did not think but simply let his body react. He was sure Marlon was trying to achieve the same—or already had.

Long moments passed, neither one willing to strike first. Caldan knew Marlon was sure of his ability; Marlon could wait for him to assume the initiative, then take it from him.

A cloud passed over the moon, blocking the light as they remained motionless, save for the slight rising of their chests as they breathed. The crowd stirred, unsure how to react, their fun for the night not starting as they wished.

"Have at him!" someone shouted, which led to outbursts from others.

"Give us a show, Marlon!"

"Don't hurt him . . . too much!"

Caldan took a step back and dropped his sword to a lower guard attitude as if content to wait a while longer, then leaped forward, lashing out with a vicious thrust aimed straight at Marlon's stomach.

Marlon's sword moved like lightning in defense. He brushed Caldan's blade aside and brought his sword around in a straight cut across Caldan's middle, which Caldan only just managed to block. Another cut and block by each of them, more careful this time as each tested the other, before Caldan drew a quick, shallow breath and launched a series of strikes . . . all parried neatly by Marlon.

Excitement hissed through the crowd. This was what they had come to see: a fight with no holding back, a real struggle between two men bent on injuring each other. One was almost a master, while the other was destined to lose and sport some ugly bruises the next day. The crowd clamored for blood, growing louder as they gave voice to their emotions. The atmosphere thickened as the tension rose.

Caldan slashed, then parried as they maneuvered around each other, thrust following feint, each block launching seamlessly into a counter.

Swords clashed with bruising force, now moving too quickly for Caldan to see. He forgot about his sword, focusing only on Marlon's movements, reacting to him and acting when he could. The dance intensified with every step, with every strike.

Caldan's breath came in gasps. His hands vibrated with every clash, and sweat dripped down his face and body. He knew Marlon was only getting started, his moves timed to perfection. Openings in Caldan's defense were ignored in favor of strikes Caldan could only awkwardly manage to parry just in time. Marlon was making sure the crowd had a show to enjoy.

Caldan's feet slid backward on the dirt. He sucked in air through his bone-dry mouth, skin burning as the fight continued, unrelenting in its pace. He knew he must lose, and that knowledge galled him, although he'd known there could have been no other outcome from the start.

By the ancestors, I'm hot! His fever reached a new pitch with every passing moment. It didn't help that he couldn't penetrate Marlon's unyielding defense. He had to finish this soon. Better to go out fighting than with a whimper.

With four quick strikes that smacked against Marlon's sword, he tried to force an opening, only to feel Marlon's tip graze against his ribs with enough force to scrape off skin.

Caldan retreated, and the crowd cheered. A slow trickle of blood slid down his torso, mixing with his sweat. Pain focused his awareness, and the next few attacks he parried neatly, managing to make his opponent skip back as his sword whistled past. Caldan shook his head to clear it. Vision blurring, his blood burned in his veins like molten metal.

Marlon took a step forward, his smile replaced by grim determination. Both swords whirled through the air, slamming together with frightening force: Marlon desperate to hurt, Caldan desperate to stay in one piece. Sweat stung his eyes, and he blinked. Marlon's defense opened in a slight opportunity; Caldan struck . . . and was thwarted. He went numb as he realized it was a trick. Marlon was toying with him.

Caldan pivoted and twisted. His blood seared through his veins, scorching his skin from the inside. Marlon's sword moved as if alive, and Caldan barely managed to sway away from its tip. Knowing he couldn't last much longer, he felt something inside him stir, and he decided on one last gamble.

Shifting to an upper attitude, Caldan lashed out—multiple cuts, feints, and thrusts coming with blinding speed. He almost relented, the strength and swiftness of his own attack bewildering him. But he saw Marlon desperately parrying the blows, barely avoiding being struck as Caldan's sword slid past his arm. A shocked look passed fleetingly across Marlon's face.

Caldan was frantic, his strength fading fast, blood pounding in his ears, sweat running in rivers down his body. He launched another series of strikes. Each one Marlon parried, but his reactions were slower and slower. Without thinking, Caldan attempted to force down Marlon's sword as it leaped at him. Seeing the opening, he lunged, and his sword tip hammered home on Marlon's torso.

CRACK!

The breaking of his sword and the cracking of Marlon's ribs echoed around the practice ground. The splintered blade drove into Marlon's chest . . . and penetrated to the hilt.

Shock gripped Caldan as he stared at what he had done.

Marlon fell, a surprised look on his face as he slumped to the ground, blood seeping from the broken sword protruding from the wound.

Around them, the students gaped in horror. With shaken expressions, some took a few steps backward, and then others rushed to Marlon's side to try to stanch the flow of blood.

Caldan sank to his knees, his mind a mass of heat and disbelief, heart hammering. He couldn't help but notice that no one rushed to his side before a wall of darkness swallowed his awareness.

CHAPTER 4

Swinging in the cold night breeze, the sign over the door of the inn squeaked back and forth, casting faint shadows from the moon around the doorway. Aidan pulled his cloak tightly around his shoulders in an attempt to reduce the wind's chill.

He glanced up at the sign, eyes narrowing in study. Painted on the wood was the face of a black goat chewing on a flower. THE BLACK GOAT was neatly painted in script below the ridiculous-looking face.

The inn was the only one for miles around. With night fallen and the cold wind biting deep, their band's leader, Lady Caitlyn, decided it would have to suffice. The timber structure seemed sound enough, although the stables were falling into disrepair, and weeds had sprouted around the buildings.

Aidan frowned. A disorderly house was often the sign of indolence, and the indolent left themselves open to evil's sway. The lure of an easy living was often irresistible to the weak-minded. But that was why people like him existed. He snorted at the direction and tone of his thoughts. He sounded too much like Caitlyn for his liking.

He turned to stare into the surrounding gloom. The dwellings and businesses crowded around the inn gave rise to a few dark streets and alleys. Out of one such alley came two men, preceded by Lady Caitlyn. The men led four horses. They approached the inn slowly, tired from many days of hard travel.

"Aidan, are the men settled?" she asked.

Caitlyn led a few dozen mercenaries she'd gathered over the years she'd been wagering her crusade. Hard men, often prone to excess; men Aidan wouldn't ordinarily associate with. But Caitlyn used whatever tool she needed to get the job done.

"Yes, my lady. A short way into the forest."

She nodded, then turned to the other two, Anshul cel Rau and Chalayan. "Have the horses stabled and combed, then come to the inn. We shall stay here for the night and be sure of an early start tomorrow. We are close to the aberrant farmhands. I can feel it."

They led the horses away into the shoddy stable, chuckling to each other after Chalayan quipped that the state of the horses' lodging wouldn't be much worse than theirs.

Caitlyn turned back to the door and stepped into the inn. Aidan followed close behind. It was typical for this remote location, the type of place they'd seen many a time over the last five years, since he'd turned eighteen and left home. It had a rough-cut wooden floor and a large stone hearth warming the room with a blazing fire. Behind the bar were barrels filled with local brews, and in front of them was a slovenly innkeeper, who appraised Caitlyn for a few moments before resuming polishing mugs with a stained rag. Patrons looked up as they entered but were quick to go back to their ale and conversations. If any were keen-eyed enough, they would have noticed the distinctive shape of swords under the new arrivals' cloaks, and the glint of finely wrought mail.

Aidan doubted any were, though.

Caitlyn moved to an empty table close to the fire and sat on a rickety chair. Aidan joined her, scanning the room for any signs of potential trouble. A plump, sweaty serving girl began an approach, weaving through an overly loud bunch of farmers.

Caitlyn nudged Aidan with her elbow. "If I had to guess by the state of this place, I'd say she's probably the innkeeper's daughter. She certainly looks the part. She should button up her shirt."

Aidan's eyes were drawn to the hint of flesh, but he stopped himself and looked away. Caitlyn was right next to him! What would she think?

"What'll ye have?" the serving girl asked in a weary voice.

Caitlyn turned to stare into the fire, so Aidan answered, not meeting the girl's eyes. "What's good?"

"Goat stew's one copper; soup's a copper as well. Ale's a copper, wine is two," the girl reeled off with a bored expression, oblivious to the question.

"Very informative, thank you," Caitlyn said. She rolled her eyes as she hooked another chair closer and rested a booted foot on it.

Aidan felt his face warm, and not from the fire. "We'll have four stews, three ales, and a wine, please."

The serving girl squinted, looking puzzled. "Begging your pardon, but are you sure you can eat all that?"

Aidan began to speak as he saw Caitlyn turn her attention on the girl. Her upraised hand stopped him before he got a word out. He could almost hear her thought: *It is always a noble's duty to be polite.*

"There will be four of us," Caitlyn said. "The other two are seeing to the horses and will be here momentarily." She slid a silver ducat onto the greasy tabletop. "Keep the difference."

In a flash, the silver coin was whisked away, and the serving girl bustled off to the kitchen.

Caitlyn reached into her satchel and placed her favorite book on the table, Troylin's *Of War and Strategy*. Just the sight of the book brought their last campaign to Aidan's mind . . .

The assault against the flesh-eating jukari's stronghold had been vicious. Bleeding and filthy—exhausted to the point of near collapse—he had managed to survive, sporting a cut to his cheek, along with Caitlyn and just a few of their followers. Smoke turned the sun red, and inside the fortress walls had been a chaotic mess of burning buildings, bodies, and blood. Their men and the jukari were broken, twisted and still, leaking crimson where they lay.

The jukari were a perverted, long-lived race created during the Shattering. Despite their powerful corruption, Caitlyn and her band had triumphed, accomplishing their complicated mission—one as dangerous as it was honorable.

Even still, Aidan had questioned her righteous cause. He knew what she sometimes thought of him: *weak of heart and stomach, too soft to see what is necessary*. Caitlyn had glared at him when he'd questioned her judgment in front of the men, as if the cut on his cheek he'd received that day were a badge that gave him authority above his station. Aidan had asked her what they were to do with the locals who had served the jukari. He'd pleaded for their lives, knowing they'd had no choice but to serve or be killed and eaten.

But to Caitlyn, sometimes death was the noble option. The *only* option. Pure. Uncompromising. One iota of compassion, one glimmer of weakness, and evil would flourish. That's what she preached, and what he didn't understand.

They are liars, each and every one of them, Caitlyn had said. *You don't take jukari prisoner, nor their turncoat servants. They chose to betray their humanity, to become tools for the destruction and enslavement of their fellow men. They are depraved through and through. Kill all of them—jukari, human—all of them*, she'd commanded Aidan. *They have given themselves over to corruption and deserve no leniency. When you seek to annihilate an absolute evil, you must destroy it absolutely. It is like a cancerous growth. Show mercy or hesitate and you leave kernels to start spreading anew.*

The order was given, the order was *obeyed*, and so ended another great day in Lady Caitlyn's life. An end to another enclave of filth. The destruction of evil—that was her sole purpose. Aidan had wept for the souls of the jukari captives, and for his own.

He started from his reverie as four mugs were deposited on the table by the grubby innkeeper. The man grunted, then went back to the bar. Caitlyn grabbed the mug that didn't have foam on top and took a swig of wine, swishing it around in her mouth as if to remove the taste of the road. She spat it into the fire, which hissed and sizzled. A few patrons looked her way at the sound but quickly went back to their own business when she glared back.

"Someone here knows about my quarry," she said firmly. "I can sense it."

Aidan swallowed. The last time Caitlyn had said something similar she'd ended up doing some forceful persuasion to get to the truth. "We should—"

The inn door banged open again and admitted cel Rau and Chalayan. Cel Rau pointed to them by the fire and the men came over, pulling out chairs and sitting.

Aidan looked them over, judging their worth as if for the first time: Chalayan the sorcerer, who would probably skin his own mother if he thought there was power in her flayed cadaver, whose goals were his own but who served them willingly for the time being; and Anshul cel Rau, a master swordsman from the treeless Steppes, whose skill with his two blades was legendary. Both had been in their company for years, and both knew, like the rest of them, there was no resting where vanquishing evil was concerned. It was often a thankless task, as many cities and towns were too self-absorbed to see the whole picture. Most people were incapable of seeing how deeply the roots of evil could grow, Caitlyn never tired of saying, and how far they could spread. Excising evil was always bloody, and the price could sometimes be high. Sometimes higher than Aidan was willing to pay; but not Caitlyn. To her, any price was worth paying to rid the world of such malevolence.

By the ancestors, "malevolence"! He was even thinking her words these days!

Chalayan looked around the inn and sniffed. "My lady, I always express confidence in your ability to know when something is awry, but perhaps this time your nose has led you astray?" He sipped his brew and grimaced. "The only thing troubling about this place is the poor quality of the ale."

Anshul cel Rau nodded, although he had downed half his ale in one go. "Too yeasty," he remarked, always a man of few words.

Caitlyn watched as he finished off the rest of his mug, then half turned on his chair to keep everyone at the inn in his sight. Both hands dropped to his sword hilts, as if he was expecting trouble from the innocuous patrons, half of whom at this time of night were too drunk to stand, let alone offer a serious threat.

"I would bet gold ducats against silver the farmers have been through here," she said. "If I were the gambling type."

Once more Aidan could almost hear her unspoken words: *Gambling is for the weak willed and the immoral.*

Chalayan shared a look with Aidan before replying. "My lady, to be honest, we don't know what the farmhands have done or to what extent they may be involved with whatever is going on."

She dismissed the sorcerer's concerns with a wave of her hand. Her eyes took on an unfocused look, as if she was remembering something from long ago. Aidan knew more about her past than he cared to. Her uncle had abused her terribly, for years. Until she'd killed him.

Caitlyn rubbed her eyes and took a breath. She looked around at them all. "Our informant Steyn sent news of strange goings-on in the nearby town of Boarsrun. His letter contained information both curious and disturbing. The locals witnessed weird behavior from two farmhands. Known to be hard up for ducats, they appeared in the town dressed in good-quality merchants' clothing, scrubbed clean, hair neatly trimmed—in stark contrast to their normally worn, dusty, and unkempt appearance. Steyn followed them late one night, when they visited a graveyard, dug a grave, and buried two shapeless bundles wrapped in canvas. Steyn unearthed the grave after the farmhands had left and found the bundles to contain corpses, shriveled and gray, human yet desiccated, as if drained of all moisture." Caitlyn paused, as if to let that sink in. "You know what that means."

Cel Rau grunted. Chalayan flicked the swordsman a glance. Aidan wanted to keep silent; he didn't want to give Caitlyn any more cause to doubt him. But—

"I don't think any of us does—"

"Evil," Caitlyn whispered.

Aidan and the others settled into silence. There was no arguing with Caitlyn when she was in one of her moods. After receiving the message, they'd ridden hard for Boarsrun, where they'd questioned Steyn and set off after the two remarkably changed farmhands, who had traveled south a few days previously. They were heading in virtually a straight line to Anasoma, which itself was strange. Usually, travelers' and merchants' routes to Anasoma were in an easterly direction toward the ocean, before turning south along the coast. The traveling was much easier due to the quality of the roads and a lesser likelihood of bandits. And while Caitlyn's party wouldn't have any issues with bandits—one look at their hardened men and the number of weapons they carried was enough to deter anyone bent on trouble—two lone farmhands might not have such an easy journey. They'd discussed long and hard why their quarry might have taken this route and couldn't think of a plausible reason. And that disturbed Caitlyn a great deal, more than Aidan thought necessary.

He swallowed a mouthful of ale and wiped his lips. A short time later, after they finished their goat stew, Caitlyn shook herself from her thoughts.

"It is time," she said quietly. "The first step to hunting evil is to show no mercy. Chalayan . . ."

The sorcerer looked at her, frowning. "Yes, Lady Caitlyn?"

"Go outside and prepare the men, then make sure no one can escape the building."

Aidan dropped his head and stared at the floorboards, his jaw clenched so hard it hurt.

Chalayan licked his lips, flicked a glance to Aidan and cel Rau, then quickly exited through the door.

"M'lady . . . Caitlyn," pleaded Aidan. "We don't have to do this."

"Of course we do. Someone here is bound to know something. We cannot tarry while evil goes unchallenged."

Aidan drew in a deep breath, hands clenched into fists under the table. Caitlyn stared at him, as if looking for any sign of dissent. She didn't need to say anything; he knew she thought he was weak.

She motioned to cel Rau, and the swordsman positioned himself by the door.

Standing, Caitlyn drew her sword, the crafted blade glowing orange with reflected flames from the fire. Aidan was struck by the thought that the hellish sight reflected Caitlyn's soul. Her fanaticism for the Good could itself be a form of evil . . .

"Listen up, everybody!" she shouted.

Voices stilled, and confused expressions intermixed with shock and anger as faces turned to her.

"We have been commissioned by the emperor to root out evil. One of you knows something, and I mean to find out who and what."

Aidan raised his eyes and toughened up his expression. He needed to support Caitlyn. It wasn't what he wanted to do, but duty first . . .

She pointed her blade at the innkeeper, who cringed back a step. "I think we'll start with you."

A SOFT DRIZZLE drifted across their camp. Dusk had fallen, and they had found a grassy patch off the road, which became their resting place for the night. A brook trickled close by, providing them and their horses with fresh water, and a few cooking fires dotted the camp.

Aidan set up a canvas covering between two saplings to keep out the wind and rain. He boiled himself some tea on the communal fire and drank it from a tin mug, both hands wrapped around it for warmth. Caitlyn was over with Chalayan; they were discussing something in hushed tones. Aidan didn't trust the sorcerer fully. Anyone with that much power bore watching.

He stared into the fire. The drizzle had been unrelenting throughout the day, and everyone was cold and ill-humored. Perhaps Caitlyn would let the men build up the fires tonight; it would give them comfort against the disheartening sprinkle. But he doubted it. *Hardship is good for the soul,* she often said. *It molds you.* Some were good men, but most were with Caitlyn only because of the rewards. Gold and silver ducats for some, other pleasures for the rest. She'd led many raids with a lot of killing. Spoils were evenly distributed, and if her men dealt harshly with those that trafficked evil, she turned a blind eye—even to what they did to the women. The first time Aidan had protested over that, she'd cut him down. *When you make a deal with evil,* Caitlyn had said, *you have to accept the consequences.*

The sound of hooves snapped his thoughts back to the present. All activity in the camp ceased for a moment, before Caitlyn met his gaze and gave a nod. She strode with determination toward the road. Aidan gulped down the rest of his tea, scalding his tongue. He collected his sword belt and strapped it on as he hurried after her. The scouts were returning, and Caitlyn liked to receive their reports in person. At least, he hoped it was their scouts, but in a strange land, you couldn't be too careful.

He made his way across the wet grass and stopped beside Caitlyn, who stood staring into the distance.

As the horses approached, Aidan gave a low whistle. The air from his mouth fogged as it came out. The temperature had dropped rapidly in the clear night sky.

He heard one of the horses snort, then an answering whistle came in response.

Beside him, Caitlyn sighed. Her hand released her sword hilt and she stretched her fingers. Aidan relaxed as well, then started, realizing he'd taken his cue from her. He shook himself. He was thinking like her, acting like her . . . but he knew he couldn't be what she'd become. He was . . . awakening. He never used to question Caitlyn, but now her intolerance and brutality were plain, and becoming worse.

A few moments later, the scouts reined their horses in and dismounted. Caitlyn nodded to both as they approached. The men were tired. Spending the day trailing someone, constantly alert and on the lookout for danger, took its toll on even seasoned veterans.

The senior scout, Watkins, stepped forward and gave a short bow to Caitlyn, then acknowledged Aidan with a short nod.

"My lady, they've stopped for the night off the road. They didn't find a very good spot and have a blazing fire going. It's like they aren't trying to keep a low profile."

Caitlyn smiled and nodded. "Thank you. Go and get yourselves a hot meal and some rest."

The two scouts shuffled toward the camp, leading their horses.

Caitlyn stood still in the drizzle, staring up the road at a tiny orange glow, the telltale sign of a fire at night.

"Why do you think they made no effort to keep their fire inconspicuous? They must know there could be bandits around."

Aidan chewed his lip, a habit Caitlyn had tried to break him of. "I can't say. You'd think farmers would have done some hunting and know some bushcraft."

"I don't think we will know until we put them to the question. Make sure the men rest up tonight so they're ready in the morning. After the last few days' hard riding to catch up with these two, we could all use the break."

"We have enough to take them now. I could gather the men and—"

Caitlyn cut him off. "In the dark and the rain? It's likely they'll hear us coming from miles away and be gone before we make their camp. No. We hit them just before dawn, hard and fast."

With a nod, Aidan agreed. "All right. You haven't led us wrong the last few years." *Do I really believe that? Her behavior is deteriorating, and I'm starting to grow tired of it.*

"I should hope not. You'll see to the men, won't you? Make sure they're squared away for the night?"

"I will, my lady, though they miss the days when you did it. You could"—he waved a hand toward the camp—"talk to them, like you used to. Show them the old you. They are looking to me more and more for commands you used to give."

"I . . . I'll think about it. I'm not as close to them as I used to be. Some of them . . . I think they don't truly understand our cause." She rubbed her temples, then caught Aidan's eyes with a firm gaze. "Remember, we must make sure to capture these two alive. No accidents. Only after they give us the answers we need will they be allowed peace."

Aidan stiffened. Next to him, Caitlyn closed her eyes. *She's waiting for my objection,* he thought. *She's not listening, but still . . .* He couldn't refrain from voicing his doubt. "My lady, do we need to . . . question people so harshly?"

His feelings of shame and embarrassment that someone he cared for thought of him as faint of heart hung in the air between them, like a physical sensation.

Caitlyn kept quiet, as if she could sense it too. She let it linger for a few moments before she answered, "You know why we have to. There are evil forces and people everywhere, and they won't hold back if they have you in a similar position. Hard tasks mean hard methods. We cannot flinch, or evil will prevail. What's the matter with you? You've seen its horrors firsthand. Together, we have observed the depths people can sink to." Her breath came in short gasps. "We cannot falter. We cannot stay our hand in trying to reach the heart of evil, no matter how distasteful the duty."

Caitlyn reached over and squeezed his shoulder. "If we show weakness, and through that failing, evil is allowed to flourish . . . then we have *failed*."

They stood still in the cold night, breath misting in the rain.

"But . . . how can we condone immoral deeds ourselves?"

She shook her head. "Not immoral deeds. *Necessary* ones. We are fighting evil, Aidan. Nothing is worse than letting a greater evil escape because we couldn't bring ourselves to pass a lesser evil. Some things must be tolerated for the greater good."

"I just . . . Sometimes I think we go too far." He stared out into the night. "As with the villagers helping the jukari. They didn't deserve to die."

Caitlyn paused again. This wasn't the first time he'd brought it up with her. "Yes, they did."

"It wasn't right."

Caitlyn narrowed her eyes and frowned. "Your compassionate nature does you credit, but we cannot falter in our duty. Don't let doubt cloud your judgment."

Aidan opened his mouth, about to object again, then closed it. There was no reasoning with her. If he pushed her too far, well . . . she'd killed others for interfering with her crusade. He didn't want to join them.

She sighed. "Come, you need rest. Let's go back to—"

In the distance, the fire erupted into flashes of light. Thunder rent the dark night. Trees cracked. A blinding white glare split the blackness. Then another.

Spots swam before Aidan's eyes. Caitlyn tugged him back toward the camp.

"Horses all!" Aidan bellowed. "Leave everything and mount up!"

And that's why she keeps me as her number two—when duty commands, I obey.

Some men stood staring at the flashes continuing in the distance. Cracking sounds and thunder reverberated in the darkness. A number of orange spots appeared—fires burning.

Caitlyn threw her saddle on her horse. Aidan did the same and tightened the cinch, while one of the men slipped the bridle on. All around the camp, men were stomping out the cooking fires and preparing their own mounts. A few horses shied at another thunderous clap.

"Let's go!" she yelled. "Gather whoever is ready, and let's get there as quick as we can."

Aidan nodded and stood in his stirrups. "All to me and the lady!" he roared. He spurred forward and out of the camp, with Caitlyn at his heels.

On the road, Aidan urged his mount to a canter, guiding it along in the dark by making sure the trees stayed on either side. Close behind rode Caitlyn and six of their men with torches, the quickest to react. He knew without looking that Anshul cel Rau and Chalayan would be among them.

They raced toward the farmhands' camp, cold wind across their faces, clouds of hot breath exhaling from the horses' nostrils. Shadows flickered across the road, and in the trees, wavering torchlight lent the dash an eerie appearance.

As they approached the fires, they saw motionless shapes in the dim light. Two forms lay on the side of the road to the left, where a stone-ringed campfire burned. There were a number of spot fires in the scrub. Three more bodies lay scattered on the road, and one farther ahead.

Steam rose from the corpses, and the scent of roasted flesh was heavy in the air. Blackened clothing had melted onto skin, faces were a mass of tiny blisters, hair burned to stubble.

Caitlyn surveyed the scene and gave a string of orders. "Find the farmhands. Bring the bodies to the campfire. We need more light."

She strode to the fire, followed by Aidan and Chalayan. Corpses were dragged across the ground to where they stood. Anshul cel Rau stayed in the background, saying nothing as usual, though he scanned the bush around them. Chalayan looked nervous, eyes constantly in motion. He clutched his trinket. After taking in the scene, the sorcerer moved away, crouching on his haunches at the side of the road.

The six bodies were examined. Scraps of unburned cloth showed their clothes were of poor quality and bore signs of heavy wear. Next to the bodies were deposited a pile of weapons, all black and warm to the touch—a few cheap swords, some knives, and a club. Whatever had killed the men had been hot enough to blacken steel.

"They're bandits," Aidan guessed.

Caitlyn grunted assent. "The farmhands, where are they?"

"These are the only bodies. The farmhands were either taken or ran off. Their horses are gone." He looked into the shadows. "From the look of what happened here, I would say they got away."

"Chalayan is spooked," Caitlyn said. "I've never seen him like this. I'm guessing the bandits bit off more than they could chew."

Aidan nodded. "I agree."

"Which means the farmhands are definitely more than they seem. And they don't hesitate to use brutal force when they need to. We have to be careful."

Caitlyn's eyes followed Chalayan, who now took a few steps toward the abandoned campfire. He knelt before it and placed a hand on the earth. After a moment, he stood and brushed his palms, a puzzled look on his face.

Caitlyn strode over to the sorcerer and took his arm, leading him away from the rest of the men. Aidan followed. Chalayan looked ashen.

"What happened here?" Caitlyn demanded in a whisper.

Chalayan shook his head. "I don't know. It's not possible."

"It bloody well is. It happened. Now what's going on?"

Chalayan shifted his weight from one foot to the other. He glanced ahead at the fires in the distance, then over to the left, where a thick tree had fallen across the road, as if pushed over. He licked his lips.

"If I were to hazard a guess . . ." he started.

"Please do," Caitlyn said.

"Then . . . this has to be alchemical. A mixture of chemicals caused a massive reaction and release of energy . . . except . . ." Chalayan hesitated.

"What is it?" Aidan asked.

"There is no residue, no smell of alchemical ingredients. And yet . . ."

"What?" Caitlyn said.

"There is a residue of sorcery." Chalayan sounded puzzled.

Caitlyn swore under her breath. "What unholy power have we unearthed? Sorcery did this?"

"No!" Chalayan hawked up some phlegm and spat it in the direction of the bodies. "I mean, it isn't possible. There *has* to be another explanation."

"But what, then?" asked Caitlyn.

Chalayan could only shake his head.

"Well, in the absence of another one, we will have to assume they are powerful sorcerers, whose abilities surpass any we have seen before." She wiped her hands on her pants. "What a mess."

Swallowing, Chalayan closed his eyes. "All around, there is sorcerous residue, as if a powerful crafting were performed, but . . . nothing like I've ever experienced." He was shaking. "It's as if someone tried to draw from their well and lost control, but when that happens, the sorcerer is consumed, and when they die, the well closes. Here, it's like a deliberate crafting." He looked at Aidan, his eyes wild.

Aidan couldn't believe what he'd heard. "A destructive crafting?"

"That's not possible," said Caitlyn.

Chalayan smiled wanly. "That's what I said." He shuddered, though at the same time he wrung his hands, and a gleam came into his eyes.

"This isn't good," Caitlyn said. "Sorcery shouldn't be used to destroy; it's against all we know. Evil cannot be allowed such an advantage."

Chalayan looked at the ground at their feet. "But we could use it, too! Think of what we could accomplish, the good we could do."

Aidan disliked the glimmer in Chalayan's eyes, and the urgency in his voice.

"No," said Caitlyn. "No good could come from this knowledge. For sorcerers to be able to unleash such power . . ." Caitlyn drew herself up. "We have found this for a reason. We must make sure this knowledge never sees the light of day, and the practitioners are destroyed."

"But—"

"No!" She cut Chalayan off and drew him close until their faces touched. "There can be no compromise with evil. Our duty is to excise these sorcerers from the world so they cannot corrupt anyone else. We must find out more about them, where they came from, where they were going, and what their purpose is.

"And then destroy them."

Aidan cleared his throat. "It might be easier to do all that after we find out more."

"We will do what we can, depending on the situation." Caitlyn looked around at her men standing away from the steaming bodies, conversing in hushed tones. "Are the farmhands close, Chalayan? Are they watching?"

The sorcerer closed his eyes for the space of five breaths. "No," he whispered. "There's no one watching. They must have ridden out hard soon after the attack."

Caitlyn nodded. "Good. Our message to the men is that this was alchemical, something you have seen before."

"Lie to them?" Aidan said. *Whatever happened to the truth at all costs?*

"We do what we must." Caitlyn stared Aidan in the eye until he looked away. "The less people know about this, the better."

Aidan crossed his arms over his chest and held himself tight. Caitlyn slapped him on the back.

"Good man," she said, and turned to the others.

"Listen up!" she shouted. "Chalayan confirms this was alchemical, some reaction. He's seen this type of thing before during his studies. Leave the bodies here. We'll go back to our camp and examine the area in the dawn light. We don't know if they left by the road or cross-country. Looks like we'll have to give them a night's head start."

Aidan could see the men were not pleased, the excitement having heated their blood. Some of them would be in a killing mood.

Or worse.

Something Caitlyn said long ago echoed in his ears. *You work with what you have, and if the tool gets the job done . . .*

CHAPTER 5

Something gray and blurry stood in Caldan's recovering consciousness. Blood throbbed in his head, and his body felt as heavy as stone. He forced himself to think, his mind to focus. Needles of pain stabbed his eyes, though the light was dim. His mouth tasted foul, and the air had an aroma of stale sweat and vomit.

"Here, drink this," someone said.

He accepted the bowl held to his lips and sipped at a warm broth until he finished it. He accepted another, which he gulped at. Little by little, strength flowed back into his body, and the pain in his head receded.

He was in a windowless room, furnished only by a stool next to the cot he lay on. On the stool were a damp rag and two empty wooden bowls. A candle burning in a nook provided the only light, and the air felt damp and thick. The blurry figure of a girl he didn't recognize stood against one wall. He managed to lift a trembling hand to his face and rub his aching eyes.

"What happened?" he tried to ask, but all that came out was a strangled croak.

"Shhh," the girl said. "Don't try to talk. They said you would be weak for a while and that you need to conserve your energy."

She folded the damp rag and placed it on his forehead, where it offered cool relief to his throbbing brow. Caldan tried to clasp her hand to thank her, but his grip slipped off. His arm felt leaden, and try as he might, he couldn't lift it again.

"I need to inform them you're conscious," she said, then left in a hurry.

Caldan heard a lock click and the thud of a bar dropping in place before he drifted off again.

WHEN HE WOKE, the pain in his head had subsided, and his body felt much lighter, as if whatever sickness had ailed him before had completely vanished. Gingerly, he levered himself to a sitting position and looked around. The room was the same, except the two previously empty bowls were now full. He reached for one and took a mouthful of cold broth.

Visions of Marlon and the blood rose unbidden. His sword embedded in Marlon's chest. What had happened? He had never seen one of those swords break, and he hadn't struck that hard, had he? He struggled to recall the fight, but the memory had split into pieces of a puzzle he couldn't put back together.

By the ancestors, what had he done? Was Marlon alive? Would Jemma forgive him? What would his punishment be? Questions, doubt, and self-recrimination went around in his mind, but he had no answers. His head swam once more, and he lay back down and fell into a dreamless sleep.

CALDAN WOKE AGAIN, and this time he sat up with no effort at all. The candle had burned to a nub. He breathed deeply of the stuffy, thick air.

There was no telling what would happen to him now. Maybe the masters would decide he had tried to kill Marlon; or perhaps they thought it was an accident, though that seemed unlikely. His eyes watered as sorrow for Jemma threatened to overwhelm him. He found it difficult to control himself, to put his feelings aside and concentrate on the mess he was in, but he had to pull himself together for his own sake. And he needed to see Jemma, to beg her forgiveness and explain he hadn't meant to hurt her brother.

Swinging off the cot, he stood on unsteady legs. He took another look around the room, noting for the first time the door had a handle but no latch on the inside. He grabbed the handle and pulled, but the door didn't budge. Locked in. *That's not good.* He staggered back to the bed and collapsed on it, one arm covering his eyes as he tried to gather his thoughts.

He heard the door click, and a figure slipped in.

"Sit down, Caldan," Master Delife said, holding up a palm to forestall any response. "You're in a predicament here. I can say that, in all my years as a master, and in my time as an initiate and brother, never has anything like this happened. The decision on what action to take was hotly debated and hard to reach agreement on, but we managed to steer the discussion in the direction we wanted. Despite the problems this will cause, it may be fortuitous for us, and for you." He paused to catch a breath and let his words sink in.

"Master, I—" Caldan began.

"Please," Delife interrupted with a shake of his head. "Many have spoken against your actions, and many others for you. I have been sent to give you the masters' judgment, which, to be honest, isn't too different from what you were going to do anyway." He moved the stool and sat down, using the wall as a backrest. The master's eyes were red with dark circles around them.

"There are a few facts of which you are unaware, Caldan. First, you have lain unconscious here for nearly two days."

"Two days? But that's . . . What's wrong with me?"

"Quite simply, we do not know. While you were unconscious, the physicians performed a few tests, but they could not come up with a cause." He rubbed his eyes with weariness. "Second, and most important, Marlon is still alive."

Caldan breathed a heavy sigh of relief. Though he hated Marlon, he didn't want him dead.

"Don't be too thankful. He's in a great deal of pain and will need a long time to recuperate after such an injury. It took all our skill, both with physiking and sorcery, to bring him back from the precipice. He was lucky. Saving Marlon took all night, and we still have not recovered."

"Two days," Caldan repeated. "I can't believe it."

"We don't know why you were unconscious for so long or, for that matter, what caused you to black out. It was one of the reasons they debated so long over what to do."

Caldan shook his head. "But I feel fine now. A bit weak but—"

"Be that as it may, there was a reason for your blackout." Master Delife hesitated. "I need to ask you something, Caldan." He produced a leather pouch and dangled it in front of him. It was the one that contained the drug and herb mixture Caldan had been taking. "Do you recognize this? It was found with your belongings."

"Yes, of course. It's mine. I've been having some aches and pains. It's not illegal."

Master Delife gave him a disapproving look. "And are you qualified to dose yourself? To know when enough is enough? Some of these things have side effects . . . like the symptoms you've experienced. Be truthful with me, Caldan; how much were you taking and how often?"

"Not much. I swear. I've been getting aches and pains everywhere, and they feel like they are down to the bone. I needed something to dull them sometimes so that I could sleep, but even then I don't take it every night."

Delife's deep brown eyes appraised him, and he clasped his hands together, obviously considering his response. "I believe you, Caldan. But you should have asked for help, not decided to self-medicate with who knows what concoction. It may have contributed to what happened, and your subsequent malaise."

Caldan wasn't so sure. Part of the reason he'd taken the medicine in the first place was because he felt the way he did during the fight. He doubted the pouch had added to it. He was about to say so when Delife asked a troubling question.

"Do you regret what resulted?"

"I . . . It wasn't my fault! I can't explain why my sword broke, and Marlon . . ."

"Everyone knows you and he don't exactly see eye to eye."

Caldan shook his head. "It's deeper than that, but I still wouldn't want to hurt him; not like this. Not almost *kill* him. I feel terrible about what's happened." Although what he mostly felt terrible about was how Jemma must now think of him. What he had done to Marlon was unforgivable; she would hate him. "It wasn't my fault," he repeated. "I didn't mean for any of this to happen."

"For all intents and purposes, an almost lethal duel with weapons," Delife said harshly. "Where the duel escalated out of control, and one of the . . . *participants* . . . was severely injured. It is hard to believe that happened by accident."

"I don't know how that happened. They were just practice swords, same as we always use. There must have been a flaw in the wood, a crack or—"

"Be that as it may," Delife said, "you have left us with a difficult issue to resolve. We cannot condone such behavior, and the fact that someone was seriously injured makes it much worse. Marlon's family is important, both to this monastery and to the island as a whole. The damage to our reputation will be severe." He stopped and turned to Caldan, drawing his shoulders back and taking a deep breath. His manner became formal, and he looked Caldan in the eye. "Believe me when I say this might be for the best, despite the circumstances. I am afraid we have no choice, and we cannot wait any longer. You have no place here with us now. Your bags have been packed. As soon as you are well enough, you will be escorted to the docks, where you will take passage on the first ship leaving for Anasoma." Delife bit his lip, as if he had more to say. Finally, he added, "Unfortunately, we had to take back the references we previously offered you."

Caldan's mouth opened, but no words came out. He slumped and lowered his head.

"Please," he managed to croak. "This place has been my life. You saved me from a bleak existence as a homeless orphan on the streets, where . . . who knows how long I would have lasted? I owe you and the monastery a debt that can't be repaid. Please . . . give me a chance to make things up to you—to everyone. I know what I've done is unforgivable, but it was an accident."

Master Delife remained unmoved. "We know you were going to leave us in a few weeks, but the reality of the situation is we cannot let you go unpunished. Surely you see that? We depend on a good many outsiders to be able to continue our work, and we cannot justify risking our relationship with them for . . . to put it bluntly, an orphan with no influential family or connections, no matter how talented he is. There can be no compromise when it comes to protecting our welfare and the continued prosperity of the monastery. And really, we are just bringing forward the day you leave by a few weeks. Count yourself lucky there wasn't any more substantial punishment. I know you understand."

Caldan didn't move, except to clench his hands into fists. They had been so good to him—the masters, the monastery—and now they were placing their wealth and well-being above him, looking to their own survival rather than the right thing to do. He felt sick, like someone had punched him in the stomach. After all this time, did he really know these monks?

The sad thing was, the more he thought about it, the more he realized he did know them.

"Oh, I understand all right."

Delife's expression turned hard. "We do what we must in these times. I, too, wish the situation were different." He looked around the room, checking to make sure no one else was there, although it was impossible for someone to be hiding. Satisfied, he said, "Here, have this." Delife handed Caldan a leather purse, and when Caldan looked inside, he saw it was half full with ducats. "You'll be allowed to take your belongings, but I didn't see many coins among them." He smiled faintly. "You'll need something to give you a start. It's not much, but it will help. It's enough to set you up with accommodation for a few days, and to buy some essentials, if you are thrifty. From then on, you'll have to make other arrangements."

Caldan squeezed the purse, the hard-edged coins digging into his palm. The masters obviously thought there was no other way, and Marlon's family could—no, *would*—make trouble for the monastery. He felt his resentment fade a little. "I don't know how it happened. I'm . . . sorry it came to this." It was the best he could muster.

"Be that as it may, it did happen, and we must face the consequences. Facing what life throws at us makes us mature. It may not be fair, but it's what shapes us. You have much potential, Caldan. It may be you are meant for greater things than we can provide here."

Trying to convince yourselves you've made the right decision. Only looking out for my *best interests, I'm sure.* But he stayed silent.

Delife regarded him for a few moments. "You've not had much time to absorb what we spoke about the other day, about your parents. But when you do, your thoughts will naturally turn to questions. Questions you will think need answers. I would caution you to be careful. Very careful. Your mother seeking answers is probably what led to the fire. And revenge . . . well, nothing good can come of it."

"I don't know what I'll do. It's all too much at the moment."

Delife nodded. "I don't envy you your problems, Caldan. There was a time when I thought, perhaps naively, that you would join our order. But the past catches up with all of us. A word of advice: if you plan on finding out about your family, your best option is to trace the origins of your trinket. Such valuable items are usually kept under tight control by those who can afford them. I would imagine records of all trinkets exist; it's just a matter of ferreting them out."

The trinket! Caldan looked around the room nervously. "Where *are* my rings? My belongings . . ."

"Don't worry, I made sure we were the ones to clear out your room. The trinket is safe, but I would suggest you find a way to secure it on your person as soon as possible."

Caldan nodded, relieved, and Delife turned to the door and opened it. A burly guard entered carrying two sacks filled to bursting, deposited them on the floor, then left.

"Your things. Look out for a guard early tomorrow morning, before the cock crows. You'll be off the island soon after sunrise. Good luck. It is a hard world out there." With one last look over his shoulder, Delife left Caldan alone.

Caldan had thought he would have a year to organize his life, whether he wanted to stay on the island or not. Only recently, that had dwindled to a mere few weeks, and now . . . it seemed he would be departing in the morning. The thought of leaving the monastery was devastating. His friends, the place he belonged, all gone.

More important, though, Jemma would hate him now. She probably couldn't stand the sight of him. He had thought of her more and more these last few months. He'd tried not to read too much into their friendship, but lately she hadn't seemed to be so far out of reach. Of course now it didn't matter, the sight of the broken sword in her brother's chest enough to dispel any thoughts of them being together. Caldan's hopes were shattered, burned to ashes and spread on the wind.

For long moments, he stared at his belongings. He gave a cursory look inside the sacks to make sure everything he owned was there, but his heart wasn't in it, as it would have been if he were embarking for the mainland of his own free will. He slipped his rings into his smallclothes and vowed to find a better place to secure them. They were the only things he had from his parents, and both were precious to him, more than whatever else was in these bags.

He folded some of the clothes he had pulled out so they wouldn't rumple too much, repacked them on top of the rest of his belongings, and tied the sacks securely.

CALDAN SAT UP suddenly, sure he had been asleep for a few hours. Something had woken him, but what?

A knock sounded at the door.

"Did you hear me? Get up! You're leaving soon. Get your stuff together."

Caldan's heart thudded in his chest. *Soon?*

"Oi! You deaf? Did you hear me?"

"Yes," Caldan yelled. "I heard you."

He struggled into a wrinkled shirt. "Do I have time to get a few things? I need to buy some bits and pieces for the trip."

"Straight to the docks with you. Orders is orders."

There was much he wanted to do before he left, but clearly he was out of time. There were a few masters he wanted to talk to, say farewell to, thank for their friendship and everything they had done for him. And Jemma . . . He still needed to talk to her, to explain his side of the story, and now that chance was gone. He sighed and stood up, only then noticing a folded piece of parchment that must have been slipped under the door while he was asleep. He picked it up as the door opened. Two guards stood there, one holding a lantern.

"C'mon. Get your stuff and get going. We ain't got much time. Ship's leaving at dawn, so get a move on."

Caldan stuffed the parchment into his pants pocket, grabbed his sacks, and left the only life he'd ever really known.

CHAPTER 6

Caldan strode down the wooden wharf and stopped before a moored ship loading supplies and merchants' goods for its return journey to the city of Anasoma. Swaying in the harbor's swell, the ship looked like any other he had seen. And yet, he couldn't help but feel it was an ominous sight—mostly because he would never have boarded it if he had a choice.

Behind him, one of his two guards cleared his throat and took a step closer.

Caldan turned around to take in the view from the wharf, of the city and the monastery. "I know. Don't worry yourself. I just want one last look at this place."

He breathed deeply of the sea air, redolent with fish and tar; and from a warehouse with signage declaring it was owned by the Five Oceans Mercantile Concern came the odor of spices and coffee. A cold early morning wind had picked up, and sea salt prickled his skin.

Fully laden, the two-masted ship sat low in the water. Figures scuttled over the deck in the dawn light, busy preparing for departure. The name *Loretta* was painted in large yellow letters on the stern.

"Best be off with you," one of the guards said. "We need to make sure you board and are taken into the captain's care. All this gawking about is delaying our breakfast."

Caldan gritted his teeth. "How inconsiderate of me."

His two hungry escorts following close, he walked up the gangplank and onto the deck. They stood there a few moments watching the activity around the ship. There was an older sailor sorting broken pieces of rope in one corner, while the strong smell of vinegar came from another scrubbing the deck with a coarse-bristled brush.

It wasn't long before someone deigned to notice them: a small, deeply tanned girl, who looked around twenty, with her black hair tied in a tail that hung halfway down her back. She was dressed like all the other sailors in rough cloth, worn and stained by hard work at sea.

"Is this the prisoner?" she asked, looking past Caldan to the guards.

"I'm no prisoner," he responded with heat. "Where would you get that idea?"

"The two guards keeping an eye on you, for starters, plus the fact we've been paid to take someone into custody and make sure he doesn't slip off before we leave. That would make you a prisoner." She smiled at him, revealing even white teeth.

"I-I—" he stuttered. "Look, I'm not a prisoner. It was an accident. I'm just . . ."

"Sure it was." She motioned the guards to the wharf. "You lads can go now. Leave him with me."

"You sure you're all right on your own with him?"

The girl gestured around her at the sailors. "Plenty of help to hand, if I need assistance. The crew wouldn't want anything to happen to one of their own."

"Fair enough." With a final look at Caldan and the girl, the guards stomped down the gangplank.

"Well now . . . what are we going to do with you?" the girl asked.

"I've never been on a ship before. Never had to," Caldan said.

She raised her eyebrows at him. "It was a rhetorical question. And one you didn't really answer anyway."

Caldan grimaced. His thoughts were skittering all over the place. "It's been a trying couple of days. I'm a bit lost."

"I think we all know how that feels sometimes." A shadow passed across her face, but it was gone in an instant. "I'm Miranda. Best we take you to see the captain. She can give you the once-over and let you know how things stand on the ship for your journey. Well, couple of days, anyway. Guess that's not much of a journey. Though since you've never been on a ship before, it might seem like one." She looked at someone behind him and held up a hand. "I can take him from here. He seems harmless enough."

Caldan turned his head to see a brute of a sailor standing right behind him, a wooden belaying pin in one calloused hand. Judging by the look in his eyes and the scars on his knuckles, he knew how to use it.

Turning back to Miranda, Caldan asked, "Is this necessary? I'm not a criminal. Look, just show me to my cabin and I'll be out of your hair."

"Sure you will," she said. "We need to show you around first, so you know where things are—for eating, the crapper, stuff like that."

Caldan was taken aback. No girl he had been around before would have said such a thing, or even *referred* to a bodily function in conversation. If Miranda noticed, she didn't show it, continuing on.

"And to see the captain, of course. She likes to have a chat with all the passengers."

"Let's go, then." Caldan just wanted to get this over with. A clean cut was always the best. He began to walk toward the door that led inside the ship.

Miranda stopped him before he had taken a few steps, her eyes hard. "We go where and when I say, got it? Ships can be a dangerous place for the inexperienced, and I won't have you injured when you're in my care. Many a lubber has hurt himself doing something stupid."

Like wounding a rich boy at a monastery, he thought bitterly.

She gestured for him to follow and sauntered toward a smaller door on the other side of the ship.

Caldan followed her, ducking under the low doorway. Inside, warm air smelling of tar and sweat washed over him.

"Hope your delicate nostrils aren't offended," Miranda commented as she continued down some stairs.

She showed him around the insides of the ship, marking areas where he was not allowed to go unless escorted—crew areas, the hold, and the galley—and where he was allowed to—the common area, the "crappers," and his own tiny bunk.

Barely wide enough for him to squeeze into, it was sectioned off from the rest of the room with a thin curtain. Seven other bunks were in the same room, and there wasn't much in the way of privacy.

"Throw your stuff in here," she said, indicating his bunk. "Can't get better than this for you, with what we're paid." She winked at him.

Caldan smiled grimly. "I can't complain. It's not like I have a choice." He placed his sacks on the bunk and closed the curtain.

Miranda looked at him, tilting her head to the side. "All right then, let's see the captain. Follow me."

She led him down a corridor and around a corner, ending at a closed door, which had chips and deep gouges in it. She noticed him looking at them. "They were here when the captain purchased her. She thinks the ship may have been taken by pirates at one time." She shrugged. "But who knows?"

She banged hard on the door with a fist, and, without waiting for an answer, opened it and walked into the captain's quarters. Caldan followed her inside.

The captain sat at ease behind a desk strewn with maps held down by stone paperweights, a couple of books, and some brass nautical instruments Caldan didn't recognize. Her skin was tanned but lighter than the girl's, and her shoulders were broader. Lines around her eyes and mouth proclaimed her older, probably around forty. Her booted feet were propped up on the desk, and she held a mug with steam pluming from it. A strong smell of coffee permeated the room.

Miranda opened her mouth to speak, but before she could, the captain waved her to silence. She took a sip of coffee and grimaced at the taste.

"Cook forgot the honey again. Bastard," she muttered. She brought the mug to her lips and blew steam off the top.

Behind her, dawn light streamed in through open windows. A cool breeze aired the cabin, which stank less than the rest of the ship—but only a bit.

The captain reached over and placed her mug carefully on the desk, folded her arms across her chest, and looked directly at Caldan.

"I'm Captain Charlotte," she began. "This is my ship. I've been owner of the *Loretta* for ten years, and I'm the law here. You go where and when I say, got it?"

Caldan noted the words were almost exactly the same as the girl had said to him earlier. She must have borrowed it from the captain's speech to all passengers. He glanced behind him, and Miranda looked at the floor, a slight flush rising to her cheeks.

"Still, you look harmless enough. Growing out of your clothes, are you? Don't they take care of that at the monastery?"

He heard Miranda snigger behind him, then cover it with a cough.

The captain frowned at her. "Enough of that, Miranda. Some manners, if you please."

"Sorry, Captain," Miranda said.

Captain Charlotte grunted at her. "Don't think that act fools me. You're as bad as the rest of the crew sometimes."

"Sorry, ma'am."

"I'm sure you are." Charlotte turned cold eyes on Caldan. "Anyway, don't make any trouble with the crew, because you know who I'll support. We've been paid to take you to Anasoma, and I plan to make this trip as uneventful as I want every trip to be. Cross me, and you'll go over the side for the sharks. Am I clear?"

Caldan looked her in the eye and nodded. He wasn't pleased with the way he'd been dismissed and sent away from the monastery, but he wasn't going to do anything rash. There was time ahead to take a look at his situation.

"Good. Miranda, get him squared away in his bunk. We leave within the hour, and we both have work to do." She waved them away and settled back in her chair, reaching for her mug.

Miranda grabbed Caldan's arm and pulled him out the door, closing it behind her. "That went well," she said. "She must have taken a liking to you."

"It went well? Is she always that blunt?"

"Always . . . well, except when she's had a bit to drink." She hesitated. "But anyways, shouldn't be talking about her to you. Let's get you back to your bunk, for the time being. When we set sail, you can come up on the deck. Crew won't like you around when we depart; you might get underfoot." She gave him a sidelong smile. "And maybe puking your guts up."

Caldan grimaced as they continued on to his bunk area, where she left him. He drew the curtain open, shuffled his sacks around to clear a comfortable space, and lay down.

He remembered the folded piece of parchment he'd found and stuffed into a pocket in a rush. It felt rough in his hands, and a daub of candle wax held it closed, but no seal had been embedded into it. Breaking it open, he unfolded the parchment and recognized Jemma's flowing script:

Dear Caldan,

No one is allowed to see you, so I bribed the guard to deliver this letter, and I hope it reaches you. I know you would never hurt Marlon on purpose, and although his wounds are serious and distress me deeply, I do not blame you.

It was pure luck we found out they were sending you away without an opportunity to say good-bye, and I needed you to know I didn't think the worst of you for what happened. The physikers tell me Marlon will recover, but it will take time. He will need constant care, which I will have to provide. I'll have to stop attending lessons, which is annoying, but I'm unable to do anything about it until Marlon's made some progress. Family must come first. My parents would want me to look after Marlon to the exclusion of all else.

They say you will not be allowed back on the island, and for that I'm sorry. I know this will hit you hard—more so than anyone else who studies here. This place has been your life, and it is difficult to leave things that are precious to us; but life throws us challenges indiscriminately, and it is for us to overcome them.

A lump formed in his throat, making it difficult to swallow. The words blurred in his vision, and he rubbed his eyes.

But I'm rambling, and I'm sure you have your own troubles to occupy your mind. I will miss your friendship and your warmth.

With fond memories, Jemma

Caldan folded the parchment with slow, reverent movements and slipped it back into his pocket. He stared at the flimsy curtain separating him from the room. He was relieved she didn't blame him for Marlon's wounds, but despite what she had written, he couldn't help but wonder whether Jemma would ever forgive him for ruining her freedom.

The swaying back and forth of the ship relaxed him, though it was only a small swell in the harbor. He was sure the two-day trip would be pleasant, if his stomach remained settled.

The reality of his situation kept intruding on his thoughts, and he wondered how much he could stand before his mind couldn't handle it anymore. The life he knew was gone as surely and as quickly as smoke blown away in the wind.

He squeezed his eyes shut and rubbed them hard with his palms. *Unfair* was the word that kept coming to his mind. But the truth was, he had been more fortunate than many others. More than he had any right to expect. Perhaps this new part of his life would change him; perhaps the experience would give him a greater understanding of the world, a new perspective.

He took a few deep breaths of the musty air and found he couldn't lie still. Pushing himself out of the bunk, he headed up to watch the ship sail in the dawn.

Caldan emerged on the deck to see crew members in a flurry of activity. Finding a corner out of everyone's way, he leaned against the gunwale. The fresh sea breeze ruffled his hair, giving relief after the fusty air below.

Captain Charlotte and Miranda stood by the wheel. Both were quiet and peered out into the harbor.

"We must profit by this wind," he heard the captain say. "Is all in readiness?"

"Yes, ma'am," Miranda replied.

"Then be so good as to tell me why Rigger Darcy is swaying back and forth as if three sheets to the wind."

"Bloody ancestors," cursed Miranda. "Rigger Darcy, you drunken bastard," she yelled, red-faced. "Get your sorry ass back belowdecks right now! Jonas, get up there and replace him."

"Right you are, ma'am," said another sailor as he passed a swaying Darcy on his way to the mast.

Miranda looked like she was about to burst, lips pursed tightly and nostrils flaring.

"Sorry, Captain. I should have checked on Darcy. We know what he's like with a bit of shore leave."

"Yes, you should have. Never mind. What's done is done. Pay better attention next time."

Miranda gave a quick, embarrassed nod.

"I will ask again. Is all in readiness?"

Miranda paused before replying, her gaze taking in the deck, the masts, sails, and crew members, and stopping on Caldan for a second before moving on. Caldan held his breath, sure she was going to send him below while they left, but to his surprise she didn't.

"Yes, ma'am. All is ready."

"Good, then we will make sail." Captain Charlotte raised her voice to carry across the ship. "Make sail. All hands to make sail."

There was a great deal of shouting and stomping of feet from the crew members as they hurried to their places.

"Silence, please," yelled the captain.

All the crew of the *Loretta* stood still, poised in dead silence. The ship lay in the harbor, gently rocking to and fro in the morning swell, waves lapping at the side.

Charlotte stood still as well, judging the wind. She paused for a few moments.

"Away aloft," she cried. Her call was repeated up and down the ship, and immediately the shrouds were covered in men and women racing upward, as nimble and at home as monkeys in trees.

As Charlotte unleashed a slew of orders, the crew on the yards untied the lines furling the sails, and sheets of canvas dropped with a whoosh. Ropes were stretched home and secured.

The *Loretta* heeled over slightly as a push from the wind filled her sails. Another push, then she inched forward until the motion became a steady drive. She was under way, gradually gathering speed as she moved away from the docks, the noise of her slicing through the water gaining in strength.

Caldan looked back at the docks, his gaze traveling up into the city and finally coming to rest on the monastery. He turned his head to the open sea breeze to hide the expression on his face, his eyes burning as he fumed against the way he'd been treated. Salty spray from the ship's passage through the water soaked his face. He didn't move or shield his face, allowing it to erase any sign of the tears that fell.

He lost track of time as he stood at the gunwale staring out at the water, pointedly not looking back at the island dwindling into the distance. Any thoughts he pushed aside in an effort to ease the pain.

The sun had risen into a cloudless sky and now beat down upon the deck. His eyes hurt from the glare off the water. To give them a rest, and to cool down, he headed back to his bunk, passing crew members on the way. They all ignored him, busy with their own tasks.

Beyond finding cheap accommodation and work, Caldan had no thoughts on what he would do when he reached the mainland. He was sure his situation wouldn't become dire, since he had gained a lot of skills and knowledge at the monastery, but he knew he had better find some work as soon as possible.

Well, no point worrying until he made it to Anasoma and decided whether it was somewhere he wanted to stay at all.

Shaking himself from his reverie, he upended both sacks, spilling his belongings onto the bunk. Such a meager collection of possessions to mark his life.

He slumped back, overcome with weariness. Too much had happened in a short space of time, and he was exhausted, both physically and emotionally. He rubbed his aching eyes. He needed rest and time to think, to come to grips with all that had happened, but he doubted he would have much time after landing in Anasoma. This short trip at sea might be good fortune in disguise and give him a chance to gather his thoughts.

He repacked his things, shoved the sacks to the floor, and spent the next few hours lying in his bunk, eyes closed, rocking gently from side to side with the ship. He wasn't feeling ill, which surprised him, but when a crewman came to alert him that the midday meal was ready, he begged off. He was hungry but in no mood to make small talk with strangers, who would have all sorts of questions.

CALDAN DRIFTED OFF, and before he knew it, he was being shaken awake. He brushed away the offending hand and sat up, groggy. Miranda stood there, hands crossed over her chest, and stared at him with a disapproving look on her face.

"Heard you haven't eaten anything all day," she said.

"Eh?" Caldan was still half-asleep. "What's it to you?"

"We want to make sure all our passengers are well. Wouldn't get any repeat business if we didn't check in on them now and again." She took a step back. "Are you sick?"

"No, not at all. I just needed some rest, and I'm not hungry." His stomach chose that moment to let out a large rumble, belying his words. He grinned sheepishly. "I guess I've been overruled."

Miranda smiled back. "Come on. We can rustle you up something to eat. You've been down here all day, and the sun is setting. I'm not surprised you're hungry."

Caldan followed her through the ship to the galley. She rummaged around and made up a wooden plate for him with a heel of coarse-grained bread, a withered apple, and a few slices of cold charred meat. The cook's treatment when preparing the meat hadn't left many clues as to what type of animal it had come from, but Caldan wasn't fussy. His stomach grumbled again as he took the plate from Miranda, and she motioned for him to follow.

"Wait," he said. "Could I have a bit more, please?"

She raised an eyebrow and gestured for him to help himself. "Sure. Just leave some for the rest of us."

He grabbed another apple and a few more slices of meat, plus a skin of water. "That should be enough. Let's go."

She looked at his heaped plate and shrugged.

On deck, she led him to a sheltered corner and gestured for him to start eating. She leaned her elbows on the gunwale and looked out to where the sun had set.

"Oh bother, we missed the sunset."

To Caldan, her words were tinged with irony, and he glanced at her. Surely she saw the sunset every day? His eyes drifted from her face to her figure beneath her clothes. She looked toned and athletic . . . He stopped himself staring before she caught him, and turned his attention to his food.

"Thank you," he said. "For the food, I mean." He stuffed a slice of the meat in his mouth and chewed ravenously. Was it beef? It could have been goat, but he couldn't tell. "I'm always thankful for food," he mumbled around his mouthful. "When I was young, I never had enough."

At his words, Miranda gave him a sharp look; then distress crossed her face, and she looked away out to sea. "I know what that's like," she said in a subdued voice.

Caldan remained silent, not wanting to bother her further, and ate with a will, finishing the plate quickly. The bread was stale, but mixed with some water it became chewable enough to get down.

"Um . . . any chance I could have some more?"

Miranda laughed, showing dimples in her cheeks, which he

thought quite becoming. He would never have guessed when he first met her she had this other side. She'd seemed far too serious before.

"My, you were hungry." She looked pointedly at the tight sleeves on his shirt. "Not turning into a jukari, are you?" she joked, referring to the wild creatures that could be found in some mountain ranges. They were rumored to be twice as big as a grown man, and twice as hairy.

He was sure she wasn't referring to hairiness. "I don't think so, not today, anyway. At least I hope not!" They shared a laugh and a short companionable silence before Caldan spoke again.

"I was serious, you know. Do you have any vegetables, green leafy ones? I've been craving green things for a while."

"Perhaps you're turning into a rabbit?"

Caldan's thoughts flashed back to the fight, and his sword penetrating Marlon's chest. His smile faltered. He knew he was changing somehow: becoming bigger, stronger than others his age. You only had to look at what he'd done to Marlon: the strength that had driven his practice sword home. No, if he was turning into something it was more likely a jukari than a rabbit.

He left that unsaid, though, simply saying, "Come on." He led the way back to the galley, his long strides causing Miranda to hurry to catch up.

She pointed out some greens, and he filled his plate with leaves, munching on some between handfuls. With a shake of her head, Miranda leaned against a table.

"I've never seen someone eat so much."

Caldan shrugged, a slight flush suffusing his face. "I'm still growing."

Miranda raised her eyebrows. "You'd better stop before you can't fit through doorways. Anyway, this is only a short trip, and we do it often, so there isn't any need to provision with dried foods and the hard bread. We stock up at each port. It keeps the crew happier than some others I can tell you about. Our captain is considerate, though the fresh food costs more. You're welcome to eat as much as you want, as long as the crew don't start complaining."

"Thanks. I can't explain it—it's only been a month or so I've been as hungry as this. I think I must be having a late growth spurt," he said, finishing off the plate of greens.

"I guess you must be." She fiddled with a lock of her hair that had come loose, twirling it around a finger. Caldan saw a question in her eyes, but she seemed nervous to ask it. Eventually, though, she said, "How come you were forced to leave?"

And there it was. Caldan hesitated. The subject was still raw, but he felt like he needed to talk about it to someone. Miranda seemed pleasant and wanted to listen. *What can it hurt?*

"I caused an accident. Someone was bullying me. It went too far. He forced me to get angry, then challenged me to a fight. The students sometimes settle things that way. It was only with wooden practice swords, but . . ." He trailed off and breathed deeply a few times. "I must have lost my temper. I hit him too hard in the heat of the fight. My sword broke, and . . . I don't know what happened. It went into his chest." Caldan closed his eyes at the look of shock on Miranda's face. "I didn't mean for it to happen."

"Is he alive?"

"Yes. They say he will recover, in time." He opened his eyes and looked at her again. "It was all a blur. And a mistake. I shouldn't have gotten angry. It's . . . more the hurt I caused my friends and the people who have been my family for so long."

"Well, no one died, and you're not a thief. I can tell the captain and crew the prisoner isn't all bad, and we can rest easy."

Caldan could tell she was trying to put him at ease, but his mood had soured once more.

I guess it's still too soon.

"I'll go back to my bunk and rest. Thank you for your kindness." He nodded his thanks and left her leaning against the table.

CHAPTER 7

Caldan woke early the next morning, roused from sleep by the noise of crew members moving about. With a sniff, he realized part of the stink in the cabin was him—he hadn't washed in days, and stale sweat clung to him and his clothes. Deciding to do something about it, he fished out a change of clothes and made his way on deck.

In the thin light, the sun started to peek over the horizon. A flat sea greeted him. Not a breath of wind ruffled the sails.

An old crew member walked the deck with a tray of steaming mugs, handing one to each sailor on duty. He caught sight of Caldan and offered him one; it was filled with strong coffee. He gave a toothless smile and wandered off to finish handing out his mugs.

There were two crewmen close by, both sipping from mugs. Caldan swallowed a mouthful of coffee and sputtered at the taste. Obviously, the cook had forgotten to cut the bitterness with honey again.

"Flat as a lake out there, Sharkey," one of the sailors said—a man barely older than Caldan, with scraggly stubble passing for a mustache.

"True, Conall, that it is." Sharkey, an older sailor with skin like tanned leather, hawked up some phlegm and spat over the side. "Looks likely we won't make Anasoma as quick as usual."

"Yep," Conall drawled. "Captain will probably have us working on the ship, though. No rest for the wicked."

"She'll want us to work out the kinks that've settled in the last few weeks. We ain't seen any action on the sea, and what with the three-day layoff in Eremite, reckon a few of the crew might be getting complacent."

"Excuse me." Caldan took a few steps toward them. "Sorry to trouble you, but where can I wash up?"

Two pairs of curious eyes turned to appraise him.

"You that killer we got on board?" Sharkey said.

"What? No! I haven't killed anyone."

"I heard you ran someone through in a duel. Clean and cold as you like." Sharkey made a thrusting motion with one arm.

"Careful now," Conall chimed in. "Don't get on his bad side, or you might be food for the sharks!"

"Ha! Will take more than a young'n like this boy to best me. And besides, I eats sharks for breakfast. How I got me name."

"Please!" the younger sailor said. "Your mom could beat you the first fifteen years of your life."

"Into the crappers with ya! Was more like thirteen!"

Both men laughed heartily. Conall wiped his eye, then Sharkey addressed Caldan.

"Pay no mind, young sir, we's just having a joke. Seen a lot of bad stuff in our time, so we's got to make light where we can. No offense."

Caldan didn't know how to respond. His face burned with embarrassment. Sharkey looked at him with something close to pity.

"Don't be ashamed, boy. We's heard it was an accident. Wash up, you said?"

Caldan nodded, not trusting himself to speak.

"Back there. You see that bucket with a rope attached? Fetch yourself some seawater and use the sponge there. Don't be shy seein' we're on deck. A small ship means doing away with some privacy. You get used to it."

"I'm telling you, we shouldn't keep taking sponges from the sea," Conall said.

Sharkey rolled his eyes. "Here we go again."

"It makes sense, I'm telling you."

"No, it doesn't."

"Sponges soak up water, and if the sponges from the seabed are all taken up, what happens?" Conall looked at Caldan. "Hey? What do you think?"

"I couldn't guess," Caldan said.

"Why, the sea level will rise, of course! The cities will be flooded!"

Sharkey smacked Conall on the back of his head with a flat palm and almost spilled the coffee from his mug in the process.

"Shut up, you moron. It's bad enough I have to work with you, let alone listen to your crap."

"I reckon it's true," Conall said, rubbing the back of his head.

Caldan sidled away slowly. "Thanks. I'll wash up now."

"You're welcome. Pay no mind to this ignorant twit. Oh, and another thing. Rinse off the seawater with some fresh, or you'll be dry and scratchy all day." He nodded farewell, and they turned back to looking out at the sea while draining the contents of their mugs.

Hauling the bucket over the side, Caldan drew up some seawater. He didn't have soap, so he would have to make do. *Another thing to go onto my list of essentials.* He stripped off his shirt but left his pants on. The crewmen might be used to a lack of privacy but he wasn't, and he certainly wouldn't be caught standing on deck with his plums out. Plus his trinket was hidden in his smallclothes.

The seawater felt cold but pleasant. After rubbing his skin vigorously with the rough sponge, he refilled the bucket and tipped it over his head, then again. As he stood, dripping onto the deck, a sudden gust of wind blew, fading to a light breeze. He lifted his arms, closed his eyes, and allowed the wind to swirl over him as he listened to the creak of the ship and the gulls circling overhead.

He heard a crunch behind him and opened his eyes, turning to see Miranda sitting cross-legged on the deck, munching an apple and appraising him.

"Good morning," she chirped and took another bite.

"Good morning to you, too," he replied, embarrassed she had been watching him. He hastily put on his clean shirt, struggling to get the tight sleeves over his arms, and placed the sponge and bucket against the gunwale. "Is something wrong?"

"No, not at all," Miranda said. "Just taking in the fresh air and sights. Glad you washed up. I wasn't going to say anything yesterday"— she wrinkled her nose—"but you did smell a bit."

"I didn't get a chance to do a lot of things before I had to leave, and I was . . . confined for a few days. It feels good to be clean again."

In fact, it felt very good. The saltwater and scrub had left his skin raw and tingly, as if he had scoured away old skin to reveal new.

Miranda looked him up and down. "You must have done a lot of exercise back there. The monastery kept you fit."

"Yes. They . . . the monks liked to keep the students active. They said a healthy body helped nurture a healthy mind. But I think they just wanted the students worn out so they were less trouble. We mostly studied inside, though, less strenuous subjects."

"Hmm . . . If you say so."

Caldan stood still and allowed the morning breeze to slowly evaporate the moisture from his skin. While not strong enough to cause many ripples on the sea, it was enough to send the occasional sail flapping. He checked on Miranda. She was still there looking at him and had nibbled her apple down to nothing. Soon, all that was left were a few seeds and the stem, which she tossed over the side.

"Here, you'll need this," she said, and slid a waterskin across the deck.

His skin felt tight, and he remembered the crewman's advice to rinse with freshwater. He splashed it across his face and arms, rubbing with his hands to remove the sea salt. Under his shirt, his skin felt prickly, but he wasn't about to undress in front of Miranda.

"Thanks." He took a swig of the water and rinsed his mouth.

"A couple of crewmen said we'll be delayed because of the lack of wind."

"Conall and Sharkey? I daresay they didn't lack for any wind," she said. "But yes, this weather isn't speeding us along, as you can see. Care to share what's left in your mug?"

He passed her the dregs, a few mouthfuls that he hoped hadn't been splashed with saltwater while he washed. She nodded her thanks, brought the mug to her lips, and took a swallow, then tilted it to finish it off.

"Ah! Nothing like someone else's cold coffee in the morning. I think I'll get a refill of fresh stuff. Be seeing you later, I'm sure." She headed down below.

Caldan spent the rest of the morning wandering around the ship, both abovedecks and below. Abovedecks, most of the crew looked idle, the lack of wind meaning they didn't have much to do. For the most part, they were relaxing. A few impromptu dice and card games had sprung up, with the participants keeping a sharp eye out for Captain Charlotte. He nodded greetings to the crew who caught his eye as he passed. Some returned the courtesy, while others never responded or avoided him altogether.

The constant moving of the deck and swaying to and fro were peculiar to Caldan, and always he could hear wood creaking and ropes groaning, even in the flat water. His sword training from the monastery had gone some way to helping him cope with the rolling of the ship, but the mild swell was an easy introduction to walking on deck. No sign he would succumb to seasickness yet, for which he was thankful.

By late afternoon, Caldan was sitting cross-legged in the shade, his back leaning against the gunwale. His arms were sore from exposure to the sun, and he ached with thirst. He took a swig of water from a skin. Warm and tasting like leather, it wasn't the best, but it was a welcome relief.

Throughout the day, whenever he was sure no one was looking, he found his fingers returning to touch the rings where they snuggled in his smallclothes. And that, in turn, kept his mind on trinkets.

His studies had touched on the subject, but there had been none for the students to examine, so they could only rely on a few old written reports and the knowledge of the masters.

Trinkets were all created thousands of years ago, before the Shattering had destroyed much of the accumulated knowledge practiced by sorcerers. The objects took many different forms, though most were jewelry, since they could be easily worn to keep them safe, but also to have them close at hand, as many were passive. Their influence extended only a small way, generally to whoever wore them. Sorcerers had been able to craft other objects of power but none like trinkets. Before the Shattering, the wealthy and powerful were usually the sole possessors of trinkets, but after the ensuing chaos, many found their way into ordinary hands, whether by purchase, luck, or more diabolical means. The exclusivity of owning such items became a mark of wealth and influence among all sections of society. Many were now pieces of jewelry with their own family stories attached, handed down from generation to generation and kept secret. Due to their sorcerous capacity—in some cases usable by people without talent—and their intrinsic rarity, they were highly valued. Poor families kept theirs hidden, and the wealthy locked them up as securely as they could. In most cases, it meant that trinkets were rarely seen, lest they become targets for thieves.

Caldan's trinket was his only clue to tracing his own family history. And it might get him killed. The thought frustrated him. Delife had told him to be careful of digging too deep, but if he didn't look at all, it was simply a ring, because other than being valuable, it was of no practical use to him—especially if he couldn't unravel its function, something the monks had been unable to do the whole time they had had it in their possession.

Caldan sighed. He had no idea how he was going to use his trinket to find out more about his parents—and he knew he couldn't sell it— so all he could do was hope that in such a big city as Anasoma there was someone who could help.

CHAPTER 8

Miranda joined Caldan on deck as he lay on his back on wood still warm from the sun and watched the stars. From the corner of his eye, he saw her take her time approaching him, making plenty of noise, giving him a chance to indicate if he didn't feel like company. When he didn't object, she sat cross-legged near him, then suggested he spar with the crew in the morning.

"What?" exclaimed Caldan.

"I said, tomorrow, if the winds are still down, the captain wants—"

"I heard what you said," he interrupted Miranda. "I wasn't asking you to repeat it."

"So why did you? Never mind. The crew needs to get in a bit of sword practice in case there's trouble, and she . . . well, I thought you could join in."

Caldan remembered his sword slamming into Marlon's chest, and he shook his head. He couldn't face sparring so soon after the accident.

Clearly Miranda didn't notice, because she kept on. "It would break the monotony. You don't do much except mope around."

"I don't mope."

"If you say so." Miranda looked away, but not before he noted a smirk on her face. "Listen, if you want to let everything get the better of you and sulk around for days, then fine, I can't stop you. But if you've been truthful with us about what happened—"

"I've told you the truth."

"—then you should focus on putting the past behind you and look at what's ahead."

Caldan gave her an annoyed look. She was only a few years older and giving him advice? "I've had enough of people lecturing me. I think I know what's best for me. I'll leave the sword fighting behind and find normal work in Anasoma."

Miranda looked at him like he was something unpleasant she had trodden in. "That easily? You have no idea what a big city can be like."

"I have no idea?"

"Yes. Believe me when I say that if you don't have street smarts, you might not make it past the docks district after we land."

"I've read about Anasoma, you know. I know what to expect."

Miranda sighed, obviously exasperated. "Listen. Reading and knowing isn't the same. You can't read something and think you know how to survive in one of the roughest parts of the empire."

"That's nonsense. Anasoma is an extraordinary city! People from all walks of life live together in harmony, and the greatest scholars and minds travel there to collaborate together, to exchange ideas." He waved his hands in excitement. "The nobles respect the lower classes for the work they do, and the working classes know the nobles' work is essential as well."

Miranda was now staring at him like he had grown a second head . . . and maybe a third. Then she burst out laughing.

"You really have no idea, do you? The docks district is run by *gangs*, who are mostly controlled by merchants. The lowest and most desperate prostitutes ply their trade there." Her voice caught in her throat, all laughter gone, and she briefly cast her eyes at the deck before continuing. "Bad things can happen to the unwary."

Caldan shook his head in disbelief. "I don't know what experiences you've had there, but they can't have been normal."

"I didn't have any 'experiences' there, but I know what the place is like. Everyone does."

"Well, thanks for the warning." He had heard, and read, about problems in the main cities of the Mahruse Empire. *But surely the emperor is doing something about it. After all, every emperor has ensured continued prosperity for his people.* He'd read about their achievements. And yet . . . "I'll take the proper precautions when I'm there," he said earnestly.

"I'm sure you will." She didn't sound sure at all. He decided not to press it.

"Anyway, back to what you were asking before. I can't do it."

"Practice with us?"

"Yes."

"I see. No—actually, I don't. Why not?"

"I can't." A bloody wooden sword arose unbidden in his mind, his own blood-soaked hand holding the hilt. He banished the vision with a shake of his head. "I just can't."

"Because of what happened?"

"I . . . yes."

Miranda shifted closer and rested a hand on his arm. Her feather-light touch felt hot on his skin, which was chilled by the cool night air.

"It's all right, really. If you don't want to, then don't."

She withdrew her hand and stood, leaning against the gunwale. After a moment, Caldan joined her, and they both looked out into the blackness of the sea.

"I don't think I'll stay much longer on this ship," she said, surprising him.

"Why not? It looks like you've found a good place here, with a decent captain. Why would you leave?"

"It's not for me, the traveling and the changes. Oh, it might feel fine for a while, but I know it isn't the life for me. I did it to escape, anyway." She glanced at him briefly, and he didn't know whether to pry or not.

"Care to tell me more? I'm a good listener."

Miranda laughed. "No you aren't, and you just proved it."

Caldan let out a laugh, too. He couldn't help it. "I guess I did." He was glad the sun had sunk below the horizon and it was dark out at sea.

She straightened, wiped her hands on her pants, then ran her fingers through her hair. "Well, I'm turning in. Think about what I said, please. Books may not contain the whole truth." And with that, she walked off.

Caldan wasn't sure what to think of Miranda. She looked very much at home on the ship yet admitted it wasn't a life she wanted or could stay with for long. It unnerved him a bit that someone who seemed so settled wasn't where she wanted to be, and it made him think about his own situation. What he would do, he decided, was find an inn to stay at until he got back on his feet. He could present himself to the guilds, to the nobles as well, and should have no trouble finding a position to which he was suited. From there, with a secure and safe arrangement, he would have time to consider what his options were.

He just hoped that wasn't as difficult as Miranda made it seem. He thought back to what she'd said. If even half of it was true, then there was much he needed to learn. He was willing to concede that living on the island at the monastery could have skewed his views, and it was stupid to think that having experienced one particular place, all others would be the same.

And there was the fact that—according to the masters—his parents had fled some danger on the mainland. His books had said nothing about that.

Unconsciously, one hand moved to touch the trinket and the bone ring, now hanging around his neck from a chain that he had bought from one of the sailors. He missed his parents . . . and his sister, whom he had never really had a chance to know. His eyes grew moist, and he squeezed them shut, rubbing them with his fingers. A certain resolve fell over him. Why they had been killed was a mystery, and maybe he would never find the answer. But he had to make an effort. For his parents, and for his sister's sake. There was little chance that whoever had done this to them could be brought to justice, but perhaps he could find them and . . .

And what? Revenge? He frowned, examining the word and all it implied. Certainly, the masters wouldn't approve. And he wasn't the kind of person who would kill someone in cold blood. But there was also no one else to mourn his family. No one left to avenge them but him.

Shaking his head, he sighed. For all he knew, he wouldn't be able to find out anything about his parents, and these bloody thoughts were just dark fantasies.

Yet, that's all he had. To leave everything behind and start afresh, or dwell on the past, possibly repeating the mistakes his parents made—those were his choices. Would following the trail lead him to death? He didn't know. But he did know he couldn't let it rest. It wasn't in his nature. Perhaps the masters had known this, too.

Caldan withdrew from the deck to his bunk. Though he hadn't done much all day, he was bone-weary.

CHAPTER 9

Glowing a fierce orange, the setting sun bled through the weed-strewn streets of the deserted town. Warm evening winds blew dust across the nearby fields, then into the surrounding forest.

It was the fields that had halted Caitlyn and her men before they continued into the dusty, ramshackle buildings of the town. They had been recently plowed and planted. Small green shoots sprouted from the broken soil, while at the nearby stream a waterwheel turned lazily. Despite the town appearing empty, the waterwheel bore signs of recent repairs: new bindings around joints, recently replaced struts.

According to the scouts, the two farmhands they were following had entered the town a few hours ago. After the nighttime skirmish the farmhands had with the bandits, the scouts had spent the day attempting to find their trail. Of course, by now Aidan knew they were no ordinary farmhands, and most likely sorcerers. Dangerous ones too, judging by their actions. Caitlyn didn't usually like to go after rogue sorcerers herself. Normally, she'd notify the Protectors, but for whatever reason, she wouldn't this time. It was like she could no longer let go, as if her obsession had her in a choke hold and she had no choice but to press on, take all the responsibility herself. Or was the explanation simpler? After all, the Protectors were miles away, and there was no telling what these rogues would get up to if they weren't stopped at once.

Crouched on a rise covered in tall grass between the forest and the fields, Caitlyn lay in watch. Next to her, Aidan was on his stomach, and behind him, Chalayan sat cross-legged. Purple butterflies flew among them and in the fields, landing on their clothes.

Dry grass rustled as the sorcerer fidgeted. He had been on edge since they'd found the charred bodies of whoever had been pursuing the farmhands. Finding their trail had been more difficult than Aidan would have thought—sorcery again, most likely—and Caitlyn's scouts were hard-pressed keeping them in the right direction.

Now they had apparently caught up with them, if the actions of this town were any indication. The scouts had told Caitlyn that there had been some movement in the town, but no one had left. A few women and men had moved between houses and the large barn near the center. And no farmers had visited the fields.

Heat from the ground seeped into Aidan's body. He breathed in warm air. The scent of soil and grass tickled his nostrils, making them itch.

Caitlyn muttered something unintelligible under her breath.

"What was that?" Aidan whispered.

"This will be a night where good triumphs over evil. I'm sure something's amiss, and I'm never wrong—" After breaking off, Caitlyn squeezed her eyes shut, her breath coming in harsh gasps.

"My lady," whispered Aidan urgently. "What is it?"

She waved him away. "Memories. I'll never be rid of them. Chalayan," she called, loud enough to carry. "Can you sense anything from the town? Any sorcery?"

The sorcerer shook his head. The thin braids of hair over his ears swung gently, each tied with a different colored cord. Aidan knew this man, and he was worried.

"What is it?" Caitlyn asked.

Chalayan, whose skill Aidan hadn't seen defeated in all their campaigns, rubbed his arms and looked away. His was a mix of raw talent, conventional sorcery, and tribal lore, and they took his feel for sorcery over anyone's in the Sorcerers' Guild. Caitlyn's commission from the emperor gave them much authority and a certain amount of leeway. Enough so they didn't have to drag one of the emperor's pet sorcerers around with them. Or any of the Protectors with their rules.

"Chalayan . . ." Caitlyn warned.

"I need more time," he replied tersely.

Caitlyn crawled on her belly over to the sorcerer, who shivered despite the warm air. "What is it?"

"A moment, please."

Chalayan cleared a patch of grass and scratched two symbols into the dirt, meaningless to Aidan. The sorcerer lifted his right hand, hesitated, then drew another symbol. He whispered a few words, guttural and raw, then closed his eyes. Motionless, he sat there. They waited.

Chalayan's eyeballs moved under his lids. Sweat poured from his face and dripped onto the dirt, eagerly sucked in by the dry earth. With a suddenness that startled Aidan, he opened his eyes and, with a quick stroke, erased the runes.

"This place," he whispered. "I fear it."

Aidan froze. *Nothing frightens this man.*

Chalayan pulled up some grass and twisted it around his fingers. "It . . . Powerful sorcery has been done here, for many years. This place feels wrong."

"Of course it does, Chalayan—there's evil there. We can handle it." Caitlyn smiled at him and settled a hand on his arm.

"No—it's more than that. Deeper than what we've faced before. Those two men are in there somewhere. And I still don't know how they did the things they did."

Caitlyn looked toward the town. "They don't know we're here. We will catch them by surprise."

Aidan stirred from his spot, taking a step toward them. "We can't.

We have no idea how many there are, their strength, or what resources they have."

"We can," said Caitlyn firmly. "And we will."

Aidan cursed under his breath. "My lady, if you would—"

"No. Surprise is the key this time."

"But—"

"Aidan," snapped Caitlyn. "I have decided." She glared at him.

She has lost it, Aidan thought. *She's starting to see me as a liability. And maybe Chalayan.* He was worried, angry, and conflicted all at once. But duty demanded he back down.

She rose to a crouch and shuffled back toward the camp, slapping her pants and shirt, puffs of dust rising with each hit.

Aidan watched Caitlyn go down toward the men. *Scum. Murdering bastards. Rapists. Why's she so concerned with evil everywhere, but blind to what's under her nose?*

He turned to Chalayan. "What is it, my friend? I can feel it: a sense of foreboding. What's causing it?"

"Maybe nothing. Maybe everything." The sorcerer raised his trinket to his lips. "This is a bad place."

Without another word, he left Aidan on the rise among the butterflies.

THE SUN DIPPED below the hills after what felt like an interminable wait. Stars twinkled in the night sky.

Aidan stood next to Caitlyn as she gathered the men and outlined her plan.

"Listen up. Four teams, each approaching the town from a different direction, each team to spread out and look for signs of life as you converge on the center. Head toward the large barn. You should be able to see it over the tops of the other buildings. Make no noise, and keep an eye out for anything strange, anything that will give us an idea as to what's going on."

She cleared her throat and continued. Aidan could see she made an effort to meet the eyes of each man as they stood around her. Some fidgeted, the nervous subconscious movements of men who inwardly dreaded the fighting they knew was to come. Some wore tight smiles or outright grins, those who relished the bloodshed and violence that usually came with one of her crusades.

"We don't know what we're dealing with here, and you all saw what happened to the bandits. We think they have an alchemical mixture that explodes and burns, but . . ." She spread her hands. "We can't say for sure."

Murmurs arose at her statement.

"What this means," she said loudly, "is that we need to retain the element of surprise. They have no idea we're here, and I want to keep it that way for as long as possible."

"Can't Chalayan protect us from the alchemy?" asked Hannes as he scratched his gray beard.

All eyes turned to the sorcerer, who shook his head.

"I'll be with one group," he said. "I can't be with all four, and even for the group I'm with, I can offer only minimal protection. The power of the . . . explosions . . . I doubt I could hold out for long." He glanced at Caitlyn, then looked away.

Caitlyn slowly walked the circle of men facing her. "You all know why we are here. We have the cause of righteousness on our side, as we always have, and like so many other times before, we will be victorious. Trust your own skills and those of your fellow men. We have faced malevolent creations from before the Shattering, and depraved men who placed no value on human life. Each time we prevailed!"

Barely, in the case of the jukari. It wasn't an experience Aidan wanted to repeat anytime soon.

Caitlyn continued. "And we will again, for our cause is just . . . and right."

Her eyes shone in the moonlight, and many nods and muted whisperings greeted her words. Once more she had them—they were ready to fight for her, no matter what. Aidan could feel the strength of her conviction. Only, this time it felt wrong . . . as if Caitlyn had veered down a dangerous path.

With a wave, Caitlyn dismissed the men, who shuffled off in all directions to finish packing their gear and gather in their assigned groups.

Aidan approached her, followed closely by Chalayan and Anshul cel Rau. The three of them stayed with Caitlyn's group, as always.

Chalayan looked wan in the faint light, and Anshul adjusted his swords in their scabbards for the third time since Caitlyn had begun her speech. He looked around with a flicker of unease. Clearly, Chalayan's obvious apprehension had spread, and even the swordsman had grown nervous.

Aidan pondered the situation. His palms were sweaty just standing near the sorcerer and the swordsman, as if his mind was picking up signs of their unease and vibrating in tune. Both Chalayan and cel Rau stared at him.

Caitlyn smiled at him lopsidedly. "What is it?" she asked.

He hesitated. *Say it, you coward.* "Chalayan says this is a bad place, and with what happened to the bandits . . . I think we should scout the town longer, see what we are up against."

Her disappointment was almost palpable. "My Aidan. Always cautious, always willing to stand back and deliberate while evil lives on."

"It's not that, my lady. We have no idea—"

"We cut it off, Aidan. Cauterize it before it spreads like gangrene. Wait, and it's too late."

CHAPTER 10

For the entire day the seas remained calm, and Caldan spent his time on deck moving around as the shadows did to keep cool. He leaned against the gunwale and watched the beginning of the crew's sword practice. So far they were below average at best, and many would struggle against the students at the monastery. The thought of his home and the pang of loss that accompanied it caught him off guard; they were quickly followed by an image of Marlon lying bloody on the ground. Caldan flinched and turned his back on the practice bouts. As he did, a cabin boy approached, stating that the captain required his presence.

Captain Charlotte waved him to a chair and made small talk, but it wasn't long before she unlocked a chest and carefully removed an exquisite Dominion set. It was made from eight different types of wood, both the three boards and the pieces. Caldan recognized rosewood, maple, oak, walnut, and one lacewood piece. Three other types he didn't know.

She didn't have to say a word.

For the next few hours they played Dominion without pause, Caldan eager to lose himself and forget about everything else.

He watched the captain sit on her armchair across the desk in front of him. The sun had set outside, and a welcome breeze began to blow. Her elbows rested on her knees as she intently examined the problem laid out on the Dominion board.

"It's a trap, isn't it?" she asked, eyeing Caldan.

He shrugged. "You have to consider that, of course."

Initially, he'd wondered why she had summoned him, then realized that, like the crewmen, she was bored with the lack of breeze and needed a diversion to while away the time.

"What are the woods used in your set?" he asked.

"Don't try to distract me," she said. "I know what you're up to."

"I wasn't—"

"Of course you were. Everyone tries something to give them an edge."

"I don't need an edge."

Charlotte gave him a penetrating stare. "Is that because I'm no competition?"

"Yes . . . I mean no . . . I mean it's been enjoyable playing with you."

"Relax," she said. She returned to the board, muttering under her breath. In the last few hours they had managed two games of an abridged version playable on her set. She had lost both soundly, and in this third game she wasn't going to fare any better.

After another few minutes examining the board, she sat back, scratched her cheek, and poured out another measure of rum for her and Caldan. They had both consumed enough to be pleasantly warm, even with the cool evening breeze coming in the open windows.

"I'm usually quite good at this, you know," she said.

"You are good. It's just that you don't see the patterns before it's too late."

"And you don't have any tact," she said sharply.

Caldan put his hands up in apology.

Charlotte frowned and crossed her arms, then shook her head with a rueful grin. "I'm sorry. I'm not used to losing. Seriously, though—I've won a fair few ducats on games, so I think I see the patterns fine. I won this set in a contest." She cradled one of the pieces and ran her fingers along the grain of the wood. "Maybe I'm having an off day."

Caldan nodded. "Maybe," he said with a shrug.

She leaned forward and, with quick economical movements, shifted two of her pieces. "There. See what you make of that!"

Caldan studied the changes for a few moments, then let a smile show.

"Amused?" asked Charlotte, taking another sip of rum.

Caldan shook his head. "No. Interested, not amused. You know, it wasn't a trap."

With a start, Charlotte coughed rum back into her cup. She wiped her mouth with her sleeve, looked at Caldan for a moment, then smirked.

"Ha-ha! You almost had me there. Of course it's a trap."

Caldan used his turn to move two of his pieces. He placed each with precision, just so on the board. He sat back in his chair and gazed out the window at the stars appearing in the night sky.

Charlotte peered closely at the board. A few minutes passed without a word being spoken by either of them.

"Well," she said, shoulders slumping. "That *is* interesting. You must have set that up close to the start of the game."

"It's an old strategy we were taught. Apparently, it was first used around four hundred years ago."

"It's not old if you've never seen it."

"I guess that's true. But anyone can read books on Dominion and study strategies for themselves. That one is from *Essays on Dominion*, and it's also detailed in *Morals of Dominion*."

Charlotte stared at him, astonished. "Have you read those books?"

"Yes, all the students do. Why? What's wrong?"

"I've *heard* of them, but they're both extremely rare. The only copies thought to have survived are said to be owned by the emperor himself and the Sorcerers' Guild. To have seen them, let alone read them . . ." She trailed off, shaking her head.

"The monks have a large library, and their scribes copy many books for the students to study. I would offer to show you one day, but . . . I fear that's not possible now."

"Maybe I'll visit the monastery next time I'm in port." She turned her attention back to the board and breathed out heavily, the corners of her mouth turned down in disappointment. "I was sure I had it worked out." Her face lit up, and she smiled. "I know just the people to use it on!" she said and laughed, her unabashed enjoyment of losing to a new strategy causing Caldan to join in.

"You're different from what I expected," Charlotte said after a short, companionable silence, where the only noise was the creak of the ship's timbers as it swayed to and fro in the strengthening breeze.

"What did you expect?" He didn't like the idea of other people thinking him a criminal, which is what they'd believed, according to Miranda.

"I wasn't told much, other than someone had been exiled from the monastery for an unspecified reason. It was natural to assume someone who has been exiled is fairly . . . unsavory."

Caldan nodded in agreement. "With me it was . . . well, all about money and influence, which hurts, to be honest. I injured a son from a wealthy family, and they could have withdrawn their children from the monastery, along with their support. They could also have made life hard for the masters by influencing other families to withdraw students or funding. The masters did what they thought was best, for themselves."

"I hate to say it, but it makes sense. Money makes the world go 'round. What are you going to do when we make port in Anasoma?"

Caldan stared into his cup. "I don't know. I have some ducats, but not many. I thought I'd find work as a tutor to a wealthy family, or as a scholar with one of the guilds. I'm not really sure."

"How much do you have?"

"A small purse," he replied carefully.

She raised her eyebrows at him and waved a hand around. "I own this ship. A small purse wouldn't interest me, even if I were a thief."

Caldan felt blood rush to his face. "Sorry, I . . . I'm a bit out of my depth here."

Charlotte grunted and sat back, crossing her legs. "But you said you injured the son of a wealthy family. I wouldn't have thought that other families in the city would welcome you if they knew about the circumstances of your exile."

Caldan brought his cup to his mouth and smelled the dark rum. Suddenly, he didn't feel like drinking anymore. "I hadn't thought they'd react like that," he admitted. "But now you mention it . . . Well, I don't need them anyway. I'm sure one of the guilds will take me in."

"If that's the route you want to go, sure." There was something in her voice, though, that caught Caldan's attention. She confirmed his suspicions when she said, "You know . . . there are places in Anasoma, and the rest of the empire, where you can win ducats playing Dominion. Either from prizes or betting on matches. And there are competitions sponsored by nobles and wealthy families, as well as the Autumn Festival games, which are coming up soon. Forget about the other competitions there, the archery, horsemanship, swordsmanship. If you entered the Dominion competition . . ." She let her voice trail off, then continued. "Someone with your skill could not only win some coins, but might come to the attention of one of the noble families or the guilds. People hold a lot of value in a good player, as you know." She must have seen something in his face, because she added, "Maybe you don't. Regardless, could be an opportunity, if you can take it. Don't underestimate yourself. It's been a long time since I was soundly beaten three games to none." She grinned ruefully. "A very long time."

"They offer prize money to the winners?"

"Not just the winners—for places as well. If someone performs exceptionally, nobles or wealthy merchants may hand out ducats as a reward. I heard a hundred years ago a man called Kelhak thoroughly trounced all comers in the Dominion contest. He won the first prize and literally had bulging purses thrown at him from the crowd."

"Kelhak? Are you sure?"

"Yes, that's what I was told his name was. Why?"

"Kelhak used to be a student at the monastery, like me, except from a wealthy family. He was exiled as well, though for reasons the monks never talk about. He was a gifted Dominion player, and some of his games are studied by the students today."

"I didn't know that."

"What happened to him after the festival?"

"No idea. He disappeared. Some say he was taken in by a noble family; others say he left with a caravan heading north. Can't say I've heard anything of him since that time. Maybe he just found a nice girl and settled down." She chortled. "Anyway, one more drink before I head topside to check on the crew." She reached for the rum bottle, but in her inebriated state knocked it off the edge of the desk. She made an awkward grab and missed.

Caldan lunged for the bottle, catching and twisting it upright before it had fallen a handspan below the top of the desk.

"I thought it was gone, for sure," exclaimed Charlotte. "I could see myself picking up broken glass and my cabin smelling of rum for a week. Thank you."

"Don't mention it," Caldan said.

"Quick reflexes you have there. I wouldn't have thought someone could move so fast."

"Just lucky, I guess."

"No, I've seen people move fast—master bladesmen and the like— and you moved quicker than any I've seen." She waved her cup for him to refill.

He obliged. "I doubt it. My swordplay is average. Any of the masters and top students at the monastery could best me."

She looked unconvinced. "You should enter the sword contest as well. No point being modest when you could earn some coins and a reputation."

Caldan shook his head. "There are plenty of better swordsmen than me. I don't doubt they will be vying for coins and a 'reputation,' as you say, at this festival."

"It can't hurt to try anyway, can it?"

"I . . . don't know if I will." *But I do know what happened the last time I held a sword.* "Right now, I can't bring myself to join in when the crew are exercising. I doubt I could win without training, and I just don't think I'll be practicing anytime soon."

"I can understand why you're reluctant, but you should still do some training—forms, exercises, the like. In the city it could come in handy. Some sections are not exactly the most law abiding. You could say they are downright dangerous. Though carrying a sword is forbidden in the city without special dispensation; some men carry sturdy walking sticks instead." She tapped the side of her nose. A mischievous smile touched her face. "Of course, you could always take on the life of a treasure hunter. Outside of the empire and surrounding kingdoms there are lands in which leftovers from the Shattering flourish—jukari and the like. Treasure hunters can make a living searching old ruins in the hope of finding valuable craftings or trinkets. It's risky, obviously—not many of them find a fortune. But enough do to keep them returning. Someone like you, trained by the monks in sorcery and bladework, could do well at such a venture. A slice of luck and you'd be a rich man."

Caldan laughed and shook his head. "I'll think about it." He could see from her expression she saw straight through his evasion. "All right," he relented. "I'll take your advice seriously, I promise."

"You're an intelligent young man, and I wouldn't want to see you maimed or dead because you were too stubborn." She smiled at him. "If I were ten years younger . . ."

Again Caldan blushed, and she laughed at his discomfort. He might have thrown her for a loop in Dominion, but she'd more than managed to put him off balance a few times herself. He decided to make a polite withdrawal and stood.

"I've taken up enough of your time. I'm sure you need to get on deck and make certain everything is well."

Charlotte stood, unsteady on her feet. "Yes, with the breeze strengthening I'd better see they put more sail on. Go on, have something to eat and think on what I said."

AFTER CALDAN HAD left, Charlotte stared at the Dominion board.

A polite knock on the door woke her from her reverie. Miranda poked her head in.

"How did the games go?" she asked, frowning. "You were playing for a long time."

She's jealous and has taken a liking to Caldan. Once I would have warned her off the boy, but now . . . now she's old enough to make her own decisions. "Not bad. If you think being defeated three games in a row is not bad."

Miranda's expression brightened. "Ha-ha!" she crowed. "Did you win any coins off him?"

"No. He beat *me.*"

"What? That's—"

"Enough." Charlotte glared at her. "You asked to play sailor on this trip, against my advice, so act like one." *Such a strange one. She's made enough ducats to set herself up for life, and she wants to play at slumming it.* "Get on deck and tell them I'm coming up for an inspection. Ancestors help you if anything's out of place."

Miranda swallowed and nodded. "Aye." She withdrew her head and closed the door.

Charlotte paused to glance ruefully at the Dominion board. She collected a light woolen cloak from the back of the door and headed up on deck.

CHAPTER 11

As they approached the pier, Caldan thought the memory of the corpse floating in the swell would stay with him for the rest of his life. It was pale and bloated, too small to be an adult. The *Loretta* passed by close enough that many of the crew stopped to stare. Occasionally, the corpse jerked down, as if being pulled, and the longer he watched, the redder the water around it became, like a pool of ink spreading across a page.

Soon after they left the body in their wake, a boat with two men launched from the docks ahead and rowed toward it. They pulled alongside the corpse and used metal hooks attached to long wooden poles to retrieve the remains. And remains they were, as by the time the boat arrived it didn't look like a body anymore as much as a mangled mess. Small sharks made their home in the harbor, and this morning they had found a feast.

On deck, Caldan looked away from the sight. The famed city of Anasoma wasn't the pristine pride of the empire he had believed it would be. Miranda had tried to explain this to him, but nothing drove new knowledge home like a good example. A bloated corpse welcoming him had certainly forced him to look at the city in a different light.

Around the wharf the *Loretta* had tied up to, debris and rubbish drifted on the surface of the water. Seaweed, raw sewage, dead fish, leaves and sticks, and the odd piece of clothing all combined to form a disgusting scum. On the wharf next to theirs he could see disheveled children hanging over the side, plumbing the water with a three-pronged hook attached to a thin rope. The items they found and stashed in a wicker basket didn't look like anything he would have considered keeping. Luckily, a stiff breeze from the sea blew most of the reek of the flotsam away, but he could imagine what the stench would be like on a hot summer's day.

A short way inland, atop towers poking over the roofs of buildings, he could just make out trebuchets and other siege engines. A forest of masts surrounded their ship, rocking gently in the swell: boats of all types and in all states of repair, old and new, some disheveled from storms at sea and a lack of maintenance, while others sparkled as if launched only yesterday.

The wooden wharves projected into the harbor and were long enough to accommodate two or three ships on each side.

"They's built for incoming merchant ships," Sharkey said from behind him. "Got to keep 'em separate from them run-of-the-mill fishing vessels and make it easy for officials to split them off and inspect. You got four docking areas in Anasoma: the merchants, where the *Loretta* berths with the rest of the trading ships; the fisheries, where the trawlers and netters dock—hardworking they are—and three stone piers for the nobles' and emperor's ships. And then there's the Cemetery to the north. Old ships well past their time and left to rot." Sharkey spat over the gunwale into the water. "Hundreds of 'em, lashed together, wrecks and hulls that still float but wouldn't last on the open sea. I've heard people live in them. Like a floating slum."

Conall stood beside Sharkey, spooling a coil of rope. As he finished, he looked around furtively, then prodded the neatly stowed rope into a loose mess and proceeded to re-coil it again, obviously avoiding real work.

Sharkey snorted in disgust at the young sailor, though he wasn't doing anything either. "You'll get caught one day, Conall, and the captain won't go easy on ya."

"Everyone else is busy; I'd just get in their way."

Sharkey shook his head and turned back to Caldan.

"Have you seen Miranda?" Caldan asked. "I wanted to . . . er . . ."

Sharkey winked and leered at him. "I know what you're thinking, lad. But she's related to the captain, so you'd best keep your hands off or Captain Charlotte will remove them herself!"

Both Conall and Sharkey chuckled as Caldan felt blood suffuse his face.

"I just wanted to say good-bye."

"'Course ya did. Well, she's got duties to perform."

Caldan nodded and thanked Sharkey, realizing their conversation with him was just another excuse to avoid work.

After docking, the crew ran out a gangplank, then busied themselves with squaring away and untying the cargo. Two guards from the Harbor Watch had taken position at the end of their gangplank, waiting patiently for customs officials. No one would be able to leave the ship until docking and customs duties were paid.

Caldan's sacks lay at his feet. He had to consciously stop his hand from checking that his rings were still secure around his neck.

Having been eager to arrive at Anasoma and see the city, now Caldan strangely welcomed the delay at the docks. The difference and peculiarity of the place confused him, as if the rules that had previously governed his entire reality might not apply here. It was disconcerting, to say the least. It was far from the shining city he'd thought it would be.

It took an hour before two officious-looking men strode up the gangplank and onto the ship. They were escorted by four grim-faced Harbor Watch guards. Captain Charlotte, forewarned of their arrival as they came down the pier, was on deck to greet them. Both men withdrew parchment from flat leather cases they carried, and one

used a wooden pen with a metal nib to make notes. They all disappeared belowdecks for a cargo inspection and what Caldan suspected
also involved a bribe. Leaving, the officials handed the captain a piece
of parchment detailing the goods inspected and the Harbor Watch's
approval for her to dock and trade. On her way back belowdecks,
Charlotte nodded for Caldan to disembark and drew close for a quick
word.

"You're fine to go, now the inspection's over." She blew out a breath
in relief, eyes squinted in the sun.

"Thank you," Caldan replied. "I assume everything went well. You
didn't expect any trouble, did you?"

"Depends on what they found." She winked at him as she hooked
her thumbs into her belt. "Some of them are more trouble than others, think they can bend the rules to try and make some extra ducats.
If you know the rules yourself, things go smoother."

Caldan nodded at the wisdom. *As it is with most situations.* "Any
advice for the city?" He pointed his chin at the pier.

"Yes: don't linger in the docks district, if you can avoid it. Dockside, they call it. Head straight up that main street in front of the
pier and keep going until you see a largish intersection with two
taverns. One, the Willing Mermaid, is a rough place, but the other
is better, the Otter. You should be able to get a room for the night, if
not longer, at a reasonable price."

"Thank you. I'll do that."

"And try not to be polite all the time. Some people will think it's
odd."

He raised his eyebrows but nodded all the same. "And mark me as
someone who can be taken advantage of?"

"Exactly. You catch on quick."

"It's an obvious conclusion."

"Not to everyone, Caldan, not to everyone. One other thing: the
room should be about four copper ducats for the night. The farther
into the city you go, the higher prices get. I daresay you'll want to
spend as little as possible until you can set yourself up with a steady
income."

His coin pouch rested inside his pants, tied to his belt and tucked in. Hard to access, but better than having a cutpurse steal it.

"And you might want to visit the purified land inside the city walls, to the west. You can't miss it. For someone like you, I imagine it would be intriguing."

"There's one inside the city walls?" said Caldan, shocked. Patches of purified land were scattered around the empire and the surrounding kingdoms. They were places where sorcery, crafting, and trinkets didn't function, areas so blighted by sorcerous forces during the Shattering that they were anathema to all who could access their wells. He had read that stepping inside a section of purified land was an experience that left many sorcerers trembling and weak, though it was probably only because they couldn't access their wells, which was what made them who they were.

"Go and see. You should be open to new experiences." Charlotte shuffled her feet and glanced out to sea before looking back at him. "Well, good luck."

"Do you know where Miranda is? I thought she would come up on deck so I could say my farewells."

"She's helping ready some cargo for unloading. I thought you two had a chat last night."

"We did, and we said good-bye. I thought . . . oh, never mind." Caldan didn't know what he was doing delaying his departure, except he would have liked to see Miranda one more time.

Charlotte placed a hand gently on his shoulder. "Don't worry yourself. You have much to sort out in the next few days. It's no easy thing settling into a new place. I don't envy you."

Caldan held out his hand. "I had better go. It was a pleasure meeting you, Captain."

Her hand enfolded his in a firm, warm grip.

"Likewise. And the name's Charlotte. We're in port here periodically, so if you have time to drop by for some Dominion practice, I won't mind."

"That would be good."

With a final nod, he walked down to the wharf and wound his way through piles of barrels, crates, and a few horse-drawn wagons until it ended and the streets of Dockside began.

Redbrick buildings with large warehouse doors and narrow windows, stained with salt residue, lined the street. Weeds poked through on the roofs, which were old, tiles cracked and missing. A few buildings had tradesmen at work, scraping off years of dirt and salt and replacing broken roofing.

The street thronged with people—sailors, teamsters, brawny men used for loading and unloading—and no one looked happy. Well-dressed merchants passed by in a rush, heads down—on important business, no doubt. The street continued over several bridges spanning canals that led off into the distance, with two larger bridges crossing over brown rivers.

The stench of the flotsam in the harbor rolled over Caldan. The breeze off the water he had been thankful for now brought the full impact to his nostrils. He held a hand up to his nose and coughed. A sailor mending a net sneered at him.

The city itself extended as far as his eyes could see. Roofs, terraces, domes, and towers stretched away from him until they became lost in a haze. The rooftops were dotted with green patches and trees. Some open terrace gardens, he thought, though most looked to be weeds and moss. Four Harbor Watch guards stood at a corner, formidable in their worn leather armor with cruel-looking clubs, scanning the crowd. He gave them a wide berth.

He set off across the cobbles, weaving through the crowd and up the closest main street as Charlotte had suggested. A faded, painted sign was attached to one building: CUTTLEFISH STREET, it proclaimed in plain script. Caldan walked past, keeping close to the left wall, avoiding the gutter of sludge running down the edge of the street. He made slow progress, passing side streets and narrow alleys. Buildings were either run-down homes for Dockside residents, cheap inns and taverns, or shops and businesses. Many of the doorways contained small braziers, along with brightly decorated bowls filled with nuts or milk. Most of the braziers contained only ash, but some exuded smoke as they burned offerings. Ah . . . the Ghost Festival. The people on

Eremite did something similar, but the monks didn't follow such superstitions.

A number of times he had to press against a wall when wagons passed, and once a group of men and women in chains shuffled by, dirt-covered prisoners reeking of stale sweat and urine. Vacant eyes stared ahead or at the ground. Guards prodded a man when he stumbled to his knees and took too long to regain his feet. A woman in the crowd spat in their direction, disgust on her face. A young bystander sneered at her and looked about to say something when his companions dragged him away.

The emperor's soldiers were posted on many corners. Many carried bows with quivers full of arrows on their backs. At one corner, an old man was arguing with a young noble who'd taken offense when he'd inadvertently been stumbled into. Despite the man's frailness, the soldiers prodded him with their clubs.

"Move along," one said, obviously taking the noble's side.

"Bloody Quivers," muttered the old man as he tottered past Caldan.

Twice the soldiers—Quivers, apparently—stopped him to ask his name and business. When they were satisfied with his answers, he was allowed to continue without any fuss.

Soon, the street opened up onto a large intersection. As Captain Charlotte had said, there were two inns, with the other corner positions taken up by a blacksmith and a leatherworker. It was obvious from the sign for the Willing Mermaid the place catered to rougher types. It was dirty, rusty, and lewd. He grinned at the salacious sign but headed into the Otter, pausing inside the door to allow his eyes to adjust to the gloom. All the tables were empty, as was the space behind the bar.

A wiry man, thin-lipped and greasy-haired, emerged from behind a hanging, which concealed a doorway.

"Good day, sir. May I be of service?" He looked Caldan up and down, and his mouth twitched. "Perhaps the Willing Mermaid across the way might be more to your taste?"

"A friend of mine, Captain Charlotte of the *Loretta*, recommended this place."

At the mention of the captain's name, the innkeeper's expression brightened. "Oh, of course. A lovely lady." He rubbed his hands together. "Are you after lodging or merely some victuals?"

"Both, if food is included with the rooms. I don't mind staying in your least expensive room as I don't hold much store in luxuries."

"Of course, sir. Let me check." The innkeeper walked behind the bar and drew out a shallow wooden box containing a number of keys. He plucked one out and handed it to Caldan. "This one should do you nicely. A bargain at six copper ducats a night. And I'm afraid it's a few hours until the next meal."

Caldan fingered his purse, the only coins he could count on for the foreseeable future. "That's fine. But six ducats? Captain Charlotte led me to believe four would be sufficient."

"For a friend of hers, I can manage with four, though taxes are high these days. How long will you be staying?"

"I'm not sure. At least a week, possibly longer. Depends on how quickly I find work."

"Ah! You'll want to try the traders' quarter—the guilds and the noticeboards are there. You can read, can't you?"

"Yes."

After exchanging a few more pleasantries, the innkeeper led Caldan to his room, making small talk on the way. It was a clean space with a barred window overlooking a narrow alley. A cot with a straw mattress was the only furniture, and if he stretched his arms out, Caldan was sure he could touch both walls.

There was much to do. First things first. He needed to spend some coins on essentials if he was to have a good start in this new place. It would be best to buy what he needed as soon as possible.

He left the room, locking the door behind him. The lock was simple, and Caldan had no doubt that anyone who wanted to enter his room while he wasn't there would be able to do so easily. Another problem to take care of, but at the moment, he didn't have anything worth stealing. Nothing except his trinket, that is, but he planned to always keep that hidden on his person anyway.

Leaving the Otter, he asked directions and quickly found his way to an outside market set up in a common square. The area was packed with stalls and wagons. Some appeared more permanent than others, while many of the wagons looked as if local farmers had brought them into the city for the day to sell produce. Meat—both raw and cooked—fruit and vegetables, cloth and clothes, pottery, hats, and a hundred other essentials were all on display.

Unlike on Eremite, here both men and women dressed in a mix of fashions, probably from other parts of the empire. The men wore pants, as they did on Eremite, but they topped them with garishly colored shirts and bright-buttoned overcoats. Not a few sported hats. The women's clothes were more diverse, from short skirts to dresses, pants, and shirts; while some just had a long ribbon wound around their torsos and upper arms. It was all he could do not to stare.

He made his way to where a haze of smoke hung in the air and mouthwatering smells of cooking wafted into the crowd. Passing by a few stalls, including one that sold honeyed crickets and grubs on skewers, he decided on one that had roast pig, which came sliced and wrapped in flatbread.

"One, please," said Caldan, pointing to the bread and meat bundle a man leaving the stall was biting into. Handing over the asking price from his dwindling supply of coins wasn't easy. Triple what he thought it would be and enough to buy him a good meal in Eremite. So far, the city wasn't living up to everything he expected. The meat was fatty and chewy, but at least tasted as good as it smelled. He finished off his lunch, and an hour later he was headed back to the Otter with a few packages, which he had placed in a leather satchel to replace his sacks.

Back in his room, he took stock of his purchases. A secondhand razor, soap, a dozen sheets of good-quality parchment, ink and quill, a handful of metal tacks, and a knife. The razor and soap he would use later when he found a public bathhouse. At the price the Otter charged for its only bath, he wasn't going to use it anytime soon. After what he'd spent today, his purse was depressingly depleted.

Taking great care, Caldan cut two squares of parchment from a sheet, each half the size of his palm. Uncapping the ink, he lay on the floor, the only flat surface to work on, and penned four glyphs on each square, all close to the corners. With two tacks dead center of the squares, he pinned one on the edge of the door near the lock and one opposite it on the frame. They would last a few days, which was enough for the time being. Whenever he left his room, he could activate them, and they would create an attraction between the door and the frame, so even if the door wasn't locked, it wouldn't open. A simple yet effective locking device, but one easily broken by another sorcerer, given time.

Caldan yawned and rubbed his eyes. Although it was now only late afternoon, he was tired. Strange surroundings, the odd sights, and the stresses of a new city combined to wear away at him. He lay on his cot for a short nap, intending to rise later and work out where he should visit tomorrow to find employment, but he was soon fast asleep.

TWO DAYS LATER, Caldan was still at the Otter, purse even emptier. To say his first two days had been an unmitigated disaster wouldn't be far from the truth.

Sitting at a table, he sipped a mug of pear cider while waiting for the food he had ordered: sheep stew, the cheapest item on the menu.

The dining room was busy tonight. If the shopkeepers and the patrons could be believed, all the inns would be busier from now on as people arrived for the Autumn Festival. Earlier that morning, the innkeeper had tried to increase the rent for his tiny room, citing the huge upcoming demand. Caldan argued it would hardly be in demand due to its small size and lack of proper furnishings, and he managed to persuade the innkeeper to keep to their current arrangement for a few more days.

He didn't have any idea how much longer he would be staying, and so far his search for work of any kind had proven fruitless. The day after arriving, he had thrown off his trepidation and visited the traders' quarter to ferret out any prospects that might be available. In the morning, he approached a number of the guilds that he thought might have a use for someone who could read and write, could calculate numbers, and was well educated in history and crafting. The tradesmen's guilds, which included carpenters, stonemasons, leather-workers, and weavers, to name a few, were interested in his reading, writing, and numbers aptitudes, but wouldn't hire him unless he was a member of the Scribes' or Bookkeepers' Guilds. Off he went to find the Scribes' and Bookkeepers' Guilds, who both said it was unlikely they would recognize someone trained outside of the city, but it did happen. After a short interview with a journeyman from each guild, they both decided his knowledge was not deep enough to warrant further testing and verification, so he would not be recognized. Additionally, the usual age to enter a guild was young, twelve or thirteen, and a long period of apprenticeship and testing was required before reaching journeyman status. Although Caldan was well versed in a number of subjects and disciplines, his knowledge was nowhere near the standard required of a journeyman, and due to his age, none would take him as an apprentice.

Merchant guilds were his next option the day after, but to his chagrin he met with the same story as the day before. Wherever he went, he was directed to a different location in the traders' quarter: the unskilled laborers' market.

By the time he arrived it was midday, and one look at the dispir-ited and disheveled men standing around hoping for the chance of a day's work was enough to halt him in his tracks. They were dressed in ragged clothes that were more patches and holes than original mate-rial, and they had grubby, thin faces. He wasn't desperate yet and hoped he never would be. He turned and quickly left the groups of men huddled against the walls out of the wind, wondering how he was going to survive after his meager store of coins ran out. The path those men were on—well, it looked like it wasn't a path at all but a dead-end street. They were barely surviving hand to mouth every day, standing around hoping for enough work to buy enough food to stay alive. Caldan wondered where they slept at night, and what happened to them in the winter when the cold wind off the ocean must chill to the bone.

For the remainder of the day until sunset he'd wandered around the city. He didn't remember much of the afternoon, as his thoughts were on survival and examining options to procure a few more coins to get him through a few more days. His situation wasn't anywhere near as desperate as that of the unskilled laborers, but he feared his store of coins wouldn't last long, especially with the Autumn Festival likely to push up the price of food and accommodation.

Thoughts buzzing in circles and not getting anywhere, he'd wandered back to the Otter as night fell and taken a chair at a table to wait for dinner.

Caldan vowed the pear cider he nursed would be his last luxury until he found a steady stream of income. It galled him to think, with all the years he had spent at the monastery, he hadn't been able to find someone who could use his skills.

But when he thought of the students at the monastery, he realized that was exactly the objective of the monks. It made sense to him now. The monastery had built a reputation as a place of learning, where diverse skills and knowledge could be taught in one place, rather than noble families having to hire many different tutors. Their children could be sent there for a year or more to gain an understanding of a huge range of different subjects and aspects of life. Further education in whatever business or subject their parents wanted could be given when their children returned home. Most of the unfortunates taken in by the monks, like himself, rarely left the island and stayed on at the monastery, so providing them with skills to survive in the outside world wasn't a consideration.

Caldan snorted into his cup, which brought sweet cider fumes to his face. The inn's only waitress—he didn't know her name—plonked a bowl of sheep stew in front of him, along with a wooden spoon and a loaf of bread. He nodded thanks, but she had already turned to deliver another meal to the table next to his. Despite looking unappealing—a bowl of greasy brown gravy with chunks of meat in it—the stew was tasty. Spices disguised the strong mutton flavor and added a heat he found pleasant, as long as a drink was nearby to wash it down. Caldan savored his stew, taking small bites of meat and gravy with bread and sipping his cider.

A man and a woman were occupied in a game of Dominion in one corner, using the inn's own board and pieces. Four silver coins glinted beside the board, so the stakes were high. Caldan decided against going over to watch and instead listened to snatches of various conversations around the room.

Two merchants near him were leaning across their table, heads together, and despite the constant hum, Caldan was able to clearly hear what they were saying.

" . . . thought I'd be able to fetch a higher price for the goods, a few ducats more per item, but they wouldn't budge. Bloody head trader was made of stone."

"Typical. They've got their fingers everywhere. I heard they bought a warehouse by the docks and a few more properties around it. Soon you'll need to pay them to store your goods as well."

"Wouldn't surprise me. They've been growing stronger for years now. Hardly seem to put a step wrong in the market."

With nothing of interest in that conversation, Caldan let his ears wander to pick out some other chatter.

" . . . hard road that one, coming down from the mountains. That's why I always come to the Autumn Festival a bit early like. Too many carts and wagons on the narrow passes make it dangerous."

" . . . so I says to the beggar, 'If you want a copper, you have to earn it, so do what I said and you'll get your ducat!' Ha-ha-ha! She ran off."

" . . . The children are fine, thank you for asking. My littlest one is starting to walk."

Caldan's ears pricked up at one conversation. "I heard the competition in the festival will be pretty fierce this year. A master bladesman from the Steppes has entered the lists, and the ambassador from the Sotharle Union of Cities has come for the Dominion contest. What I wouldn't give to see him matched against the emperor's chancellor!"

"Ha! Unlikely to happen. They'll try to have him knocked out in the qualifying matches."

"Still, wouldn't it be a sight to see the old pompous ass getting beat by the upstart cities?"

"Isn't going to happen. He's won every contest the last few years.

As much as I dislike the dried-out old bird, he knows what he's doing."

Caldan had read about the lands surrounding the empire, but it was odd, and strangely exciting, to hear them spoken about by people who might have even been there. The Sotharle Union of Cities was far to the northwest, and the Steppes to the southwest, populated by mostly nomadic tribes he'd only read of. Hundreds of years ago, the empire had tried to claim the lush grasslands of the Steppes for itself, succeeding only marginally before having its nose bloodied by the fierce people living there. He thought back to what Captain Charlotte had said about treasure hunters finding their fortune in the wilds. Still not something he could see himself doing, but with his prospects what they were, he might have to seriously consider it.

Caldan's thoughts turned back to Dominion as the inn grew noisier. Usually, any discussion involving the game would have him looking to join in and while away a few hours with like-minded people. But not tonight. He was too tired from the last few days and disheartened at the start of his new life in Anasoma. Still, he did have an inkling as to what line of inquiry he could follow up next. He could always do as Charlotte had suggested and enter a few of the competitions at the Autumn Festival. But doing well enough to earn a purse of ducats was chancy indeed, and relying on luck to survive didn't appeal to him. He could try his hand at winning some coins playing Dominion against people frequenting the inns around the area, but somehow it didn't feel right. Taking ducats from people who hadn't had his advantages of practicing against masters, and rare books to study from—no, it was unfair. He would take that path only as a last resort.

He swallowed the rest of his pear cider in a few quick gulps then stood, intending to head back to his room and work on some patterns and exercises with crafting. That was his next idea, to approach the Sorcerers' Guild and see if they could find a use for his talents in that area. From his lessons at the monastery, he knew he had skill and was one of the few able to access his well. It was a long shot, just like with the other guilds, but what choice did he have?

When he was halfway across the room, his eyes wandered to the

Dominion game continuing in the corner between the man, who was sitting back with a satisfied smile on his face, and the woman, who grimaced at the board. She was overmatched and in some difficulty. Her first tier looked solid, but her pieces on the second and third tiers were in disarray. If she kept going like this, the game would be over soon. Her eyes kept flicking to the silver coins beside the board as she thought about her next move and chewed on a fingernail. By the look of her clothes, she wasn't as well off as the man opposite her, and she looked like she found the stakes of the game distressing once it had turned against her.

On an impulse, Caldan quickly skirted through the crowd and up to his room, where he jotted a few sentences on a piece of parchment. Exiting, he descended the stairs and beckoned to the waitress, then tasked her with delivering the folded parchment to the lady playing Dominion. The waitress winked at him and giggled, then sauntered off toward the players.

Let her think what she wants, thought Caldan, shaking his head on the way back to his room, not lingering to see if the note was delivered to the lady or what her reaction was.

He had drifted off to sleep when a knock on his door woke him to a semiconscious state. Half thinking he was dreaming, he lay there listening, and a few moments later the knock came again. Stumbling to the door, he made sure his improvised crafting lock was still active, brushing his hand across both pieces of paper. A light vibration and warmth told him the sorcery was still working, but he could feel it wasn't as strong as two days ago. The paper couldn't hold the forces much longer.

"Hello?" he said. "Who is it?"

There was a hesitation from the person on the other side. "You sent me a note. I need to talk to you."

Caldan passed his hand over the crafting, this time whispering a few words. As he spoke, the vibration and warmth died away, leaving an odor that reminded him of lemons. He should have known the lady might try to find out where the note had come from.

He turned the key in the lock and pulled the door open halfway.

"Good evening," he said, stifling a yawn. "Sorry, I was asleep. No need to thank me for the note. I thought you might need some help. You looked like the game meant a lot more to you than it did to your opponent."

She stood in the hallway, an annoyed expression on her face. "I wasn't going to thank you. Here's your note back." She held out the folded piece of parchment.

"But . . . why? I saw your position, and it definitely looked like you needed help."

"Looks can be deceiving. Here, take it back." She pressed the note into his hand.

"So you came up to tell me you didn't need my advice?"

"I came up because I wanted to tell you your solution to salvage the game *was* elegant. Will you be playing at the Autumn Festival?"

Caldan's thoughts were trying to catch up to the conversation. "Um . . . no. I mean, I'm not sure yet."

"That's good. The less competition the better."

He frowned, not able to get past something. *She was clearly going to lose that game.* "Why didn't you need my help?"

"Because I didn't *want* to win. I lost that game, but *luckily* managed to win the next two against him, after he upped the stakes." She smiled a wry, lopsided smile. "I will say, he was terribly upset at losing so many silver ducats, but you should only bet what you can afford to lose, I always say."

He finally woke up to her game. "I see . . . You make your living playing Dominion?"

"Of a sort," she replied. "Listen, it's late and I need to sleep. I came to offer some advice: passing hints or strategies might be acceptable for friendly games, but when ducats are involved, it's best you keep to yourself. If he had thought I was cheating, it would have gone badly for me . . . and you. At the very least I wouldn't have been able to keep the coins. So stay out of others' business, please."

Caldan hadn't realized he could have caused trouble for her, but thinking about it now, of course he could have. It was stupid of him, and he thought back to the advice Charlotte had given him about being too polite.

"Um . . . if it helps, I think the serving girl thought I was propositioning you." He felt himself blushing. "I'm sure she didn't think there was anything else to the note."

The lady sighed. "That's good, I suppose. As long as my reputation stays clean in regards to Dominion, I don't care what people think. I can see you're new to Anasoma. Think before you act, that's all." She turned on her heel and disappeared down the hall, descending the stairs to the common room.

Caldan closed the door, reactivated his crafted lock, and lay back on his cot, hands behind his head.

Stupid, he thought. Of course someone might have thought she was cheating if they had seen the note. Maybe the stress of the last few days was affecting him.

CHAPTER 12

With a loud *clunk*, the bolt slid home in the thick door, and Amerdan paused to catch his breath. The streets outside were filled with smoke, and his eyes, nose, and throat felt choked with the smell of burning. He brushed through the beaded curtain covering the doorway, and its tiny bells tinkled. He had arranged the colored beads to display a string of red flowers over a yellow background and attached a silver bell to every fifth strand—not fourth or sixth; he'd made quite certain of that. They were welcome bells for customers arriving, warning bells for him.

It was the last day of the Ghost Festival, when the spirits of the ancestors supposedly came back to visit the living. Priests performed rituals to absolve their sufferings, and regular folk left food offerings to appease them. The more spiritual observers made their own stick and straw figures, representing ancestors and people they had known, and burned them with incense, hoping this would ward against any danger the spirits posed. Anyone they had wronged or harmed was differentiated by a few windings of black cloth around the neck.

Today was the last chance households had to light fires and inciner-ate symbolic offerings to the ghosts, to make sure they didn't come into their homes and bring bad luck. Most people built their fires in front of their dwellings, thinking the ghosts were more likely to enter that way. The smoke from so many fires was starting to get on his nerves; too many people had placed too many wrapped offerings on the flames. Burnt food, burnt parchment, burnt cloth all assailed his nostrils, mingled with the cloying stench of fragrant woods. He was just glad to be back at his shop and leaving it all behind.

He took a few deep breaths to get rid of any lingering odor, wiped the back of his hand across his nose, and blinked to remove the sore-ness from his eyes.

His shop stood empty. Still and silent. He moved behind the pol-ished counter, as always keeping an eye out for anything untoward. There were people out there who wouldn't understand what he did, and though he was always careful, the smallest slip could be his undoing. He reached up and gently grasped Dotty. Just the touch of the gray rag doll roused the specters of his sisters. They'd adored Dotty. But they were all dead now, and that was a long time ago. He cradled her in one arm and walked out the back door into the courtyard. His pigs grunted and nuzzled the pen. They were still hungry.

He'd set up a brazier next to the well, with kindling and coke ready to be ignited. Amerdan liked to use coke for this day; it burned hot and bright, and never left anything behind. He didn't like untidiness.

He carefully placed Dotty on the lip of the well. She sat there look-ing at him expectantly.

"There you go," he murmured.

Thank you.

"You're welcome."

The night was cloudy, cold. Sounds from the neighboring street floated to his ears: people passing by on the way to or coming from a party; the clinking of plates from next door, where dinner was being served; the drunken laugh of someone who had made too merry; and snorts from his five pigs. The courtyard was dark, save for glimmers from the lanterns of passersby reflected over the walls. He stood still, letting the cold of the night wash over him and absorbing some of the calm it lent.

What are you going to do about the Sorcerers' Guild, Amerdan? Nothing, as usual?

Amerdan regarded Dotty with a sidelong glance. "Bloody sorcerers," he cursed. Telling him what to do, what he could sell. As if they had ownership of all the rare earths in the world, even those not in their possession. He was violating the law, so they'd said, and had to cease selling the sorcerous raw materials. "They'll pay," he vowed.

When? Dotty seemed to say. *We want them punished.*

"Soon."

You know what they did to us.

Amerdan closed his eyes for a few moments as memories of what the sorcerer had done to his sisters washed over him. Their screams. Their blood. So much blood. His hands trembled, and he clasped them together until the shakes subsided.

Enough, he decided. He produced a packet and extracted a firestick. With a flick of his wrist, he scraped it on the well and the phosphorus ignited. Soon, a fire crackled in the brazier.

Amerdan waited patiently until he judged it hot enough, then spoke into the shadows.

"Revered ancestors, be my protection against the wickedness and snares of the ghosts, those who wander the eternal twilight between our world and yours. Help them find peace, and guide them away from here, where their spirits may linger to do harm."

He bent to a wicker basket by his feet and withdrew a handful of tiny stick figures. He'd made them all over the last few days, labored over every last detail. Each had different clothes made from winding strips of cloth around its legs, torso, and arms. Colored beads for eyes were glued to small wooden heads, and he'd even attached lifelike hair. There were seventeen in all.

One by one, Amerdan took each figure, looked into its eyes, and repeated a short phrase, making sure to name the figure.

The first, the effigy of a man with green bead eyes, went into the brazier. Flames licked greedily at the offering.

"Christophe Morrow, rest in peace. Do not search for me, do not come for me. My life and soul are barred to you, now and forever." Amerdan's voice quavered. *You deserved worse than burning.* For killing Amerdan's sisters the sorcerer should have died a thousand gruesome deaths. He spat onto the figure as the flames consumed it.

He waited until the hated effigy had burned completely before continuing. The second figure went into the brazier, a woman with a short brown skirt.

"Lydia Fortescue, rest in peace." *My first lover. She should never have doubted me.* "Do not search for me, do not come for me. My life and soul are barred to you, now and forever."

Again, he watched until the figure had been consumed by the fire before continuing, and one by one the pile of wooden figures slowly diminished. He waited a few minutes for each one to be fully burned and the smoke to dissipate. By the time he reached for the seventeenth and final figure, an hour had passed.

He held the last figure tightly for a moment, then stroked the few strands of hair on its head. Two strips of red cloth had been tied as a belt and a ribbon around its head. He threw it onto the glowing coals and gritted his teeth as it began to burn.

Such a sweet young girl. Barely an appetizer for my pigs. See, the poor hogs are still hungry.

"Daphne, rest in peace. Do not search for me, do not come for me. My life and soul are barred to you, now and forever."

He remained still, one hand clutching the trinket pendant around his neck he'd taken from the sorcerer, as he watched the coals and the wavy heat emanating from them.

A loud shout outside from a boisterous reveler broke his contemplation, and he shook himself. The cold night air had chilled him, despite the brazier. Only then did he become aware of someone pounding on his front door.

Dotty was looking at him with her bead eyes. *It's one of them.*

"No. It can't be. They gave me a week." He grabbed Dotty, shoved her inside his shirt, and rushed into his shop. The banging continued as he unbolted the door, to reveal a scrawny young man, barely of an age to shave, Amerdan reckoned, and garbed in threadbare loose-fitting clothes. He had the sallow complexion of someone who spent a great deal of time indoors. He reeked of dust, old books, and stale sweat.

"What are you—"

"Ah, you *are* open!" The young man started to take a step inside but halted when Amerdan moved to block his path.

He carries the stench of sorcery. "I'm closed for the day. That was why the door was locked."

"So early? Never mind. I know you've been told to stop selling certain minerals and ores by the Sorcerers' Guild."

"What of it?"

"Well, I was hoping to take some off your hands so it's not a complete loss. There are a few things I could use in my studies. I'm an apprentice sorcerer, you see. But"—he spread his hands—"I find I am rather short of ducats." He looked at the floor.

Straight off the farm, this one, thought Amerdan. Recently apprenticed or indentured, and finding city living more expensive than he was accustomed to. And come here to take advantage of him. *Bloody sorcerers. All as bad as each other.* At his thought, Dotty squirmed inside his shirt, reminding him. Reminding him of what that bastard had done to his sisters, had almost done to him.

Amerdan punched the apprentice in the stomach. Air whooshed from the man's mouth, and he folded like a piece of paper. On his hands and knees like a dog, he gaped at Amerdan, opening and closing his mouth like a fish out of water. Amerdan moved behind him and kicked him in the plums. While the sorcerer was retching, Amerdan dragged him fully inside, slammed the door, and slid the bolt home.

Grabbing him by his lanky, greasy hair and his trouser belt, Amerdan dragged him into his back room and downstairs to the basement.

He threw the apprentice into the room at the bottom, then stood still for a few moments, breathing in the atmosphere. Warm and humid. Fragrant with sweat and urine, and fear. The air was . . . bliss. He remained unmoving, letting it surround and cover him, soaking up the flavors, savoring their essence. The air was alive with promise. He would be transformed again, like so many other times. Goose bumps rose on his arms.

A groan came from ahead of him, disturbing his serenity. Amerdan moved to a wall and used a firestick to light a nearby lamp, allowing a glimmer of light to peel away a layer of darkness.

The apprentice—no, the thing; the vessel to be drained—lay on the stone floor, hands clutching its groin. Its eyes followed him with fear.

Usually, he had to be ready. Had to be prepared. Everything had to be just right.

Not tonight. The sorcerers had made sure of that. Come into his shop, ordered him to stop selling! Who did they think they were? And now . . . this would-be sorcerer was going to make amends.

Amerdan placed Dotty on the shelf beside the lamp, where she could see everything. Her bead eyes stared deeply into his. She was ready. And so was he.

"Puh . . . please," the thing moaned. "Why . . . are . . . you . . . doing . . . this?"

Amerdan stayed quiet. Watching. Savoring its fear.

"Please," the thing repeated. "My master . . . will come looking for me . . . He'll find you." It stopped for a moment to regain strength. "He'll kill you . . . for this outrage. And I'll see . . . you burn."

"Hush. You don't know the truth of things. Lesser creatures seldom realize their limitations. It's what makes them . . . insignificant."

Amerdan drew out a long, thin blade from the sheath on his belt and held it to the light, checking for imperfections. A habit. He knew there would be none; he took great care with his implements.

"Why?" it rasped. "You can't do this. They'll come looking for me."

Amerdan turned to regard the thing. "Why?" he repeated, toneless and uninterested. Always, the vessels had the same questions, unimaginative and unintelligent. And this thing was supposedly a great mind, an apprenticed sorcerer, no less. He shook his head. Talents and abilities wasted on useless constructs of flesh and bone. They were undeserving, and ultimately their weakness held them back from greatness. They could not rise above their base desires and transform themselves, as he had. The sorcerer who had killed his sisters had been foolish enough to reveal his secret. And Amerdan had taken it from him, along with his life. Since then many more vessels with talents he considered worthy had added their paltry essences to his pool.

He removed his shirt and dropped it on the floor, then ran his hands over his chiseled torso, crisscrossed with scars. A reminder of his awakening, carved into his flesh by the foul sorcerer.

His trinket hung around his neck, where it glowed brighter than the light from the lamp.

He had been born much like them, ignorant and unaware. Oblivious to his flaws and to the flaws of those around him. But he'd been tested. Scourged. Made anew. Forged into something else. Something stronger. Greater.

In the blink of an eye, he leaped across the room to sit astride the thing. It gasped at his speed and strength. His knees gripped its sides tight, and its eyes followed the trail of the shining knife, which swam in front of its face. A firm quick slice and the knife withdrew. The vessel screamed. Hot red blood dripped from the wound on its forehead.

Amerdan wiped his hand on the cut, smearing sticky crimson wetness on his palm. He gripped the spherical trinket around his throat tight with the blood-smeared hand.

Only the sound of the vessel's harsh breath pierced the silence.

It knew what was coming. In the end, they all did.

Amerdan's hand around the trinket glowed red, then orange, then yellow, as a bright light emanated from the pendant and shone through his flesh.

"Please," the thing sniveled. "What's happ—"

Its breath was cut off as Amerdan dropped the knife and clamped its throat shut. Brutal strength squeezed, and cartilage cracked.

"Hush. You are a vessel, and I shall partake of you. You will become part of someone greater than you can imagine."

The need filled Amerdan, sending a shiver down his spine. Goose bumps rose on his skin; hairs stood on end.

Shining through the confines of flesh and bone, the light grew incandescent.

The vessel groaned wordlessly, an internal howl colored by pain and loss. A faint radiance rose from its skin, growing stronger with each passing moment. A thread of glittering white light reached from Amerdan's glowing hand to the vessel. It grew to a cord the thickness of a thumb. Pulses traveled up the cord from the vessel to the trinket, where they were absorbed. Amerdan's eyes squeezed tight, leaking tears.

The skin covering the vessel turned gray, then shrank and cracked, leached of vitality. With a convulsive shudder, Amerdan shrieked as the cord vanished, leaving the room dim. Shadows flickered from the lamp.

He collapsed on top of the desiccated thing, panting. He lay still, regaining strength.

Amerdan levered himself to a kneeling position, the gray shrunken corpse between his knees.

He laughed, the full, throaty, relieved laugh of someone who was alive after a trial he hadn't expected to survive.

He looked toward Dotty, wiping tears from his eyes and cheeks. "We endure, again."

In the flickering light, Dotty winked at him. His sisters could see him evolving. He laughed again, pleased.

With a roar, he threw his head back and shouted to the heavens through the stone above him. The muscles on his arms and torso, veined and bulging, strained to their limit, shiny with sweat.

"Again I suffer and survive!" he yelled. "Again I drink and receive what I require." His arms stretched to the ceiling, one dripping a scarlet ribbon of blood.

"I am bound." His heart pumped wildly in his chest.

"I am shriven."

"I am unrivaled." He dropped his arms and gaze to the gray corpse.

"I am many . . . I am transformed," he gasped, exhausted.

From the table, where she was sitting in shadows, Dotty's eyes held the glint of a smile.

LATER IN THE night, Amerdan emerged from his dark cellar, the body of the apprentice flopped lifelessly over one shoulder. Whistling tunelessly, he locked the door that led to his hidden room and replaced the wall hanging.

He stood in the yard and looked up into the night sky. Moonlight shone upon his face, and he imagined he could feel its luminous power infuse him. A fancy, nothing more. There was only one way to take in power that he knew. And only the talented were worthy to make a sacrifice of themselves for his purpose.

There were not many he felt were worthy enough to transfer to him.

He stopped at the pig sty. Snuffles and grunts greeted him. Daphne had whetted their appetite, but now it was time for the main course.

He shouldered the lifeless corpse into the pen, then turned and walked back inside. Excited squeals and tearing sounds followed him.

CHAPTER 13

aldan rolled onto his side again and pushed his thin blanket away. He had tossed and turned for the whole night as he drifted in and out of a restless sleep. His muscles protested as he rose and stretched before drinking a few mouthfuls from a flask of heavily watered wine he had bought. It quenched his thirst but left a sour taste in his mouth. He missed the plain drinking water at the monastery, but most of the water in the city couldn't be trusted, despite the aqueducts, so many people drank ale or watered wine instead.

Dawn began to brighten the dirty window of his room, and he felt a restless need to get out and stretch his legs before breakfast. Descending the stairs, he passed through the empty common room and out onto the street, which was virtually deserted at this hour, except for one or two early risers. Without thinking, he headed left and walked toward Dockside. Since arriving he hadn't been back there, and now he wondered if perhaps it looked and felt better in the morning light.

Streets and buildings he passed looked completely different, coming as he was from another direction, and it gave him an eerie feeling of being in a strange new place.

Anasoma was big, large enough that it was almost a day's walk from one end of the city to the other. Even if you took the main roads, there was always traffic, which slowed your progress. To Caldan, it was too big, with too much traffic and too many people, and the roads were too chaotic. Walking early showed him another side of the city, one more peaceful, despite the smells of urine, smoke, and sweat lingering in the air. The scattering of people he passed in the street still kept their eyes to themselves, though.

Without the usual crowds, it wasn't long before he reached the docks. The Otter was much closer to the water than he'd thought. Ships bobbed in the swell, decks deserted save for a skeleton crew on watch aboard each vessel. At the end of the closest wharf, he could see the *Loretta* was still in port. He decided against a visit, since most likely everyone would be still asleep—or drunk in a tavern somewhere.

A few dirty, shapeless lumps lay behind stacks of crates covered with canvas—homeless men having found somewhere out of the wind to sleep the night. Soon they would be lined up at the docks, hoping a ship would be in need of cheap labor.

Caldan walked along the dock front before heading down a side street, eager to explore the city and see what this district had to offer. A few turns later, winding through an alley between two stone buildings, he came upon a plaza with six exits, the windows and balconies overlooking the space all shuttered tight. Choosing a passage at random, he ducked into a series of narrow alleys. Garbage had piled up here and there, and the smell of something rotten filled his nostrils.

Turning, he started back the way he had come, but a man stepped from a dark alcove filled with rubbish. He was broad shouldered and had wild eyes that bulged from under a mop of black hair. Dirt smudged his face, and patches of skin showed through his ragged clothes.

"Hi there!" the man called, eyes flicking left and right. "You lost?"

A scrape behind Caldan alerted him, and he twisted his head to see two more men emerge from garbage piles against the walls. They moved to block the alley.

"Yeah," one of them said. "Looks to me like he needs some help, Zeke." He smiled, showing brown teeth.

"No names, idiot!" the first man said.

Not good, thought Caldan. He retreated a few steps until his back brushed the side wall, trying to keep all three in view. "I'm not lost; just took a wrong turn. Sorry to bother you, gentlemen."

"Ooh, *gentlemen,* is it?" the third ragged man said as they came closer, forming a semicircle around him. All of them now had feral grins pasted on their faces.

Caldan's hand felt for his half-full purse, the only ducats he had left, but he wasn't in a position to bargain. "Here," he gasped, "take it. I don't want any trouble."

Zeke's expression turned sour, and he sneered. The other two took a step closer, almost in unison. They must have done this before. "Well, thank you kindly for offering us what we can take anyway. Is that a joke? 'Cause we don't think it's funny, do we, boys?"

They all laughed as Zeke snatched the purse from Caldan's hand, and practiced fingers felt through the material. His expression darkened.

"What's this? There ain't hardly any coins in here! That's it. You ain't going nowhere. Nails, grab his arm. You too, Sticky."

"Thought you said no names," Sticky said.

"Yeah, well, you gave him mine, didn't ya?" Zeke said.

Zeke's two cronies stepped in and grasped Caldan's arms.

"It's all I have. Take it and leave me alone." Caldan became acutely aware that he hadn't thought to obtain a weapon of any kind as so far nothing in Anasoma had been cause for alarm. Swords were forbidden, but he wished he had purchased a heavy walking stick.

Zeke stepped forward and, before Caldan could react, elbowed him hard in the head. Caldan's ears rang, and the buildings tilted wildly around him. His legs felt like jelly, but the two men held him upright. He could smell their rotten breath and the rancid odor of their bodies.

"You bloody shit!" Zeke shouted. "Think you can walk here in our territory and get off with a few coins? You boys know what happens when someone can't pay the toll." Zeke backed off a few steps and picked up a length of thick wooden plank.

"We sure do, boss." Sticky guffawed as he took a firmer grip on Caldan's arm.

"That's right," Nails said, putting the squeeze on Caldan's elbow. "You shouldn't come here if you don't belong, and if you can't pay us proper, you gets a beating."

Caldan tensed and shook his head, trying to clear the fog from his mind. Zeke came at him with the plank held in both hands.

Fear and anger boiled up inside Caldan. He jerked his arms together, and to his surprise, Nails and Sticky stumbled and thumped into each other in front of him. Zeke tried to check his swing, but the plank thudded into Sticky with a crack, eliciting a yelp of pain and shock.

Caldan lashed out with his knee, hitting Nails in the stomach and dropping him like a stone.

Zeke slammed Caldan into the wall. He gasped for breath. A fist caught him on the side of the head. He went to his knees, blood roaring in his ears, right arm twisted behind his back in Sticky's wiry grip.

"You bastard!" Zeke bellowed, face turning red. "I'm gonna smash your face in!" He stepped back to make room and swung the plank.

Splintered wood hit Caldan in the cheek, knocking his head back into the wall. Burning pain spread from the wound. Coppery blood flooded his mouth, and his vision blurred.

He shook his head and looked up to see Zeke take a step back. The plank moved for another strike.

Caldan's left hand clenched into a fist and struck Sticky in the plums with a sickening thump. The thug squawked and fell to the ground, curled into a ball, both hands clutched between his legs.

Caldan dropped on top of him. The wind of the plank passing above his head ruffled his hair. It hit the wall, and the jarring impact drove it out of Zeke's hands.

Rolling off Sticky, Caldan staggered to his feet. Zeke clenched and unclenched his fists. Both Nails and Sticky were down, Nails sucking in lungfuls of air to get his wind back, Sticky whimpering like a dying dog.

Zeke's expression had gone wilder. "Oh, you're really gonna get it now. You're gonna wish you weren't born."

Caldan eyed the exit to the alley back the way he had come. If he could get enough room to slip free . . .

No time . . .

Zeke rushed at him, arms outstretched. Caldan pivoted and lashed out with a fist. His knuckles cracked, and a sharp pain exploded in his hand. Zeke went down, holding his head.

Caldan staggered to the other side of the alley and leaned against the wall. Something warm trickled down the side of his face where the plank had hit him. He wiped at it, and his hand came away scarlet. Drops of blood dripped onto the ground. He couldn't focus on what to do next.

Zeke stood, face twisted into a murderous sneer, and hauled Nails to his feet. "You're bloody dead now. I'm gonna kill you!"

Caldan steadied himself, wiping his hands on his pants. Zeke and Nails moved to either side.

A shout came from Caldan's left. "Halt! Harbor Watch! What's going on here?"

Zeke and Nails reacted instantly, grabbing Sticky and dragging him as fast as possible down the alley away from the voice.

Caldan collapsed against the wall as the pounding of booted feet came closer. Two pairs stopped in front of him, while another three continued past in a halfhearted shuffle.

A few moments later, they returned empty-handed, and all five pairs of boots stood around him in a semicircle.

"What are you up to?" asked a gruff voice.

Caldan looked up into five hard faces. Rough and weathered, the men were clothed in boiled leather, and metal-shod batons hung from their belts.

"They robbed me," he croaked. He couldn't feel one side of his face. "You alone?"

Caldan nodded, wincing at the pain in his head.

"Then of course they did. What are you doing in this area alone? Don't you know better?"

"Apparently not," Caldan said. "I just wanted a walk, to explore a bit."

All five men shook their heads at him in disgust. One spat into a pile of garbage.

"Well, that's stupid."

"Yep," another one said.

Caldan hung his head. Something wet he had sat on started seeping into his pants.

"Listen, you're obviously new here, so I'll give you some advice. Stay to the main streets, preferably with friends, and don't wander around at night or early morning."

"Can't you catch them? They took my purse, all my ducats."

"They're long gone. We catch them in the act or we don't catch them at all."

Caldan rubbed his burning eyes. He felt a quiver in his voice as he replied. "That's it? Walk away and forget about them?"

"We don't have time to search the streets. That's the way things are. Ain't no use complaining. We stopped you getting killed, didn't we?"

Caldan nodded, causing another sharp pain in his head. He thought it wise not to move it for a while. "I suppose." He stared at his bloody hand.

The watchman in charge gestured, and strong arms lifted him to his feet, where he wobbled unsteadily.

"You feeling right enough to walk?"

"I'll walk out of here, that's for sure," Caldan said. He wanted to leave the reek of the alley and the whole morning far behind him.

"We'll make sure you get back to the main street, then you're on your own."

"He don't look too good, Sergeant. Maybe we oughta take him to a physiker."

"Crap. I guess we better. Elpidia isn't far from here. Let's go, and make sure he doesn't lag behind."

Firm hands grabbed Caldan again, and he let himself be led

through twists and turns of alleys. The group briefly traveled along a main street, where morning passersby gawked at them.

They stopped at the brightly painted red door of a narrow house. A window to the street showed floral curtains and hanging bunches of dried herbs.

A heavy fist banged on the door, and a face showed in the window, then quickly disappeared. The door opened to reveal a middle-aged woman dressed in drab brown workmanlike pants and tunic, and an apron with many pockets.

"Harbor Watch," she greeted the men in a serious tone. "What's happened here?"

"Elpidia, sorry to bother you. Some idiot got beat up. There's a bit of blood."

"I can see that."

"Thought you might want to take a look at him. He isn't too steady on his feet."

"Right. Bring him in, then."

Caldan half lurched and was half dragged into a front room and sat on a rickety chair, which creaked alarmingly under his weight.

"Heavy bastard. Wouldn't o' thought it."

"Yep."

A glare from Elpidia quieted their talk.

"Watch your mouths, gents," admonished the sergeant. "Well, we best be off. Got a lot of work to do."

Elpidia placed her hands on her hips. "I'm sure you have." Her expression softened. "You did the right thing."

The sergeant tilted his head to her. "C'mon, gents, let's get back to it."

Their murmuring faded as they left the room and closed the door behind them, leaving Caldan slumped in the chair.

A lamp gave some light, and he risked turning his head to look around.

"Don't move," came Elpidia's voice from behind him. She sounded softer once the guards had left. "I'll get some water to wash your face and something to help with the pain."

Banging sounds came from the back, then Elpidia appeared carrying a wooden bowl and some rags. From a pocket, she produced a vial, which she held out.

"Drink this. It's for the pain."

Caldan swallowed the contents. He recognized the bitter taste from his studies as a mild sedative and painkiller.

Dragging a stool close, Elpidia sat and busied herself rinsing a steaming rag.

"You don't say much, do you?" she said.

Caldan grimaced. "Sorry. It's been a tough morning."

"Looks like it." She placed a hand firmly on his jaw and turned his head to the side. She wiped at the blood on his face. The rag was hot on his skin, and a pungent herb odor came from the steam.

"Let me know if it hurts. There's a long gash here. Your skin has split."

"I was hit with a plank." He felt woozy. "I think the sedative has worked. I'm feeling . . . numb."

"Good." Elpidia didn't pause with her cleaning of the wound on his cheek and the skin around it. She tugged his face with each stroke, but the pain was bearable.

"The good news is, it doesn't look serious. I can stitch it up for you. I sewed my own curtains, so it shouldn't look too bad." She probed around the wound with a finger. "There's bruising already. Lucky your cheekbone wasn't cracked. Any other injuries?"

Caldan shook his head. "Only bruises, I think. And my pride." Through his mild daze, he noticed Elpidia had a rash that ran from her left ear down her neck.

She smiled briefly before resuming her businesslike expression. "You're not from around here, are you?"

"No. It must be obvious. The Harbor Watch said so as well."

"It's in your speech and bearing. Even slumped in the chair, your posture is different. You look"—she struggled to find the word—"grounded. Maybe that's not the right word." She stood. "Hang on." She moved to a table and opened a jar, dabbing a pungent ointment onto her rash before disappearing again through a curtain covering a doorway.

A gurgling from one side of the room caught Caldan's attention. Balanced on a metal tripod, a flask filled with yellowish liquid bubbled away, a clear distillate dripping into a glass vial. A sharp, disagreeable odor came from the yellow liquid. On the same table sat a dozen other bottles, all filled with different-colored liquids and meticulously labeled.

Elpidia returned and noticed his interest. She sat back down on the stool next to him, cradling a cloth pouch in each hand. She inclined her head toward the bubbling liquid.

"Distillations for my work. Mostly I sell potions for various ailments, like digestive problems, joint pain, fevers."

"It smells like King's Water. Acidic."

Elpidia blinked. She moved a hand to scratch the rash on her neck, then stopped, as if thinking better of it. "You know something of alchemy?"

"A little. Where I am from, they taught us some. Funny, I wouldn't have thought King's Water would be any use for a physiker. They used to think it part of creating an elixir of life, since it can dissolve gold."

"You mean they don't anymore?" Elpidia queried, frowning at him.

"The book *Great Secrets of Alchemy* argues drinking potable gold to confer longevity is a falsehood."

"I've heard of the book but don't have a copy. Where did you read it?"

"When I was first learning about alchemy. I didn't have a talent for it, though. Burned my fingers a few times and spilled too much." *Sore fingers, hot liquid pooling on the floor, the brother in charge smacking him on the back of his head while Jemma tried in vain to stop laughing. . .*

His shoulders slumped at the memory.

"You okay?"

"Yes—sorry. Anyway, after they found I had more talent for crafting and metallurgy, I concentrated on those." He paused. "I'm rambling, aren't I? Must be the sedative."

"It's fine. You'll have to stay here awhile for it to wear off some before I let you go." Elpidia moved to another table and measured out quantities of dried and powdered herbs into the first cloth pouch.

"So, tell me, what does *Great Secrets of Alchemy* say is the secret of longevity?" She paused to wipe her brow with a white kerchief. Small beads of sweat had appeared, although the room was cool.

"That there isn't one, at least using alchemical means. It theorizes that a combination of alchemy and crafting would be able to slow aging and cure serious diseases, and there are the stories of people living longer before the Shattering. But if it was true, the knowledge has been lost."

Elpidia looked troubled. "Interesting. Though I think I'll stick to making a living first. Someone else can waste their time experimenting for an elixir of life."

Caldan started. He hadn't thought about how he would pay her. "Ah, there is a problem," he began.

"You can't pay?"

"I'm afraid so." Caldan hung his head.

"Don't worry. That's why the Watch brought you here." She withdrew a needle and thread from the second pouch, along with a vial of clear liquid. "Most herbalists and physikers in the city receive a small stipend from the emperor's councillors. It's to cover us when things like this happen." She deftly threaded the needle, then dangled it by the thread into the colorless liquid. "Some good things do happen in Anasoma. Hold still."

She pinched the skin of his cut together and began stitching it closed. Caldan gritted his teeth at the sharp pain, wincing as she sewed stitches into his cheek with deft motions.

"There, just like sewing a hem."

"Thank you." The side of Caldan's face felt tight and sore.

"You'll need to come back in ten days for me to take the stitches out—unless you want to do it yourself, that is?"

The thought of pulling thread out of his own skin didn't appeal to Caldan. "I think I'd rather let you do it."

Elpidia nodded. "Suit yourself. I'm here most of the day, so come back anytime. If I don't answer, don't wander down any side alleys to kill time before I come back."

"Funny," he said, although nothing felt humorous at the moment. "I won't."

She handed him the first cloth pouch, now full of her herb mixture.

"Make a tea with this, twice daily. A pinch will do, enough to cover a ducat-sized area on your palm. Use three fingers to pinch the measure, not two."

"Got it, a pinch two times a day. Thank you again." He struggled for a moment to stand up but slumped back into the chair.

"Sit and don't move," Elpidia said. "Rest awhile until the sedative wears off."

Caldan acquiesced without complaint. The numbing effect of the sedative made the chair feel comfortable, like a well-worn pair of boots fitting to perfection. He closed his eyes and listened to Elpidia bustle around.

He nodded off but woke as she shook his shoulder. "You awake?"

"Yes, sorry." Caldan yawned. "Feels like a day has passed already."

"It's only midmorning."

This time, he managed to stand without too much difficulty, though his head remained foggy. Swaying, he clutched the back of the chair for support.

"You need to take it easy. Go home and rest for a few days."

Caldan gave a hollow laugh. "My room is paid until today, and all my coins are gone. I could try to sell some of my belongings, but something tells me I won't get much for them." He ran a hand over his face and head, feeling his scratchy stubble. "Sorry, I shouldn't bother you with my troubles."

Elpidia frowned, her eyes narrowing. "We all have troubles. Sometimes it helps to talk about them."

Caldan staggered a few steps to the door, and by the time he reached it, his head felt clearer and his legs steadier. "I would guess that my story isn't too far removed from many others who come to Anasoma. But it does feel like I've had a run of bad luck."

"There is a hospice a few streets back, up the hill. You could see if they can take you in."

Caldan nodded his appreciation. "Again, thank you. You have been too kind. I made some friends on the ship that brought me here, so I will see if I can stay with them until they leave." He bowed his head and stepped outside, closing the door firmly behind him.

People swarmed in the street, though he did notice that the few who passed close gave him a wide berth. They obviously knew the physiker's house and thought he might have an illness that was catching. He supposed the sight of him in a blood-smeared tunic, with a bruised face and freshly stitched scar, didn't help either.

A weight dragged on Caldan as he shuffled down the street toward the docks. The walk took longer than expected, probably because he was still sluggish from the sedative. Facing Captain Charlotte and begging for a bunk until the ship left port wasn't his idea of returning the friendship she had shown, but it wasn't as if he had much choice.

At the docks, he braced himself in the cold wind blowing from the sea. The day had turned out to be the coldest yet since his arrival, a sign the season was turning. Restless waves churned white with foam, and spray splashed over the wharves. Dark clouds rolled overhead, and the city was in for a good soaking, if he was any judge of the weather.

Huddled in alcoves and behind boxes and bales, the homeless laborers braved the icy wind for the chance of a few coins or food. Poor, desperate men.

Caldan made his way along the docks to the wharf where the *Loretta* had berthed, head lowered to keep the chilly droplets of spray out of his face. At least the air was fresh now, the usual stench of the docks blown inland.

At the end of the wharf, he stopped. The *Loretta*'s berth stood empty.

CHAPTER 14

Vasile tugged at the tight, starched white collar he was forced to wear while adjudicating and looked out from his desk over the multitude of heads waiting patiently—and impatiently—for a magistrate to review their complaints. The chambers were large enough to hold several hundred petitioners; however, their high ceilings and hard stone walls meant any noise was amplified, and after a day of constant clamor, he never failed to develop a headache. Mostly unwashed bodies baking in the hot room left the atmosphere fuggy and rank and only exacerbated the problem.

Long benches had been set up in rows for people to sit on, but they were overcrowded, and some of the less fussy petitioners had chosen to sit on the floor with their backs resting against the wall.

Pinching the bridge of his nose, Vasile closed his eyes for a few moments, then beckoned one of the servants over. A bead of sweat trailed from his forehead to the tip of his nose. He wiped it off.

"Could I have some more water, please?"

The young girl nodded and hurried off to the kitchens. He would have preferred a cold glass of wine, but unfortunately drinking on the job wasn't allowed. He clasped his hands tightly on his lap under his desk to stop them shaking. *Yes . . . a nice cool refreshing wine, with beads of condensation on the outside of the glass. Perfect.* He licked his lips.

The servant returned with a mug of water, which he took before dismissing her with a wave of his hand. A few gulps later, he felt marginally better, although the constant din had not abated, nor had the ache in his head.

Vasile steeled himself and picked up his assignment sheet for the day. He had seen six cases already, and it was only midmorning. He knew any of the other magistrates would have been hard-pressed to see more than three or four.

Nodding to an attendant, he indicated he was ready for the next petitioner. The man, with a thin guard in tow, consulted his list and wandered off into the crowd.

A thin guard? Aren't they supposed to be burly or big? He frowned and let the thought trail off.

The attendant returned moments later with two rough-looking men. Farmer types, by the look of their dusty and patched homespun clothes. Both were large men, formed from hard work. The shorter one clutched a worn cloth hat, wringing it like the neck of a chicken he wanted for his supper. They both shuffled closer. The tall farmer looked angry, while the one with the hat fidgeted nervously.

Vasile groaned. Perhaps this dispute was over a missing chicken. *What other fascinating cases will come before me today?*

"State your case," the attendant intoned.

The shorter farmer's eyes darted from Vasile, whom he had been staring at, to the attendant and back again. He gave his hat an extra-hard twist.

"To you?" he asked the attendant.

"No, to me," Vasile said in an exasperated tone.

"Oh, sorry, Sir Magistrate. Um . . ." He trailed off. "Well, one of my cows gone missin'."

Cows, not chickens. Close, though. Maybe I can have roast chicken for supper tonight. Vasile licked his lips. *White wine goes well with poultry . . .* With a start, he dragged his attention back to the case.

"And?"

"Well, like, she gone missin', and I couldn't find her nowhere."

Vasile blinked.

"I looked and looked, but she ain't nowhere to be found. Then, a few days later, I heard about Shale here, how he's bragging in town to all about how he's slaughtered one of his cows since he has too many and been eating like a king, and will be for weeks, and salting meat ready for winter. So I said to myself, that's funny, funny odd, you know, since I don't reckon no one in their right mind would do that so early afore the season changed and—"

"Yes, yes," interrupted Vasile. "You are accusing Shale here of stealing your cow and slaughtering it for meat."

The shorter farmer shifted his weight from foot to foot, all the while staring at the floor. "I reckon I am."

"That ain't true!" exclaimed Shale, the alleged cow thief. "It was one of mine, old and sick. She wasn't gonna last, so I made use of her, like any of us would've done. How you gonna show the good magistrate here it was yours and not mine?"

The other farmer's hat looked like it was going to break apart in his hands, but he straightened and didn't back down. "We all of us know what you're like, Shale. Don't think we don't know!"

Vasile held up a hand, and the guard stepped forward. The two farmers hushed and glared at each other, red-faced.

Not like that skinny man is going to do anything if these two decide to fight. He almost smiled at the sight.

"Shale," Vasile asked, "did you steal the cow, and did you slaughter it?"

"No, sir, I didn't."

Vasile took a deep breath and let it out slowly. "Shale, look at me." He waited until the tall farmer looked him in the eye. "This is a place where the truth is paramount."

"Para-what?" said Shale.

"Of utmost importance."

"Oh . . ."

"I am going to ask you again: Did you steal the cow?"

"No, sir. Like I said afore, I didn't."

Vasile sat back in his padded chair and shifted his aching legs. "Well, good Shale, let me tell you something. I don't believe you."

Shale's jaw dropped, and the shorter farmer's eyes widened.

"In fact, I believe this other man here is right."

"No, sir, it ain't so."

"It *is* so." He turned to the other farmer. "How much was the cow worth?"

For a few moments, the farmer couldn't speak, then managed, "Thank you, good Magistrate, thank you."

Vasile waved his thanks away. "How much?"

"Could maybe've gotten two gold ducats for her, if I'd've wanted to sell her."

"Fine. I hereby convict Shale of stealing property and the destruction of said property. Shale, you are to pay compensation to—whatever your name is—of two gold ducats, and a further two as a fine payable to the attendant."

"Here now!" shouted Shale. "That ain't fair. I ain't done nothin'." His eyes shifted to everyone around him: Vasile, the guard, the attendant. "It's not true!" His hands clenched into fists.

"You, Shale, are a liar," Vasile stated firmly. He nodded to the guard and attendant, who escorted him to a side room.

Shale struggled initially, but less and less as they moved away and he came to terms with being caught.

The shorter farmer still stood there, looking at a loss for what to do now. He was probably stunned his case was over so quickly and that he would be compensated.

"You can follow them. They will make sure you get your ducats."

The man nodded his thanks and turned to leave, then stopped and faced Vasile.

"Please, sir, if I may?"

"Yes?"

"What . . . I mean, how did you know?"

Vasile reached for his mug and took another gulp of water. "We deal in truth here. In this place, truth becomes evident. Let your family, your village know." *That will do for him,* thought Vasile.

The farmer nodded. "I will. Thank you, sir." He turned his back and followed the others to collect his gold.

AND SO THE day passed for Vasile, case after case, petition after petition, each one more or less as stupid or sordid as the rest. After weeks and weeks of the same stories day in and day out, Vasile found himself worn out by the monotony of it all, numb to the people who came looking for justice at the magistrate's hand. He couldn't remember the faces of the last few petitioners. Even the face of the grateful farmer with the missing cow had faded to a fuzzy blur in his memory. It was no wonder most magistrates worked only a few days a week, citing other responsibilities.

It was the sentencing that grated on Vasile the most. His discretion was extremely limited in most cases, as there was a standard list of punishments for crimes and misdemeanors, according to the emperor's laws. Sometimes he wished the penalties were not so harsh. Giving a man with a family dependent on him a year's hard labor in a work gang for stealing a loaf of bread was, in his opinion, far too harsh. But the laws were inflexible, and the emperor himself, may he live forever, decreed the punishments to be just. And who was Vasile to disagree? Besides, work gangs were required all over the empire to build the emperor's projects, from roads to dams and fortifications, and the emperor's palaces.

Vasile drew himself up from a slouch. His buttocks had gone numb, and his legs ached. Twisting his hips from side to side, he tried to work some feeling into them with little success.

The light in the vaulted room had dimmed substantially during the last case he had seen, and he was looking forward to heading to his favorite tavern for a drink or two—or more if he felt like it, which he usually did.

His attendant broke his thoughts. "Last up for the day," the man droned with a voice already weary. "William Voltain and his case against the Five Oceans Mercantile Concern, represented by Luphildern Quiss, one of their head traders."

Vasile groaned inwardly. Any case involving nobles and one of the major trading houses was likely to be complex, tedious, and fraught with intricate issues. The ache in his head throbbed harder, and he debated postponing the case until morning. No, best to at least hear the initial complaint and get some of the preliminaries out of the way.

Once again, two men approached his desk flanked by the attendant and the thin guard. Both were dressed in fine-quality clothes tailored to fit their frames. He guessed the one with extra lace at the sleeves and throat to be the noble William, and the crests on the gold buttons of his purple vest confirmed his guess. The other one must be the representative of the Five Oceans Mercantile Concern: nondescript brown hair, fair skinned, a trifle thin, but otherwise unremarkable.

William fidgeted, straightening his clothes and brushing specks of dust from his sleeves, while the trader stood relaxed and calm.

"State your case," the attendant said in a bored tone.

"Ahem." The noble cleared his throat nervously. "My name is William Voltain of the House of Voltain." He paused as if expecting a response from Vasile. When none was forthcoming, he gave a slight frown but continued. "I am presenting myself before you as a representative of the House of Voltain in a matter of utmost importance." Again a pause.

"Pray continue," said Vasile. *Quickly, please.*

"It concerns a warehouse property of substantial size on the dock front, which, by its very dimensions and location on Cuttlefish Street facing the docks, is quite valuable to whoever is in possession of the title. My grievance with the company is based on certain inalienable facts about the events leading up to their purchase of said warehouse, on the eve of when my own deal to secure purchase of the property was to be concluded." William became noticeably distressed as his speech went on and stopped to raise a handkerchief to his mouth, as if to cover his distaste.

"Furthermore, it has come to my attention that the use to which the warehouse has been put, while not illegal, certainly raises doubts as to the decency and integrity of the Five Oceans Mercantile Concern."

As William uttered these words, the company's representative looked sharply at him and stared intensely for a few heartbeats before resuming his previous casual attitude.

"What use has the warehouse been put to?" asked Vasile.

"Um . . . I am not sure, but rumors have reached my ears of furtive comings and goings at all hours of the night, and I myself have seen a covered wagon entering the property in the early morning."

Vasile clicked his tongue in annoyance. "What you are saying is that you have no idea. You have seen a wagon entering the warehouse. Do not wagons often come and go from warehouses?"

William looked perplexed. "But surely you can see such activity is suspicious?"

"Actually, no, sir. I deal in truths and evidence. Do you have proof anything untoward is occurring there?"

"Not proof, exactly . . . Suspicions."

"I cannot entertain suspicions without credible proof, so obtain some or dispense with allegations of impropriety for the duration of this case. Am I clear?"

William's lips pressed into a thin line, and he nodded once, not pleased at all. He swallowed a few times.

"Well—ahem—then I will without delay outline the grievance I am bringing to you today."

"Please do." *For all our sakes.*

"A number of weeks ago, it came to my attention that the property on Cuttlefish Street would be coming up for sale." He stopped to wipe his brow with his handkerchief. "Through my agents, I was able to verbally secure possession of the warehouse from the owner, and the exchange of title for a sum of ducats was only a formality to be carried out in due course, once all details had been agreed to by both parties."

Vasile found his head tilting forward in boredom at William's words. Another squabble over a property title, and no doubt a lot of hearsay and *he said, they said* was on the horizon. He rubbed tired eyes.

"However," William continued, "the day we were to exchange title and ducats, we found a different situation. To my amazement, this man's company"—he glared at Quiss—"had somehow taken possession of the property and title, and the previous owner had packed up and left for parts unknown. As you can see, there was no alternative for me other than to bring this case to the magistrates, who I am sure will deliberate the matter and come to the obvious and satisfactory conclusion."

Vasile looked up. "Indeed, we will come to a conclusion." He saw William smile, assuming the matter was all but settled. *He thinks his noble status means he has a right to trample over the less fortunate, but before Vasile, nothing could be further from the truth. Still, with this case, maybe he has something . . .*

"Does the representative of the Five Oceans Mercantile Concern have anything to say?" asked Vasile.

The tall man took a step forward. "My name is Luphildern Quiss, and I am by position and aptitude a head trader for the company." His voice was incongruously firm and melodic.

"An odd name. I don't recognize the provenance."

"Indeed, many of the company's senior shareholders originate from a small city quite a way inland. You would not have heard of it." He spread his hands self-deprecatingly. "The property in question also came to our attention, much as it did to that of House Voltain, and for reasons he has stated, we were also interested in purchasing the title. Alas for William, our offer was accepted over his by the owner, due to it being substantially higher."

"That's outrageous," interjected William. "The owner was adamant he would not accept another offer, and our verbal agreement was binding."

Interesting, thought Vasile. Both were telling the truth, but as he knew all too well, you could speak what you *thought* was the truth and not be correct.

"Sir William, you believe the owner agreed to sell you the property, no matter what other offers were made."

"Yes," came the reply. *Truth.*

"And Sir Quiss, you state the owner did in fact sell to your company for a price substantially above Sir Voltain's."

"That is correct." *Truth again.*

"So the owner must have changed his mind and accepted the higher offer."

"I simply cannot believe this happened," exclaimed William. "The man had a long-standing relationship with my family, and we had both mutually benefited from many business deals. He would not have changed his mind without some coercion." *Truth again.*

"Ah," exclaimed Vasile. "You are accusing the Five Oceans Mercantile Concern of bringing pressure to bear on the owner in some manner such that he felt he had no choice but to accept their offer or suffer dire consequences?"

William nodded. "That is my belief, yes." *And yet again.*

"And where is your proof?"

"I beg your pardon?"

"I believe that *you* believe you are correct. But *I* am yet to be convinced that what you believe is actually the truth and that you have proof of said facts. Do you follow me now?"

"I do, yes . . . ahem . . ." William coughed into his handkerchief. "Unfortunately, all I have to go on are the actions of the owner before and after the event, and my own feelings as to the situation."

"I see," said Vasile. He turned to the trader. "And you, Sir Quiss, do you deny any such underhanded maneuvering on the part of your company?"

"I most certainly do, and I object in the strongest possible terms that Sir William would suggest such a thing without being able to prove his claims."

Vasile paused. Sir Quiss was lying.

On the surface, there wasn't anything Vasile could do. The deal was sealed, and the previous owner was evidently uncontactable. All William Voltain and his house had lost was a business opportunity, which Vasile was sure they had plenty of. Why would Quiss be lying about the method of obtaining the property? And why would his company need to resort to such measures? He decided to probe a little further.

"The warehouse itself, Sir William, you said it is on Cuttlefish Street, correct?"

"Yes, across from the docks, a prime position."

"But there is nothing else remarkable about it, apart from the location?"

"Not that I can think of."

"And, Sir Quiss, there is nothing else that would have made the property essential to your company acquiring it?"

"No."

Interesting—a lie.

"Gentlemen," interrupted the attendant, "I am afraid we are out of time for today." He gestured to the dimness of the room, and the other petitioners, who had been waiting all day, reluctantly filing out the door.

Vasile shifted his weight in his chair again. "Tomorrow morning, I expect both of you here, as soon as the building opens for the day."

Sir Voltain nodded curtly and took a step away from Sir Quiss before giving him a disapproving look and turning on his heel. He hurried across the emptying room.

Sir Quiss had a smile on his face. "Good day," he said to Vasile before he too turned and, with an unhurried walk, exited the building.

IT WAS LATE evening. Vasile sat at a table alone, elbows resting on the surface, careful to avoid the spilled puddle of wine in front of him. Although he had downed a drink or two more than was advisable, the puddle hadn't been made by him, but by a drunk patron who had decided he needed to talk to Vasile. After Vasile pointedly ignored him, the man had left, and, the inn being the place it was, the puddle remained.

Smoke filled the air, irritating his eyes, which he frequently rubbed. The smell of sour beer, wine, and puke mingled to create an unpleasant aroma. A few oil lamps around the walls did little to brighten the room. The main source of heat was a stone fireplace burning peat.

Although it was late, two men were deep in conversation at a table, while at another, three men had been playing cards for some time.

Vasile gazed into his cup, which had a few mouthfuls of cheap wine left. He fished out his brass timepiece, a gift from his wife, careful not to look at the inscription inside when he opened it. Sixth hour of the night. Dawn was five or so hours away. He knew he should have left a while ago but couldn't bring himself to go home to an empty room. Clicking the cover shut, he slipped the watch into his pocket and swirled the dregs of wine in the cup. He should leave the wine and go home. Really he should.

But knowing and doing were two different things.

A blurred shadow appeared on the table, flickering in the dim light. Vasile looked up to register a middle-aged man in gray wool clothing, a serious look on his ruddy, bearded face. Despite the quality clothes, he had a rough look about him, a hardness.

"Vasile Lauris," the man said.

"Good evening. I am afraid you have the better of me, Sir . . . ?"

Without asking for permission, the man pulled over a stool and sat opposite Vasile. He dropped four copper ducats on the table. A moment later, a serving girl arrived bearing two cups of wine, which she unceremoniously set in front of him before scooping up the coins.

"Let me buy you a drink," the stranger said, pushing one of the cups toward Vasile. "The house red. We believe it is your drink of choice these days."

Vasile hesitated. He made it a point never to drink so much he couldn't function the next day, and one more wine would put him close to the edge. But a free drink was a free drink.

"What's your name?" he asked.

The man shook his head. "Names can be dangerous to know, and I prefer to remain anonymous."

Vasile scratched his head, shrugged, and picked up the cup. "To your health," he said and took a sip. "So who is the 'we' you mentioned?"

"They said you were sharp, though I have to admit, in your current state, I thought you wouldn't be thinking too clearly."

"What's wrong with my current state?" protested Vasile.

"Why, nothing. Nothing at all." The man looked around the room, as if searching for something.

Vasile started to feel edgy. "Let me get to business, then," the man continued. "I am a representative of the Five Oceans Mercantile Concern. We believe there is a case you are currently undertaking in your responsibilities as a magistrate, whereby the good name of our company is being besmirched by the petty and unwarranted grievances of William Voltain." He stopped, as if uttering such a long speech were foreign to him. His cup of wine was in one hand, but he hadn't sipped from it, even to wet his lips.

What a waste of perfectly . . . terrible wine.

"And if I am? I'm unable to discuss any . . . particulars of petitions . . . with strangers, especially when they claim to represent one of the parties . . . without offering any substan-substantiation of such a claim."

Vasile slurred a couple of words but thought on the whole he had done well. *Can't these people leave me alone? There will be plenty of time to annoy me tomorrow.*

The man's expression remained impassive. "I will be forthright with you. My company is concerned about the damage this case has done, and may continue to do, to our reputation. We believe that a quick resolution in our favor is the best outcome, and in return for such we are prepared to offer substantial compensation. You see"—he leaned in closer to emphasize his point—"this case doesn't benefit anyone, even William Voltain, although he would disagree. We want to see as little damage done to us and to good William as possible. What is the harm in that?"

He drew a bulging purse out and placed it on the table. Coins jingled.

Vasile eyed it. "A bribe, is it?"

After the lies today in the magistrates' building, and the half lies this man was spouting, he wasn't sure he wanted to be mixed up in this case.

"No. Compensation for services rendered. We all want the same thing. Justice for the wronged, swiftly and firmly delivered. Trifling cases such as this one shouldn't be taking up your time, especially when it is evident William Voltain is upset he was bested in a business deal."

Vasile knew this wasn't right and he should say something, but his mind was fuddled with drink.

"Compensation?" he managed. "To dismiss the case?"

"To have the correct judgment swiftly delivered tomorrow morning, so you can move on to weightier matters. Like cows and such." The stranger smiled.

Vasile's blood rose, and his cheeks felt hot. He stood up abruptly, knocking his stool over behind him.

"I will not take your ducats," he said through clenched teeth. "Keep your coins and get out. I do not take kindly to being called corrupt."

The man remained still, looking up at him. "My pardon, Vasile. It was our understanding that you were in a position to take such a generous offer. Indeed, it is our understanding you might be in need of some ducats, what with your fall from grace and your house in such disrepair."

Vasile felt his blood boiling in his ears. He shoved the purse back at the man.

"Leave now. You know nothing about me. How can you know me? My home and my position are no concern of yours."

"I think you should reconsider."

"I think you should get out. Immediately."

The man grimaced, collected the purse, and stood. "So be it. We are not left with any choice." He nodded to Vasile. "Good evening, then." He turned and walked out of the inn, leaving Vasile fuming and wound as tight as his watch.

He rubbed his face with both hands. *By the emperor*, he seethed, *what's going on?*

IT BEGAN LIKE every day at the magistrates' building Vasile could remember: an aching head from the night before; too-bright light streaming in from the windows. His attendant poured a mug of water, which Vasile gulped as if he had spent a day in the desert. Petitioners filed in after their wait outside, and the low murmur of their chatter started to build.

Vasile coughed into his fist repeatedly and wished he hadn't accepted the free cup of wine last night. Wished the whole sordid episode hadn't happened. He closed his eyes to rest them and found he wanted to keep them shut.

"First order of business today," the attendant intoned too loudly for Vasile's liking. "Continuation of the petition of William Voltain against the Five Oceans Mercantile Concern."

Vasile opened his eyes to find the innocuous Luphildern Quiss standing tall in front of him next to the attendant. Of William Voltain there was no sign.

"Ahem . . . Magistrate Lauris," said the attendant. "Sir Voltain is not here . . . er . . ."

"Yes, I can see that," snapped Vasile. He winced at the pain in his head and took a deep breath. "We'll wait for him to arrive. No doubt he has been delayed in the morning crowd."

The attendant nodded, as did Quiss. Such a calm, inoffensive man, thought Vasile. He had to be party to the deeds of last night, surely. Or maybe he wasn't. Perhaps his superiors acted without informing him. All these complications made his head hurt worse.

They waited for a few minutes. Vasile checked his pocket watch. They waited a few more. The attendant shifted his weight and looked at Vasile. Vasile pointedly ignored him. More time passed.

The flat voice of Quiss broke into Vasile's thoughts. "Magistrate Lauris, we have been waiting quite some time. I believe this demonstrates the lack of importance Sir Voltain places on this matter. He has no proof of any misdeeds on our part, and his absence today shows he knows his petition will not be decided in his favor."

"Really?" responded Vasile. "I actually have a few more questions for both of you."

A fleeting look of surprise crossed Quiss's face, to be quickly replaced by curiosity. He gave a short bow. "I will be happy to answer any questions you have once Sir Voltain arrives."

During this exchange, a messenger hurried up to the attendant, who conversed with him in hushed tones. The attendant's mouth opened, and his eyes widened.

"Magistrate Lauris, the messenger has delivered news of import to the case."

Vasile waved a hand. "Go on."

"This morning, Sir Voltain did not emerge from his rooms for breakfast," the attendant said, voice grave. "The household staff, becoming concerned, entered his rooms, where they found Sir Voltain dead. He hanged himself from a crossbeam sometime in the night."

Vasile put a hand to his forehead. He groaned as the pain in his head doubled in intensity. He could feel the eyes of the attendant and Quiss on him, waiting for a response. He looked up at Quiss, whose face was composed, bland even. But Vasile saw the corners of his mouth turn up slightly in the suggestion of a smile. The words of the stranger last night echoed in his thoughts.

So be it. We are not left with any choice.

Complications like this he could do without. He would need to proceed with caution.

Gripping the arms of his chair hard, he spoke. "Due to these unfortunate circumstances, the petition brought by Sir Voltain has no sponsor. As such, it is my duty to inform you the petition has been suspended. If another sponsor appears to take up the petition, then the case will recommence." He stopped, considered what to say next.

"Luphildern Quiss, you have heard my pronouncement and are free to leave."

The representative of the Five Oceans Mercantile Concern looked straight at Vasile and raised his eyebrows. "Such unfortunate news," he said. "Who would have thought Sir Voltain would be overcome by the misfortunes of his . . . fortune? Still, I am pleased with the outcome for my company, however the verdict was reached."

"The petition is not dismissed, merely suspended. Another sponsor from House Voltain may desire to continue with it sometime in the future."

Quiss shrugged. "I'm confident they will see where their best interests lie in the matter. This whole episode has inconvenienced all of us, some more than others."

Vasile knew he was telling the truth, and his heart beat faster. "'Inconvenienced' is a mild word for a death."

"I can offer no more to someone who was a stranger to me. Misfortune or death can come upon someone so quickly these days; choices one makes that may seem reasonable and appropriate at the time can lead to unforeseen consequences." Quiss gave a quick smile. "But I am sure we won't be seeing each other again, Magistrate Lauris. Good day." He turned on his heel and walked away through the crowd.

Vasile took a few deep breaths, heart racing.

The attendant stared at the back of the departing trader, then shook himself and addressed Vasile. "That was cold of him. He could have at least feigned some sorrow or sympathy for Sir Voltain."

"Yes . . . well . . . these merchant types only care if it involves ducats." Vasile swallowed.

From all the lies told yesterday, he was sure the face of the petition presented to him was not the whole story. What secret was so important they would attempt to bribe him, and when that failed, kill someone to stop the case in its tracks? The problem was, Vasile wasn't the type to let something like this rest. He valued the truth more than any man he knew. His talent for telling lies and truth apart made sure of this. And what these people had done to an innocent man to cover their . . . Vasile paused. They had not committed a crime, at least as it pertained to the petition brought to him. In fact, in all probability, he would have had to rule in their favor.

Vasile gathered himself and told the attendant to bring the petitioner for the next case. Perhaps if he threw himself into his work he would forget Luphildern Quiss and the Five Oceans Mercantile Concern.

But he knew he would remember, and he knew he couldn't let it rest.

CHAPTER 15

P assing people who barely registered, Caldan walked through the crowded streets in a daze. A few he bumped into stopped their protests before they began or broke off early when they saw the look in his eyes and his bruised, scarred face.

The owner of the Otter showed concern at his state, but Caldan brushed off his questions. He needed a rest to recuperate. He lurched up the stairs to his room.

Moving his hand across the vertical door crack, he whispered words of unbinding that would disable his crafted lock. No vibration or smell of lemons came to him this time. Cursing, he turned the key in the lock and entered.

His belongings remained as he had left them. The room looked untouched. Quickly, he relocked the door and checked his crafting. All that remained were the two tacks driven into the wood, along with a few fragments of burnt parchment. At his feet, ashes littered the floor, stirred by a faint draft coming from the gap under the door. As with all craftings, the forces guided through this one had ultimately proven too much for the material used. Still, it had served him well, and it wasn't too much bother to create another.

Caldan caught himself and paused. He wouldn't need to create another, since he couldn't pay for the room, which meant he couldn't stay.

His thoughts were jumbled, churning in his head like clouds during an unforgiving storm. Sucking in deep breaths, he tried to calm himself, his palm resting on the door, creating a steadiness he could focus on. He had no ducats whatsoever, no loose coins around his room he could spend on another night's accommodation at the Otter. His possessions consisted of the clothes he wore and a couple of changes, a leather satchel, and the odds and ends he had purchased the other day.

His trinket weighed against his neck, worth a fortune, but he would never sell it. Not even if he found himself homeless and starving on the streets.

First things first . . .

Turning his back to the door, he collected his possessions and packed his leather satchel, taking his time to fold his clothes and neatly stow the parchment so it wouldn't crease. He replaced his bloodstained shirt with a fresh one—although it was smaller, so he self-consciously squeezed into it, remembering Miranda's amusement at the tight fit the last time he had worn it. He slipped his knife into a pocket. It was small and unnoticeable, and he felt safer with it after his morning run-in with the street thugs.

Caldan shouldered the satchel and exited the room. On the way out, he attracted the innkeeper's eye, telling him he was trying his luck at the Sorcerers' Guild and would hopefully return later. The man wished him well before turning to a waiting well-dressed lady, a new customer.

Caldan stepped out into the midday sun and headed in the general direction he knew the traders' quarter to be located, sticking to main avenues so as not to become lost. He knew there was another square off the main one in which the more influential guilds congregated, and he desperately needed to find work before the day was out. His stomach felt hollow, and unless his luck changed he would be sleeping on the streets.

His progress was slow, as he still felt out of sorts after the attack and the subsequent dose of sedative. Sleep and a hearty meal would set him right, but they might be a long time coming.

Stop thinking about food, he admonished himself. *It's making it worse.*

By midafternoon, he arrived at the cobbled square bordered by buildings that housed the public offices of the more prestigious guilds and organizations, including that of the Sorcerers' Guild. He lingered in the afternoon sun, leaning against a wall and surveying the building from across the square.

Truth be told, he was delaying entering the intimidating entrance—huge metal doors covered with intricate runes, framed by a stone doorway. Designed to overawe, it was doing its job well. He saw a number of people head toward the gleaming doors, then veer off and busy themselves at a stall close by or continue walking out of the square. *People like me,* he supposed, *who have never been inside before and need some time to gather enough courage to enter.* Caldan recognized some of the runes carved into the doors, glyphs of strength twined into barrier wards, but there were many he couldn't identify.

Butterflies fluttered in his stomach. He worried about his ragged and bruised appearance, too—he needed to make a good impression. But there wasn't much he could do about how he looked, so with a deep breath, he straightened up, pulled his shoulders back, and crossed the square.

On the other side of the metal doors was a vestibule once designed to be a waiting room, with stone benches on the side walls. It now looked to be used as a cloakroom. Hats and cloaks hung from wooden stands arranged around the room. A boy stood as Caldan entered. About to speak, he stopped when he saw Caldan wasn't wearing a cloak or hat to take charge of.

"I take it I go through?" Caldan said, gesturing to the inner door on the other side of the chamber.

"Yes, sir. Um . . . are you sure you are at the right place?" The boy stared at Caldan's battered face and lingered on his newly stitched scar.

"I am. This is the Sorcerers' Guild, is it not?"

"Yes, sir. It's just . . . sorry, never mind. Go inside. The apprentice at the desk will help you."

"Thank you." Caldan opened the doors, and cooler air from inside wafted over him.

The walls were unadorned beige stone, lit by an overhead cluster of crafted sorcerous globes. A young man sat behind a long wooden desk absorbed in a book, one of several in front of him. A corridor ran off from each side, and from down one came the muted sound of voices.

After a pause, the young man looked up from his book, blinking at Caldan and his obvious state of injury.

"May I help you?" he asked, with the same hesitation the previous boy had shown.

"I'm here to see a senior sorcerer."

"I think a physiker would be of more use . . ."

"I'm here to test for admission," Caldan said as firmly as he could.

The young man looked him over and nodded. "Indeed. You'll have to pardon me—we rarely have people wander in from the street for admission." He paused for a moment. "I'll see if someone can talk to you."

He tugged twice on a thin rope dangling from the ceiling, and a bell sounded somewhere inside the building. A short time later, another boy appeared, and a quick hushed conversation ensued. The new boy ran back down a corridor, sandals slapping on the stone.

"Just another moment, sir," the young man behind the desk said. "Someone should come to see you when they have time. Take a seat." He gestured to a long bench and returned to reading his book.

Too nervous to sit, Caldan wandered around the room, satchel weighing on his shoulder. His face burned, and the skin felt stretched tight across the cut. He waited.

And waited.

Men and women entered and left periodically. Only a few waited with him, and those not for long. Tired of standing, he took a seat on the bench.

After what felt like an hour, he approached the clerk at the desk again.

"Excuse me."

The man looked up with an annoyed expression. "Yes?"

"Will it be much longer?"

"Got something more important to do, have you?"

"No, it's been a while, and I thought—"

"Someone will come and see you when they are free. You don't wander in and expect everyone to drop what they are doing and rush out here to serve you, do you?"

"No, I . . . Never mind." Caldan went back to sitting on the bench. From the corner of his eye, he saw the young man shake his head at him.

Another hour passed, to Caldan's increasing frustration. The day was growing late, and he needed to find some food. His stomach growled. He was physically and mentally drained from the eventful and exhausting day, but still the wait dragged on. He felt like he had been stuck in this stuffy room for far too long. His stomach growled again. The clerk glanced up from his book, then busied himself with his note writing. He had been jotting down notes for the last hour. *Scratch, scratch.* The sound of his quill on the parchment had begun to irritate Caldan.

Just as he was about to give up, the messenger boy returned. "Please, sir," he said, approaching Caldan. "Follow me."

It's almost as if they knew I'd reached my limit, he thought.

But Caldan simply nodded and followed the boy down a corridor. They passed a few closed doors until they reached one indistinguishable from the others. The boy rapped his knuckles on the door, said, "There you go," to Caldan, and ran off.

"Enter," came a deep voice from within.

Caldan entered the room. In a chair behind a desk sat a pale, gaunt, middle-aged man. Light coming through a window glinted from a round metal object he was studying. Glancing up at Caldan, he placed it on the desk and said, "So you want to become a sorcerer?" He motioned Caldan to take a seat in one of two overstuffed armchairs.

After the long wait, Caldan's mind felt sluggish, and it took him a bit to get his thoughts straight. Finally, though, he said, "I have a talent for it, along with many other skills. I'm well versed in alchemy, metallurgy and smith-crafting, and history, as well as some medicine, and numbers. I can read and write a fair hand and am passable with the sword. I can also play a skilled game of Dominion." Caldan threw that in there on impulse. The link between great Dominion players and great sorcerers was well known.

"Well, don't tell me everything at once. You won't find any need for sword fighting here," the man responded disparagingly. "Is that how you were cut?"

"No, sir. I was waylaid this morning near the docks. There was some trouble with a few thieves. The Harbor Watch ran them off."

"Hmm." The sorcerer nodded. "Rough district. Right, let's get started then. What's your name?"

"Caldan, sir."

"Why didn't you use crafting to defend yourself and give them a few broken bones for their trouble?" He waved his hands and wiggled his fingers in what Caldan understood was meant to be an uneducated person's idea of a sorcerous gesture.

Caldan assumed from his bearing he was a sorcerer, and possibly a master. But he didn't want to access his own well to confirm his guess without permission. And after his last question, Caldan wasn't so sure. Was he a master? He was clearly testing Caldan with such a ridiculous inquiry.

"Sorcery on the spur of the moment is virtually unachievable. There has to be some preparation."

"Go on."

"Defensive wards are possible, but destructive sorcery is impossible."

"Why didn't you ward yourself against the attack, then?"

Caldan spread his hands, palms up. "Wards are generally tricky and take time to activate, so I have heard. If I had known I was going to be attacked, and if I had the materials—*and* if prior to the attack I had a few moments to access my well and empower a crafting—then yes, I could have warded myself." He hesitated. "But I have not yet been shown how to do this."

"Could you smith-craft a shield that you can activate in the time it takes to blink?"

"Well," Caldan said slowly, giving himself time to think. "The crafting would have to be made of metal, probably an alloy. It would have to absorb the forces directed at it, so . . . no, it couldn't do that. Wait . . . maybe it could be completed with a secondary locking shaping . . . I'm not sure, sorry."

The sorcerer waved a hand in dismissal of his apology. "Don't worry. It took greater minds than yours a long time to discover how to solve that puzzle. But once solved, like all breakthroughs, it all seems relatively easy in hindsight."

Caldan nodded. The sorcerer shifted his weight in his chair.

"Young man, how old are you?"

"I come of age in a few months, sir."

"That's old to be seeking an apprenticeship. You know that, don't you?"

"Sir, I grew up on Eremite and have studied at the Monastery of the Seven Paths for a few years."

The man raised his eyebrows, though Caldan couldn't tell whether he was impressed or skeptical of his claim.

"I have many skills, but the monks do not go into great depth with anyone except their most talented initiates."

"I'm aware of the monastery, and the arrangement they have to educate the sons and daughters of some noble houses. You haven't run away, have you?"

"No. I'm an orphan. The monks took me in when I was young."

"That explains your shaved head. Why should we accept someone a few years past the age we usually take apprentices?"

"Truthfully, sir, as I said, crafting isn't my only skill. It may be I can work in some capacity other than as an apprentice—an assistant, perhaps? All I ask is for you to consider favorably what I can do and see if I can fit in somewhere. Please."

The sorcerer's expression remained unchanged. Again he shifted in his armchair. "One moment." He closed his eyes and sat still, unmoving except for his chest rising and falling with each breath. He gave a few twitches, then opened his eyes.

"You have a strong well, straight and not as rough as most."

"So the monks told me, since I can't sense my own."

"You can sense others?"

"Yes. I know not many can, but I have that talent."

"That's rare. Show me what you can do, crafting-wise."

"Excuse me?"

"Show me a crafting you've completed, or craft something for me here and now."

Caldan hesitated, then placed his leather satchel on the desk and removed two square sheets of parchment, his ink, and his quill. The sorcerer's eyes narrowed, and he leaned forward to watch Caldan's work.

Bending over the table, Caldan drew with swift, smooth strokes, the quill scratching on the parchment. Soon he had covered the parchment in thumbnail-sized glyphs, evenly spaced. He had an idea, a variation of the ward he had placed on his room door at the Otter. Finished with this part of his crafting, he began to fold the paper, creasing some folds firmly and others only lightly, working as fast as he dared.

"You can craft with paper," observed the sorcerer.

"Yes. This shouldn't take long."

"I hope not." Caldan glanced up to see if the man was angry, but if anything he seemed amused.

A few final folds, and Caldan held up a box with a lid in his palm. Without asking permission, he scooped up the round metal object the man had been examining when he entered the room, placed it into the box, and closed the lid. Accessing his well, he linked to his crafting and felt a vibration from the box.

"There."

"Well? What is it? Paper isn't the best medium, you know. It won't last long."

"I know, but it's quick and easy to carry around."

The sorcerer harrumphed and held out his hand. Caldan gave him the box, which he shook. A faint rattle came from inside. Slipping a nail under the lid, the sorcerer tried to pry it open, but to his surprise it didn't move. He pressed the box between both palms and grunted with exertion, but it stayed uncrushed. He gave Caldan an amused look.

"Interesting. Open it, please."

"Sure." Caldan stopped. "Um . . . I forgot . . . in my rush . . ." He felt heat flood to his face. A stupid mistake, which could cost him dearly.

"You didn't include a way to unbind your crafting? That's a novice error."

"Yes, I agree. I'm sorry."

"What will I tell Master Giske about his crafted metal ball? He wants it back tomorrow."

Caldan wilted inside. "I don't know. Maybe you need more time to study it?" he said dubiously. "The paper should degrade quickly, as there is a strong force flowing through it."

The sorcerer sighed and placed Caldan's improvised warded box on his desk. "Well, at least you have some talent. I would guess the box won't last the night." He scratched his cheek. "How far along were your metallurgy and smith-crafting studies?"

"I don't have a guide to go on," said Caldan with an apologetic shrug. "The monks taught what they taught, and they weren't ones for letting their students look too far ahead. But I can run through some of what I know."

"Start with what you think the difference between smith-crafting and blacksmithing is."

Caldan took a deep breath, smiling inwardly, careful not to let it show. The monks had been thorough in teaching the difference between the two—their first lesson in the subjects—which they repeated frequently as students progressed.

"Blacksmithing, or simple smith-craft, as Lucidous refers to it in *The Complete Forged Metalwork*"—Caldan glanced at the sorcerer, hoping his reference to the famous text would elicit a response, but the man merely grunted—"is essentially forging and shaping iron using a hammer and anvil. It's more complex than that but not much.

It's for creating mundane utensils for day-to-day use, such as horseshoes, plows, axes. Simple work." He saw the master nod in agreement. "Smith-crafting, on the other hand, uses metallurgy. By extracting metals from different ores, and purifying and alloying metals whose properties are different to iron, one can create useful objects, generally using much finer tools, kilns, and molds."

The sorcerer gave him a thoughtful look. "What would you class as a useful object? Isn't a horseshoe useful?"

Caught off guard, Caldan hesitated before replying. "Yes, of course," he said slowly, giving himself time to organize his thoughts. "Um . . . what I meant was that anyone could be apprenticed as a blacksmith and learn their trade, as working with iron does not require a great deal of innate skill, whereas metallurgy requires a much deeper knowledge of many different metals and alloys, and their properties. Smith-crafting is more delicate, using molds, wire, inlays. Metallurgy combined with smith-crafting—and further combined with crafting—can create some of the most beautiful and useful objects known." His voice had gained confidence throughout, and he finished firmly.

The sorcerer frowned. "I expect most apprentices to know as much. It's good you do." He cleared his throat. "What percentage of carbon is combined with iron to make steel?"

"About two percent," Caldan rattled off. An easy one.

"And how does the carbon make the iron stronger?"

Caldan gave him a puzzled look. "Er . . . I don't know. I don't think anyone knows."

The master nodded with a rueful grin. "Thought I might ask anyway, in case you had any theories. What gives the reddish tint to rose gold?" he added quickly.

"Copper," replied Caldan without thinking.

"In what ores would you find platinum?"

"Copper, maybe nickel."

The sorcerer paused for a moment. "If you were to make a crafting out of gold, how would you strengthen the metal so it wasn't soft?"

"You could add some rare metals to make it harder, but they would be expensive. More than the gold itself." He racked his brain. "I don't know any other way. Shaping glyphs on the object wouldn't work, but—"

"It wouldn't? Why not? Isn't that how trinkets are crafted?"

"That's the prevailing theory, but I don't think it's correct."

"Really, and why not? What insights do you have that wiser scholars and sorcerers have not been able to work out themselves?"

"Well . . ." *How do I answer what no one has in hundreds of years?* The man was looking at him, and a moment of hesitation set in before he realized he had nothing to lose. "Well," Caldan repeated, "you can't craft a loop into the object to reinforce its hardness to withstand those same forces coursing through it. The crafting would make the object harder, then harder again, then harder—an infinite loop. It would crack or crumble, maybe melt."

"Indeed, or worse. So how are trinkets made?"

The question took Caldan aback. No one knew how to craft trinkets. The knowledge had been lost long ago. He resisted the urge to reach up and touch the weight of his own trinket, the ring resting heavily against his chest. "I haven't the foggiest," he said.

That gained a small smile and a nod of agreement from the sorcerer, who remained quiet for a moment, then spoke. "Well, let me know if you figure it out." He leaned back in his chair and crossed his arms. "Give me a moment to think."

Caldan bobbed his head. "Thank you, sir." He sat patiently while the man took some time to decide his fate.

After what felt like a few minutes, but was probably only one, the sorcerer spoke. "It is plain you know theory well and can improvise on the spot, albeit there was a problem with your paper crafting."

Caldan opened his mouth to protest but stopped as the man held up a hand. "I know, having the test sprung upon you, the stress . . . I have heard plenty of excuses before, and they don't hide the fact that it is inherently flawed. I can't even open it." He slammed a hand onto the paper box with a thump, and it retained its shape. "Ow!" he exclaimed.

"That was the point, sir."

"Well taken, then."

Caldan waited expectantly.

Finally, "I have made my decision. I think we can use someone like you—not as an apprentice, though. All the masters have enough apprentices after the last intake, but people with talent pop up occasionally. If you prove you can work hard, there could be an opportunity for you to be taken on. No promises, though."

Relief swept through Caldan. "Thank you, that's wonderful!"

"Wages are two coppers a week for the first four weeks. If we are satisfied after that and you decide to stay, it's four coppers a week. It's not much, I know, but room and board are included. Agreed?"

"Yes, agreed . . . sir."

The sorcerer eyed him thoughtfully, then held a hand out. "My name is Master Garren. Welcome to the Sorcerers' Guild."

CHAPTER 16

Caldan clasped Master Garren's hand warmly. Great relief flowed through him, and for a while he couldn't speak.

Master Garren grinned at him. "You might not thank me in a few months. The work for new arrivals, apprentices or not, is hard."

"That's no problem. I want to learn more."

"Ah, well you won't be learning much for a while. Helping out the masters and the staff with the upkeep of the building will be your lot for some time. The other masters—depending on how much time they can spare for you—will determine your progress in other areas. Unless you show an aptitude far in excess of what I have seen today."

Caldan's shoulders drooped, but inside he felt positive about the opportunity he now had to be involved with the sorcerers and learn as much as he could. And to have a roof over his head and food. He would never have thought such simple things would elicit so much emotion from him.

"I will write you a letter to be presented back here in five days."

"Excuse me?" Caldan asked in shock. "Five days?"

"Yes, I have to organize a few things. It's not as simple as snapping your fingers." Master Garren punctuated his words by clicking the fingers of his right hand.

"I see." Caldan hesitated. He needed somewhere to stay and food to eat, or he might turn up in five days worse for wear than he was now. "Ah . . . there is a slight problem."

Master Garren snorted. "Come on, out with it."

"I was robbed in the attack this morning," Caldan said with a sheepish grin. "All my ducats were taken, and my room at the inn was only paid until today."

"So you have no coins, no place to stay, and no way to eat?"

"Yes. It's embarrassing, but I could use some help. Not coins. I can work to repay you. Whatever odd jobs or such, I am willing to do my best."

"Hmmm . . . I have to say, you don't look like any of the usual apprentices we take on here. They tend to be bookish types, pale and scrawny or overweight, not as robust and athletic as yourself."

"The monks teach that physical discipline is connected to mental discipline. Exercise and strenuous activity are encouraged."

"Be that as it may, as I said earlier, we can't take you on as an apprentice. You can work for food and board until we can conduct some proper testing of your talent and abilities, then we'll decide what training you require and how you can best be utilized." He gave Caldan a stern look. "Nothing is for free in this world. You will be worked hard, perhaps harder than you have ever worked. And all we do is for the good of the guild. Your wants and needs come secondary to that. Do I make myself clear?"

Caldan swallowed. "Yes, sir. I understand."

He didn't know what he was getting into, but he needed some direction and stability for the time being. He realized he hadn't known what he wanted since his expulsion from the monastery and subsequent troubles. He had been focused on finding something, any work to survive after his coins ran out. He hadn't stopped to think about what he really desired. Now it appeared his choice had been made for him out of necessity.

The master drew out a mechanical watch from a pocket and read the time.

"It's late now. You'll have to follow me. I'll leave you with someone who can put you to use, and find you a meal and a place to sleep tonight."

Relief flooded through Caldan for the second time. "Thank you. I appreciate this."

"As I said—you may not in time. Follow me. I'll have to see who is available to take charge of you . . . The Protectors have space, so we'll go and see Master Simmon. Oh, before I forget." He scribbled briefly on a sheet of his own parchment from the desk, then blew gently on it to dry the ink. Folding it in half, he handed the note to Caldan. "Proof for you to show anyone who asks," he explained.

Garren led him out of the room and farther down the corridor, then across an open courtyard. Dusk had fallen, and two glimmering stars peeked from the night above.

Down another corridor, they exited through thick double doors into a huge open space. A cobbled path arrowed out in front of them, splitting an immaculate lawn dotted with shrubs and trees. The path forked toward the end as it approached another set of double doors. Master Garren hurried down the right path, through a section bordered by gray stone cubes every few yards, each big enough to sit on comfortably.

They continued through a gap in the building surrounding the garden and strode through the brief darkness. On the other side lay a torchlit courtyard, this one paved with flat sand-colored stone slabs. The guild was obviously much larger and more extensive than the public façade showing onto the square revealed.

Garren led him across the yard. Five circles were marked off with white chalk, the largest fifteen yards wide, much like the dueling circle used at the monastery for sword training. Caldan realized that was almost certainly what these were.

They entered a dormitory. Narrow beds poked into the room from both side walls, each with a trunk at the foot. The room looked clean, and the beds were made up with linen sheets and gray woolen blankets.

A muscular man with a trim black beard stood at the far end, conversing with a boy sweeping the floor.

"Ah! Master Simmon," Master Garren said. "A delivery for you." He sounded amused.

The bearded man broke off his conversation and appraised them both. Gray eyes roved over them, lingering on Caldan but not stopping on his bruised and scarred face. He took a few steps in their direction, fluid, like water running downhill.

"Master Garren, I would have thought you would be at supper by now." Master Simmon's voice was surprisingly smooth for someone so intimidating.

He has a swordsman's bearing, thought Caldan. *Calm but tight, as if ready for anything.*

Caldan opened his senses and reached out to evaluate Simmon's well. It felt constricted and narrow, not at all what he would have expected from a master sorcerer. Perhaps the Protectors valued other skills over crafting.

A subtle vibration tugged at the edges of his awareness. Simmon wore two thin silver rings on his fingers, and a silver amulet around his neck. Caldan's heart raced. They were trinkets. And the master also wore a rune-covered bracelet, probably his own crafting.

Garren laughed. "Not yet. I have one last task to finish. This is Caldan, a new recruit."

Simmon stared at Caldan, then looked back at Garren, expressionless. "What do you mean, 'new recruit'?"

Caldan tried to fade into the background.

"That's what I'm getting to. I haven't placed him yet, and he needs somewhere to stay for a few days, until I get him sorted out. I thought he could stay here with the apprentices, for the time being."

"Really?" drawled Simmon. "Not with the journeymen sorcerers? Or with the staff?"

"I thought there would be less chance for him to get into trouble here. It's more . . . organized."

Simmon gave a wry smile. "That it is," he agreed. "Leave him with me. When do you need him back?"

"I'll try for the day after tomorrow; if not, then definitely the day after. I'll send a boy to pick him up."

"Fair enough. I'll find something to keep him occupied."

"Excellent!" Master Garren beamed. He turned to Caldan. "Well, that's you settled in."

Hardly, thought Caldan. But he wasn't about to argue, so he just smiled instead. "Thank you again, Master Garren. I'm extremely grateful to you."

Garren waved a hand in dismissal. "No thanks needed. Work hard, and do your best. Listen to Simmon here, and I'll see you in a few days."

"Yes, sir. I will."

With a short nod to the other master, Garren turned and walked out of the dormitory.

Simmon gestured Caldan over to a bed with no linen on it. "Take this one. It's close to the door, with the extra traffic that brings, but it'll do you for a few days. Sheets are in the trunk, and you can lock your possessions in it. Key is in the lock."

Caldan slipped his satchel from his shoulder onto the bed. "Thank you."

"What happened to your face? A fight?"

"Yes, sir, with some thieves in Dockside. I was hit with a plank."

Simmon shook his head in disgust. "Bloody Harbor Watch should be keeping the area safer for everyone."

"They did save me." Caldan felt he had to interject on their behalf; he wouldn't like to do their job himself. "If they hadn't come along, I doubt I'd be here now. I'd probably be floating in the harbor instead." *Like the bobbing corpse I saw on the way in.*

Simmon didn't look convinced. "So—what's your story . . . besides taking ill-advised tours of Dockside?" He glanced sharply at the other boy, who had stopped sweeping the floor and stood staring at them. Seeing the master's look, he quickly returned to his work, head down.

"Nothing special. I grew up on Eremite and felt I needed to see more of the world."

Caldan knew telling the truth might generate more questions.

Best to keep a low profile until he knew more about the place and sorcerers—the Protectors as well. He didn't think telling them he had been exiled for almost killing someone would be a good start.

"Careful, I see. That's good, but sooner or later we will know everything there is to know about you. If there is anything bad, you should tell us first, before we find out on our own."

"Good advice. Thank you, sir. Well, I was raised by the monks at the monastery there after my parents . . . died."

Simmon nodded sympathetically. "They took you in?"

"Yes. I think they hoped I would eventually become one of them, teaching there or doing some other work to help the monastery. But it didn't work out."

"You studied there, though? Like the nobles' sons and daughters who go there for tutelage?"

"Among other things, yes. I joined in classes when I could. I learned about a range of subjects and disciplines. But as I found out when I arrived, a good overall education and set of skills didn't exactly set me up to be able to make a living here."

"Ah, too old to become an apprentice and not enough proficiency in any single skill?"

Caldan shrugged. "I'm sure Master Garren will find something for me. He made me give him a demonstration of my crafting skill, and it must have impressed him enough."

"Crafting as well? What else did you study?"

"Alchemy, metallurgy, Dominion, the Way of the Sword, some medicine, history . . ." He trailed off.

"I see. But nothing in enough depth that would allow you to step off the boat and take up a profession to earn a living." It wasn't a question.

Caldan shifted uncomfortably on his feet and kept quiet.

"What are your strengths?" asked Simmon.

"Dominion and crafting," answered Caldan without hesitation. "Then probably metallurgy and the Way of the Sword."

"An interesting mix. The Way of the Sword—I haven't heard it called that for a long time. Not since—" He broke off and shook his head. "Have you heard of Kelhak? He came from the monastery as well, won the Dominion tournament at the Autumn Festival a long time ago."

"I have—a bit more of late, too. He had a different reputation at the monastery, though. Exiled for something . . ." Something clicked at that moment for Caldan: Kelhak had been exiled, too, and his indiscretion wasn't sinister or immoral. Maybe in a few years rumors about Caldan would be circulating among the students at the monastery.

"Hmm. Do you know what Master Garren has in mind for you?"

"Probably helping out the masters. He mentioned I might get a chance to join some classes after a while."

"Maybe, if you show an aptitude for a particular skill. It sounds like yours is crafting. You can access your well every time you try?"

"Yes, though there wasn't much of a focus on it at the monastery. Most students didn't have the talent, or had it weakly, so they taught more theory than practice."

Simmon said nothing. Three young apprentices entered the dormitory. They saw the master standing there and hurriedly removed some books from their chests and left as quickly as possible.

"May I ask something, Master Simmon?" Caldan said.

"Go ahead."

"Is there a library or archives? I mean, I'm sure there is, but would I be able to have access to it?"

"Yes, there is one for apprentices, and I don't see why not. Any of this lot will be able to show you where it is," he said, gesturing to the dorm room. "Why?"

Caldan wasn't going to tell him about his trinket and his desire to track down his family history, so he quickly put together something believable. "I want to study as much as I can, in whatever spare time I have. Maybe if I can learn more, I can be of more use to Master Garren."

"Commendable, but you only have a couple of days before he returns for you, and you look like you need some rest." Simmon gestured at Caldan's bruised face. "Take it easy for a while, recover. For now, let's get you some food. Leave your stuff here, and lock it up."

Caldan complied and waited for the master to continue.

"Follow me. I'll show you where supper is being served. You'll take all your meals there."

The meal hall was located close to the dormitory and was mostly empty. There were large tables dotted with a few clusters of young boys and girls—apprentices, he guessed. He also saw a few older men and women. Two men dressed in dark robes conversed in hushed tones at the end of the hall.

Supper consisted of a bowl of boiled greens, a few slices of peppery lamb, a chunk of coarse-grained bread, and a mug of weak brown ale.

Caldan was left on his own to finish his meal, with instructions to return to the dormitory and have a good night's sleep. He ate slowly, though he was famished, savoring each mouthful. He had never gone a day without food, not even overnight. He felt the meal significant and reflected on how the day could have finished if he hadn't been accepted. He'd be on the streets, in the dark, wandering around with no place to go. As he swallowed each mouthful and sipped his ale, he thought about the homeless men at the docks, and vowed he would never end up like them.

CHAPTER 17

Puzzled stares and the occasional curious look from the apprentices greeted Caldan as they were all woken with the dawn by a clanging bell. One of the older boys introduced himself as Oskar and showed Caldan to the water pump and washing trough, where they all splashed their faces and rinsed their hands. The water was refreshingly warm in the cool morning air. After a quick breakfast of bread, boiled eggs, and hot tea, he was pointed in the direction of Master Simmon and found him poring over a thick ledger, penning a few words here and there on different pages.

Simmon passed him on to a shy young girl in a worn apron. She took him to a storeroom and supplied him with a broom, dustpan, and cleaning rag, and gave him directions to sweep and tidy the meal hall where the apprentices and he had eaten.

Aside from the sweeping and cleaning duties, Caldan reckoned his first few days at the Sorcerers' Guild went smoothly. He was assigned plenty of odd jobs: tidying the classrooms; pumping and carrying buckets of water to the kitchens, dormitories, and masters' quarters;

unloading wagons of grain and various foodstuffs; and beating the dust out of stored blankets to ready them for the winter. Not exciting, but better than being on the street.

That said, being taken on by the sorcerers had so far proven to be a disappointment. He was no stranger to hard work, but although the tasks they had him performing were tedious, they were not arduous. He knew he could do these chores, but he also knew he could do more—much more.

On a few occasions, he noticed Master Simmon watching him, checking up on him, no doubt. No Master Garren, though, and that meant there was no change in sight.

The only good news was that whatever healing herbs Elpidia had given to him had succeeded in helping his bruises to heal faster than he thought possible. Within a day they had faded to yellow, and on the second day had virtually disappeared. The soreness had vanished too, and his skin no longer felt tight from the stitches in his cheek. He would have to find out what herbs she had prescribed for him.

EVERY AFTERNOON, WITHOUT fail, the apprentices of all ages and levels gathered to exercise and train. Mornings were reserved for the less active training and classes, or so Caldan was told. He had no idea what they studied, or why. But he could observe them during the afternoons, and they always began with a long run through the internal gardens and corridors, followed by strengthening exercises, then instruction on sword technique. Journeymen and masters drilled the young apprentices mercilessly, not holding back when they sparred with each other. Sweat and bruises ended each afternoon's session, with the odd trickle of blood from a blow pulled too late. He understood the sword training was akin to the monastery's guiding principle of unifying body and mind, though some would think it passing strange for sorcerers, especially considering Garren's comments when Caldan was first interviewed.

On the afternoon of Caldan's third day, he was directed to sweep the packed dirt area used by the apprentices as an exercise and sparring ground. For sword training, a good grip for the feet was necessary, so he took special care with the task, gathering any stray leaves that had fallen into the circles.

There was still no sign of Master Garren, but Caldan had come to welcome the mind-numbing nature of his work. Since his expulsion from the monastery, his mind had been restless, his thoughts skittering this way and that. He hardly knew what he was thinking from one moment to the next, though for some reason his thoughts often drifted to the girl Miranda he'd met on board the *Loretta*. Each time they did he felt embarrassed and guilty. What would Jemma think of him?

He had been wrenched from a stable reality to an unstable situation in which he had no control. A few days where he could relax and not worry, not think about what was happening and what was going to happen, had served to ground him and bring his whirling thoughts under control.

The apprentices filed in and separated into groups, stretching and limbering up. Journeymen selected pairs, who sparred with each other, four pairs for the smaller circles and one for the large circle. Caldan understood the purpose of the smaller circles as opposed to the larger one: to keep the combatants close together, pushing at each other so the tension and confrontation was short and intense. Step outside the circle, and you lost the fight. Only the larger one left enough room to disengage and back away, to gather for another phase. In the small circles, the close pressure was relentless, and finesse was often the first casualty. Inside the large circle, combatants could let loose the flowing forms of the sword; they were free to engage and then disengage, to show their expertise. Swordplay here was graceful, stylish, polished. In the smaller circles, it became brutal and vicious.

Caldan slipped to the side, keeping to the shadows. He wouldn't be missed for some time, and he wanted to watch the apprentices train. It felt like months since he had held a practice sword himself, though only two weeks had passed. He still felt queasy just thinking about holding a sword, but the trauma of what he'd done to Marlon was receding at last.

Despite the cool nights, the days were still warm, and Caldan was grateful for his spot out of the sun. He positioned himself next to a stack of empty barrels and took the opportunity to sit on one. Back leaning against the wall, legs dangling over the side, he watched the sport.

Caldan estimated there were close to fifty young apprentices gathered in the courtyard, as well as a dozen older journeymen and three masters, with roughly a third of both ranks women. The disparity in the numbers of younger to older apprentices puzzled him. Did they fail and expel so many that in a few years only a fraction remained? Was what they were learning so difficult or arduous that such a winnowing was needed? Or were there apprentices somewhere else, sent for additional training as they got older?

The staccato clash of wooden practice swords brought Caldan back to the present. He could see that the younger apprentices were of vastly differing skill levels. The masters tried to pair them up with a partner of similar ability, but sometimes the gap in skill was too great, and the match ended in short order. Best of three touches; no blows to the head, hands, or groin, as far as Caldan could tell.

One older apprentice, bigger than his fellows, took delight in pulling his blows too late to prevent most of the impact when they landed. From their pained expressions during and after the matches, it was clear his opponents were not happy to be facing him. A couple of the masters frowned at the apprentice whenever he landed an overly hard blow, but they didn't stop the bouts.

He caught Caldan staring at him and sneered. Caldan shook his head and looked away. No point in antagonizing anyone; he would be gone from here as soon as Master Garren returned.

Disappointed expressions and pleased looks ended each practice match, the sparring at the smaller circles finishing much quicker than the large-circle fights. The overall skill of the apprentices was not as high as Caldan had thought it would be. Some of the older apprentices approached the practice with a workmanlike attitude, as if practicing a skill they would rarely use and just going through the motions.

"What do you think?" asked a voice right beside Caldan. He turned to find Master Simmon leaning against the wall next to him.

"You startled me. I didn't see you there."

Simmon shrugged. "You weren't supposed to." He crossed his arms and looked out at the apprentices. "You're older than most of them and have studied sword fighting. What do you think of their skill?"

Caldan struggled to come up with something polite to say, shifting his weight on the barrel, finding a more comfortable position to gain time to think. "They're . . . fine. There's a broad range of skills out there. Some are better than others." He didn't know why the master was talking to him and hoped it wasn't another test of some kind.

"Very diplomatic of you." Simmon continued to gaze out at the apprentices, eyes shifting from one practice bout to another. "But not really helpful. Give me an honest opinion."

You asked for it. "Most are barely adequate. I mean, they are still young, but I don't see many that move fluidly, that look like they have a talent for the sword. See that one there." He pointed to a boy with reddish hair. "He might have some talent, but it's too soon to tell. I'd have to watch him a bit more to see. The only others that are good are the older journeymen and the masters."

Across the courtyard, the bigger apprentice landed a hard blow on a skinny boy, who fell to the dirt, clutching both hands to his stomach. Caldan wrinkled his nose disapprovingly at the unnecessary force.

Simmon barely seemed to notice the use of violence and the defeated apprentice's suffering. "No one fails his or her apprenticeship with the Sorcerers' Guild based on sword work. But apprentices with good sword skills are considered for the Protectors once they become journeymen."

"What is it the Protectors do?" asked Caldan.

"You said you studied history."

"Yes, but there isn't a lot of writing on the Protectors. All I know is that you're the sorcerers' martial arm, like guards."

A snort of amusement from Simmon followed his statement. "Then you *really* don't know much about us and what we do. Guards . . ." He trailed off, shaking his head. "You'll learn more later from the masters, if you get to work with them. There are many different roles in the Protectors, as there are within all professions, including the sorcerers. Sword skill is valuable for certain tasks, just as skill in crafting is for others."

"You practice crafting as well?"

"Indeed. The Protectors know a lot about crafting; we're sorcerers, after all." Simmon stopped abruptly, as if about to say more but thinking better of it. "The older apprentices whose talents lie in other areas obviously don't need to come to all of these practice sessions." He gestured with one hand to the ones who had, two of whom were struggling to land a blow on each other. "But they must at least be able to keep to an acceptable standard."

"And that's acceptable?"

Master Simmon again pierced him with a hard look. "Think you can do better?"

So much for wanting my honesty. "Yes. I think I can." He waited for Simmon to get angry. So what the master said next surprised him.

"At least you say what you think. Come on, let's see how you do." He strode past a group of apprentices watching one of the matches.

More excited than nervous, Caldan levered himself off the barrel and followed closely in Simmon's wake. *Finally—a chance to do something other than sweep.*

Simmon stopped at the edge of the larger circle, waiting for the match in progress to finish. A few apprentices eyed Caldan as he stood behind the master. Some whispered to each other and pointed in his direction.

A brief spatter of applause and a few cheers signaled the end of the match. Not as many as usual, though. All eyes had turned to Simmon and Caldan, wondering what was happening. Caldan felt himself propelled forward as Simmon turned and gripped his shoulder hard, then forced him into the clear space. Simmon took the two practice swords from the pair who stood there still panting and sweating in the afternoon sun. He handed one to Caldan, who accepted it reluctantly. The feel of the sword in his hand brought back memories of Marlon, and his stomach roiled.

"Who am I fighting?" he asked reluctantly.

Simmon grinned and stepped back a few yards, sweeping his sword in front of him in a classic guard position.

"Me," he replied, executing a lunge straight for Caldan's chest.

A shift in Simmon's posture alerted Caldan to the attack, and his own sword whipped up in time to deflect the blade, though it came faster than any he had seen today. He leaped back. Simmon slashed at his neck. Caldan sidestepped and jerked his sword up in defense. Wood came together with a sharp crack. Their blades met again in a tentative probing.

Caldan started sweating, heart hammering and blood pumping hard. The grip of his sword felt slick in his sweaty palms. Cheers and shouts from the apprentices faded to a faint buzz, barely audible.

Simmon took three steps to his right in an arc, always keeping the same distance from Caldan, but the way he moved didn't seem right.

Simmon's muscles tensed, then he grunted and leaped forward, both feet leaving the ground. His sword swooped down from behind him in a wide curve. To Caldan, he looked like he moved at three-quarters speed.

Blades met again as Caldan parried Simmon's attacks with an ease he hadn't thought possible. An opening came, but Caldan, puzzled with what was happening, halted his attack.

Is Simmon trying to trick me? Make me think I have a chance against a master of the Protectors? Or is he setting me up in front of the apprentices?

No matter what was going on, Caldan saw each of the attacks and feints in Simmon's next combination as if he knew where the sword would be before it moved. Two thrusts he parried, two feints he ignored, and two cuts he moved to avoid.

A frown appeared on Simmon's face.

Caldan drove his sword toward Simmon's neck, then switched the direction at the last instant to sweep into his side. Simmon couldn't adjust in time, and Caldan's blade hit him above the hip. A touch.

They stopped and stared, each as surprised as the other.

"One to you." Simmon's voice rang clearly in the yard.

The shouts of the apprentices hushed to silence. All their eyes were on Caldan and the master.

Caldan moved and reacted faster than ever before. He wasn't better or more skilled—he couldn't be. He'd been only middling with the blade at best.

By the ancestors, what is happening?

Simmon's sword darted in as he renewed his attacks. Caldan countered all with ease. Simmon's technique was perfect, his attacks focused and faultless, his defense exceptional. But he couldn't handle Caldan's newfound speed and the swiftness of his reactions.

Caldan countered as fast as he could—faster, clearly—a simple three-slash combination. Taught early on in sword training, the attack and the defense against it were mastered early by all and included in the practice forms.

Yet his third cut of the combination hit home on Simmon's shoulder, Caldan struggling to pull the blow he thought would never land.

Both the master and Caldan stepped back, swords lowered.

"Two to you," growled Simmon. A curious look had replaced his surprised expression. "We have a victor."

Best of three touches, of course. The bout was over. *Thank the ancestors for that,* thought Caldan. *I'm not sure what would have happened had it gone on any longer.*

Simmon gave him a thoughtful look, then turned to address the crowd of apprentices.

"Let this be a lesson to you all," he said, deep voice rising to drown the excited buzz. "Never underestimate an opponent, as there's always someone stronger, faster, and more skilled than yourself. Expect the unexpected, then you'll never be surprised." His gaze passed over them all as he turned in a circle.

"Enough for today. Everyone practice forms for an hour, then study until the evening meal." He gestured for Caldan to move out of the circle with him and leaned close so that the others couldn't hear. "Any reason you kept your skill a secret?" he asked quietly.

"I didn't. I mean, sorcerers don't need sword skill, right? It's only for exercise and to have fun."

"Fun?" Simmon repeated. He looked Caldan in the eye. "Most of the apprentices probably didn't even follow the fight, it was so fast. I struggled from the beginning. I couldn't believe I didn't get a touch on you at the start." He paused to think, brushing sweat off his nose and running a hand through his black hair.

"How long did Master Garren see you for, when you came here to ask about work?"

"Not that long. He asked some questions, and I gave him a crafting demonstration, which didn't work out well."

"How old were you when the monastery took you in?"

Caldan didn't want to talk about that time, or how long it took the monks to get him to speak again. "Seven," he said. "What's this have to do with anything?"

Simmon held a hand up. "Easy—you're not in trouble. I just want to figure out some things. They took you in, and you studied with them until now, or you worked for your keep?"

Caldan shook his head. He didn't understand. Wooden swords whooshed through the air around them as the apprentices practiced forms. Despite the flurry of activity, he could feel their curious gazes on him.

"A bit of both. They were kind to me, after . . ." His throat choked up. "After they took me in." *After my parents were murdered.*

Simmon nodded in understanding. "You were working and learning from them for the last ten years?"

"They didn't mind what I studied. I joined in lessons with the students when I wanted, except I didn't have to pass exams. Sometimes it was just me and one of the monks discussing theory or practicing."

"The Way of the Sword, crafting, alchemy. And Dominion as well?"

"Yes."

Simmon rubbed his beard. "You have spent ten years living and training at one of the institutions with a great reputation for teaching, so much so that nobles pay for their children to study under the monks. And Garren, I mean Master Garren, didn't question you on this?"

"No, Master. And I hadn't thought it was anything worth going into much detail about."

Simmon sighed. "All right." He looked around at the apprentices, frowning in thought. "I want to talk to you more about this later. I think Master Garren wasn't thorough enough when he interviewed you. You should think about what's just happened, and what we've been talking about. Take the rest of the afternoon off. Whatever tasks you have, finish them tomorrow." Simmon turned to leave. "This has taken up enough of your time, and mine."

Still out of sorts from the practice match, Caldan nodded and slipped through the groups of apprentices, leaving his sword in a pile with the other spares.

Most apprentices were looking at him now, some staring and some with furtive glances. Many whispered to their colleagues as he passed.

"Back to work!" Simmon shouted, and the apprentices guiltily resumed their forms.

Many of them still took surreptitious glances at Caldan.

They don't know why I'm here, and now I just defeated one of their masters in sword practice. He could only guess what the rumors were about him now, especially with his scarred cheek. He needed some time to think, to get away from the crowded courtyard. He also felt slightly sick and his muscles were trembling—whatever had happened left a lingering effect he didn't like the feel of. He wished Delife hadn't taken his old pouch of medicine, but he could always obtain more.

Caldan hurried through one of the corridors and into the large garden he had crossed with Garren when he first came here. Finding a shady spot under a leafy tree, he lay down.

Grass poked into his back and arms through his clothes, but the smell of the lawn and plants around him, and the relative silence away from the Protectors' quarters, served to put him at ease. Slowly, he relaxed, eyes closed, breathing in the warm afternoon air.

"YOU'RE A HARD man to find!" A chirpy female voice woke him.

He opened his eyes to see Miranda above him, looking down with a frown on her face.

"Asleep during the day. Captain Charlotte would have you whipped!"

She brushed a strand of hair from her face. No longer dressed in her usual rough sailor's clothes, she wore a dark red dress with a wide brown leather belt cinched around her narrow waist.

Caldan struggled to a sitting position. "Oh!" he exclaimed. "You." He wasn't awake yet, and his thoughts were muddled.

Miranda's expression changed to a warm smile, slightly embarrassed. "If I wasn't the forgiving type, I'd think you forgot my name."

"Miranda. Sorry, I was . . . resting my eyes." He managed to stand, but wobbled, the grass uneven under his feet. "What are you . . . I thought the *Loretta* had left. I saw its berth empty."

"Pleased to see you again, too. And may I say your appearance has improved," she commented. Her hand came up to touch his injured cheek, and her tone softened. "What happened?"

Caldan's face felt hot as he blushed. He turned away from her hand, skin tingling where she had touched him.

"I wandered where I shouldn't have and was robbed. It's not as bad as it looks."

"It looks like it happened weeks ago, not recently." Miranda's stare was puzzled. "Those stitches need to come out, or the skin will grow over them."

"The physiker said to come back in ten days. It's hardly been three."

"I've seen some wounds on the ship, and helped stitch up cuts after fights, and I think they need to come out now. Come on, do you have some spare time? What am I talking about—I just found you napping. I'm sure you can spare a few minutes. I can have the stitches out quicker than you can say 'ouch.'" She grinned.

"I think I'd rather the physiker took them out."

Miranda gave an amused, lilting laugh. "A professional hand is needed, is it? I know when I'm not wanted."

"No, it's just that . . ." More firmly, he said "It's not that I don't trust you."

"It's that you would rather a professional did it?"

It's just that I can't think with you so close. She looked different to Caldan. Out of her rough cotton pants and shirt, and clothed in what must be her good dress—he thought she was pretty before, but now she looked . . . striking. His heart hammered in his chest.

"Yes. She'll have some ointment to help the scar heal, you see."

"Of course."

I've disappointed her. He couldn't think of anything he wanted to do less. Hoping to get her mind off that, he asked, "How did you find me?"

"Captain Charlotte told me she'd suggested the Otter to you, so I checked there, and the innkeeper told me the last he spoke to you, the Sorcerers' Guild was your destination. He sounded quite concerned that you hadn't returned. Told me I should check down by the docks among the unskilled laborers."

Caldan shook his head, face grim. "They're a sorry lot. It must be hard for them here. So I'm glad things turned out for the best for me. How did you get in here?"

Miranda laughed, cheeks dimpling. "By asking young boys eager to impress an older woman, and a ducat or two in the right palms."

She seemed amused by her ability to wander into the Sorcerers' Guild unescorted.

Caldan gathered himself, holding out his arm for her. "Shall we go for a walk?"

She nodded and took his arm, and they made their way off the grass and onto the paved path.

Miranda wrinkled her nose. "You smell. Been doing some exercise?"

Caldan suddenly became very aware of his ruffled state—his wrinkled, sweaty clothes that hadn't had a proper wash for some time.

"It's been a strange day," he said.

Miranda raised her eyebrows.

"I'll explain some other time. You didn't answer my question," Caldan said. "What happened to the *Loretta*? Why didn't you sail with her?"

Shadow overlaid the path, as the sun had dipped below the top of the tall walls. They passed through patches of sunlight that shone through gaps between buildings.

Miranda took a while to reply. Caldan thought she discarded several answers before speaking.

"That life, at sea, it wasn't for me. The *Loretta* was a fine place for a while. It let me get myself together. Captain Charlotte . . . I couldn't have asked for a more understanding person. She's my second cousin." She broke off and swallowed. "But I grew up in the city, and that's where I'm more comfortable." Miranda went quiet.

Caldan let her be.

They strolled through an opening at the end of the garden and down a wide corridor. As they exited through a doorway onto a crowded street, she continued.

"I have some ducats saved, and I want to settle down, maybe open my own business, if I can." She laughed. "But you probably think that's silly."

"No, not at all. Trust me—I'm in no position to judge *anyone*." He squeezed her arm briefly in reassurance, and she smiled. "What sort of business?"

"Trading. It's what I know from my time on the *Loretta*. In truth, I may need to find a job and earn some more ducats before I have enough. Rent in Anasoma isn't cheap."

They wound their way down a main street, Caldan directing them toward Dockside in the general direction of Elpidia's house. As they passed through the Barrows district, the houses and shops grew less salubrious. Food stalls stretched along one side street teeming and noisy with an early evening crowd.

Joining the Highroad, Caldan and Miranda found the walk to Dockside still took some time, though the wide street allowed ample room for pedestrians, carts, and overburdened donkeys. The city was so big. Caldan still couldn't believe the size of it.

The transition into Dockside was noticeable. Where the large buildings and warehouses lining the docks themselves were in relatively good condition, farther back and down the side streets, worn and dilapidated houses were in abundance. Stretched multistory wooden buildings leaned over alleys, and makeshift walkways connected their roofs.

"Inside isn't usually as bad as the outside," Miranda remarked—she must have noticed his expression. "People don't care about appearances, especially when they are renting. It's inside where they take care the most."

"What about the bridges?" Caldan pointed to a walkway spanning an alley.

"Another Highroad, in a manner of speaking. Sometimes it's easier to go over the buildings than come down to the streets."

"A thieves' road?"

"Sometimes. Not everyone here is dishonest or a thief."

"I know, I just . . . The place is confusing for me. I'm not used to it."

Miranda patted him on the arm. "Don't worry. It'll grow on you."

He just wasn't sure he *wanted* it to, but said nothing.

A while later—after a few wrong turns, and after asking for directions from a passing matron with four children in tow—they stood before Elpidia's red door. Following his polite knock, Elpidia ushered them inside, frowning at Miranda, and gestured for Caldan to sit with ill-concealed impatience.

"Why are you back so soon?" she asked as Caldan settled into the chair with a creak. Elpidia glanced at the chair. "Don't break it," she said, then turned the knob of an oil lamp. Its flame brightened, pushing back some of the shadows. She moved to her fireplace and struck a small stick against the stone. Light flared, and she used the flame to ignite a stack of kindling, upon which sat two logs. A faint phosphorous odor penetrated the room.

"Now," she said. "I assume there's a problem, so what is it? Did—" She broke off and peered at his cheek. "What happened? Where did your bruises go?" She leaned over Caldan, one hand turning his cheek to the light from the lamp. She brushed a finger over his scar. "Hmmm," she murmured thoughtfully and stepped back.

"I heal quickly," he said. "And the herbs you gave me must have helped."

"Those stitches need to come out. The cut has closed already. It's much further along than usual for such a wound."

"I told you," Miranda chimed in.

"Wait here. I'll need some instruments." Elpidia disappeared behind the curtain into her back room.

Miranda leaned against the side of the fireplace and held her hands out to the flames. "It's been a while since I've been able to do this," she said. "Fire on a ship isn't a good idea. I didn't realize I missed it so much."

"The monks didn't allow themselves any heating in winter," Caldan said. "They thought some sacrifices hardened the body and the mind. Of course, the paying students were allowed fires whenever they wanted."

Miranda gave him a curious look, then returned her gaze to the flickering flames. "They have to survive, the same as everyone else. You can't blame them for choosing to teach what they are good at rather than fade into poverty. It's helped them survive, and from what you have said, they haven't lost their identity."

"True. Sometimes I wish I was back there."

Miranda gave him a prickly look he couldn't interpret.

Elpidia returned carrying a bottle of colorless liquid, a cloth, a sharp knife, and some tweezers. She dragged a low stool close to Caldan.

"Hold still," she said in a flat professional tone. She dampened a corner of the cloth with the colorless liquid and wiped both the knife and tweezers.

Caldan felt sharp pains in his cheek as she pulled the stitches out enough to slip the knife under to cut them. With sharp jerks, she pulled out the thread. As the last stitch came free, she used the damp cloth to wipe the cut.

"Ow!" Caldan exclaimed as the alcohol stung his cheek.

"Don't be a baby," both Miranda and Elpidia said at once. Miranda laughed, while Elpidia only gave a tight smile.

Caldan scowled.

Elpidia examined the scar as she continued to wipe his cheek. "The wound looks well on the way to healing. I don't know if it's because you are young or my herbs are better than I thought, but it looks like there won't be much of a scar soon." She pursed her lips thoughtfully, then gave a slight shake of her head. She glanced down at the red-stained cloth in her hand. "Have you always healed so quickly? When did you first notice it?"

"I don't know what you mean," Caldan said, puzzled at her insistent tone. "It mustn't have been that bad a cut."

Elpidia's eyes narrowed and she grunted softly. "Anyway, I've got work to do. And I'm sure you both have something better to do than wait around here."

Caldan stood, and the chair let out another creak. "Thank you, Elpidia. For your help and time. I hope I won't be back here soon."

"I'm sure you mean that in a nice way," Elpidia said.

"Yes—sorry. I didn't mean it the way it sounded. I meant—"

Elpidia cut him off with a wave of her hand. "I know what you meant."

Miranda moved from her position by the fireplace and headed to the front door. "Come on, Caldan, we need to be going," she said.

He wasn't sure why she was hurrying them out, but the physiker was clearly eager for them to leave, and he couldn't think of a reason to tarry. "Thanks again, Elpidia," Caldan said. "Farewell."

"WELL," REMARKED MIRANDA with a deprecating look at the door. "She wasn't too friendly. For someone who makes her living helping sick people, you'd think she would smile more or make small talk."

"Ease up on her, Miranda. She did good work on the stitching." Caldan nudged her with his shoulder to soften his words.

Miranda sniffed. "I suppose she has to deal with a lot of ill and wounded people. It would probably make me unfeeling as well." She looked around the street. "Why don't we have something to eat? Daylight's fading now, and I'm famished."

Caldan nodded in agreement before he could stop himself. Empty pockets meant he couldn't afford to pay for a meal for himself, let alone for two, and the two copper ducats he should receive after his first week wasn't a fortune either. "Wait . . . I can't. I've been eating at the meal hall where I am now, and don't know anywhere in the city to go. And . . . I have to admit that all my coins were stolen a few days ago. It's how my face got hurt in the first place." He hung his head in shame, not daring to look her in the eye.

"Everything?" asked Miranda in an incredulous tone. "Were you carrying it all with you? Didn't you take what you needed and leave the rest safe in your room?"

"Yes, everything." For some reason, her questions angered him a bit. *I'm the one who was robbed.* "I wasn't thinking. I guess I'm just as naive as you first thought on the *Loretta*."

She pulled him to the side of the street and looked directly at him. Her eyes softened, and he could feel his anger dissipating even before she spoke. "I'm sorry, Caldan—that was unkind of me. How about this idea? I'll buy you dinner, but you have to promise to return the favor when you come into some coins. Deal?" She looked expectantly at Caldan, who thought for a moment.

"I guess so." He didn't like the idea of being in someone's debt, but he liked Miranda, so the thought of another future dinner with her was enticing.

"Good." She squeezed his arm. "I know where to go, a place that's clean and serves a good menu." She looked at him slyly. "If you like eel."

"Eel?"

"Yes. You know, the wriggly kind."

"Sounds . . . interesting." *Sounds disgusting.*

Miranda laughed and directed him down a side street, using pressure on his arm to guide him. Earthenware products stretched the length of the road, spilling out of shop doorways that were still open despite the late hour. A girl with ragged hair watched them pass from her position sitting atop a large urn, chewing what looked like shiny grasshoppers skewered on a stick.

Miranda sniggered at him and smacked her lips. "Roasted grasshoppers covered in honey. Crunchy and sweet."

The girl looked to be enjoying them, but Caldan wasn't convinced. "If you say so."

"I do. Hang on." Miranda stopped at a corner and peered down the cross street to the right. The pottery gave way to crowded food stalls, which lined the buildings on either side. Fragrant smoke drifted from low-burning braziers cooking the various foods on offer.

"This is the place. Come on." Miranda strode ahead down the middle of the street, shifting her hips to avoid the many people at the stalls.

Caldan only moved his eyes from Miranda to watch where he was going after he bumped into a man smoking a pipe.

"My apologies, sir," he mumbled.

The man's hand went to his purse, and finding it still secure, he gave a curt nod before moving on.

Caldan followed Miranda's weaving outline but had difficulty negotiating the crowded street. She edged ahead, her slight figure allowing her to twist into spaces his bulk couldn't. She glanced over her shoulder a few times to make sure he was still there. He increased his pace, despite the crowd, and saw her stop in front of a building.

She smiled as he approached. "This is it," she said, gesturing to an orange door.

Above her, a sign denoted the place as CAMILD'S HOUSE OF EELS in bold black letters. BEST EELS THIS SIDE OF THE RIVER SOP. On it, two eels twined around each other above a frying pan.

Caldan's trepidation must have shown on his face, because Miranda rolled her eyes, grabbed his hand, and pulled him through the door.

They entered, and Miranda nodded to a serving boy, who smiled in recognition. She followed the boy through a doorway into a large, low room filled with dark wooden booths, seats padded with cloth. A single lamp suspended over each table gave the place enough light to see by but still left it in semidarkness.

As they sat in a booth, a waiter wearing a black apron appeared, greeted them briefly, and left a chalkboard covered in script on the table.

"Ah, let's see what the special is today," Miranda said, and grabbed the board. Her eyes roved down it, squinting in the dim light. She paused and frowned at Caldan.

"Maybe not," she muttered and turned back to the board.

"What?"

"I don't think you'd like that dish."

I'm not sure I'm going to like any *of these dishes.*

"What is it?"

"Lamprey braised in ginger, vinegar, and salt with a blood sauce."

That's disgusting, thought Caldan. "Blood sauce?" He thought a lamprey was a type of eel, but wasn't sure.

"They chop its head off, squeeze the fluid out, and use it to make a sauce. With chopped onions, red wine—that sort of thing."

"Sounds . . . revolting."

Miranda stopped reading and looked at him. "That's why I decided you wouldn't like it."

"Can't I choose my own dish?"

She shook her head and winked. "No. I'm paying, so I'm choosing."

Caldan fidgeted in his seat while Miranda deliberated. Muted conversations from other diners reached his ears, and another waiter passed close by their table carrying a tray of steaming plates. The aroma of freshly baked bread, garlic, wine, and a spicy odor he didn't recognize wafted past. He could hear Miranda humming to herself.

"Ah, Miranda?"

"Yes?" She didn't look up.

"Are you sure you can afford this place? I mean, we can go somewhere less expensive, if you like."

Miranda waved a hand and shook her head. "It's all right, I know the cook. I come here a lot when I'm in port." She paused. "When I had shore leave," she corrected. "Now, shh. I'm trying to decide."

Caldan fingered the dark tabletop, tracing the grain. He looked around the room, but the high screens separating the tables didn't allow him a view of the other patrons.

"Will you stop fidgeting!" exclaimed Miranda.

"Sorry, I was just . . . taking in the atmosphere." *And trying not to think about Miranda sitting so close, or the fact that I probably look—and smell—like a vagrant, or that I'm about to eat a meal that would scare the ancestors . . .*

Miranda held the chalkboard in the air above her for a few

moments, then placed it on the edge of the table. The waiter reappeared and bowed slightly from the waist again. He collected the board and waited silently.

"We'll have the spicy eels with noodles and the baked eel with bay leaves. Could we also have two glasses of Camild's red wine, please?"

The waiter nodded and withdrew without saying a word.

"Don't they talk?" asked Caldan.

"Actually, they do, just not usually to customers. Gives the place a reputation of privacy, somewhere you can be intimate and not be disturbed."

Intimate. For some reason, that word made him uncomfortable. Desperate, he said the first thing that came to mind. "How come you haven't cursed yet?"

"Pardon?"

"On the *Loretta,* you cursed like a . . . sailor." Caldan grinned at Miranda's annoyed frown. "But you don't seem to talk like that now. Don't tell me you were faking it?"

She shrugged. "I might have been."

"Then who is the real you: the sailor or the lady in front of me?"

"Both, of course." Miranda's throaty laugh filled their booth. "On the ship, well, they expect a certain type of behavior. And it wasn't a stretch for me to act it up. They wouldn't have respected someone who didn't curse like one of them."

Their waiter returned and deposited two pewter goblets on the table. The only sound he made was the rustle of his clothes. Miranda picked up her goblet, tilted it in Caldan's direction, then took a sip. She swallowed, eyes closed, and a smile spread across her face.

"Excellent," she murmured. "Cheap but still good. Go ahead, try it."

Caldan took a mouthful of the fruity wine. To him, it didn't taste too different from any other wine. He could see the slightest disappointment cross her eyes at his lack of appreciation. He took another sip and made a show of enjoying it. Miranda relaxed.

"And now?" Caldan prompted.

Miranda twisted her goblet by the stem. "Like I said, that life wasn't for me, so I don't have to act."

"Everyone acts."

"Everyone?"

"Yes, no one shows their true self to strangers. Even to friends."

"I guess that's true, if you think about it. It's sad, though." Miranda took another sip from her goblet.

"Sad? In what way?"

"That people don't show who they really are to others, even friends and family. That's sad. Can you ever know someone, then?" She shrugged.

"If you trust someone, you wouldn't act with them. Like married couples."

Miranda scoffed. "Caldan, you have no idea. Sometimes married couples are the worst."

"Why?"

"Because they want to keep each other happy, or at least try and keep the relationship smooth. That means hiding more, in some cases."

"You're too cynical."

"That's coming from you, who says everyone acts? Maybe I am. But then again, I've seen a lot." She broke eye contact and stared down at the table. "A lot more than you, I'd wager," she said quietly. "My mother . . . before she died . . . had worked the only way an unskilled woman could at the docks. It was enough to keep us in our one rented room and in food, but that was all. I was nine when I realized my mother wasn't like the other mothers."

I've upset her again. Very smooth, Caldan. He'd stirred painful memories in her. He knew enough, at least, to determine that now wasn't the time to press her further. He tried another tack.

"I'm sorry."

Miranda gave him a wan smile and shrugged.

"So what made you come looking for me?" Caldan said.

She wrinkled her brow and gave Caldan a long, searching look. "After I decided to leave the *Loretta*, I spoke with Captain Charlotte. I didn't want to go back to the city where I grew up for . . . well, for a few reasons. She gave me some good advice, but in a way that made it harder for me as well. Too many options can confuse you sometimes." Miranda paused and brushed a lock of hair over an ear with her fingers. "But staying in Anasoma felt like the right decision. There's plenty of work if you aren't fussy, and plenty of opportunity, if you have some ducats and a plan. It's a huge city and a good place to try and make a living in. Then I thought about you, and that we are in similar situations, and two heads are better than one. Maybe not so much your head," she said, but her tone was light. "Anyway, a friendly face and someone to share expenses with could make starting out here a lot easier. I decided to see if you wanted some help. We could work together, and settling in would be easier for both of us." She lowered her eyes to the table and cleared her throat.

Caldan considered what she'd said for some time. The silence stretched on as she expected him to say something, but he didn't have much to offer for his side of such an arrangement.

"That's kind of you. I mean, it's a good idea, and normally I wouldn't hesitate, but . . ."

"You don't think we should help each other out?"

Caldan's smile slipped a little, and he toyed with his goblet. He wanted to accept Miranda's offer, but . . . his decision to trace the origins of his trinket and what he might unearth could be dangerous. As it had proved to be for his parents and sister. To bring Miranda into that without her knowledge would be unconscionable. And that left him with the question of whether or not he should tell her—was he ready to tell *anyone* yet?

"Look, Miranda," he said, "the fact is, I don't have anything much to contribute. I don't have any ducats, I have no idea what I'm doing with the sorcerers, and I don't even have a room to stay in at the moment. I'm sleeping in a dormitory with apprentices years younger than me. And on top of that, I have other business I need to conduct. Information I need . . . no, *have* to find out." He sat silently for a moment.

"Caldan, what is it?" she asked. "What is this 'other business'?"

He looked at her and couldn't help notice how earnest she looked. How much she seemed to truly care what he was about to say next. He wasn't used to someone being really interested in what he had to say. Not the monks, certainly not the other students—not even Jemma.

Maybe this is an act, too. But even so, it's one I want to believe in. Someone to share even a little with. Guess it's now or never . . .

"I never really knew my parents. That's why I grew up in the monastery. They . . . died . . . when I was young." He shifted uncomfortably in his seat. "Recently, I found out they were murdered."

Miranda gave an anguished gasp, the blood draining from her face. She reached across the table and took Caldan's hand in hers. "I'm so sorry, truly. That's awful."

Caldan nodded slowly, eyes downcast. "All I have of theirs is a ring, which is . . . distinctive . . ." He trailed off, uncertain whether to tell Miranda the whole story.

"Is it . . . a trinket?" she asked, frowning slightly.

Surprised at her guess, Caldan nodded before he could stop himself. "Yes. Please don't tell anyone."

She smiled disarmingly. "It'll be our secret."

"When the monks gave me the ring, they told me about my parents' past, which was that they worked for the empire. But it isn't enough. I wish it was, but . . . I need to find out more about them. Who they were, where they came from. Perhaps it will lead me to understand what happened to them, or it could lead me into danger. And that's the problem: I just don't know." He cleared his throat. "It could be dangerous, and I wouldn't"—he looked directly into her eyes—"*couldn't* bring you into something that might lead to you being hurt or worse. Do you see?"

Miranda gave his hand a gentle squeeze and nodded. "I do. I'm glad you felt able to tell me."

"It wouldn't be fair to you otherwise, and I wouldn't do that to you."

"No, you wouldn't, and that's unusual. You're an interesting man, Caldan." She released his hand and leaned back, giving him an appraising stare. Finally she said, "I agree."

"Excuse me?"

"I agree to help you, unless things get rough. Then we can decide whether to continue or to run."

"Ah . . . thank you, but I wasn't actually asking you to help—"

"No thanks needed," interrupted Miranda. "I'm sure I'll be able to help you. I know a few people who know others. Information here can be remarkably easy to obtain, if you have the right contacts . . . and the ducats."

Caldan scratched his head and frowned. This wasn't going the way he thought it would. "Really, I don't have much to go on—"

"All the more reason to work together."

"I guess so . . ."

"I know so. I'm not saying I'll follow you to hell and back, or vow revenge if you get yourself killed."

"Let's hope it doesn't come to that."

"But what I'm saying is that I *can* help. You follow whatever trails you have, and I can find out what I can and introduce you to people whose business it is to know other people's business." She shrugged. "Simple, and hardly dangerous."

With a half smile, Caldan nodded. She made sense, and if he had any inkling the situation was deteriorating or was likely to, he would distance himself from her.

"Then I agree as well," he replied. "Though, as to your business, I'm afraid all I can offer is a friendly face and someone to talk to."

Miranda's expression improved, and she smiled. Caldan felt the room become brighter and warmer.

"Great! I'm still working out what I'm going to do anyway. And I'm sure you're selling yourself short. Either way, I've found a place for myself, and from working with the captain I have some contacts with the merchants and traders. There are lots of ducats to be made, if you don't mind risks."

She broke off as their waiter appeared. He placed two steaming bowls and a basket covered with a thin cloth on the table. The smell of freshly baked, hot bread came from the basket, and Caldan's stomach rumbled. He glanced at Miranda, and she rolled her eyes. The waiter left two empty plates for them as well as pewter forks and spoons.

Miranda rubbed her hands together. She slid one of the empty plates across the table to him and proceeded to scoop out portions of both eel dishes. "Let's eat. Pass me some bread, please."

He removed the cloth and placed one of the thick slices on her plate.

"It's best eaten when it's hot, so don't worry if you can't hold a conversation for a while."

Not exactly what I'm worried about, he thought as he eyed his dish warily.

For some time they enjoyed a companionable silence as they demolished both bowls of eel. To Caldan's surprise, he found himself enjoying the dishes, including the noodles and bread. Miranda's eyes sparkled with amusement as she watched him take pleasure in eating eel for the first time. Following her lead, he used bread crusts to scrape his plate and soak up the remaining sauce.

"Well," Miranda said after she finished her last crust of bread. "That was good."

Caldan nodded. "It really was."

"You don't have to act so surprised. If we're going to be partners, you're going to have to learn to trust me more."

He could only laugh at that.

"Now you have a task to complete for the next time we meet."

"Excuse me?"

"To find as good a place to eat, of course!"

"That might take a while. I have to earn some ducats first before I can return the favor."

Miranda leaned her elbows on the table, goblet held in both hands. She swirled her wine. "If it takes a while, you'd just better make sure it serves good food. Too much anticipation could lead to high expectations."

"I'll strive to meet your lofty standards."

"Ha. Why don't you just focus on getting settled, then, and we can figure out the future later."

"Sounds perfect." Caldan raised his goblet. "To the future," he toasted.

Miranda touched her goblet to his. "To the future." She smiled at him. "It's getting late. What time do you need to get back? I could show you some more of the city. It isn't all bad, you know."

Caldan grimaced. "I'm with the young apprentices at the moment, in their dormitory. They sleep earlier than I would like."

"Oh ho! An early night, up with the dawn?"

"Yes. Any day now I should be out of there. One of the masters, Master Garren, is placing me somewhere, then I hope to have my own room."

"Somewhere?"

Caldan opened his hands in a gesture of despondence. After his troubles finding any employment at all, he felt quite good about the sorcerers, but he could understand Miranda's puzzlement that he didn't have a firm idea what he would be doing.

"He had to find a place for me. I'm too old to become an apprentice, but too inexperienced to be a journeyman. I mean, I had to beg him to let me stay until he sorted something out."

"He must think you're good, then, or he wouldn't have gone to so much trouble."

"Maybe. He seemed impressed, except for the mistake I made."

"What mistake?"

Caldan hesitated. "I crafted something because he asked it. But I forgot an essential part, so it didn't work as planned."

Miranda sniggered and then they both laughed. They caught each other's eyes, then looked away at the same time.

"What's it like?" she finally asked. "Crafting, I mean. It's sorcery, isn't it?"

"Yes. It's . . . hard to describe." Caldan paused to scratch his itchy cheek. He stopped at Miranda's frown. "I know, don't scratch it, or it won't heal properly."

"I wasn't about to say that," she said with feigned innocence.

He smiled and looked at Miranda, catching himself as his gaze traveled down to the smooth skin of her neck. He took a deep breath. "Anyway, it's like making something with your hands. That's why it's called crafting."

"But it's sorcery?" she persisted.

"It is, or rather it's like a *part* of sorcery. You see, it also takes some skill at woodworking or metalworking to be able to create an item that functions the way you want it to. The item itself is used to both shape and anchor the forces you want, and it has to be able to resist the wear of those same forces. The longer you need your crafting to last, the harder the materials have to be, and the more expensive. Except some sorcerers are able to mitigate this, somehow."

"Which means you couldn't set yourself up as a sorcerer and start your own business crafting items unless you had a lot of ducats for the materials, right?"

"Exactly . . . plus the Sorcerers' Guild wouldn't allow it. Not that it would matter—you wouldn't be very good without access to the resources they have. The library, the knowledge from past experiments, the training and discipline they offer."

"What about fighting with sorcery? Shooting fire from your fingers, that sort of thing?" She held her hands up and pointed all her fingers in his direction.

Caldan laughed and shook his head. "They're all myths. No one can do destructive sorcery. People say it was possible before the Shattering, but I think the stories were made up. Tales from before the Shattering are just that, tales. Sorcery is only used to create useful lasting items and tools, like trinkets—although even they aren't able to be made anymore; the knowledge has been lost." His hand strayed to his neck, where his own trinket rested against his skin.

Miranda looked thoughtful. "It stands to reason, though, that if trinkets exist but the knowledge of creating them has been lost, then maybe that's what happened with the destructive sorcery. That it's possible, but the knowledge has been lost."

Caldan pursed his lips. "Maybe, but I don't see it that way. Trinkets have to be craftings we just don't understand anymore. Because we can still craft and trinkets exist, then we can assume they're related. But there's nothing comparable to destructive sorcery, so it makes no sense that it's been lost forever. It makes more sense that it never existed in the first place."

"But the skill of how to make trinkets has been lost. So why couldn't the same happen with destructive sorcery?"

"Well, yes, but . . . the chaos around the Shattering caused a great deal of expertise to be lost, but many sorcerers from that time did all they could to preserve their knowledge. If there was something as important as destructive sorcery, surely there would at least be mention of it, even if it was 'lost' so as not to surface again. There's no mention of it in any of the texts I've read, only in fanciful tales."

"Oh well, so no fairy-tale evil sorcerers?"

"I'm afraid not. We're all good guys." Caldan grinned at her, and she laughed.

"Well, do you have to be going soon or . . . ?" Miranda left the question hanging.

"Oh. Yes, I should get back. I'm sure someone would have been looking for me to give me more work, and it's probably past the apprentices' curfew. I wouldn't want anyone to think I've gone missing."

"That's all right. We can see some of the sights another day. Walking around doesn't cost any coins, so we can do it whenever you have some time free."

Miranda stood and led Caldan down an aisle between tables while fishing at her belt for coins. At the entrance, their waiter appeared, and she passed him a handful of ducats. Caldan couldn't see their color, but he was sure the place wasn't cheap. Both the decor and the food assured him of that.

Night had fallen, and a cool breeze gusted up the road, chilling Caldan through his shirt. Lanterns at each food stall and the glowing coals from their braziers lit the street, giving the place a warm, welcoming feel, despite the wind.

Miranda folded her arms across her chest for warmth and blew out a breath.

Caldan looked both ways down the street, surprised people were still out. The crowd and noise were a marked change from inside the restaurant. He offered Miranda his arm again.

"Can I walk you home?"

Miranda shook her head. "Don't worry, I can make my own way

from here." She smiled at him to make sure he understood nothing was wrong. "I know where you are now, so I'll come and see you again in a few days, after you are more properly settled in. And I should have a contact for you by then. I presume you are searching for someone who can assist in the Sorcerers' Guild?"

He nodded in agreement, and she continued.

"If you need to get word to me, come here to Camild's and leave a message. They'll make sure I get it."

Caldan shuffled his feet and looked out at the street. "Well, good night." He turned to Miranda and found her holding out her hand. He took it, and she shook his with a surprisingly strong grip.

"Good night, Caldan. I had a really nice time."

"Me too," he replied lamely, wondering what she meant.

She used his hand to pull him closer, grunting with the effort.

"You're a heavy bastard," she cursed. "Sorry, old habits and all that." She patted him on the cheek, taking care to avoid his wound. "Don't make me regret finding you. I'll see you soon, in a few days." She released her grip and stepped back.

"I won't. I'll repay you for the meal as soon as I can."

"That's not what I meant," she said, and the way she looked at him was distracting. She ran a hand through her dark hair. "I'll see you soon."

"Thank you for dinner. And for the company," added Caldan.

"You're welcome. Good-bye." She moved to walk away before stopping. "Oh, and one more thing. Don't keep shaving your head. Let your hair grow. I think it'll look good on you."

With a final farewell, she turned on her heel and strode into the crowd, heading south toward the river Sop.

Caldan stood and watched until he lost sight of her in the throng, then wove his own way through the crowd north toward the High-road. He had a long trek back to the dormitory, but it was a fine night for a walk to collect his thoughts.

The cold air helped cool his burning cheeks, too.

CHAPTER 18

Vasile woke, hands raised in defense, alone in bed among tousled sheets and with sweaty, rubbery limbs. His palms covered his face as he wept.

"I know, I know," he groaned. One hand moved to caress the empty space next to him, and for the briefest moment he thought he could smell her perfume. "Why couldn't you understand?" he whispered. He didn't expect an answer. None had come to him since his life had crumbled to dust.

He hadn't slept well since his encounter at the inn and the subsequent news of the death of Lord Voltain. A lesser man would count his blessings and move on, while a greater man would take action against his enemies.

It seems I'm neither.

Vasile savored the thought. A few months ago he would have drunk himself senseless and not cared a whit for the Five Oceans Mercantile Concern or the death of Sir Voltain. These days, his loss paralyzed him in more ways than one. Two years ago he would have had the truth out of anyone in his way, and the facts of the matter would be laid out for all to see. As he quoted at the magistrates' chamber every day, truth was paramount.

Truth can hurt, can be blind to consequences. Truth can cut. Truth can sever. He had always known that about truth. Too late, though, he had realized that those in power often didn't *want* the truth. They wanted a semblance of truth, as long as it fit their own machinations.

Truth when it is convenient.

But he couldn't stop. Couldn't stop picking at the truth. Everyone lied. The chancellors, merchants, his friends, his wife. *And I have to know. Couldn't they see?* Which is why he had to pick and pick. Truth was paramount, so he had believed.

And here he was.

He rubbed weary eyes and spat on the floor, scratching his five-day-old stubble. He was normal again. Just like that. Too bad the low had been so . . . degrading. He could have done without it.

His thoughts ran back to the previous weeks. What had changed him?

Sir Voltain's death, without a doubt. He hadn't liked Sir Voltain, but at least the nobleman hadn't lied. He had told the *truth*. Which led the magistrate to another truth: he found he had a distaste for being threatened. Broken, without much to live for, still Vasile discovered within himself a reluctance to be bullied. To be prodded like a cow.

He was tired. Tired of drinking, tired of prevaricating, tired of the lies all men told.

His thoughts turned to the last weeks and the incidents that had awoken him from what seemed a deep, oppressive dream. He reckoned his resources: not many ducats; enough that he could survive for a few days, though not enough to pay bribes, if required. Contacts; he had a few left still, even if they weren't as forthcoming as before his fall. He pursed his lips. And he had himself, his own abilities.

He snorted softly. His talent had destroyed everything he had ever valued. With a shake of his head, he moved his thoughts away from the hurtful feelings he was trying to avoid. He shuffled them to the back of his mind. They wouldn't help him here, far from it.

Perhaps this was how many of the criminals paraded before him felt. Cornered, bereft of options, a desperation lending their plans an edge of recklessness. Certainly, some of their schemes looked farcical when they were brought in front of him, even to the offenders themselves.

Consequences were a strange beast, sometimes obvious, sometimes hidden, more often than not different from those expected.

Vasile nodded to himself, realizing he had only himself now, and whatever sparse resources he could marshal. He fingered the few ducats he had in his pocket. His resources were meager. Another problem.

Now I can begin again. Problem is, he told himself, *I have no idea where to start.*

By the time he left his house he was shaved and dressed in his second-best set of clothes. Under one arm he carried his bedsheets wrapped around a pile of dirty laundry. He dropped the bundle at a local widow's, who had a small business washing for those too lazy or too busy to do it themselves.

A bit of both, I'll admit.

He made a brief visit to a bathhouse situated a few streets from his home and left refreshed, skin and hair feeling cleaner than they had in years, and teeth scrubbed with a piece of cloth dipped in salt. The attendant at the baths also recommended chewing spice balls periodically, and on his advice, Vasile purchased a bag.

A short time later, he walked up the steps into the magistrates' court, past throngs of petitioners waiting to be heard, then into his shared office, where his desk was piled high with paperwork. His assistant, Ozra, bolted upright from the chair in which he sat. To Vasile, it looked suspiciously like he had been asleep.

"S-Sir," Ozra stammered. "We thought you weren't coming in today, that you had been . . . taken ill with what has ailed you these past months."

Been a drunkard, you mean. Thank you for the diplomacy.

"Taken ill . . . yes, I believe I've thrown off that particular sickness," he said. "Indeed, in the end I am made of sterner stuff than most would believe."

"Sir . . . Very good, sir!" Ozra gestured to a pile of documents with one hand while stifling a yawn with the other. "There's much to get through today. May I draw your attention to the case of—"

"Not now," Vasile said. "I'm afraid some urgent business has come up, and I must take a leave of absence."

"A leave of absence, sir?" He looked Vasile up and down, taking in his clean and orderly appearance with a puzzled look.

Vasile nodded. "I'll write a missive to the chief magistrate telling her I'll be taking one." *And then take it—whether she agrees or not.*

He hastily penned a brief letter to his superior. Folding the missive in half, he handed it to his attendant, who took it tentatively. "Deliver this, will you, please?" he asked, sure the man would take some time—something he was counting on so the chief magistrate wouldn't have a chance to stop him.

Ozra nodded and looked at the letter. "If I may, sir . . ." He hesitated before continuing. "You did a good job here, much better than any I have seen during my time. I hope to see you back."

Maybe he had been too hard on him. Vasile placed a hand on Ozra's shoulder, then surprised him with a brief hug. Startled, Ozra almost dropped the letter.

With a tight smile, Vasile turned and walked out of the office. In the street outside, he stopped, looking left and right.

A rumbling stomach decided his next course of action for him. A meal would do wonders for his state of mind and give him time to think about his next step.

Soon he was sitting at the Copper Kettle, a close-by tavern he'd frequented often the last few months when he had a break from the proceedings of the magistrates' court. The tavern keeper, Angut, gave him a hearty welcome as Vasile entered.

"Good sir," Angut bellowed across the mostly empty room. "A great pleasure to see you again. Please have a seat. I'll bring you your usual."

Vasile stopped him as he turned for the bar. "No," he said firmly. "Not today. Some almond milk and the roast fowl, please. I'm a little delicate today."

Angut tapped a finger against his nose and gave a knowing smile.

"Of course. Haven't we all been there? Shan't be long." He bustled off through the door to the kitchen, and Vasile chose a seat well away from his usual spot near the bar.

A short time later his thoughts were interrupted by the tavern keeper depositing a large mug filled with a white liquid in front of him, and a plate of crispy brown chicken smelling of herbs.

Vasile set to with a will, devouring the flesh of the bird one piece after another, picking the bones clean with shining, greasy fingers. The almond milk he could have done without, except it was reputedly cleansing. He glanced to the wine barrels at the bar, then back to his plate. With deliberate care, he raised the mug to his lips and took a deep swallow.

Time to get his thoughts in order. Quiss and the Five Oceans Mercantile Concern would have to be his starting point. They were involved in something that either Quiss or his superiors considered important enough to kill for. The unfortunate William Voltain's accusation that he had come across information showing that the warehouse was being put to disreputable use probably had an element of truth to it. Their attempt to bribe Vasile to alter the outcome of the case in their favor supported this.

Vasile looked at his greasy fingers and pulled a creased handkerchief from a pocket to wipe them. The remaining dregs of his almond milk sat there.

Cursing, he swallowed them in one gulp and slammed the mug onto the table, wiping the back of his hand across his lips.

CHAPTER 19

As he stood shirtless and half-asleep in the predawn chill, pumping water for the apprentices, Caldan knew today marked a change for him.

Late last night, after he'd sneaked into the dark dormitory, one of the apprentices had whispered that Master Garren had been looking for him and had had a heated discussion with Master Simmon.

Caldan wasn't sure why they had argued, but reasoned it was probably because he couldn't be found. From what he had seen, Master Garren was busy and couldn't waste time looking for him.

An apprentice Caldan recognized as Owen—the sandy-haired, cheeky lad who had whispered to him last night of Master Garren—sidled up to him and washed his hands and face in the trough.

"You'd better see Master Simmon as soon as possible, I reckon," Owen blurted. "He didn't look pleased when Master Garren left."

"Thanks. I'll do that after breakfast. Do you think it'll be porridge again?"

Owen snorted in disgust. "Hope not. They usually wait until the weather gets colder before they start serving it every morning." He glanced up at Caldan, then quickly looked away.

Caldan sighed and kept pumping the handle. He didn't think they would forget yesterday's display in a hurry. Young people were impressionable, and he didn't want them looking up to him or following him around like Marlon's friends did.

After a hurried meal of porridge—*sorry, Owen*—Caldan made his way back to the dormitory. Master Simmon was wandering around the practice yard, running a critical eye over the area. Seeing Caldan, he beckoned him over.

"Master Garren came here last night, looking for you," Simmon began without preamble.

"I heard. Am I to collect my things and meet him somewhere today?"

Simmon shook his head. "No. There has been a change of plan."

"What! Am I not wanted now? What did he say?"

"Easy," he said, holding his hands up in front of him. "It's nothing like that. Walk with me to my study. I'll explain everything there."

A wave of relief fell over Caldan, and he followed the older journeyman to his study. Much like Garren's room, it had two windows overlooking the garden, and there were two armchairs and a desk, but in addition to these, three solid ironbound chests stood against one wall. On the desk sat a vase filled with wildflowers, looking out of place in Master Simmon's room.

The master smiled. "Strange to find wildflowers in my room?"

"Yes." He didn't know what else to say.

"My wife and daughter picked them for me. My wife doesn't like the thought of me spending time in a cold stone room without anything to brighten it up, despite the fact there's a whole garden outside. I promised I'd keep them on my desk." He caught Caldan's eye. "And as a Protector, I always keep to what I promise."

Caldan was about to reply when there was a sharp knock on the door.

Simmon gave it an irritated look. "Come in!" he barked.

The door opened to reveal a porcine, gray-haired man with the clothing and insignia of a master. Caldan hadn't seen him before.

"What is it, Alfrede? Can't you see I'm busy?"

Master Alfrede glanced at Caldan dismissively before addressing Simmon.

"One of my apprentices has disappeared. You need to find him."

Frowning, Simmon looked annoyed and troubled at the same time. "Are you sure you weren't . . . too hard on him?"

"What do these apprentices expect when they come here anyway? There's no coddling in the real world."

"I'll come and see you after this. I won't be long."

"He was last seen heading to buy supplies. If you can—"

"I'll see you after this," Simmon said flatly.

Alfrede's lips pressed together and his eyes narrowed. "Well, I wouldn't want to keep you." He turned in a huff and slammed the door behind him.

As the master left, Caldan noticed a vibration in the air radiating from the glyphs etched into the iron bands on the chests. None of the three boxes had a discernible lock.

"Can you feel the craftings?" asked Simmon, noticing his expression.

"Yes." The vibration from the chests made his skin itch, and Caldan scratched an arm.

"Not many can. That's another mark in your favor."

"Am I being tested?"

"Always." Simmon sat at his desk. "Sit, please."

"Master Simmon," said Caldan as he lowered himself into the chair. "Is Master Garren upset I was missing when he came for me?"

"No, not at all."

"Then . . . I was told he looked upset . . ."

"He was. But not for that reason." Simmon sat thoughtfully for a few moments. "Remember when we talked about the Protectors? How I told you that your perception of them was wrong?"

Caldan shifted in his chair. "Yes," he said cautiously, not really sure where this line of questioning was going.

"Tell me again what you think we do?"

"I thought you were a martial faction of the Sorcerers' Guild, those with crafting talent who were not so . . . bookish, I guess you could say. You focus on protection wards and can look after yourselves, not to mention safeguarding the security of the Sorcerers' Guild."

Master Simmon smoothed his short beard with his hand. His thin silver ring and bracelet trinkets tugged at Caldan's awareness.

"We do all that, and that's what the outside world sees of the Protectors. But it's not the whole picture."

Caldan eyed Simmon warily. He still didn't understand what Simmon was talking about, but clearly there was more than met the eye to this master Protector. Caldan knew he was an expert swordsman and sorcerer, and one confident enough to openly wear two trinkets. And he didn't think Simmon was a Protector because he was untalented in crafting—his initial assumption about most of the men in that group. If anything, Simmon was far from a novice, if the three chests were his work.

He said I'm always being tested. So what is this test?

Almost unconsciously, Caldan opened his senses and reached out to judge the strength of Simmon's well again. As before, the tear of his well felt like a wound, narrow and rough. But he sensed something else this time, as if the well were deliberately constricted.

Is he hiding the real strength of his talent? Why would anyone do that? Perhaps just as important: How?

Simmon looked thoughtful. "What did you sense?" he asked abruptly.

"Your well is narrow, constricted. Judging by that, I wouldn't have thought your ability in crafting was strong, but . . ." Caldan hesitated.

"Continue. What else?"

"It's as if your well has been disguised to appear smaller than it is. You are hiding your strength."

"Hmm . . . you can see that?"

"Yes."

"Very interesting." Simmon's gaze became piercing. "Bear with me while I tell you more of our history. I believe you will find it answers what I'm sure are the many questions you have. And when I am done, you'll see what happened with Master Garren to make him so upset. Okay?" He paused, as if expecting a response.

"Sure," Caldan said, not sure at all, but realizing he would never understand this otherwise.

Simmon held Caldan's gaze for a long moment, then slowly nodded, as if coming to a decision. "Good. What I am about to say can't leave this room. It's between you and me. Some things are too dangerous to be known. To be honest, no one would believe you if you ran off and spread tales around the city anyway, but I must have your oath you won't. Do I have it?"

"Yes. I swear."

"I thought you would—and I'm glad. I feel what I'm about to tell you could help you make a very important decision."

"What decision?"

"Ah, I get ahead of myself." Simmon looked down and rubbed his bracelet trinket. "Let me start with what I promised: a bit more about the Protectors. What you know and see of the Protectors is only part of our role, not the sum of what we do or even our main purpose. I can't tell you everything, but I can let you know a few pieces of our history.

"What do you know of the Shattering?" Simmon asked. He held up a hand to stop Caldan's reply. "No, wait. I won't ask any more questions. I'll explain. You know, through being taught and all you have read, that sorcery can only be used for helpful, constructive purposes, correct?"

"Yes. I'm sure most people with talent have tried to start fires or light a candle, but it doesn't work that way."

"Right. And when one of your craftings wears away, what happens? When the material it is made from can no longer withstand the forces flowing through it? It erodes, right? As if it was decaying or burning."

"Yes."

"You could say it is destroyed by virulent forces?"

"Yes . . . I guess you could say that."

Simmon leaned forward again, intently. "Constructive sorcery is what today's talented sorcerers study, and untalented ones, too. But contrary to what is commonly known, there are ways to harness crafting to unleash destructive forces."

Caldan's mouth opened in shock. He quickly closed it. "Then why have I never heard about this until now? How come I never see it?"

"Because it is dangerous, and we go to great lengths to see that it doesn't become common knowledge. Imagine every sorcerer, no matter who they were, able to hurl fire, to boil the blood of those facing them. Power to destroy also corrupts those who wield it. Destructive sorcery isn't easy, but for a sorcerer of talent, it isn't hard, either. The forces are there to be unleashed. You don't have to shape them as much, or craft objects to control them, because they are gone in moments. Constructive sorcery is actually harder. To control and shape the forces into a specific function takes much more skill." Simmon paused for breath. His voice had become more passionate with each sentence. "Remember, it's easier to destroy than it is to create. Such is always the way of nature—that no matter what is created, it always falls apart to nothing.

"The problem is, though, that that also applies to people. There will always be those without morals—the weak of will—who let their base desires override any resistance to what they know is the wrong action to take. And there are those who, by some design, are unable to see they are on the wrong path, who lack the empathy of normal people.

"And that's where we come in.

"The Protectors were formed after the Shattering to monitor and contain the use of destructive sorcery. It was felt—rightly, I believe—that some things are too dangerous to be known, and it's the Protectors' mission to make sure such knowledge is either removed or concealed. To ensure those without qualms—as well as those without the control—will not be able to use it for their own purpose, to the detriment of others."

Caldan's mind reeled. *Destructive sorcery. And the Protectors knew it existed!*

"Rumors of rogue sorcerers always surface," continued Simmon.

"Most of them are just that—rumors created by bored or drunk people for their own amusement. Some, however, are not rumors, and that's where we come in."

"Surely you don't hunt down sorcerers for making discoveries?"

Simmon's gaze hardened. "Not for 'making discoveries,' as you put it. For choosing a particular path, one that could destroy more than themselves."

"But—"

"I know it seems like we're stifling knowledge," Simmon said, cutting Caldan off, "but believe me, you aren't the first to make such objections. Imagine a world where all sorcerers could summon fire or cold, shatter stone or steel. Imagine the chaos! How do you decide who can be trusted to do the right thing, to use such power only for the good of society? And that's if it was out in the open! A few hidden people are worse. They almost always see it as a means to an end, a way of dominating others with violence. The Protectors will not allow that."

Caldan nodded, not trusting himself to speak yet. It made sense, if what Simmon said was true—and he had no reason to lie about something like this. But destructive sorcery? Hidden for thousands of years from everyone? It was a lot to swallow all at once. And what really threw him was this: Why tell him? He had only just arrived. He was a nobody—not even a member of the guild.

A sneaking suspicion dawned on him.

"Master Simmon, why are you telling me all this?"

"Quite simply, I want you to become an apprentice in the Protectors."

And there it is. Caldan had no words.

Simmon continued. "I can guarantee it will be far more rewarding than what Master Garren had planned for you."

And that's why he was so upset. Something didn't quite add up, though.

"But aren't I his? I mean, not as property, but he accepted me first."

"Ah," Simmon said, smiling rather smugly. "But I outrank Master Garren."

There was rank among the masters?

But that was the least of his concerns. *Me . . . a Protector?* The idea conflicted inside him, the uncertainty of being up to the task warring with the pride of being asked. Caldan remained silent, taking a few moments to gather his thoughts. Eventually he said, "Are you sure you want *me*, though? I've only just come here, and I didn't serve an apprenticeship . . ." Caldan trailed off.

"I know all that, Caldan. And yet I asked you anyway. Yes, we still need to work out what your strengths and weaknesses are, then we can decide what further training you need. But I've never been wrong at judging someone, and I know you have what is needed to be a Protector—your demonstration with the sword would have been enough to convince me even without your other potential."

Caldan blushed. "That was a stroke of luck. I've never been in a real sword fight or worn a sword outside practice sessions."

Simmon waved a hand dismissively. "Very few Protectors have been in a real sword fight. We like to keep everyone prepared, though. And you're already more prepared than most."

Caldan wasn't a fool, and he could sense Simmon wasn't telling the whole story. Which was to be expected. The master wasn't going to trust someone he barely knew with all of the secrets of the Protectors. No doubt the further Caldan progressed within the Protectors, the more knowledge he would be entrusted with.

"I'd still be able to study crafting?"

"Master Garren had arranged a minor role of assisting the masters for you, and possibly receiving some training, if your time permitted. At a wage of four coppers a week, I believe?"

Caldan nodded in agreement. "And you are offering something similar?"

"Not at all." Before Caldan could protest, Simmon continued. "You will *definitely* take lessons in crafting—it's one of the most important skills a Protector must know. As I said before, we need to determine what extra training you require, so that takes priority. I can assure you that for crafting, as well as numerous other subjects, training will be ongoing. And wages will be a silver ducat a week." Simmon's eyes bored into Caldan's. "I trust that will be sufficient?"

A *silver ducat!* Ten coppers a week. More than twice what Garren had offered him. Caldan recognized a sweetener to a deal when he saw one. *And I'll learn more under Simmon, too.*

Simmon stood and stepped around from behind his desk, his movements economical and smooth. "Do we have an agreement?" he asked, and held out his hand.

For the first time since he sat down, Caldan didn't hesitate. He clasped Simmon's hand in his own, feeling the strength in the master's grip.

Simmon smiled and clapped him on the shoulder. "Good. Master Garren was upset at losing you because of the crafting display you performed for him. He was impressed but didn't know what to make of it, which was why it took him so long to find a place for you."

"It was a paper box," protested Caldan weakly. "Nothing extraordinary."

"It's a rare thing to be able to craft with paper and for the object to last longer than an hour or two. A useful talent only a few masters have. His loss is the Protectors' gain."

I hope so, Caldan thought, a bit nervous again. "What now? Do I move from the dormitory to somewhere else?"

"Of course. You'll need to stay with us. The room will be small, mind you, nothing extravagant. You'll also need to set yourself up with some gear and equipment. The senior Protectors will provide you with a list of what's required."

Caldan's face fell. Where was he going to get the ducats to pay for what he needed? He couldn't ask Miranda for a loan, and she was the only person he knew in the city. He doubted a moneylender would loan him anything since he didn't have collateral. Even if they did, he'd have no way of paying back the extortionate interest they charged.

"You don't have any ducats, do you?" Simmon surmised at Caldan's crestfallen expression.

"No," said Caldan with a hint of shame. "I'm sure I can save some from my wages. Maybe find another way to earn some coins while I'm training."

"That won't do. You can't concentrate if you are worrying about not having the proper equipment and how to earn enough ducats to buy it." He opened a drawer in his desk and rummaged around, withdrawing a cloth purse much like the one stolen from Caldan only a few days ago. It felt like months ago, so much had changed since then.

"Here." Simmon tossed Caldan the coin purse, which he caught with a faint clink. "Pay me back as soon as you can. And I mean sooner rather than later. Don't let on I did this for you, either. Can't have people think I play favorites."

But you are, aren't you—playing favorites, that is. Why, though? Even as he thanked him, Caldan couldn't help but be suspicious of what Simmon was holding back. *I can't let this opportunity go to my head.*

"One more thing, Caldan. I know it seems like this is just a way to earn ducats, but think about what it means. For a lot of us it becomes far more than a job. Go now. See one of the senior Protectors. I spoke to a couple of them earlier, and by now word will have spread. They'll have a room made up for you and that list."

"You were that confident I'd agree?"

Simmon shrugged. "Pretty much. As I said, I'm a good judge of character." He waved a hand at Caldan. "Go on, you'll need the rest of the day to settle in and buy some gear."

Caldan gripped the purse in one hand and, with a nod to Master Simmon, exited the room with a spring in his step. He had found somewhere he could continue his training, and he wasn't destitute anymore.

In debt, sure, but not destitute.

CHAPTER 20

idan felt Anshul cel Rau grab his arm and tug him to a halt. They ducked into the nearby doorway of yet another deserted house. A musty odor wafted out, like all the other houses they had encountered so far in the town.

"Let's check one more," said the swordsman, and Aidan nodded.

Inside, the house appeared as all the others had, as if the occupants had left in the middle of whatever they had been doing. On a table sat four plates, four sets of eating utensils, four mugs. A platter in the center held the remains of a meal: a leg bone and some dried scraps of unidentifiable vegetables. All the surfaces were covered in a fine layer of dust.

Aidan motioned for them to leave, and they joined Caitlyn outside.

"Same again, my lady," whispered Aidan. "Not a soul around and dust covering everything."

She sniffed and wrinkled her nose. "Perhaps they didn't fight what came for them but joined it, like many would these days."

Aidan glanced at cel Rau. "Perhaps they didn't have a chance to resist."

Caitlyn shook her head. "Everyone has a chance, unless they are weak. Let's keep going."

They moved silently into the night, their group spread out along five streets, all traveling parallel to each other.

So far, they had not heard a sound from the other groups, which meant they should be making similar progress. Caitlyn and her men were getting closer to their quarry, who, if luck wasn't with them, would be surrounded before they had an inkling anything was amiss.

Ahead, a hiss from Chalayan brought them to a halt again. Caitlyn motioned Aidan and cel Rau to follow as she sidled up to the sorcerer.

"What is it?" she asked, pitching her voice low.

The sorcerer's face was beaded with sweat, and he trembled. "Something . . . ahead . . ."

"What?" whispered Caitlyn.

"Give me time," snapped Chalayan back at her.

Caitlyn glared at him.

"There's something . . . old here," said Chalayan.

"Old? What do you mean?"

"Sorcery. Years old. Yet traces of it still remain. Such power . . ." His voice trailed off.

Caitlyn touched Chalayan's shoulder. "Not recent, then? Good. Nothing for us to worry about."

"No! There's something else, more recent, ahead of us. A crafting. I think it crosses the street."

"A trap?"

The sorcerer shook his head. "Wait." He whispered a few words and squinted. One of his crafted amulets around his neck flashed briefly.

"It's . . . a trigger. An alarm."

"Ancestors' shadow!" cursed Caitlyn. "Across the street?"

Chalayan nodded then went back to staring ahead.

"All the streets are probably guarded the same way," Caitlyn said.

"I agree," said Aidan. "We need to stop the men going forward until we can find a way around or deactivate the crafting." He expected Caitlyn to disagree.

"We can't stop all of them without giving away our positions," said Caitlyn.

"They'll be given away anyway, if the alarms are tripped."

"We don't *know* there is more than one."

"It makes sense that—"

Caitlyn made a short chopping motion with one hand. "Enough. There isn't time. One of the other groups will trip an alarm soon. We have to move quickly."

What had gotten into her? She wasn't normally so rash. Aidan had no idea why she had changed so much, but he didn't like who she had become. "My lady, please, if we can—"

"No. We move now." She drew her sword and waved it above her head. "Forward, men!" she shouted. "For the emperor!" She rushed ahead, leaving Chalayan, Aidan, and cel Rau behind. Men surged around them, following Caitlyn toward the center of the town.

Chalayan gave Aidan a grim smile. "Once more, my friends. Let's hope she pulls this one off as well."

"One day her luck will run out," said cel Rau.

Aidan clapped both on the back. "Let's hope it isn't tonight."

They sprinted down the street in Caitlyn's wake.

FLASHES OF LIGHT flickered across the town. The sun peeked over the hills to the east.

Aidan dragged the unconscious form of Chalayan through the doorway of a deserted house and collapsed on the floor. Two of the sorcerer's amulets had melted into the skin around his neck, but the shield he'd generated to cover them had sufficed. He had lost consciousness soon after.

Aidan drew a waterskin from his belt and gulped a few mouthfuls. Dirt covered his face along with his clothes. Spots of blood dotted him from head to toe—the blood of his own men as they had been blown into small pieces with sorcery.

He coughed, then dragged himself to the open doorway. The street was empty. In the distance, screams sounded. More than half their men were down, from what he had been able to determine, with a grand total of three sorcerers on the other side killed.

Twenty men dead. One sorcerer left. A high price.

He needed to rest.

Aidan arranged Chalayan as comfortably as he could.

"I'll have to leave you here for a while," he said to his unconscious friend. The sorcerer didn't stir. "I'll be back soon," he promised.

They had met the same sorceries that destroyed the bandits, but Chalayan's own had saved many of them. Mundane resistance had consisted of mainly untrained men and women, easily dispatched by Caitlyn's experienced men, and professional mercenaries who had surrendered once a few sorcerers and most of their comrades were killed or subdued.

Aidan lifted the crossbow he'd taken from a dead man. Ranged weapons usually proved effective against sorcerers, as long as they weren't given a chance to shield themselves, but against these ones they hadn't done much. Somehow, they had shields up all the time. Still, it was better than trying to get close enough to swing his sword. All the men who had tried that were dead.

Leaving Chalayan there for the time being, he crouched low and exited the building, moving forward in a scuttle.

Aidan approached the barn as quickly as he could, which wasn't fast, wincing with every step on his bruised leg. A short time ago, Caitlyn and cel Rau had fought their way to the large barn in the center of the town. What resistance they encountered had seemed intent on falling back to that position and protecting it.

He limped up to Caitlyn, who knelt on the ground, sword resting on her thighs. Anshul cel Rau stood before her, both his swords stained red. Caitlyn and the swordsman were covered in dirt and spots of blood like Aidan was, though only on one side, as if they'd been shielded from the blast. Bodies lay around them, some blackened and steaming and others in pools of blood dripping from open wounds. A few gave distraught moans. One moved a hand.

"We have to kill him; he's the only one left," Aidan heard Caitlyn say as he approached. "With Chalayan unconscious, someone needs to make a bold move, take him down before he realizes what's happening."

Cel Rau nodded grimly, knuckles white as he gripped the hilts of his swords.

"What's the situation?" asked Aidan.

Caitlyn rubbed her eyes and wiped her hands on her arms. She succeeded only in smearing the blood and dirt on her sleeves.

"The last sorcerer is on the run, retreating south along the road. Our men on that side . . ." She shook her head. "We couldn't have known there were more than the two we were following."

"If we'd waited longer—"

"We didn't have time!" screamed Caitlyn. "More could have come, and we would be in a worse position." Spittle flew from her mouth.

Aidan squeezed his eyes shut for a moment and clenched his teeth. Caitlyn wasn't acting rationally, and he was sure she wouldn't have made the same decision months ago. She looked lost, as if her increasing obsession with evil had finally unhinged her.

"We should have waited," Aidan repeated.

"We struck while we had the advantage of surprise, and that's the last I will hear of it."

She turned to cel Rau. "Go. You know what to do. Kill the sorcerer. He should be weakened by now."

"Should be?" Aidan protested. "I think we should consolidate here, look to our wounded, and regroup."

Caitlyn stood, ignoring him. "Go, cel Rau. Evil cannot be allowed to escape."

The swordsman nodded reluctantly, then loped off down the nearest street, heading south to where smoke filled the sky.

"What about the wounded here? We should see to them."

"No. They failed. Leave them. We don't have time. We need to see what's in the barn, what they value so highly." She beckoned Aidan to follow and limped toward the barn door. Blood dripped behind her from a gash in her thigh.

Aidan paused to look around at the dead and wounded littering the ground. With a shake of his head, he limped after Lady Caitlyn.

Caitlyn struggled with one of the massive doors that confronted them. Aidan helped her, and together they managed to open a gap wide enough to slip through.

As he followed Caitlyn inside, Aidan sniffed at the strange smell—spices overlaid with an herbal tartness, combined with a festering rotting scent and piss and excrement. And porridge. He swore he could smell porridge. He blinked, eyes adjusting to the lack of light.

Lined up along the room were heavy wooden cots, four rows of twenty. On most of the cots lay women, hands and ankles tied with strips of leather, skin raw and bleeding where the straps met flesh. All the women were pregnant, some close to term. In one corner of the gruesome room stood a cooking fire, on which sat a huge steaming iron pot.

Closest to them lay a pale-skinned woman; black hair hung limply over the side of her cot, and her belly was swollen with child. Her eyes opened, and she looked at them.

"Please," she whispered. "Water."

"Aidan, get some water," commanded Caitlyn. "We need to hear what she has to say."

At the sound of her voice, heads turned to stare at them. Some of the women began crying. A few begged for release; some made no sound.

Aidan grabbed his half-full waterskin and knelt beside the woman.

"Shhh. There, there, it's all right. You're safe now." He splashed water into her mouth. "We need to cut her bindings."

"We'll do no such thing until we confirm she isn't working with them."

Aidan was shaking his head before she'd finished. Where had her mercy gone? Was this a symptom of what ailed her? "See what condition they are in? How could they be helping?"

Caitlyn glared at him. "Be it on your head."

With four quick cuts of his knife, he freed the woman from the leather straps. The muscles in her arms and legs were withered and slack. Her body trembled, and she shook her head. "Please . . . they will . . . come . . . back . . ." She reached over and grabbed Aidan's hand with surprising strength. "You must kill us all."

"Good idea," said Caitlyn.

Aidan clenched his teeth. "No, don't worry. We're here now. You can rest easy."

"You don't . . . understand." The woman's eyes closed. "We've been . . . here years."

"Shh. You're safe now. We'll help you all. The sorce—"

"No! They'll come back. You cannot stay."

Aidan smoothed her hair. Strands came out in his hand. "What happened here? What happened to you?"

The woman let out a low keening moan. "Years we have been here. Tied up . . ." She swallowed. "The sorcerers, they . . . make us have babies. I . . . don't want to live like this." Tears rolled down her face. "Please."

Aidan cleared his throat. "Do you know why they do this?" he asked.

She shook her head. "They only say . . . they need them." She sank down to the cot, exhausted, still clutching his hand.

Aidan pried the woman's fingers off as gently as he could. "Rest," he said.

He bent to retrieve his crossbow and walked over to the cooking fire to remove himself from the sight of the woman. Caitlyn stared at her before coming to join him. In the pot on the fire bubbled porridge.

"I've seen this before," he said grimly.

"Seen what?"

He gestured toward the women on the cots. "This . . . wasting. An old man in my village couldn't walk or move much. Too old, I guess. He lived on gruel and whatever the women brought him. Months went by, and eventually he wasted away to skin and bones. He didn't use his muscles, so they deteriorated."

Caitlyn's mouth drew into a thin line, and she hugged her chest. "That's what she meant," she said flatly. "Never to leave their cots, to walk around. To lie there eating this shit and have babies."

"By the ancestors, I could kill someone." Aidan wiped at his watering eyes. "We need to free them all, get some wagons to take them away from here, someplace safe."

"And where is safe? These men, whatever they are, have to be stopped." Caitlyn drew in a deep breath, then another.

With a sudden movement, the woman turned to face them, her emaciated neck struggling to keep her head steady, and she grimaced in pain. "Run!" she croaked. "Get away from here. They'll be coming."

Three thunderous claps reached their ears, each closer than the one before. Outside, shouting erupted, and men screamed.

Aidan ran toward the open door. "Let's go!" he roared.

Chaos had broken out. Plumes of smoke billowed from the south, where the men had been in pursuit of the last sorcerer. Now, they rushed back toward the barn with fearful looks on their faces, clutching wounds of blackened skin. Seeing Caitlyn and Aidan, they staggered toward them.

"M'lady," one said. His face had a large burn down one side, and he squinted in agony. "More sorcerers. The men are trying to hold them, but I fear they won't last long."

Aidan exchanged a look with Caitlyn. The pregnant woman had been right.

"Right, here's the plan," Caitlyn said. "Aidan, you gather up all the men you can, help the wounded who can walk, and meet back here as soon as you can."

He nodded.

"You three," she continued, "we passed a house over there stocked with supplies. Come with me, and we will grab what we can. I have an idea the sorcerers won't like. Go now, quickly."

Aidan loped off as fast as he could, while the men followed Caitlyn. He wasn't sure what she had planned, but he hoped it was good. Their situation looked dire.

He kept to the sides of the streets and peeked around each corner before he turned it or crossed an intersection. He hurried to the smoke plumes as quickly as he could. Whenever he passed one of the men, wounded and retreating, he gave him instructions to head for the barn and help Caitlyn.

Thunder rang out, hurting his ears. A fresh cloud of smoke rose ahead of him. The roar of crackling flames sounded in the distance.

He ducked down at the corner of a house. Charred black bodies were everywhere. He swallowed, breathing harshly. None of them moved.

A makeshift barricade had been erected using a cart and crates. Now the cart lay in burning pieces, wood from the crates scattered around. Through the smoke and fire walked three figures, all surrounded by a shimmering haze. One he recognized as the last sorcerer they'd been pursuing. The other two were new, a man and a woman. She said something and laughed; the others joined in.

Aidan ducked back behind the corner, with his hands clenched down on the crossbow. Three sorcerers, when they thought only one was left. Straining, he managed to draw back the string and cock the mechanism. He loaded a bolt. Maybe he could take one out before . . . No, they were shielded. He cursed under his breath.

Making his decision, he turned and limped back toward the barn. With any luck, the sorcerers would be wary and take their time searching the streets for any signs of ambush. It might be a while before they made it to the barn. There was a good chance the women could still be rescued.

His leg gave a spasm of pain, like a knife jabbing into the muscle. Gritting his teeth, he kept going, leaving the sorcerers behind.

Caitlyn's men were in chaos around the barn. Two wagons stood near it, while men ran in all directions, loading one wagon with supplies and the other with some of the pregnant women. All were wounded in some way or another, all with makeshift bandages over legs, arms, chests, faces. One man's face was covered in blisters, his left eye white like a boiled egg.

Caitlyn directed two men carrying a barrel. Three more barrels lay on their sides against the barn walls, their contents spilling onto the ground. It ran thick and viscous and yellow—oil. They dropped the barrel next to the door and headed back to the wagons. Caitlyn disappeared inside the barn.

Aidan looked over at the men. They started hitching the wagons to four skittish horses. A few others with injuries had dragged themselves into the wagons. He limped over to Rikard, who stood by the closest wagon checking the axle.

"What's happening here? What are you doing with the oil?"

Rikard hawked and spat on the ground, shaking his head. "No time to save them all. We gotta do something so the sorcerers don't get them. Might be easier on them this way. Lady's orders."

Aidan turned to the barn in horror. Oil puddled against the walls, along the whole side of the building.

"By the ancestors!" he cursed. *She sent me away so she could organize this without my interference. She doesn't trust me anymore.*

Caitlyn appeared through the open doors carrying a flaming torch. She took a few steps toward him, then stopped, seeing the look on his face.

"I'm sorry, Aidan," she said. "There isn't any other way. We can't take them all with us."

He took a hesitant step toward her. "Don't do this," he pleaded. "We can come back, enlist more men, and—"

"No time," she interrupted. "They won't stay here. They'll move somewhere else, and we will never find them again."

"Caitlyn . . . My lady, please, we can't do this. We need to draw the line somewhere."

Caitlyn's expression turned dark. "We must do what we can to stop evil where we find it." She backed a step toward the barn.

He had to do something to prevent this horror. Aidan sank to his knees. "But where do *we* stop?" he shouted. "They deserve to live. We have to try and rescue them!"

"Sometimes we have to make hard decisions."

"This isn't a hard decision!"

Caitlyn shook her head. "Oh, Aidan, you are blind. If we leave these women, they'll continue to give the sorcerers whatever they want, whatever they're getting from them. We can't take all of them with us, so we must destroy the ones remaining. Who knows what evil is inside them?" She took another step toward the barn.

Aidan raised his crossbow, pointing it at her chest. He knew one thing: she had to be stopped. His voice came out as a dry croak. "Please, don't make me do this."

Caitlyn looked at the crossbow and hesitated, then gave a low laugh. "You won't do it. I know you too well. You'll come to realize this is the right thing to do."

"It isn't right," he said through gritted teeth. "It can't be right."

"Always the weak one." She backed toward the barn.

Aidan pressed the crossbow trigger.

The bolt punched through Caitlyn's mail shirt and slammed into her chest with a thud. A look of surprise appeared on her face. She sank to her knees, and the torch dropped to the ground in a shower of sparks, thankfully missing the oil. She looked at Aidan. One hand came up to touch the bolt. Blood seeped between her fingers.

"I'm sorry," he whispered to her. "I couldn't let you do it." Tears ran down his face. The crossbow slipped from limp fingers.

Caitlyn fell forward, then rolled to one side, hands clutching at the ground.

Two men rushed past him and slid to a stop over Caitlyn, checking for signs of life. One shook his head.

The world moved as if through water, slowly, sounds muted. Aidan felt a vibration through the ground. All heads turned to look in one direction—south.

Some men approached Aidan at a run. They took his arms and dragged him along the ground toward the wagons.

He was thrown onto the bed of a wagon. It jerked, then moved forward, gathering speed.

Caitlyn lay outside the barn, leaking onto the dry dirt, burning torch by her side.

The barn stood untouched.

CHAPTER 21

Caldan trudged down the corridor toward his room. He passed a senior apprentice about his own age, who didn't acknowledge his nod. Some of them had been ignoring him since he arrived a week ago. It seemed unless you slogged through the lessons and trials of the apprentices, they didn't look at you as an equal.

At the moment, he couldn't care less. He was too tired and dirty to concern himself with making friends right now. His clothes and skin felt dry and scratchy after a day spent helping in the furnaces, where young sorcery apprentices practiced casting metals into crafting items. His lips tasted of salt from his own sweat.

Ducking into his room, he rummaged through his clothes and darted off to the washing area to clean up before the evening meal. With a few ducats, he had purchased some pants and shirts, ones that fit better than his old clothes. As well as the clothing, he bought a number of items needed to participate in the lessons and practice sessions he had been assigned: carving tools for both wood and wax, and a bundle of candles for reading in his room at night. All the purchases left a sizable dent in his purse, which didn't contain his own coins to start with.

Caldan headed for the evening meal. As usual, he sat alone, the senior apprentices pointedly ignoring him as they came in and talked in groups. He wolfed down his meal of a thick mutton stew with bread and hot cider, and then left.

No windows opened into the library because the sunlight damaged the books, so all apprentices used the sorcerous globes left on a table inside the door for light to see by. Shelves of books stretched away into the darkness. The air inside felt dry and smelled of parchment, leather, and decay. There were desks around the room, at each of which sat two apprentices with their own globes, reading from books.

Surprisingly, the library here was much smaller than he'd imagined. With more sorcerers and apprentices in residence than he'd ever thought possible in one place, he had hoped the library would be enormous and overflowing with books on all subjects, but it wasn't the case. Far from being a repository of knowledge on a multitude of subject matters, the library contained books that mostly dealt with crafting, with sections set aside for Dominion, politics, and history. It was a disappointment. The library at the monastery was at least ten times the size and covered a much larger range of subjects. Any idea he'd had of trying to research his trinket for information on where it and his family had come from had evaporated when he'd entered the library for the first time a few days before.

He felt sure there must be another library. One that held other texts only the master sorcerers and Protectors had access to. The more valuable knowledge wasn't going to be left around for any apprentice to read so he could try his hand at something that could very well kill him.

One startling problem was a lack of any definitive text on trinkets. There were a few that dealt in generalities; sometimes they were mere collections of rumors. On a few occasions, Caldan had read outright falsehoods, from what he understood of crafting, in these books.

He doubted there was much to be learned in this library, at least for him. Still, he wanted to be sure, so he spent some time poring over titles and flicking through the tomes.

After an hour, he gave up. He'd been here three times in as many days, and like during his previous visits, he felt he had wasted his time. He replaced the books he had been looking at—*Principles of the Craft* and the poorly researched *Secrets of Trinkets*, with a sigh.

Useless. All these books held nothing for him.

Rubbing sore eyes, he abandoned the library for his room. The hard schedule the Protectors had him following the last few days left him tired and irritable, though his muscles weren't as sore as he expected.

Small miracles, he supposed.

He gathered up his cloak—yet another recent purchase—and slipped through the dark corridors on his way to the Yawning Rabbit Inn.

The Yawning Rabbit lay close to the keep and many of the guilds. Its doors faced out onto the cobbled courtyard where Caldan had first seen the public offices of the Sorcerers' Guild. Due to its close proximity and fine food and drinks, it was a favored haunt of the apprentices from rich families and masters from many of the guilds.

Listening to some of the apprentices, he had heard of a healthy Dominion competition running there, where anyone could play as long as they had a willing opponent—and coins they were willing to wager. Caldan was going to try his hand and see if he could win enough ducats to repay Master Simmon.

He also owed Miranda a dinner, a debt he was even more eager to be free of . . . although for very different reasons.

As he approached, the doorman eyed him for a few moments, then gave him a nod. He stood a foot over Caldan's height, and his arms looked as if they could crush rocks. Caldan exhaled in relief.

He entered the establishment and walked over to a long bar that took up most of one wall. Arched doorways opened onto a central courtyard, in which stood a large pond. Bronze turtles poured water from their mouths, while Caldan caught glimpses of fish between lilies on the surface. Several staircases led up to a second floor. Oil lamps and two blazing fireplaces lit the room. He could smell ale and smoke, along with aromas wafting from dishes waiters carried as they rushed past. At this time, the crowd was thin, but owing to the size of the building there was still a surprising number of people here. Caldan picked out masters from different guilds, including two who looked to be sorcerers; a number of nobles; and a few merchants and traders. Tables seating four were situated randomly around the room. He noted a number of card games were in progress at these.

Stepping up to the bar, Caldan caught the eye of a serving girl in a white apron and ordered a cider—his second of the night, but he expected to make this one last since he would need his wits about him. She returned promptly with a tankard, and he slid a copper ducat across the bar. She frowned, then indicated another coin was needed. He dutifully slid a second coin alongside the first. *I'm definitely going to have to make this cider last a long time.* He took a sip and leaned back on the bar to take in the atmosphere.

Time passed, and the level in Caldan's tankard dropped to half, even with his cautious sipping. Serving men and women came in and out of a swinging door, laden with trays crowded with mouthwateringly fine-smelling dishes: lamb chops in a red wine sauce, roast pork with crackling skin, heavily spiced stews eaten with loaves of fresh-baked bread. The aromas were so inviting, he marked the place as an option to take Miranda to repay her for the meal they had shared. Not as select as her choice, but if he ever had enough coins, this was a definite possibility.

A loud bark of laughter broke his reverie. The crowd was swelling as the evening progressed.

Caldan judged the time to be about right. He headed across the room and up a set of stairs leading to the second floor. This level also consisted of archways opening onto the space in the center, though balconies jutted over the courtyard. Dominion boards of varying quality took up half the floor space.

Caldan made a circuit of the entire second floor, taking note of the players engaged in Dominion, as well as the onlookers. Smoke drifted into the night air from spiced tobacco pipes. One man held a twig bushy with green leaves he occasionally picked off and stuffed into his mouth to chew. Nobles and sons of nobles, merchants, and scholars all brushed shoulders as they passed one another.

On one wall was a chalkboard with the names of different people and numbers. A polite inquiry and he was told it was the odds board for wagering on who would win the upcoming Dominion competition at the Autumn Festival. At a table under the board sat a sweating, rotund man surrounded by pieces of paper, ink, a pen, and a dark-colored candle. *That must be the bookmaker.* Caldan watched open-mouthed as a man approached the bookmaker and placed a stack of gold ducats on the table. In return, the bookmaker scribbled on a piece of parchment and finished it off by affixing his seal to the chit with the purple wax. The seal was attached to his belt by a sturdy chain.

Laughter and shouts punctuated the steady din of conversation. One man, a wealthy noble by the look of him, stood and cursed loudly at a number of moves made by his opponent, a pretty woman with red hair. His face was red, and he clenched his fists for a few moments, then two hefty bouncers appeared behind him. He fished a purse from his waist, threw it onto the Dominion board, and pushed his way through the crowd gathered around his table.

"It's the same every night for him," a quiet voice said by Caldan's side.

He turned and took in the speaker, a slim, thin man with a graying goatee. One hand rested on his belt, while the other held a glass of clear liquid with a cherry at the bottom. His shirt was an expensive weave with silver buttons.

A man of some means.

The man gave a stiff bow from the waist. "Some people don't know their limitations, eh? Allow me to introduce myself. Izak Fourie, at your service. You're new here, no?"

"I am," he replied warily. "I'm Caldan. Do you come here to watch, or do you play matches as well?"

Izak Fourie waved his drink in the direction of the closest game. "A little of both, though mostly I wager on matches. I'm afraid I don't have the talent of some of the regular players, and most know it." He shrugged. "But we all have to make do with what we have, am I correct?"

"Yes," agreed Caldan, as he thought this was expected from him. "So . . . how do you bet on the matches? Is there someone else that takes bets, like that gentleman over there?" He pointed to the man under the chalkboard.

Izak frowned for a moment, then smirked. "'Gentleman?' I guess you might call him that. You can bet with him, if you have enough coin. More often wagers are made between two people and witnessed by the house. You see the attendants?"

Having them pointed out now, Caldan was surprised he'd missed men standing at each table, dressed in the same livery as the waiters downstairs, only of a finer cut.

"I'm guessing that since the house witnesses wagers, it takes a cut?"

"Exactly." Izak smiled. "Ten percent of the winnings. You didn't think this place existed solely because of the owners' love of the game, did you?" He laughed softly.

"No, but I'm always open to being pleasantly surprised."

Izak laughed again. He sipped his drink. "By my beard, this stuff is good!" The tip of his tongue came out and licked his lips. "I take it you are new to our fine city as well?"

Izak was a strange man, but seemed friendly enough.

Which is why there's no way I'll be trusting him anytime soon.

"Somewhat new," replied Caldan cautiously. "I have a role with the Sorcerers' Guild." He wasn't sure why this man had taken an interest in him, but he doubted it was solely to be courteous.

"Really? A role?" Izak drawled. "How interesting." He coughed onto the back of his hand, then nodded to a game starting a few tables away. "Come, shall we observe this match and provide commentary?"

"Why not?" Caldan said, and they found a position standing behind one of the players.

As play started, Izak nudged Caldan with his elbow and leaned in close. "I happen to know both players. Both are regulars here and at a number of other establishments. They are quite skillful."

Caldan studied the board as each player handed a scrap of parchment to the attendant, on which they had written their first seven moves so these couldn't be changed. As with any battle, the first moves were planned in advance without knowledge of your enemy's strategy. Only after that could each player adjust their own tactics to account for their opponent's.

From the opening moves the man in front of them fell behind in the scoring, and as the match progressed, his position became more and more untenable, and he fell further behind.

By this stage a number of other observers had joined them, and after a short whispered conversation between two of them, one shouted, "Two silvers on Lord Schalk, at two to one."

The bet lingered in the smoky air until a woman opposite them piped up. "Done. Witnessed?" All turned to the attendant, who nodded at both the woman and the man who had announced the original wager.

Caldan frowned. "Doesn't that distract the players?"

"Part of the game, my friend. Playing under added pressure. Of course, when the betting gets frantic toward the end of some of the better matches, the players can be put off." He shrugged. "That's just the way it is."

This was all new to Caldan, so he withheld further comment. Friendly banter between players and people looking on he was used to, but knowing people were betting on you—and how much—would be unnerving.

Play continued, and Lord Schalk—the man they stood behind—did slightly better, winning back a few points. Still, he would go into the third phase behind by a fair margin, and it would take a canny player to claw his way ahead.

Izak leaned close to Caldan. "I know it looks bad right now, but Schalk here is a fine player, and although he's behind, it is knowledge of the board that separates out the great players."

"I agree. We'll see what happens next."

For Lord Schalk, the third phase went well at first, considering the disadvantage he started with. His opponent played cautiously—too cautiously, in Caldan's opinion—and allowed Schalk some leeway to consolidate his positions. Then, as if realizing his mistake, he made a series of moves that pushed at Schalk's pieces, feigning an attack on multiple fronts, which drew a response, then broke through at a weakness created. Schalk scrambled to defend.

"Ah . . . I think Lord Schalk's game has been lost," said Izak softly to Caldan.

By now the crowd around the board had swelled considerably. A number of people made wagers, shouting over the heads of the players and confirming with the attendant.

But to Caldan, the board didn't look right. Something niggled at the back of his mind—a few of Schalk's pieces left behind, seemingly neglected when his others were forced backward to defend. After a few moments, Caldan nodded to himself. He recognized the scrambling defense and subsequent attack coming. It was detailed in *Morals of Dominion*, in a chapter on whether someone at such a disadvantage in the game was entitled to a victory, and how victory could be achieved.

"Five silver ducats for Powell to win against Lord Schalk," announced Izak loudly from Caldan's side, holding up a hand.

Caldan hissed between his teeth and grimaced.

"What?" said Izak. "I know Schalk, and he can't come back from this. It's a safe bet."

Caldan pulled Izak's arm down. "No, it's not," he said hastily. "Don't bet against him. Either he's a better player than you think, or he's been studying."

Izak eyed the board and pieces dubiously, then stroked his goatee. "You think Schalk will win? Why do you say that?"

"It depends on what he knows, but I've read about this strategy before."

"You read about it? Are you sure?" asked Izak with a penetrating stare.

"I am. Here." He reached into his purse, drew out a silver ducat of his own, and passed it to Izak. "Wager this for me, on Schalk to win."

Izak frowned, then nodded. He cleared his throat and raised his arm.

"Ten silver ducats on Lord Schalk to win!" he boomed, adding nine of his own to Caldan's one. A few laughs greeted his announcement.

Lord Schalk paused to look behind him at Izak, then returned to the game.

"Keep your coins, Izak. We know you lost big the other night, and chasing down losses will only make things worse!" shouted a young nobleman.

Izak smiled and laughed. "Too scared, eh?" he returned. "How about twenty silvers? Is that enough to interest anyone?"

Caldan winced. Twenty silver ducats was a large sum, and Izak, whom he had only just met, was trusting Caldan's instincts against what looked like a certain loss.

I'm not sure what Izak will do to me should Schalk not win the game, but I doubt he'll take too kindly to losing a considerable amount of silver.

"I'll take that wager!" replied the young noble. "Witness, please!"

The attendant nodded at both men, mentally recording the wager. Izak raised his glass in a silent toast to the young noble, who grinned back. Heated conversations rose from around the table in the wake of the wager.

And now it was too late, and all Caldan could do was watch the fate of the game . . . and his newfound "friend."

Suddenly, the air in the room felt thick and stifling. Caldan was sure he was right, but if he wasn't, he would lose a silver he could ill afford to, and probably make an enemy. He swallowed and the sides of his throat stuck together. He gulped the dregs of his cider, barely tasting the liquid.

"You'd better be right," Izak said over the din.

Tell me something I don't know.

Caldan caught sight of Powell frowning at them.

Schalk motioned to the attendant and announced he would use all five of his extra moves at once. Earlier, his opponent had used three of his own.

Positions of his pieces were reversed, and some changed tiers on the board. Schalk used his moves to disrupt Powell's forces and consolidate his own positions.

Caldan held his breath. This was the crucial point in Schalk's borrowed strategy. The aim was to cause your opponent to panic and make rash decisions, leading to dubious moves. If he did, you had a chance. If he didn't, then he still had the advantage after recovering and uniting his forces.

But those are definitely the moves I would have made, he thought, analyzing Schalk's new positions. *Now it's up to Powell to fall into the trap . . . or for me to plan my escape.*

Powell leaned forward in his seat, gaze shifting from the board to Schalk and back again. Caldan saw the moment panic set in. Powell licked his lips and motioned to use his last two extra moves. His forces were currently too scattered to take advantage; they would be wasted. He drew some of his pieces in to consolidate against an attack.

*And that *was *the critical mistake.*

From their vantage point, Caldan saw Schalk's shoulders relax in relief, and that sight almost caused the same reaction in him. From there, the game progressed steadily in Schalk's favor. His forces mopped up the territory left vacant and gained in power. With a few hard-fought skirmishes here and there, he captured or turned Powell's isolated pieces.

The game was won in short order.

Powell yielded when it was obvious to all he had lost. Schalk had come back from a seemingly impossible situation to victory.

Schalk's friends and acquaintances crowded around him, congratulating him on a fine game. Powell stood and stared at the board, then with a short bow to Schalk left the table for the bar.

With barely concealed ill grace, the young nobleman who had taken Izak's wager passed him a handful of silver coins, and a further two to the attendant. Izak thanked him profusely—much more than was polite, rubbing the loss in.

"Heh! That'll shut him up for a while," Izak said to Caldan with a pleased grin on his face. He threw back his drink and chewed on the cherry, spitting the stone into the glass. "An interesting start to the night, my new friend." He handed Caldan three silver ducats, thought for a moment, then handed him another. "With my thanks," he said, brushing off Caldan's protest. "After all, without meeting you, I would be down a few silvers rather than up so many. A fortuitous and prosperous meeting for us both."

"Thank you. Still, I wasn't sure Lord Schalk had that plan in mind."

"Well, he did, and we both took advantage of your insight. Come." He clapped Caldan on the shoulder. "Let's refresh our drinks and watch another game."

They pushed through the crowd to the bar, and Izak hailed a waitress. "Another for myself—and get my new friend here whatever he likes as well."

Caldan hesitated. He needed a clear head, but after the stress of that last game, he also needed a drink.

"What's wrong?" asked Izak.

"I'll probably be playing later, once I get a feel for the place, so something weak, if they have it." He eyed the bottles dubiously.

"A glass of the pear cider, then." Izak motioned to the waitress. "It doesn't have much of a kick, and you can drink it all night. Fruit, you see. It's good for you." He winked at Caldan.

Two glasses plonked onto the bar, and Izak handed the waitress some copper ducats with a broad grin, which she returned.

"I should find out more about her," Izak murmured softly, sipping at his drink.

Caldan thought he'd misheard him. "Pardon?" he said, leaning closer to hear him over the din.

"Nothing. I'm feeling the effects of my drinks already. Pardon me."

Caldan nodded. "Certainly." He craned his neck to see around the figures of a couple who blocked their view of a game in progress. It was a contest between two competent amateurs with a lot of suggestions from the surrounding crowd, something he hadn't seen happening in the harder games.

He sipped his pear cider, finding it pleasantly tart and not at all strong. "I'm going to walk around, see if there are any interesting games going on."

"Good idea," replied Izak, glancing in the direction of the waitress who had served them drinks. "I'll join you." He drew out a perfumed handkerchief and wiped his face.

Caldan had to excuse himself a few times as he negotiated his way through groups of people chatting and drinking around Dominion boards, Izak in tow. He disregarded three disorganized games before his eyes alighted on a board set up to begin a game, with a slender, severe-looking lady sitting in one of the playing chairs.

She was dressed in plain dark pants and a shirt closed with mother-of-pearl buttons, hair tied in an intricate tight braid. She lounged back on her chair, fingering an earring with one hand while holding a glass of wine in the other, pointedly ignoring a number of men standing around as if they expected a game to start at any time, despite the lack of an opponent.

She gazed at the board with an uninterested expression, wrinkled her nose, then sipped her wine, grimacing at the taste.

"I wouldn't bother with her," commented Izak. "She hasn't lost a game for quite some time. The Lady Felicienne is quite adept at Dominion, as you would expect from someone in her position."

"And what position would that be?"

Izak stroked his goatee. "Her official title is Third Adjudicator, which in itself is fairly innocuous, a title that shows her place in the hierarchy. Her role, though, is to run a department that deals in information."

Caldan thought quietly for a moment. This was interesting news and quite possibly something he could turn to his advantage. "So . . . spying?"

"Oh no, nothing as crass as that. I daresay if we knew who headed up the emperor's spies, we wouldn't be around long." Izak chuckled. "No, her department keeps its eyes and ears open, keeps its fingers on the pulse of what is happening around the empire, as well as with the guilds and other organizations."

Interesting. As casually as he could, Caldan said, "So, if, for example, I wanted to trace the origins of a trinket and where it was now, she could help?"

Izak raised his eyebrows. "Oh, she could do that, and more. The empire tracks all trinkets and who owns them, so I've heard. If you wanted information that valuable, she would be one you could go to. Though I doubt you'd like the price she would ask, even if you could get her to agree to your request."

"Expensive?"

"No, she has all the ducats she could need. She would ask for favors or keep you in her debt until you were of use." Izak shuddered. "Not to my liking."

Caldan chewed a thumbnail, ignoring Izak's questioning look. Did he dare approach this woman? He had hardly any ducats to offer, but if what Izak said were true, she wouldn't be after coin. An opportunity like this was unlikely to arise again, and what could she ask of him anyway?

"Well," said Izak. "I need another drink." He looked around the room. "Ah, there she is. Do you mind if I . . ." His voice trailed off, and he waved in the direction of the bar.

"Of course not."

"I'll join you in a bit." Izak again drew out his perfumed handkerchief and wiped his face, then with a wave disappeared into the crowd.

Turning back to the Dominion table, Caldan approached. Chances like these were few and far between. Best he took this one in both hands, if he could.

"Excuse me," he began. Lady Felicienne arched one eyebrow at him but didn't speak. This close, Caldan could see small pocked scars on her cheeks. "I see you're in need of an opponent, and I'd be glad to give you a match. If you would like . . . I mean . . . if that's what you're here for."

A number of the people around the table stopped their conversation to listen. Lady Felicienne toyed with an earring while she appraised him. Caldan had the feeling she didn't miss much as her gaze took in his clothes and the stubble on his head, lingering on the scar on his cheek. He noticed her eyes flick over his shoulder in the direction Izak had headed, then back to him.

"Why not?" she agreed in an amused tone. She sat up and waved at the empty chair across from her. "Please, be seated. What are you wagering?"

Caldan hesitated then reached into his coin pouch. *Can't risk too much.* He withdrew two silver ducats and placed them on the table.

"Two silvers," he said as firmly as he could manage, heart pounding.

Behind him, someone coughed, and he heard a snicker. Lady Felicienne looked at the coins, blinked, then looked at him.

"I don't know if I can cover such an amount," she replied, deadpan.

"And something else."

"Oh?"

"I need information. If I win, I'll get to ask you questions I believe you can help me with."

"Information about what?" she said, hand creeping up to fiddle with her earring again.

"I'd rather not say here." Caldan gestured to the crowded room.

"Then how am I to judge whether what else you are offering is sufficient to cover it?"

"I haven't offered anything yet."

"Yes, and that's a problem. So you are betting unspecified services against unspecified information?"

Caldan was clearly out of his depth. "Yes, I suppose. I don't know what I could offer that you would be interested in. I guess you'd be a better judge of that."

Felicienne looked him up and down and smiled. "Indeed." She sat back into her chair and tapped a cheek with a finger, eyes never leaving Caldan's.

"Tell you what," she said eventually. "I'll take up your challenge. These dullards loitering around waiting for someone better than them to take me on are boring me to tears."

Caldan glanced at the people standing about. A few glared at the lady, but some had smirks of their own as they politely ignored her rudeness.

"Well . . . thank you. I'll sit down."

"Please do. It might make playing hard otherwise." She leaned forward, placing two silver ducats directly on top of Caldan's. "I don't believe anyone has thanked me before for accepting a challenge."

Caldan could feel her eyes on him as he sat, scraping his chair on the floor when he moved it closer to the board. A woman tittered in the background.

Felicienne put a hand in the air and was soon approached by one of the spare attendants bearing two scraps of paper and writing implements. They each took a piece and scrawled their first seven opening moves, then handed it back.

The man studied both before placing each faceup on the top tier for them both to see. Lady Felicienne smiled.

Caldan grimaced.

The first phase of the game had begun.

LADY FELICIENNE LOUNGED in her padded chair, at ease with her progression in the game, a glass of bright green liquid in one hand. She barely glanced at the board, her main focus of attention the crowd gathered around their table—other players, patrons, even a couple of the serving staff on a short break from their duties.

Caldan knew she didn't have to stare at the board because the pieces, positions, and state of play would be foremost in her mind; they were in his. He gathered that her nonchalant pose was for the benefit of her reputation.

In the hour their game had progressed, he'd learned a little about her from whispers reaching his ears, spoken in hushed and often awed tones by people in the crowd.

Lady Felicienne Shyrise, a Third Adjudicator to the emperor himself. As one woman he overheard put it, shy by name but not by nature. She'd traveled from the capital to Anasoma in order to attend every Autumn Festival for the last five years, to compete in the Dominion tournament. Caldan hadn't heard anything else of value, unless what she liked to drink or eat was considered valuable information here.

He drew his attention back to the board. Something wasn't quite right with Lady Felicienne's last three moves, but he couldn't put his finger on what bothered him. Her attempted feint then attack did nothing to improve her position, though the projected power of her pieces moved slightly to another direction. He scratched his head and shifted in his chair.

On his right, Izak shouldered his way through the crowd toward him, face flushed and glowing with a sheen of sweat. Half of his shirt was untucked from his pants. Stopping to apologize briefly to a couple he had barged between, he approached Caldan with a broad grin. He leaned close and whispered. "You could have found someone easier for your first game here, no?"

Caldan half smiled apologetically and spread his hands. "The table was free, and she was waiting for an opponent."

"That might have told you something, if you'd thought about it." Izak wiped his brow with his kerchief. "Still, an interesting game, from what I can see."

"Are you all right? You're a bit flustered."

Izak grinned and winked. "Quite all right, thank you. I had a . . . chat . . . with the waitress. Perhaps a refreshing drink is called for." He straightened up and signaled to a hovering waiter. Izak handed him a few coins and gave him some instructions, then leaned back down to Caldan.

"It might not be any of my business, but have you placed a wager on the game?"

"Yes, two silvers." Caldan saw Izak's eyes widen.

Izak coughed into his hand. "Two silvers. She must have been bored."

"Pardon?"

"Nothing. You realize you'll lose? I mean, she is one of the best players in the empire."

"Is she?" Caldan frowned. Her play had been excellent, but he had seen better. And played better himself. "I wouldn't say she has the upper hand."

Izak gestured at the board. "Of course she has. Look at the game. Are you blind?" Izak shook his head. "I'm sorry, that was harsh. Can you not see she is in a winning position?"

"It just looks like it. She is almost where I want her."

"Forgive me if I sound skeptical."

A waiter appeared at his elbow bearing a wooden tray. Izak passed Caldan another glass of the pear cider and availed himself of his own drink, something that looked like mud with a spoon in it.

"Ah! Just the thing to replenish the reserves," Izak exclaimed.

Caldan watched as Izak swallowed a few spoonfuls of the thick brown substance. A comment from behind Izak made him turn with a laugh and hold the glass and spoon in the air. A few ribald cheers followed his display.

Caldan shook his head in confusion and returned to the game. He had much to learn about this place.

Lady Felicienne stared at him. Her eyes moved from the Dominion board to Caldan and back again. She placed her drink on a side table and leaned forward to study the game, hands clasped in front of her, eyes narrowed with concentration. She looked . . . annoyed.

She finally senses something isn't right, Caldan thought. He hoped she didn't grasp his plan until too late.

Someone jostled Caldan's right shoulder and his drink spilled. Izak.

"Oh bloody . . . I mean . . . excuse me. My apologies." He had found a chair somewhere and managed to drag it through the crowd and place it next to Caldan's. He sat himself down with an audible sigh of relief, clutching his now-empty glass with smears of the mudlike substance inside. A strong smell of herbs and spices reached Caldan, emanating from the glass.

"Medicinal?" Caldan inquired.

"Oh . . . yes. Good for what ails you, replenishing your strength, that sort of thing."

Caldan studied the board again but kept an eye on Lady Felicienne. Knowing your opponent and figuring out what they had inferred about your play was as important as the moves themselves.

"You think you have the upper hand?"

Caldan sighed softly. Izak was distracting him. He meant well, but it wasn't going to help his game.

"It depends on the next few moves, on whether she has worked anything out and can reorganize her defense."

"If I make a modest wager of my own, I won't regret betting on you?"

"Anything can happen, as well you know, but I think she won't catch on in time. I wish I had wagered more now."

Izak stood abruptly. "Well, time for another drink. I can't sit around here all evening distracting you." He disappeared into the crowd.

Caldan's opponent had played an outstanding game, and if she realized his plan in the next few moves, things wouldn't go well for him. The pieces were in a delicate balance at the moment.

Felicienne moved three of her pieces. He held his breath as she used two of her extra moves. She sat motionless, not breathing, staring at the board. Caldan hardly dared breathe himself. She half stood to move one piece on the second tier, paused, then moved another.

He let out a long slow breath. She hadn't seen through his ruse to the heart of his plan. Her moves were logical—as she saw them—but in the end served only to destabilize her position further.

Caldan gathered himself, but before making his moves studied the board and pieces. It was when you were at your most confident that things were likely to go wrong. Concentrate too much on your own game and you could miss vital aspects of your opponent's.

A bump on his shoulder told him Izak had returned with another drink, a yellowish spirit in a bulbous glass. His face was still flushed, probably because of the alcohol he had consumed.

"Here you go. Thank me later." Izak handed him a piece of paper. On it was written *C. 2G, T7, LF 15-1* with a scribbled signature under a dark wax seal.

Caldan frowned at the cryptic writing. "What's this?"

The attendant approached and asked to see the paper. Caldan handed it over while Izak smiled. The attendant scrutinized the paper then, satisfied they weren't cheating, handed it back with a nod.

Izak held another piece of paper in his other hand. "It's your wager, and this is mine. You can give me the ducats I spent placing the bet later, after you win."

"My what?" Caldan said loudly, turning heads in the crowd. He tugged Izak's arm through his coat and drew him closer. "You made a wager in my name? For how much?"

Izak squirmed in his grasp. "Easy, lad, you've quite a grip there. I'd like to use this arm later."

"How much?" grated Caldan.

"It says right there. Two gold. Have to make the most when the odds are good. If you win, they'll come down a bit."

Caldan sat stunned. *Two gold ducats. I don't have two gold ducats.*

"What's the problem? You think you'll win," explained Izak. "We'll both make out like bandits. No one here seriously thinks she will lose."

Caldan clenched a fist. The one holding Izak by the arm. Izak's mouth opened in pain.

"I don't *have* two gold ducats. Let alone two to spare on a wager."

Izak tried to pry Caldan's fingers off his arm. "Steady on, eh? I'm sure you said you wanted to win some ducats tonight."

"Not by betting coins I don't have. What happens if I lose?" In debt two gold ducats and unspecified services to Lady Felicienne. His stomach churned.

"I thought you said you'd win?"

"I . . . it's . . . probably. But that's not the point. What if I don't? I can't pay."

"Hmmm." Izak blinked. "Then you'll probably go to prison or the work gangs. Owww!" He clutched at Caldan's hand on his arm. "Let go!"

"What does the paper say?" demanded Caldan.

"Well, C—that's you, Caldan. Two G, that's obvious . . ." He glanced at Caldan, whose expression made him quickly return to the paper. "Um, T seven—that's table seven. This table. LF is the dear lady here. And the last numbers are the odds. Fifteen to one." He swallowed. "So . . . that's thirty gold to you, if you win, less three as commission."

Caldan shook his head in disgust, then released Izak's arm.

"Is there a problem, gentlemen?" Lady Felicienne's words drifted across the Dominion table to them.

Caldan quailed inside, and Izak went as still as a statue.

"No . . . not at all," replied Caldan. "A friendly disagreement."

Felicienne wrinkled her nose. "Ah, the worst kind." Her eyes shifted to Izak, then returned to Caldan. "Has Izak done something regrettable?"

"Almost certainly," Caldan said, eliciting a smile from the lady.

"I hope you placed a wager on me." She smiled at Caldan. "I'm about to crack this egg open, and about time, too. For two silvers, I wasn't expecting this much resistance."

A pain in his jaw made Caldan aware he was grinding his teeth. Hard. *Two gold and more in debt if I don't win, and Lady Felicienne making light of the game.* His face was hot, and the air around the table had gone stale, the crowd surrounding them too close for comfort. He shut his eyes and took a few deep breaths.

"Are you all right?" came Izak's voice, as if from a distance.

Opening his eyes, Caldan shook his head. "No, not really. Especially if I lose."

"But you said you'd win."

Izak was beginning to annoy him. "No, I didn't."

"You did. You said—"

"Can you please be quiet? I have to concentrate."

"Oh, of course." Izak held a finger to his lips. "You can count on me."

Caldan nodded. "Could you do me a favor? A glass of water would help."

"Water? What you need is a good strong drink. Something to—"

"*No.* Water, please."

"I'll be back shortly. Don't make any moves until I return." Izak weaved unsteadily through the crowd, and Caldan sighed with relief.

"Good friends, are you?" inquired Lady Felicienne. "With Izak?"

"No . . . my lady. I just met him tonight."

"My lady?" She smiled at him. "So formal?"

Caldan squirmed in his chair.

Felicienne continued. "If we ever have occasion to meet formally, you can call me 'my lady,' but here you can call me Felice."

A sharp intake of breath could be heard from a few onlookers, and a sneer appeared on Felicienne's face. "A good game deserves some reward, does it not? Though in the end, learning from a loss can also be a reward for those less skilled." She met his eye. "I look forward to those unspecified services."

Heat rose to Caldan's face at her words. He swallowed. "Felice it is. You can call me Caldan."

Felice nodded once. "And what is it you do, Caldan?" Her eyes traveled down his torso. "For someone who plays Dominion with no little skill, you seem a bit . . . muscular."

Caldan cleared his throat, embarrassed to admit to her he was only an apprentice with the Protectors. "I'm a sorcerer."

Felice raised an eyebrow at him. "Indeed. Well, a valuable calling, to be sure."

The air grew thicker with each passing moment. Caldan decided to make his move. "I believe it is my turn?"

"You would believe correctly."

Caldan nodded. "I choose to use my five extra turns now."

Felice's satisfied smile quickly turned into a scowl of confusion, brow furrowed. His normal turn plus five extra turns made it a total of six moves he could perform. Caldan stood and, in quick succession, moved his pieces over the boards.

Lady Felicienne's mouth opened in surprise.

Caldan returned to his chair and sat with a sigh of relief, the piece of paper with the wager on it clutched in a sweaty hand. Seeing Izak, he eagerly reached out for the glass of water he carried and drank it in a few gulps.

"What happened?" hissed Izak. "I told you not to make any moves until I got back!"

"I took a chance," replied Caldan. "Moved a little early, but it worked out still."

"She looks angry. At you."

Caldan studiously avoided Felice's gaze. "I take it she doesn't lose often?"

"Ah, no. Not often. Rarely, you could say." Izak looked at his empty hands. "Where did my drink go?"

"Forget your drink. We're lucky I'm not being hauled off to prison now." He glared at Izak, though Izak was peering at the Dominion board.

Izak tilted his head and blinked. "I think she has lost," he said with a tinge of wonder.

"She has, and she knows it. Luckily for both of us, since I daresay prison wouldn't be a good place to be."

"Oh, it's not so bad, once you get used to it. Excellent! A rather interesting night so far! Who do you think you should play next? We can make some coin before word of your play gets out."

"I'm not playing anyone else tonight."

"But you must! The opportunity is tonight. Tomorrow, people will be warier . . . more wary."

Lady Felicienne stood abruptly. All eyes turned to her. She gave a bow to Caldan. "I concede defeat," she said plainly. "Well played."

Gasps could be heard from the crowd, and the buzz of conversation rose in volume.

Not knowing the usual protocol, Caldan nodded in return. After hesitating a moment, he walked around the board and held out his hand. "It was a good game. I'd be happy to play you again soon."

Felicienne looked at Caldan's extended hand, then grasped it firmly. "Likewise. I do believe we'll be seeing more of each other. It's not often someone teaches me something new with Dominion. And I fear I underestimated you, which won't happen again."

Caldan gave a wry smile. "I'm sure it won't."

"I haven't come across that strategy before. It was . . . a learning experience."

"I can't claim credit," Caldan said. "It was devised a long time ago by a man called Kelhak. It's so old I think it's been forgotten."

"Ah." Felicienne gestured to the silver ducats on the table, two of Caldan's and two of hers. "Your winnings."

He thanked her and accepted the coins.

She brushed a stray strand of hair back over an ear. "There is still the matter of the unspecified information. Obviously this isn't the place, though. Izak here will know how to contact me, and I always repay my debts. I'll arrange for someone to meet you and discuss what you need. Will that be sufficient, or would you like me to provide some kind of collateral before I leave?"

"That . . . will not be necessary. I trust you."

At his words, Felice raised an eyebrow and smirked. "I believe I've learned more than enough for tonight, so will be leaving. Can I offer you an escort back to the Sorcerers' Guild?"

"Ah, no . . . thank you. I can look after myself."

Felicienne paused. "I'm sure you can." She glanced at the thinning crowd around the table. "Still, perhaps instead you can escort me to my apartments and we can discuss your needs in more detail tonight?"

Caldan heard Izak cough into a hand, then murmur something unintelligible and wander away from the table. His heart beat faster. What would Miranda think of him?

And why am I thinking of Miranda at a time like this?

"I apologize, but I must decline," he said.

"Must you?"

"Yes, my lady." She raised an eyebrow at him. "Um . . . Felice." Caldan scrabbled for an excuse. "Honestly, I don't know where I am at the moment. I'm new to the city and was lucky the sorcerers took me in."

"I would say they were lucky."

"Either way, I need some stability right now."

"Unstable, am I?" Before he could protest, she held her hand up with a smile. "I'm joking—though that's something I haven't been called before. No, I won't push, and I'm not offended. I had better be going."

She nodded and, without another word, left him standing there by the abandoned game.

Izak sidled up to him. "Well, well, well. You must have impressed her."

Caldan shook his head. He didn't know what to make of the Lady Felice. He rubbed his eyes and yawned. It felt like a long night, though it was still relatively early.

"You should have another game tonight. You need to take advantage before word of this gets out."

"No. I should be getting back. I've had enough stress for one night."

Izak sighed in resignation. Out of his coat pocket he pulled a piece of paper similar to Caldan's. "Let's go collect, then. Are you sure . . . ?"

"I'm sure. No more tonight."

Izak guided Caldan through the crowd by the arm. A few people nodded to Caldan, and one man clapped him on the back. They wound their way over to the man sitting under the chalkboard, who handed over their winnings with minimal fuss.

The cloth purse lay heavy in Caldan's hand. More ducats than he had ever had in his life, enough to pay Master Simmon back and have plenty left over. Enough to treat Miranda to a decent meal to repay her kindness.

Izak bounced his purse in his hand. "Well, if you're going to have an early night, I might do the same. Too much excitement is not good for someone my age. Except sometimes!" He laughed, and Caldan couldn't help but join in.

Declining a farewell drink, Caldan exchanged a brief good-bye with assurances that he would return to the Yawning Rabbit soon and seek Izak out.

CHAPTER 22

I t took Caldan two hours to weave his way through the morning crowds before he arrived at the place he had agreed to meet Miranda. Six days had passed following his victory over Lady Felicienne, and Caldan still felt uneasy with the gold ducats he had won, courtesy of Izak. He'd paid Master Simmon back, his largesse being met with a raised eyebrow and pointed questions as to where he had come about ducats so swiftly. Caldan had confessed, red-faced, but Simmon had merely grinned and told him not to win too much, with an explanation that some of the merchants didn't like it when sorcerers did well against them, on account they might be cheating.

A few coins Caldan spent on essentials; the remainder he secreted under his straw mattress. He had crafted another lock for his door that should stop any casual thief from entering his room.

Caldan caught sight of Miranda and waved. They had arranged to meet at an intersection in Dockside, as Miranda said she had some business to arrange and would introduce him to a contact he might be able to use to find out about his trinket.

She waved back, and Caldan lowered his arm with relief. Master Simmon had him performing a seemingly endless succession of exercises the last three days. Designed to strengthen his body, the exercise sessions left him gasping for breath and aching. Afternoons were dedicated to crafting and lessons on alchemy and history. With all this newfound activity, Caldan found his appetite returning to what it had been before he arrived, managing to put away twice as much as his fellow apprentices, to his embarrassment and their amusement.

Miranda favored him with a smile as she approached from across the street, pausing to avoid a group of children running past.

"How are you?" she asked, touching his arm. "Come on," she said before he mustered a reply. "Let's get going so we can get our business out of the way and enjoy the day."

"I'm well, apart from being sore. What have you been up to?"

"This and that. More this than that." She grinned mischievously. "I managed to secure a deal that might make some ducats, if it works out."

Caldan laughed. Miranda was always up to something. "Good. At least one of us has the sense to make an honest living."

"I didn't say it was honest," she said, grinning broader. "And what do you mean? Have you fallen into some dishonest coins since we last met?"

"Not exactly, but I could have been in a lot of trouble." He explained the night at the Yawning Rabbit.

Miranda doubled over with laughter. "Sounds like this Izak is a character."

"And then some. He didn't act stable at all. I think he likes taking risks *too* much."

"And living life to the fullest. Still, it worked out well for you in the end."

"Better than you think," he said with a grin.

"What do you mean?"

"I haven't had a chance to tell you about the Lady Felicienne."

Miranda gave him a cool look. "You met a lady?"

"Yes, at the Yawning Rabbit."

Miranda examined her nails. "Really? How nice for you. Was she pretty?"

"What? I guess so." At her deepening frown, Caldan swallowed. *Is she jealous?* On the one hand, he felt guilty about making her feel bad. On the other hand, he'd never made anyone jealous before . . .

"It wasn't like that, Miranda," he said, and was surprised to see a slight blush reach her cheeks. "She was the one I played Dominion with. She works for the emperor and has access to information."

"Ah, I see."

"Since I won, she's now in my debt."

"Really?"

"That was the bet we made. If I win, then she helps me."

"And if you lost?"

"I'm not sure . . . I kind of left it open . . ."

"Are you crazy? She could have asked anything of you!" She eyed him, and the faint blush rose to her cheeks again. "I've heard those ladies can be quite forward."

"It was all business," he said firmly. No need to discuss Lady Felicienne's request for an escort home—it was never even a consideration for him. "And it all worked out in the end. And I made a few ducats, so there's that, too."

"Does that mean dinner is in the cards soon?"

"When I find a suitable place."

"You have no idea where to go, do you?"

"Not really," he admitted with a smile.

"Well, I'm not going to help you. Ask around with the masters. I'm sure they know a few places that serve decent food."

"Good advice."

"I'm always full of good advice."

"Whether people want it or not?"

"Exactly. If they don't listen, at least I tried." She stopped and took hold of his chin, turning his cheek toward her. "Elpidia knows her stuff. The scar has faded nicely, and it hasn't been long—although there is some redness here," she said, brushing her finger along the healing cut. Taking her hand away, she said, "Remind me to see her if I ever need to have something stitched."

By the ancestors, she was beautiful. And yet, Jemma still lingered in his thoughts. *It's only been a few weeks . . .*

Caldan swallowed, feeling heat rush to his face. Her finger felt like it had left a burning trail across his skin. "How likely is that?"

"You only took a few days, so more likely than you think."

They ducked into another side street, as up ahead two carts blocked their way, amid loud protestations from both drivers and a vocal crowd. Soon Caldan could smell the sea and catch glimpses of water between buildings as they strolled down a steep street toward the harbor.

Miranda guided them through a few turns, and eventually they found themselves standing in front of a building across from the docks. Compared to many of the buildings around it, it was well maintained, with a fresh coat of whitewash on the walls. Where the building stopped, the walls continued to surround the large patch of land the trading company owned. A thick wrought-iron gate stood in the middle of the wall, while bright red double doors opened into the building proper. Fixed atop the door in raised bronze letters was a sign declaring the building home to the Five Oceans Mercantile Concern.

Miranda didn't wait to see if he followed as she strode confidently through the open door. Caldan stepped quickly after her into the opulent interior of the building. Smooth gray marble tiles paved the floor, and highly polished mahogany counters lined all three sides of the large entry room. A number of employees were behind the counters, talking with people who had business there and looking busy writing in ledgers and organizing papers. Expensive sorcerous globes hung on the walls every few yards, illuminating the room more than necessary. The odor of roasted coffee overlaid with spices pervaded the air, signifying large quantities of the costly products were close by.

He paused, awestruck at the sheer amount of ducats that had been spent to create such an impression.

"What a waste," Caldan muttered. "This doesn't look like a merchants' office. At least, it isn't what I expected."

"Shhh. They aren't just merchants," Miranda explained. "They loan ducats as well, and own businesses in the city. And not only Anasoma. No one knows for sure, but it's widely believed they are the wealthiest company in the city, if not the empire."

"They're a bank as well?"

"Yes." She stood looking around at the counters, obviously unsure of which one she needed to go to.

"May I assist you?" came a soft voice from their left.

Caldan turned to find a woman. Her blond hair was tied back, and there was a bright smile on her face. "If you can tell me what you are looking for," she said, "I can direct you to the proper counter."

"Yes, thanks," said Miranda. "I'm here to pay for some warehouse space, and to see Sir Quiss on a matter of some property."

"Excellent. I hope you're having an enjoyable day. Please, that counter over there." She gestured smoothly across the room to a man with spectacles signing and stamping some papers, flanked by two large, muscular men. "I'll let someone know to inform Sir Quiss."

"Perfect. Good day to you, too." Miranda nodded to the woman and grabbed Caldan by the arm, pulling him along with her to the counter. The lady retreated to stand by the open doors.

"Weird," remarked Miranda.

"Yes. Is her job to stand there and help people who look like they need it? Do you think she does anything else?"

"How should I know? I would hope so. Paying someone to stand around doing nothing all day seems odd."

Sizing up the burly men, Caldan didn't think anyone in their right mind would take them on. "They take money very seriously here, I suppose."

"True," Miranda said. "They have a professional operation. Which makes me feel good about getting into business with them."

They approached the bespectacled man, but before Miranda could utter a word, he spoke.

"One moment, please." He continued to sign and stamp documents, tutting at one before placing it in a pile to his left. He removed his spectacles and rubbed his nose.

"Now . . . how may I help you?" the man inquired.

"My name is Miranda, and I am here to—"

"Ah, yes, pay for some warehouse space. Now, where is that contract?" he said half to himself, and searched through one of the piles in front of him.

"Here is the payment." Miranda withdrew a purse and deposited it on the table.

"Excellent," said the man, with a thin smile. After signing the contract, he stamped the document and moved it to a different pile.

"I'm here to see Sir Quiss as well," said Miranda. "The lady over there said she would have word sent to him."

The man nodded and gestured to a group of padded chairs around a highly polished table. "Be seated, and he'll be out shortly. I'm afraid your gentleman friend here will not be able to join you in the meeting, unless he also has direct business with Sir Quiss."

"No, he doesn't." She turned to Caldan. "You'll be all right waiting here?"

"Of course."

"Good. Let's sit down."

In the middle of the table sat a bowl of sweets individually wrapped in waxy brown paper. Caldan helped himself to a couple and popped one in his mouth. Miranda sat next to him and rubbed her hands together.

"Good," remarked Caldan. "Like solid honey and spices. You should try one."

"I'm too nervous. My palms are sweaty, and I can't very well rub them on my dress."

Caldan chuckled at her.

She glared at him, then her expression softened. "This is important. If it goes to plan . . . let's just say I will have done well. And Sir Quiss, he's also the contact I mentioned to you. Merchants such as these have access to a great deal of information and have vast resources to be able to find almost anything out."

"You think they could help me trace my trinket?"

"I believe so. They have . . . leverage . . . with most of the nobles and other merchants. There isn't much they couldn't do if they turned their mind to it. I didn't mention trinkets, just that you were after information."

A figure emerged from a door behind the counter.

Caldan saw a man who was not quite a man. He looked denser than ordinary men, as if he didn't fit in the space he occupied. Harder. Caldan squeezed Miranda's arm unconsciously.

"Ow! Don't do that!"

He blinked, and the man appeared normal this time, as if Caldan's eyes had played a trick on him. "Sorry," he muttered.

The strange man spoke briefly to the bespectacled man, who motioned in their direction.

"Miranda, I don't think this is a good idea."

"What? Why? I won't be long."

He pulled her close and whispered. "I . . . don't have a good feeling about this."

"Pish," she said. " 'Don't have a good feeling.' About what? You're probably just too full of sweets. Caldan, I need this." She broke free from his grasp and stood, smiling as the man approached.

Caldan stood as well, eyeing the man, who stopped and bowed curtly to Miranda and nodded to Caldan.

"Luphildern Quiss," he announced in a curious melodic accent Caldan hadn't heard before. "Head trader for the Five Oceans Mercantile Concern, and before you ask, one of many senior traders." A fleeting smile crossed his face. "And you are Miss Miranda, I believe."

She held out her hand. "Yes, I am. Pleased to meet you."

Sir Quiss looked at her hand for a moment before extending his own. Caldan sucked in a breath between his teeth. They shook hands.

Nothing happened.

"And I'm pleased to meet you, Miss Miranda. Please, come with me. I'm afraid your gentleman friend will have to wait here."

Quiss locked eyes with him, a look of such intensity and startling penetration that it left Caldan feeling stripped bare.

He ripped his gaze away, breaking eye contact on reflex. Quiss half turned and gestured for Miranda to precede him through the door from which he had appeared.

"Thank you," she said and turned to Caldan. "I shouldn't be long. Don't eat too many sweets."

Caldan shook his head minutely. *Don't go!* his look shouted at her. Sweat prickled his skin.

She frowned at him, and her expression became annoyed. "I won't be long," she said again, and turned to walk across the room and through the door, followed closely by Quiss.

Caldan blinked, and again the man looked denser, harder. Caldan's eyes burned and he rubbed them quickly. Quiss remained the same this time, like a stain on the fabric of reality, rent and twisted. The scent of rotten fruit reached Caldan's nostrils.

He swallowed a mouthful of honeyed spice. *By the ancestors, what is going on?* He glanced around the room. Everyone else looked normal. Maybe he was seeing things, or perhaps he was too tired. No, something was wrong. Quiss wasn't a man, or he was a man but something else as well.

Caldan sat and folded his arms, staring at the door Miranda had disappeared through. *She'd better come out soon,* he thought, *or . . . or what? I'll rush in and rescue her? Miranda obviously couldn't see anything different about the man, so why can I?*

The padded chair felt uncomfortable, and he squirmed while chewing a fingernail. The wait dragged on. Something strange was happening here, and while he had no idea what it was or where to start looking, Quiss had to be the key. Caldan growled in frustration and half stood before sitting down again. It was likely the security here would stop him from going through the door.

It felt like hours passed before the door opened and Miranda walked through, followed by Sir Quiss. She looked normal, a smile plastered on her face. Caldan sighed heavily in relief, though he didn't know what he had expected to happen.

They joined him by the table, Miranda looking pleased with herself and Sir Quiss hovering expectantly.

"I believe our business is concluded, Miss Miranda," stated Quiss. "And your escort is the gentleman you told me about, the one looking for information?"

"Yes, of course. Caldan, do you want to explain to Sir Quiss?"

Caldan froze for a moment. He couldn't bring himself to show his trinket to this man. He thought furiously. "Ah . . . yes," he managed to say. "Actually, I find myself in an awkward position. The Lady Felicienne has been good enough to agree to assist me. I'm afraid I didn't have a chance to let Miranda know. I apologize for the misunderstanding." By the time he was finished, Miranda was glaring at him, red-faced and tight-lipped.

Quiss bobbed his head in a short bow. "I know of her. She should serve you well. Then, if that is all, I bid both of you good day."

"Yes, again I apologize. It was thoughtless of me."

"Yes, it was," growled Miranda.

Quiss shook his head. "No harm done. Farewell." He turned and strode away.

Caldan pulled her in close.

"Are you all right?" he whispered.

"Are *you*? Of course I am. Why wouldn't I be?"

"Didn't you see the way he looked?"

"What do you mean? He looked like a merchant."

Caldan stuck his hands in his pockets and hunched his shoulders. "No, it was more than that. He was different. I could see he didn't belong. That's why I didn't want to ask about my trinket."

Miranda frowned at him, then laughed. "Don't be silly; there's nothing wrong with him. Just a senior merchant doing business." She looked at him with worry. "Are you coming down with a fever?"

"No. I'm not." Caldan shuffled his feet, unsure how to explain to her what he had seen. Maybe it was a trick of the light. He shook his head. "Never mind," he said.

She looked at the empty bowl, which had been full of sweets. "Hungry, were you?"

Caldan went red. "I thought the other apprentices might like some." He patted two full pockets.

She gave him a disappointed look. "You don't do things like that. They are for people who are waiting."

"I was waiting," he protested.

"But . . . oh, never mind." She made a show of massaging her temples, breathing out heavily through her nose.

"This place is unsettling. Can we leave?" He wanted to get out as soon as possible. He needed time to think on what he had seen.

"I'm finished, so yes, let's go." She latched onto his arm and pulled him toward the door to the street, but Caldan didn't budge. His eyes were glued on the door. He knew he had just asked to leave, but something was making him wonder if he should follow Quiss to find out more about the man.

"Oof! You're heavy. I couldn't move you an inch. Come on."

No—now's not the time.

He fell into step beside her. She clutched his arm and drew close to him.

Caldan hurried along with her, feeling a palpable sense of relief after they exited the building. Miranda continued at a fast pace he was only too happy to keep up with, since it meant more distance between them and Quiss.

He walked by Miranda's side as she headed for the wharves. She set a brisk pace down Harrow Lane, then turned onto Spoonbill Street. Somewhere close, he could hear a baby crying. Across the way at the local communal oven, smoke poured from the chimney. Eventually they made their way up one of the long wooden jetties where ships stood idle, only one or two sailors on deck to keep watch during the day.

Gulls screeched overhead, swooping down to bicker over entrails in discarded piles as women gutted fish ready for the markets. Some birds stood on the wharves' foundation poles sticking out of the water and added their excrement to the growing piles at the top. Miranda stopped near one such pole and made to lean against it. Caldan grabbed her arm and pulled her away, pointing out the white streaks of gull guano.

Miranda gave the lone bird atop the pole the evil eye. Her smooth, sun-warmed skin felt like it was burning Caldan's palm. He let go and dropped his gaze.

"Here is fine," Miranda said. "Apart from that bloody bird, stupid thing. If only they tasted better, we wouldn't have to put up with so many." She laughed. "Oops, I'm trying not to curse."

"Don't worry. I won't tell, and I'm sure the bird won't."

"Are you making fun of me?"

"Never," he replied with a smile.

She returned one of her own, which lit up her face. "Anyway, what was all that about, back there?"

"I had a strange feeling." Caldan wasn't sure he should tell her the truth. He didn't know what was going on, why the man had looked denser than everyone else, or why that would matter. Alarming Miranda with no probable reason wouldn't do any good. "It's nothing," he found himself saying. "I don't know what came over me."

She looked at him strangely, then nodded. "Something made you react that way. If you aren't sure what it was, then that's fine. It scared me, that's all." She hugged both arms to her chest. "So . . ." Her expression brightened. "I began negotiations with the Five Oceans Mercantile Concern to sell them my building."

Caldan scratched his head in puzzlement. "Your warehouse? But you just bought it."

"I know. Isn't that great? The man who sold it to me didn't know Five Oceans had plans to buy up properties in the area as part of developing a new market and trading hub."

"And you did?"

"Yes. Someone I know knew someone who knew someone else; all gossip to them, but I saw an opportunity. Spent a good deal of time looking up who owned buildings in the area, I can tell you, and eventually I found someone willing to sell."

"Won't he be angry when he finds out?"

She waved a hand and snorted. "Maybe, but he won't want to admit being outdone by a woman and will put it down to bad luck, condescending fool."

"Congratulations are in order, then. Perhaps a celebration?"

A twinkle flashed in Miranda's eyes as they crinkled when she smiled. "Not yet. Soon. Once the deals are done, and assuming nothing goes wrong. I think a major celebration would be in order then." She grinned at him. "Come, there's something else I want to do."

She led him off the wharf and south along the harbor, chatting about everything and nothing. The sight of the denser-man had stirred something in Caldan. He answered Miranda's questions distractedly, eliciting concerned glances from her at times, but, thankfully, she didn't bring it up again.

They passed broken crab pots and netting being mended, bales of wool being readied for export, watched over by taciturn guards. Buildings became cleaner and less run-down the farther south they traveled, until they came upon the start of stone wharves replacing the wooden constructions of the poorer section, built long ago by the emperor's labor gangs.

"Here." Miranda stopped them at the beginning of a stone wharf.

A makeshift barricade had been hastily erected, behind which stood five men of the Harbor Watch and a thin-faced sorcerer Caldan didn't recognize, a senior master judging by the trinkets she wore. He had never seen so many trinkets on one person. Even without accessing his well, he could feel them, multiple vibrations at the edge of his awareness: two amulets suspended from silver chains around her neck, at least three rings among the many she wore on each hand, and possibly one or two more somewhere. She stood leaning against a crate and studied her nails.

They moved closer to the crowd pushing up against the barricade, mostly Dockside locals with nothing better to do, though a few well-dressed men and women were among them. Caldan estimated there were already more than a hundred people here gawking; a few were drinking from wineskins or bottles, faces flushed even with the cool breeze.

"What's this about? What did you want to see here?" he asked Miranda.

"Haven't you heard? See the ship at the end of the pier?" She pointed east down the stone projecting into the harbor. "The city's abuzz with news of its arrival. It's huge," she added. "And no one knows where it's from. Word on the street is it's a merchantman, albeit one no one's seen before. And then there are the cranks claiming it's the start of an invasion." She scoffed. "An invasion where no troops come ashore, and with just one ship."

Caldan gave a low whistle as he took in the size of the ship. "It looks too big, like it shouldn't hold together in heavy seas."

Armored figures stood on its deck, sunlight glinting from polished steel. Caldan squinted. Yes, one of the men had crafted glyphs and sigils covering his breastplate, and metal bands on his forearms.

"But it obviously does, though. From what I can see she's a fine piece of workmanship, that's for sure," Miranda agreed. "Gossip is she's called the *Black Lion*."

A number of other passersby paused to gape. Some moved on, while others joined the crowd.

"I never saw anything like it in any port I visited," Miranda said. "I wonder where she's from. Exciting, don't you think?"

"Yes, it is. When did it dock? Has anyone seen the crew on shore leave, spoken to them?"

"That's the weird thing—no crew have come off. At least no one has seen any of them at the taverns around here. You can see one or two occasionally on deck, but it looks like shore leave has been canceled. It's hard to get a look at what they're like from here. It's too far away to see clearly."

"Let's hope the captain doesn't have a mutiny on his hands!" Caldan said. "No shore leave for the crew on a ship that must have come a long way; they must be itching to come ashore."

"Any normal crew would be," agreed Miranda.

One of the Harbor Watch guards motioned to his fellows and approached the crowd. "Everyone settle down!" he bellowed. "No pushing."

At his words, the crowd surged forward and pressed against the barricade. He looked back at his men, then turned back to the crowd and raised both hands for calm. The sorcerer took a few steps in his direction.

"Move along now," the guard said. "You're blocking passage for other people."

Caldan couldn't see how. No one had been let through the barrier since they had arrived, and they certainly weren't blocking the usual traffic in the street.

"What are you trying to hide?" came a yell from the crowd.

"We're just looking."

Murmurs of assent followed the statement.

The guard shook his head. "Move along. We don't want any trouble."

Jeers greeted his response.

A trickle of sweat ran down the guard's cheek as the sorcerer reached his side and studied the crowd with expressionless eyes.

The buzz in the air grew louder. Caldan felt people press up against them as the throng surged forward, squashing him and Miranda against the barricade. Miranda responded with a few words under her breath Caldan couldn't catch, but he was pretty sure she was failing once again to lessen her cursing.

There was a scream, and others called out. Someone had fallen.

Caldan's gaze was drawn back to the strange ship. A shiver ran through him, and he experienced a sense of foreboding. He shrugged the feeling off. It had to be the close proximity of the sorcerer's trinkets.

Miranda grabbed Caldan's arm. "This doesn't look good. We need to get out of here."

He barely heard her over the noise.

Caldan nodded in agreement and tried to turn, but couldn't. They were wedged in. At least he could see over the crowd, but Miranda was having a worse time of it.

A bottle sailed over their heads, and the guards ducked out of the way. Glass exploded as it hit the wharf. The guard with the sorcerer nodded to her and retreated. She took a step forward.

"What's happening?" Miranda shouted.

Caldan felt the sorcerer access her well. "The sorcerer has advanced toward the crowd."

Miranda's mouth dropped open. "Oh crap," she said.

At that moment, a blue haze popped into existence around the sorcerer. One of the amulets hanging from her neck shone with bright runes. Caldan smelled hot metal, like the inside of a blacksmith's forge, and—there it was again—lemons.

Another bottle flew through the air, this one well aimed with vicious intent. It struck the sorcerer and shattered. Glass and a pale yellow liquid sprayed in all directions. Purple motes of light flowed from where the bottle had hit the sorcerer's blue haze.

She stood there unharmed, unflinching.

It was some kind of shield, it had to be. A sorcerous shield.

As the liquid dripped from the sorcerer's shield, her eyes hardened. She drew herself up and glared at the throng. Over their heads, Caldan could see groups of the Harbor Watch approaching from the north and south along the street. This wasn't a place they wanted to be.

Caldan grabbed Miranda by the arm and pushed his way back through the crowd. People pressed in from all directions, red-faced and shouting. Then at last they were clear, and just in time. Another group of the Harbor Watch marched into view, long clubs ready for action.

"Come on," he said to Miranda.

She nodded in agreement, and they ducked down a side street. A few minutes later, they stopped to gather themselves.

Caldan shook his head, perplexed. "The crowd was getting out of control. It's lucky we made it out when we did. Why did they react like that?"

"Who? The crowd or the Watch?"

"Both."

"Sometimes there are riots in the poorer districts, people protesting the emperor's taxes or whatever. The Watch breaks them up before it gets too rowdy." She thought about it for a moment. "But why now . . . I'm not sure. I didn't think a riot would break out. I just thought it would be interesting."

There was a long silence, then Caldan spoke. "Well, it definitely was *interesting*." He cleared his throat.

Miranda frowned at him. "Very funny. Anyway, did you see the flags on the ship?"

"I guess. What about them?"

"They looked to be Indryallan, although it's been a long time since I was there."

"If I remember right, that's far to the north," Caldan said. "I wonder what they're doing here."

Miranda only shrugged. He was about to say something when the strange feeling he'd had when first seeing the ship swept through him again. He shuddered. Finally, he said, "Listen—I hate to do this, but would it be okay if we meet again soon to celebrate your good fortune? I'm not feeling the best, and I think I should go, get some rest."

Miranda nodded, a concerned expression on her face. "You don't seem well, since your strange turn."

"I'm sure it's nothing," Caldan said, although it didn't feel like nothing. Still, he didn't want to worry her—not without any cause. "I'll feel better after a night's sleep." He rubbed his eyes; they burned, as if the glare and salt off the sea had irritated them. He felt exhausted.

"And I thought you were taking me to dinner," Miranda said. "Typical man!"

"We can go if you—"

"I'm teasing, Caldan. Besides, all of this today has taken more time than I thought, and you really *do* look like you're going to fall over." She sighed. "Make sure you eat something before going to bed, and drink some water. Water, mind you. Not ale or cider."

AFTER HE ARRIVED back at the guild, Caldan made a quick detour to the apprentices' dormitory. To their delight, he emptied his pockets of sweets, leaving a few for himself—they were delicious after all. Begging off from a surprise overture to stay and spend some time with them, he trudged back to his room, feet dragging, distractedly using the rails on the stairs where he would normally step up them two at a time without pause.

Once settled, Caldan lay awake, running through the day's events over and over, the meeting with Quiss and the strange ship foremost in his mind.

Sleep was a long time coming, and when it did come, it was fitful.

He woke to twisted, sweat-stained sheets, bleary eyes, and a headache.

CHAPTER 23

Sitting on his bed with a single candle for light, Caldan laid out the materials he had gathered from the guild's supply store: two yards of thin copper wire, and slender rods of hardwood.

He used his knife to cut four short sections from a rod and one longer section, then carved shallow grooves into each end. Using the knife, he bore down on the soft copper wire and cut strips as long as his little finger. He wrapped the end of one wire strip into the groove around the end of a wooden section and attached it to the longer piece. In no time at all, he had attached all four short parts to the longer one and stood it on his palm. It looked roughly like a four-legged animal with no head or tail, but those would come soon. The copper wire allowed the legs to move.

Caldan made short work of attaching a copper wire tail and a flat head, also made from bent wire. The more metal he used, the longer the crafting would last. Laying the construct on his knee, he began the painstaking process of penning runes on the surface of the parts.

He wished there was a way he could have etched runes into the copper wire, but it was too thin.

"Should have done this before attaching everything," he muttered to himself, leaning over the crafting of a dog in an awkward hunch. He thought of it as a dog, but it could have been any four-legged animal; it didn't look much like anything.

It didn't really matter, either—the shape, the function, not the representation, was what was important.

Two fingers of the candle had burned by the time he finished. He had used three separate types of ink, with many pauses to rest his cramped fingers and consider the type and function of the rune before penning each.

Closing his eyes, he accessed his well and linked it to his construct. The runes flashed brightly, then dimmed to a steady glow, barely discernible in the candlelight. The animal shivered then and, at his urging, took a tentative step forward, and another. At the edge of the windowsill, it stopped. Caldan released a breath he hadn't realized he was holding.

He eyed his construct critically. As a first attempt, it was mediocre, he decided. Round wood was hard to draw runes on. *Perhaps if both the wire strips and the wood were flat . . .* They would still be thin, and hard to draw or etch on, but that seemed like the best option going forward.

He yawned, covering his mouth with his hand. He blew out the candle, took off his boots, and then slipped under the covers.

CALDAN WATCHED HIS wire and wood crafting closely. The energy his construct drew had started fluctuating wildly, a clear sign it had become unstable and would soon burn out. The jumbled shape stirred and straightened itself out, slowly unfolding until it stood on four legs.

Sure enough, a few minutes later the wooden segments began to smoke, and the wire slowly bent under great strain. A flash of light lit his room, the wood consumed instantly once the crafting holding it together crumbled under the strain. A pile of charcoal, ash, and twisted wire remained.

Waving away threads of smoke drifting up from the pile, Caldan coughed at the caustic fumes. He scraped the remains of his crafting from the top of his desk into a sack next to it on the floor, where it joined the rest of his burnt-out craftings. Still, it had lasted five days. He was improving, and faster than he had thought possible when he was at the monastery.

His trinket weighed against his chest. The rings felt comfortable there, and he was getting used to the constant feel of them inside his shirt. He drew the neck chain off and dropped the trinket onto his palm, leaving the bone ring on the chain. The silver ring felt heavy tonight. He rubbed a finger over the surface.

He knew he needed to wear it to study the ring properly, to use his senses in different situations, to see if it reacted under certain conditions. But he still couldn't wear it openly. Not yet. The best he could do was wear it when locked in his room and while he was asleep. Not the best situations for determining if it was a passive or an active trinket, but it was all he had for the moment.

He had seen the masters openly wear trinkets, mainly for practical reasons, as they used them in their work to augment their power. He now knew the only thing stopping the masters from being robbed of their trinkets, if caught out in public, was their ability to shield themselves. A shielded sorcerer couldn't be harmed by physical means, as long as his concentration held and his crafting could withstand the strain. And this skill, this talent, was what kept the majority of trinkets in the possession of the sorcerers. Talented sorcerers couldn't be robbed or harmed unless the situation came upon them so suddenly they couldn't access their well in time. Only a few journeymen had developed the strength to shield themselves, but all the masters had. He guessed it was one of the unspoken abilities that separated them from those they taught.

If the only way he could effectively study his trinket was to wear it, then being able to shield himself had to be one of his focuses. And to that end, he had borrowed a few books from the journeymen's library, as well as paying one of the senior journeymen for a few extra lessons. Teaching knowledge above an apprentice's level wasn't forbidden, but the extra lessons hadn't been easy to arrange . . . and didn't come cheap.

For now, he would have to content himself with studying the ring in private. Caldan slipped his trinket onto his finger and opened his well. From the surface of his desk, he picked up a metal medallion, an expensive crafting required to create a shield. This one he had purchased from a senior apprentice, who Caldan had heard was amenable to creating craftings for the apprentices' personal use. From what he could tell, it was cheaply made but sufficient for his purposes until he could obtain a better one.

Sitting on his bed cross-legged, back against the cool wall, he closed his eyes and concentrated.

CHAPTER 24

An apprentice sidled up beside Caldan. He was at least five years younger than Caldan and a good deal shorter. To be fair, *all* the apprentices around Caldan were younger and shorter, another thing that singled him out and separated him from their groups.

The young boy brushed back a lock of wavy blond hair from his eyes. "Any idea why the classroom is locked?" he asked.

A few of the other apprentices turned at the question.

"I have no idea," said Caldan.

"We thought, well, I thought they might have told you something since you are . . . you know . . . older."

Caldan shook his head. "No, they don't tell me any more than they tell you. I'm just another apprentice."

The rest of the apprentices turned back to waiting in the hall outside the classroom, except the one who had asked the question. He had a curious look on his face.

"'Just another apprentice,'" the boy mimicked, and gave a short laugh. "No one your age would be accepted unless they judged you had exceptional talent."

Caldan shrugged. "Anyone with talent is usually found earlier than me, that's all. There isn't anything special about me."

The boy looked unconvinced.

"Look," said Caldan. "In and around the major cities, children are tested young, right?"

The boy nodded.

"And if they show signs of talent, they're offered an apprenticeship. There's no mystery that, in out-of-the-way places, there are children and adults who were never tested and have talent but don't know it."

"I guess so."

"So there isn't anything special about me. In fact, I'm at a disadvantage. You have years to learn and take in all you can here. I've started late and way behind anyone my age."

"But what about—"

The boy broke off as Master Theunisen approached. Theunisen withdrew a key ring held to his belt by a chain and unlocked the door. He ushered them inside, closing and locking the door after them. The apprentices moved to their desks, eager to find out what was going on. Most readied pens and paper to take notes.

Theunisen cleared his throat loudly, and the students stopped their rustling. "You're probably wondering why the door was locked, so without further delay . . ." He opened a drawer in his desk and removed a narrow wooden box covered with inlaid metal runes.

Caldan could feel the master access his well, and he also felt a number of wards on the box being disarmed. He caught the faint scent of lemons. *Why lemons?* He'd noticed the smell before, when he unbound his ward on his door. This was new, and intriguing. Was he developing a sense for when sorcery was performed? He glanced around, but no one else was sniffing. He shrugged and brought his attention back to what the master had to say.

"The lesson today is on shielding," announced Theunisen. He opened the box to reveal rows of metal amulets. All the same size and shape, they were lined up one by one in slots built into the box.

Gasps came from the apprentices. Caldan grinned. Finally, they were going to study a skill he was interested in.

Theunisen ran a finger along the amulets, then looked out at his audience.

"The good news is that you're all sufficiently advanced to begin training in shielding yourselves, which is no small achievement. But the bad news—and isn't there always?"—he chuckled—"is that it's going to take a long time for you to master this skill, for even the most basic of shields." He paused, as if to let that sink in.

A shiver of excitement ran through Caldan. Extra lessons from a few of the senior journeymen had done wonders in developing his skill, but he was missing something, he was sure. He could hold a basic physical shield for an instant, but never longer than that. The effort it took to maintain the energies flowing around him through the crafting soon caused a pain in his head, and after a few attempts, he developed a headache. The journeymen mentioned "transference" and "the shaping loop" but wouldn't be drawn out further. Caldan couldn't figure out what he was doing wrong, and it was frustrating to be so close. He suspected his tutors were holding something back, and he hoped Theunisen would fill in those missing pieces.

Theunisen walked among the apprentices, stopping at each one to hand out a shielding amulet. As he did, he continued an explanation of the lesson. The amulet felt cool in Caldan's palm.

"The reason the door was locked today, you can probably guess, is because these amulets are extremely valuable, having been crafted a long time ago at great expense. They are true craftings, and what I mean is that the best metals were used to create them, and the masters who made them were among the best of their time. They have lasted over a hundred years and are expected to last many more centuries. Not as long as trinkets, perhaps, but long enough."

He handed an amulet to the last apprentice, then returned to his desk.

"All amulets are to be accounted for, by me, at the end of each class. You'll be allowed to use them during the class, but at the end of each session they are to be returned, no exceptions. Needless to say, the penalties for anyone caught stealing one of these craftings will be severe."

A few of the apprentices nodded. Why anyone would want to steal an amulet was beyond Caldan. Well, no . . . why someone would was obvious; why they'd think they could get away with it wasn't.

Caldan examined the amulet in his hand and found it not so different from the medallion he had secreted in his room. It was of a much better quality, but the runes and bindings used were similar. At least he knew the one he had bought should be sufficient to create a shield and he hadn't been sold a flawed crafting. With a quick glance at Theunisen, Caldan opened his well and used his senses to examine the amulet. As far as he could tell, it was virtually the same as his. Which meant the problem was with him—his understanding of the forces, or a lack of ability or practice on his part.

Theunisen continued. "From now on, many of your lessons will involve using craftings, all of which are valuable and will be kept under lock and key before and after lessons. The next few months are where the talented and the not so talented will be separated out. Those who can translate theory to practice are not rare, but it is the strength and quality of your crafting that will be assessed. Some"—he glanced at Caldan—"have already shown some aptitude but must not become complacent. Stretching yourself can lead to great progress. Of course, it also has its risks.

"The key will be concentration. The theoretical classes have prepared you for this. It's all a matter of putting what you have learned into practice."

Of course, converting theory to reality isn't easy.

Reaching into his drawer again, Theunisen produced another box. Inside were two lines of balls—one set of wood, the other of iron. The smallest were the size of a pea, and the largest were fist size.

Theunisen removed the smallest wooden ball and held it up to the room between his finger and thumb. "If any of you create a shield and sustain it for more than a moment, we can use this ball to test it." With a flick of his wrist, he sent the ball sailing over their heads, where it struck the back wall with a loud clack before dropping and rolling onto the floor.

"Don't worry," he said. "It won't hurt if it hits you—at least not much, anyway." He chuckled to himself. "If your shield holds, then we can test with the next size up. These balls are a gauge of how strong your shield is. The only way test a shield is to subject it to a force. I'm afraid all of you might have some bruises over the next few months, and it will take months for you to master this crafting skill. Be prepared for hard work and a little pain. You, boy." He pointed to the closest apprentice. "Fetch, please."

The apprentice scrambled to obey. As he picked the ball up and turned back to the master, Theunisen held a hand up, indicating for him to stop.

"First, a demonstration."

There was a collective intake of breath from the apprentices. Seeing shielding sorcery was rare, unless you were able to perform it yourself.

Theunisen drew out one of the amulets. In the blink of an eye, Caldan could feel him open his well, and immediately the master became surrounded in an indistinctness, a bending and twisting of light similar to heat haze on a hot day. Apprentices gawked, and a few grinned.

"Now, throw the ball at me."

The apprentice holding the ball hesitated.

"Come now, it wouldn't hurt even if I didn't have a shield. I'm sure you've wanted to throw something at a master—here's your chance."

With a glance around the room, the apprentice drew back his arm and threw the ball at Theunisen as hard as he could.

A wave of purple motes spread out on the shield from the impact. The ball dropped to the floor.

"The sparkles you see are the energy dissipating. The momentum of the ball is transferred to the shield and is absorbed."

The haze winked out of existence, and Theunisen stood there smiling. "It took me a month to be able to shape that shield and somewhat longer to perfect maintaining it as long as I wanted." There were groans from the apprentices. "I told you—it will come; you just have to keep working at it. You already know most of the theory, though there are some things you need to figure out yourselves."

Months, thought Caldan. He could only hope it wouldn't take that long—without the shield, he'd never wear his trinket.

Theunisen rubbed his chin and scowled at the apprentices. "Here is where your lessons become harder. You must turn theory into reality and be able to maintain that reality for long periods of time. In the beginning, it will be hard, but over time it becomes easier until it requires little effort. Now, enough time wasted. Concentrate. Get to work!"

Chair legs scraped on the floor as the apprentices shifted to comfortable positions, each holding an amulet tight in one hand. The room became quiet as they concentrated.

Theunisen opened a book and started reading. It looked like he wasn't expecting anyone to be able to create a shield anytime soon.

Exasperated, Caldan rubbed his amulet and opened his well. He needed to figure out why he couldn't hold a shield for more than a moment. The structures were there and correct, he was able to access his well without any problem, and the crafting in the amulet was fine. The issue must be his understanding and application of the theory.

He closed his eyes and concentrated. He brought up a shield, and again, after a moment, it fizzled out. Opening an eye, he glanced around. All the other apprentices had their eyes closed, so no one had noticed his shield pop into and out of existence. He had worried that it might raise questions if he showed progress so early, but he dismissed that almost immediately.

It's time to forge my own path—risks be damned.

The good thing was that he was now being allotted a moment in his hectic schedule to actually study and practice, and he planned to use these lessons to see if he could work out why his shield wasn't holding for long. The time was a bonus he hadn't reckoned on having, so he was definitely going to take advantage of it.

He opened his well again and linked himself to the amulet, this time leaving his eyes open. The runes for linking glowed faintly along with the bridging runes, which allowed his well to provide energy to the crafting. The shield surrounded the individual, though some craftings could surround a much larger area, such as the craftings the sorcerers created for the empire's forges and metal cast-works.

But why did the shield only hold for such a short time?

He thought about Theunisen's purple motes of light . . . what had he said? They were his shield absorbing the energy of the projectile. *But where did that energy go? The shield took a fixed amount to maintain, didn't it?*

But how could it, if it was being used to stop external forces, like projectiles? Energy from his well must have to fluctuate, or there was a buffer of some sort. Or it could be constantly renewed from the well to maintain stability . . . which meant it had to somehow *return* energy to his well. Could it be that simple?

What if . . .

Turning the amulet over, he examined the runes on the other side. Another linking rune and more bridging runes. It also had the standard physical shielding runes and a few others. The linking rune was different, though.

He couldn't get his well to link to it. The energy wouldn't flow through from his well. He examined some of the other runes, recalling the many lessons at the monastery. And that's when inspiration hit him: *They act as a buffer, storing excess energy until it can be siphoned off so the crafting won't be damaged by spikes of force flowing through it!* So the other linking rune, *that* was the key. If the energy of the shield was to remain stable, it had to be constantly renewed. "Transference" and "the shaping loop," then—which their journeymen teachers had taught them—were the most important parts of the shield. Caldan sighed. It figured. If you started paying someone for something, they might try to string you along for a protracted time, especially if you paid well. He would just have to find someone else who wouldn't hold back information.

He looked back at the amulet.

This second linking must be in the opposite direction to the first, which means it transfers energy back into my well. But that means splitting my well into two strings . . . This wasn't a concept taught at the monastery. Either the masters there wanted apprentices to figure it out themselves, or they hadn't known.

Caldan focused on his well and *twisted* . . . like so . . . He trembled all over, and sweat prickled his skin. He'd never needed to split his well into two separate strings. His mind felt drained. Clearly the masters could create more than two strings from their wells, but he didn't think he could do it without more practice. Everything he had crafted needed only one link to his well to draw power from. Yet, the possibilities were exciting. He could see how he could create more versatile craftings with more than one string; stronger ones, too.

Caldan took a breath and tried again. As he split his well, he connected one string to the rune that powered the shield, then the other to what he thought of as the transference rune.

He felt the usual tightening of his skin, and his vision blurred as the shield sprang up around him. He smelled hot metal, as if he stood next to a forge, and again, lemons . . .

Caldan counted to ten. His shield remained. He counted to ten again. The shield stayed stable. He spread his senses out to it, feeling the flow of energy from and back into his well. Smooth and flawless, like a deep swift stream.

He could feel the shield wasn't going to collapse and dissipate. He grinned in delight. Success!

An object struck his shield and a cascade of purple sparkles spread all over him, an inch from his clothing. He felt the buffer draw them in before his shield overloaded, then dissipate them into his well. His shield held firm. Whatever had hit it hadn't been powerful enough to penetrate.

He cut both links.

All the apprentices stared at him in astonishment, while Theunisen was on his feet with a thoughtful look on his face.

Caldan shrugged. "Sorry?" he said.

Whispers started among the apprentices.

Theunisen nodded. "Would you be so kind as to retrieve the ball, please."

Caldan gave a quick nod and looked at the floor. A large wooden ball half the size of his fist lay there. Not the largest in the testing box, but almost. He swallowed.

Retrieving the ball, he moved to the front of the room and handed it to Theunisen. He made as if to go back to his desk.

"Not so fast," said Theunisen, his hand coming down on Caldan's shoulder. He turned him to face the room. "It seems one of you is learning more quickly than anticipated. Which is just as well, since he has a lot of catching up to do."

A few of the apprentices were smiling at him, some in genuine admiration. The young boy with wavy blond hair who had spoken to him before the class raised both hands and gave him a silent round of applause, grinning all the while.

"Today," Theunisen said, "you have been shown what you are all capable of with hard work and dedication. A month or so earlier than this usually happens," he said wryly, to the laughter of some apprentices.

His expression became stern. "Remember this day. This is what you are working toward. Okay, get back to work. It is the rest of you who have a lot to learn now."

At his words, the apprentices turned their attention to their own amulets with renewed vigor. Caldan felt their wells open, but no shields sprang up. He turned back to Theunisen.

"What now?" he said.

"Well, that is only the first shield you need to master. Unfortunately, I don't have amulets for the others here yet, since I didn't think they would be necessary for a while, but no matter." He shrugged. "Take the rest of the morning off. Relax and absorb what you have learned. I'll bring other shielding craftings to the next class."

"But shouldn't I stay here and practice?"

"No," Theunisen replied emphatically. "You know what you did and how the shield works. Can you honestly say you need to practice it?"

"No, I guess not. Once you know it and can do it, you know it."

"Exactly." He pushed Caldan toward the door. "Ah, I almost forgot." He held out a hand. "The amulet, if you will."

"Couldn't I keep it for a while? To study."

"No."

Worth a shot.

"But well done. You took a big step forward today."

Caldan nodded and grinned. "Thank you."

CHAPTER 25

Caldan shifted uncomfortably in his seat. The thin cushion between him and the sturdy bench was padding enough, but something else was making him prickly. He rubbed the back of his neck with one hand and scratched his head.

He leaned against the bench, his right hand touching his trinket on his middle finger, tracing over the engraved patterns. Since acquiring the shield medallion and learning how to use it, he'd decided to wear his ring in the open, despite the risk. From everything he had read, and all the information from talking to various masters, his best chance to find out the function of his ring was to wear it at all times. Some books even suggested that an affinity grew between a person and a trinket when the person wore it for extended periods. What they all said was that not knowing what you were dealing with and opening your well to a trinket could have damaging or even deadly consequences.

Although his ring felt noticeable on his hand, he realized it was probably all in his mind, the effect of wearing something he wasn't used to.

Looking around, Caldan took in the main room of the establishment in which Izak Fourie had asked to meet him for lunch. Yesterday, after meeting Miranda for a cheap evening meal at a street stall—and promising yet again that the good meal he owed her would be forthcoming soon—he had dropped into the Yawning Rabbit on the way back and had run into Izak, who pressed him into meeting the next day.

Although it was early afternoon, Izak had stated the meeting was for lunch, and for someone like Izak, it probably was. Caldan had eaten a substantial meal with the other apprentices before making his way to the eating house Izak recommended, which was indicated only by a nondescript sign depicting a bowl and a spoon.

Inside was clean and tidy. Long benches with low backs surrounded tables. A number of patrons sat in twos and threes, with a few larger groups. Caldan could pick out most of what was said around him; the place didn't lend itself to much privacy. All the patrons wore good-quality clothes, and many pieces of jewelry were in evidence. Obviously this was somewhere well-to-do folk came for a leisurely meal and idle conversation.

A jug of heavily watered wine had been placed on the table in front of him as soon as he sat down, along with two cups. He had told them he was expecting a friend to join him. He took a sip. Good wine, as far as he could tell.

His cup was half-empty when he saw Izak approach. As usual, he was dressed well: dark pants with a white linen shirt. Not a hair on his head looked out of place, and his gray goatee had been combed. Trailing behind him was a pudgy man around the same age, with a pasty, flaccid face, dark eyes, and wrinkled clothes of a much lower quality than Izak's. He was sweating slightly, Caldan noted, though the day wasn't particularly warm.

"Ah, Caldan," Izak gushed with a broad smile. "I must apologize for my lateness. I slept in and barely had time to freshen up before I had to leave. It's been weeks since we've had a proper chance to catch up."

The pudgy man stood silently behind Izak, glancing around the room, eyes lingering on the other patrons in view, hands wringing nervously.

"It has been a while," said Caldan. "My studies have kept me busy. You look fine to me. I see you brought a friend."

"Oh, of course. Allow me to introduce you to an acquaintance of mine, Sir Avigdor."

The man stepped forward and offered his hand. It felt like shaking warm porridge. Caldan nodded in greeting as Izak seated himself opposite, then looked around and raised a hand to catch a waiter's eye. Sir Avigdor also looked around the room and ran a hand down his shirt, as if to smooth the fabric. He shuffled to a seat next to Izak. Caldan sat back on his thin cushion and surreptitiously wiped his now damp hand on his pants.

Having failed to catch a waiter's eye in the few moments he had been trying, Izak rose to his feet. "Excuse me," he said. "I'll see what the delay is all about and order us something to eat. And drink." He waved a hand at them. "You two can get better acquainted." He strode off without waiting for a reply, straight to the bar.

Sir Avigdor watched him go. "I hear you play Dominion well," he said in a voice nothing like his appearance—cultured, with a hard edge. "So Izak says, and so my employer says. Sometimes Izak is right, but my employer . . . she is always right." He reached across for the jug of wine and poured a drink into the spare mug. "Do you mind?"

"Not at all." Caldan eyed him warily across the table. The pieces fell into place. "Lady Felicienne?"

Avigdor raised an eyebrow. "Good. Very good." He cleared his throat. "She is upset you've not taken her up on her . . . generous offer as yet. Izak and I are friends, however, and Lady Felicienne has prevailed upon me to have Izak meet you here. You see, she doesn't like unpaid debts, if you catch my meaning."

"I do. Could you please convey my apologies to her. My studies don't leave much time at the moment, and there were a few . . . issues I had to sort out first."

Avigdor sniffed the wine and wrinkled his nose, then sipped from his mug and grimaced. He was obviously used to better-quality wine, despite the impression his outward appearance gave.

Guess I don't know that much about wine, Caldan thought. He'd underestimated Sir Avigdor. He might dress the fool, but he clearly did it to conceal the calm, calculating mind beneath the clothes.

Avigdor put his cup down. "Ah yes, the sorcerers. I've heard their training can be hard. More than a few apprentices have left broken, physically or mentally." His gaze held Caldan's.

Caldan shrugged and tried to look nonchalant. "It's been fine. Nothing too strenuous or demanding."

"Wake at dawn, physical exercises, classes in history, geography, alchemy, medicine and . . . crafting. Nothing too strenuous or demanding?" Avigdor drawled. "Many apprentices would disagree with you, I am sure."

"I'm used to studying and training hard." Caldan searched for Izak and found him still at the bar talking to the barman. He looked back at Avigdor, who was watching him closely.

He wasn't sure he liked where this was going. "The training the Protectors put the apprentices through is hard, but as I said, I'm used to it."

"The sorcerers, you mean."

"No, I'm apprenticed with the Protectors."

Avigdor's mouth opened in shock, then closed abruptly. His lips curved into a sly smile. "An apprentice Protector, you say?" He leaned forward. "Listen, I'm all for trying to wring some advantage out of a negotiation, but you had best keep your arguments honest and not so . . ." He waved a hand in the air. "Laughable. I thought you were supposed to be an excellent Dominion player."

"Are you suggesting I'm lying?"

"Are you suggesting you're telling the truth?"

"Why would I lie? Wouldn't someone like Lady Felicienne easily discover if I misled her?"

Avigdor sat back and folded his arms across his chest, looking squarely at him. He sat quietly before reaching over and taking a swallow of his wine. Again he grimaced at the taste, shaking his head and giving a quick grin.

"I forgot myself and took another sip." He gave a deprecating laugh. "It takes a lot to unsettle me these days. But you are right—you would be a fool to lie to me . . . and my lady. So a Protector . . ."

"What's wrong with the Protectors?"

"Nothing. In fact, they are quite impressive. They have fine alchemists, sorcerers, and sword fighters among their ranks."

"Then what's so startling?"

"They don't have apprentices."

Caldan scoffed. "Of course they do. I'm one! There are apprentices everywhere. I have classes with them every day."

"Do you? With apprentice sorcerers or apprentice smith-crafters, I would judge." Avigdor looked at him intently. "Have you met another apprentice Protector?"

"Of course I have! Why . . ." His voice trailed off as he thought about it.

All the students studying sword fighting, surely they are apprentice Protectors? But if they are, why don't they room near me? Caldan had assumed it was because he joined so late, but it didn't change the fact that the rooms around his were populated by journeymen Protectors, not apprentices. He frowned. "Strange," he muttered.

"Indeed. Curious, I must say, and highly unexpected." Avigdor was nodding slowly, and Caldan knew he was storing the knowledge away. "My mistress will be interested in such news."

"Then that means she owes me double."

Avigdor coughed into a hand. "If that information wasn't free, then you shouldn't have shared it." He laughed at Caldan's embarrassment, and Caldan moved to leave. *I don't need to be laughed at by a man I hardly know.*

"Now, now—don't be so sensitive. As you said, she would have found out about you if she wanted to anyway, so what did you really reveal? Sit down, please."

Reluctantly, Caldan resumed his seat on the uncomfortable bench.

"Good. Shall we get down to business? I was told you needed information. On what?"

Caldan placed his hand on the table, fingers spread. His trinket glimmered between them.

Avigdor whistled slowly. "That's a valuable piece for an apprentice to have. If I were you, I wouldn't wear it until I could protect myself."

"I can. Don't worry about me."

"Well, it's your funeral." Avigdor leaned forward for a closer inspection. "Lions, and a knotwork pattern. Rare, I would say, but I'm not an expert on trinkets."

"But can you help me find out more about it?"

"Is that what you want information on, then?"

Caldan nodded.

"Oh yes, most certainly. We have access to Anasoma's trinket records, which mirror the capital's—albeit with a few months' delay. Descriptions, functions, owners past and present. They're all there."

Caldan breathed a sigh of relief, though he still felt nervous. This was more than he could have achieved on his own. Far more. But what would be revealed? Would the information be valuable enough to Avigdor and Felicienne that they would use it to his disadvantage? Frowning, he hesitated, then spoke. "I trust this will stay between us? I mean, whatever you find, you'll pass only to me and not anyone else?"

Avigdor's gaze grew curious. "What do you expect me to find?"

"I really don't know, but it might have led to my family being . . . killed, when I was young."

"I'm sorry to hear that. Though this makes it more interesting." He placed his hand on his heart. "I promise whatever I find will be shared with only you. And my mistress, of course."

Caldan nodded again. There wasn't much he could do about it anyway. The truth was, now that Avigdor knew what his trinket looked like, he could find the information, no matter what Caldan wanted.

"Do you need a sketch or a rubbing of the design?"

Avigdor tapped his temple with a finger. "It's all here. I have a knack for remembering details."

No doubt why Lady Felicienne keeps him in her employ.

"Give me a few days," Avigdor said. "I can send a message to Izak?"

Though Izak was friendly, Caldan wasn't sure he trusted him yet. "To the Protectors would be better, addressed to me."

"They might wonder why I would send you correspondence."

Caldan shrugged.

Amused, Avigdor continued. "Is there anything else you can tell me about its origins?"

And there's the rub: How much to tell? "All I know," Caldan began, "is that my parents and grandparents may have worked for the empire, though in what capacity, I have no idea. Other than that, I have nothing to go on."

"Well, in a few days you will have something more. If there's any information on that ring, I'll find it. And then Lady Felicienne's debt to you will be paid."

At that moment, Izak appeared at the table with a steaming pot of coffee and three glazed mugs. Beside him, a serving girl placed a tray holding two jars on the table. Each had the handle of a spoon poking out the top. Izak thanked her with a smile, then shooed her away when she inquired if they needed anything further.

"Well, I hope you two have been getting along while I was gone," Izak said.

"We were," answered Avigdor. "Coffee, I trust?"

At Izak's nod, Avigdor helped himself to a cup, went to place the pot back on the table, stopped, then poured a cup for both Izak and Caldan.

"Sorry, not used to serving other people," he said.

Izak waved his apology away. "Quite all right, my friend. Who is?" He laughed. "What was the topic of conversation before I rudely interrupted?"

Avigdor reached for both jars. "Your friend Caldan here was telling me he has become apprenticed to the Protectors."

Izak looked quickly at Avigdor and blinked a few times before his gaze moved to Caldan. "That's . . ." He cleared his throat. "Could you pass the honey and salt, please? This coffee isn't to my taste."

Avigdor passed the two jars across to Izak, who opened both and sprinkled a pinch of salt into his cup before stirring in a generous dollop of honey.

"I wasn't aware this was anything out of the ordinary," said Caldan. "There are a lot of apprentices in the guild, and I assumed a fair few were apprentice Protectors. What's wrong?"

Izak shook his head slowly. "Nothing. It's just surprising."

"Very surprising," added Avigdor.

"Hush," Izak said, and frowned at him.

"Don't hush me."

"Just drink your coffee while I explain some things to young Caldan here."

Avigdor muttered into his cup as Izak glared at him. To Caldan, they sounded like two old friends grumbling at each other. He took a sip of his own coffee. His stomach rumbled. Despite eating with the apprentices, he was already starving, but both Izak and Avigdor looked like they had no interest in eating yet. He sighed.

Izak sucked in a breath and turned to Caldan. "Are you sure you're an apprentice Protector?" he asked. "Not just an apprentice in the Sorcerers' Guild?"

"Yes. I spoke to Master Simmon at length, and he asked me to become an apprentice Protector. Those were his words. What's so strange anyway?"

"The Sorcerers' Guild has many apprentices, and all of them have talent in crafting, am I correct?"

Caldan nodded slowly. "Yes, to varying degrees. Though they all have other talents, too." He'd heard some talented apprentices went to study in the capital, paid for by the guild.

"Tell him how the Protectors choose their members," said Avigdor.

"I was getting to that," snapped Izak testily, glaring at him again. He looked at Caldan. "From what I understand, the Protectors choose from the apprentices recently promoted to journeymen, but not just the ones who are the most talented in sorcery or crafting. They also choose people who have other skills as well, including sword fighting, smith-crafting, or alchemy. Not much is known about who they choose or why, to be honest. What happened with you? What did Simmon say?"

His questions were casual, but Caldan could sense a sudden intensity to his gaze, and even Avigdor's posture straightened as Izak asked.

"What department did you say you were in? That Lady Felicienne runs?" he asked Avigdor.

The man smiled, his pasty face shiny with a thin sheen of sweat. "I didn't. And that's the best question you've asked so far." His eyes glittered with amusement. "Probably the first question you should have asked."

"Lady Felicienne is a Third Adjudicator, that much I know. But what does that mean?"

"By itself," said Avigdor, "not much. And I won't tell you all that much more. Let's just say that while we *do* gather information on all sorts of things, our real challenge is to interpret it, to make sense of the information, to piece together facts from different sources and see patterns . . . conceptual reasoning, if you will."

Patterns, thought Caldan. "Hence Lady Felicienne's interest in me, and yours. Playing Dominion is hard enough. To be good you have to be able to see patterns where others cannot."

Both Avigdor and Izak nodded.

Caldan's stomach rumbled . . . again. What was up with him? He'd just eaten a large meal. "Can we order some food?" he asked. "With the training I've been doing, I need to—"

"It's coming," interrupted Izak.

"I could use some, too," said Avigdor, patting his belly.

"You could lose some weight," commented Izak.

"And you should eat more," snapped Avigdor. "All skin and bones; no meat on you. Anyway, back to what I was saying. A good Dominion player *is* likely to excel at what we do. I say likely, not guaranteed. You see, some people . . . well, they see the patterns in Dominion but have a hard time applying the same skill to human interactions and events. Mostly, these are the same scholars you would find spending their days in a library or secreted away doing their own research. We need people who can see patterns but also are able to relate to the world outside their window."

"And Izak provides you pieces of this pattern?"

"Very good," said Avigdor, genuine admiration on his face. "Yes—Izak and I do business sometimes, in rumor, information."

Izak looked pained. "I'm not so low as to sell rumors."

Avigdor grinned, showing a set of surprisingly perfect teeth. "Call it what you will. But knowledge is power, and there are people who pay good ducats for a nice morsel."

A serving girl appeared, bearing another tray. She placed covered dishes on the table, along with a plate and a fork for each of them.

Avigdor peered at the dishes. "I hope you ordered enough for us, not as if three of you were eating."

Izak's face broke out in mock pain. "Please," he said. "Give me some credit. I know what an active youth and an . . . overindulged adult can go through. Luckily, you're paying."

Avigdor raised his eyebrows and sighed. "As usual." He lifted the lid off the dish closest to him. "What have we here, noodles?"

"Should be noodles, almond eggs, fish with onions, rabbit in wine, and some fried spinach with garlic," said Izak.

Avigdor gave an approving nod and set to with a will, taking a good portion of each before waving them to do the same. Izak waited until they were both done before taking a portion of a couple of dishes. They ate in silence for a while before Izak spoke.

"You see, Caldan," he explained through a mouthful, "I'm part of several circles—nobles, merchants, businessmen, and the like—and, well . . . if a harmless piece of information comes my way, I let Avigdor here know. As a friend."

"As a friend," repeated Caldan. "Of course."

"Good! I see you understand. And friends help each other. That's what friends are for."

"I guess, but—"

As if reading Caldan's mind, Izak said, "We're all friends here now. It's just a shame you're with the Protectors, though."

"I might have offered you a job otherwise," Avigdor added. "Yes, too bad." He eyed his clean plate and the empty dishes sadly. With a sigh, he sat back.

Caldan looked at them both, then ran a hand across his short hair. From exile to numerous job offers—life in Anasoma was suddenly rife with opportunity.

"Gentlemen," he said, finally voicing what he had arrived at as the true purpose of this meeting. "I think I shouldn't leave the Protectors after all they've done for me so far."

"Oh, I wasn't suggesting you should," said Avigdor. "More to the point, I don't think you could *leave*. You see, no one leaves the Protectors."

Caldan stared at them. "What do you mean?"

"Protectors die Protectors. Whether from old age or earlier. I've never heard of anyone leaving their ranks for any reason," said Avigdor. "Never."

Caldan shook his head. "No. There must be people who have left. Who got tired of the life, wanted to spend more time with their family or something."

Avigdor and Izak both shook their heads. It was a long moment before Izak spoke. "Be sure of what you are getting into, young Caldan. Avigdor here wouldn't take you now. He couldn't. If you swore an oath to the Protectors, then they would see you as theirs."

A silence fell over them. Caldan chewed a fingernail and thought back to what Master Simmon had said during their meeting. Simmon hadn't come out and said so, but anyone caught leaking the Protectors' secrets would have to be silenced.

"You look pale," said Izak. "Here, have a top-up, and make sure you drink it all down." He lifted the pot and poured more coffee into Caldan's cup.

Caldan gulped a couple of deep swallows, not tasting the drink.

"Listen, Caldan," said Izak. "I wouldn't be too concerned, if I were you. We don't have a lot of information about the Protectors, so it's likely we are wrong. They probably have rules or guidelines we know nothing about. It could be that people have left them, but it isn't widely known."

Caldan began to shake his head, then stopped. He remembered Master Simmon's words, and they echoed in his head. *Some things are too dangerous to be known.*

"As it is, I can only wish you luck," said Avigdor.

They spent the next few minutes in silence. Avigdor checked his pocket watch a few times, once frowning at it and shaking the case. Izak and Avigdor talked quietly between themselves, meaningless chatter, leaving Caldan alone to his thoughts.

Caldan, for his part, didn't know what to think. Was he lucky to have found a place where he was paid to continue studying what he loved, or was it a honey-coated trap? Judging by what Master Simmon said, he thought the Protectors had a noble cause, one he could identify with, especially knowing the information the master had imparted to him with such passion. Men like that were passionate only about what they believed in.

He gritted his teeth, frustrated. Maybe they were making too much of this. So far, he had been treated the same as any other apprentice. No one had given him any reason to distrust them. In fact, the masters had all been pleasant enough. Nothing to worry about, surely. Well, he would have to keep his eyes and ears open. A *sound strategy, anyway, for a new apprentice in a new city.*

The late lunch ended with small talk, of the weather and the current building projects the emperor had decreed. Avigdor commented on the recent increase in tax evaders and criminals who were sentenced to hard labor on the building projects. Izak agreed it was best to keep them off the streets and from bothering honest folk.

Caldan said nothing.

They shook hands and departed in different directions. Izak rushed off, citing an urgent appointment.

Caldan walked slowly through the streets back to his room. At this pace, he would miss his early afternoon class in metallurgy, but he already knew what they were covering anyway.

And none of it included the answers he was looking for.

CHAPTER 26

Caldan spent a good part of the next few days experimenting with his shielding medallion, trying to find out what its limits were. He kept up with his regular lessons and physical training under the watchful eyes of the journeymen and masters, but every spare chance he had he used to investigate the medallion. The engravings on this crafting were sloppy, and from his metallurgy studies he knew the metal was inferior. If he could decipher how it worked, he could make another, and probably a better one.

Caldan sat at a table in the apprentices' workshop of the smith-crafting wing. The workshop was a good forty paces square, with thick beams crossing the ceiling. A furnace lay in the center, glowing coals giving the place a warm feel to go with the heat, and the not unpleasant odor of burning coal ash filled the air.

Only a few other apprentices were in the room with Caldan, busy with their own work. Those who had the ducats to experiment with metal craftings, or those who were particularly talented, conducting research given to them by a master.

He held a piece of paper on which he had roughly sketched his medallion and the crafting runes engraved on the surface. To the right, he listed the alloy it was made from, and underneath, other variations of the alloy he thought would be better suited to the task. The monastery had been advanced in this area; indeed, he believed he could teach the masters here a few things, though thinking back to his conversation with Izak and Avigdor, he might be better off holding his knowledge close.

Caldan slid his shielding medallion under his sheet of paper to hide it from a casual observer. Opening his well, he touched the medallion with a finger and extended his senses. Touch wasn't necessary, but it helped to establish a firmer link and required less concentration. And there was less chance any of the apprentices in the room would feel what he was doing.

Unbalanced. He frowned and split his well into two, one string to examine the metals, while the other linked to the runes. Yes, the metal was strained, as if barely holding together; the glyphs did the job adequately but were rough and poorly cast. Tiny pockmarks covered the surface, where a good casting would be smooth. It was barely able to perform the function it had been designed for. And the metal felt wrong for the task; it had probably been something else melted down for the materials to save ducats.

As a shielding medallion, it sufficed; as smith-crafting, it was an abomination. All the parts were there to create a whole—the metal to withstand a well; linking and bridging runes, a basic buffer—but the object was crude. If this was the standard of the journeymen, Caldan felt for the masters and what they had to deal with.

He sighed for the poor workmanship and for his own loss of ducats on such a piece. At least it worked, if only just. And perhaps he could alter the medallion so it wasn't as unstable.

He reached across the table and chose a fine scribing tool. He considered the implement for a few moments before placing it back in its leather case. Tampering with the runes cast into the medallion would be a last resort, as too much could go wrong. Since it worked as it was, he should first look at the crafting.

Pushing his awareness into the medallion, he focused on the linkages, the streams that tied the separate parts into a whole. As he suspected, the rough glyphs combined with the flawed metal caused some linkages to be better than others, more "open" and able to carry a greater load. But as all good crafters knew, the links were only as good as the weakest one. Any differences meant the flow from someone's well would bottleneck, leading to energy bleeding, and that wasn't good. With such a rough casting, the metal could break under the strain.

Reaching deeper, Caldan connected his well to the linking runes and felt his skin tighten as the shield sprang up and surrounded him. He followed the lines of force through the links, seeing where they flowed properly and where they pooled or were impeded. One in particular stood out. The flow from his well almost stopped when it hit it; only a trickle came through. *If I can add a link, one to supplement that one . . .* Concentrating hard, he formed another in his mind and joined the two ends around the problem link.

His finger grew hot, and he snatched it back. A glow appeared through the paper covering the medallion. It burst into flames.

"By the ancestors!" cursed Caldan and slammed his left hand down on the paper. Skin sizzled.

"Argggh!"

He raced to the tempering barrels, plunging his hand into the one filled with water. Behind him, apprentices gasped in surprise, then rushed toward his bench. One splashed a bowl of water over the burning paper, which extinguished with a hiss. The room buzzed with commotion.

"Ancestors, what happened?" shouted someone.

"His paper caught alight," said another apprentice. "One moment everything was fine, and the next, flames."

Someone grasped Caldan's shoulder. "Are you hurt?"

He turned to look at the apprentice, hand stinging. "I'm fine, just an accident." His thoughts raced. What should he say? He wasn't supposed to have the medallion. A few apprentices had gathered around the table he was working at. One used a rag to wipe at the wet paper and ashes. At that moment, a journeyman came in, drawn no doubt by the commotion.

Caldan pulled his hand from the water. A red circle scored the skin of his palm. The throbbing had subsided, and his hand felt sore but not overly painful.

"Excuse me," he said to the apprentice next to him. "I'd better see the journeyman."

Caldan closed his left hand into a fist to cover the mark. He had no idea what he would say about the medallion, nor what the penalties would be for having such an object in his possession, let alone experimenting on it. Taking a deep breath, he approached his workbench, where the journeyman and a number of apprentices stood.

"Journeyman, please forgive me. I was—"

"So this is your doing?" interrupted the journeyman. "Reckless experimentation, I assume. And what's this?" He poked a finger into a hole in the table. It went in up to the second knuckle. "Unless I miss my guess, there's metal in there. Melted its way into the wood. What if it had exploded?"

"Exploded?"

"Yes. Ex-plo-ded. Don't they teach you anything these days? One thing I know they do teach you is not to try crafting anything yourself until a master has looked over the designs and the workmanship before linking it. Did you fall asleep during that lesson?"

"What? No, I—"

"Make sure you clean this mess up. I don't know what you can do with the hole in the workbench." He eyed Caldan. "You know I have to report this, attempting to construct a crafting without supervision."

"I'm sorry. I should have known better." He bowed his head in contrition, though inside he was relieved. Tampering with the medallion had caused it to melt and the paper to burn. He was down a considerable sum of ducats and now had no way to shield himself, but luckily, the metal melting had hidden the fact he'd had a working shield crafting in his possession.

"You should have, especially at your age. You need to demonstrate that you have better control of yourself."

"I should have known better," Caldan said again.

The journeyman only nodded curtly before dismissing the apprentices who had gathered around. They wandered back to their places. Their numbers had swelled since the commotion. A few in other rooms had heard, or word had passed around. Caldan saw some engaged in animated talk and hand gestures, probably enjoying a laugh at his expense.

With another dark look at Caldan, the journeyman turned and left. Caldan needed to find out what the penalties were for his transgression.

He wiped the remaining water and ash mess with a rag and poked his finger into the hole in the workbench. It touched metal at the bottom, still warm and smooth. He used a knife to retrieve the chunk. It would be worth a small amount of ducats but nowhere near the cost of the working medallion. With a sigh, he left the apprentices' workshop, sure that more than a few eyes were on his back as he walked out the door.

Now that he knew consequences could be worse than the crafting simply cracking or disintegrating, he would have to be more careful—that is, if he could get his hands on another shield crafting in the first place.

Obtaining the medallion had been expensive and, he now realized, ill-advised. Entering the Sorcerers' Guild with its resources and training was a stroke of luck he couldn't have dreamed of when his ship disembarked.

And like a fool he was endangering that opportunity.

Caldan's thoughts returned to his purse of ducats locked in his room. Not enough for another shield crafting, even if he was of a mind to purchase one. Odds were that news of his mistake today would travel like wildfire, and anyone usually willing to sell a crafting, even one as badly made as the medallion, wouldn't want to deal with him lest it be traced back to them. His chances of purchasing one from the journeymen were slim to none.

There was only one solution. He needed to draw on his own talent and construct the crafting himself.

AN HOUR LATER, he was back in his room. Materials would be a problem. The runes and design he knew well already, though it would be best if he could obtain a working crafting to model his own from. He could try to study the ones in class more closely, but it would be better if he could take it out with him as a reference.

Not likely, he thought.

Someone knocked on his door, and he opened it to reveal a solemn-looking Master Simmon.

"What have you gotten yourself into?" Simmon asked rhetorically. "Come, let's get this over with."

In the end, the whole ordeal wasn't as bad as Caldan thought. A first offense and no one injured. Penalties amounted to a stern talking-to, some extra training to "keep his mind on his development," as one master put it, and a fine of ten silver ducats. The masters wasted no time and sent him packing within minutes of seeing him.

Back in his room, Caldan sat on his bed, back against the wall. Some solid thinking was in order. The ten silver ducats hurt the most. He needed all he had to purchase the metals for his crafting, and if he couldn't use the apprentices' workshop, he was in a pickle.

His stomach rumbled, and his thoughts turned from money to food—which in turn reminded him he still owed Miranda their long-delayed dinner. Now that too would have to wait.

The day had been a complete disaster.

"AH, CALDAN, THERE you are." An apprentice sorcerer hurried up to him, slightly out of breath. She carried a leather satchel and ignored him a moment while she rummaged through it.

"I've been looking for you everywhere," continued the girl. "This came for you." She held out a sealed letter.

Caldan's breath caught in his throat.

"Take it. I haven't got all day. The rest of these need to be delivered."

He took the letter—expensive paper, smooth in his fingers—noting the plain seal of yellowish beeswax imprinted with what looked like a bird. On the front, in a neat feminine hand, was his name, *Sorcerers' Guild—Protectors*, and the words *Deliver Soonest*.

"Ahem."

He looked up to see the girl still standing there, hand outstretched, palm up. She raised her eyebrows at him.

"Oh, sorry," Caldan said as he fumbled in his pocket for his coin pouch, taking out a copper ducat and handing it over.

The girl smiled before turning heel and hurrying off.

Caldan turned the letter over, noting nothing unusual, apart from the quality paper. He didn't recognize the seal, but there was only one letter he was expecting.

Lady Felicienne.

Abandoning his errand, Caldan scurried back to his room, closing and locking the door behind him. He sat on his bed, broke the seal, and drew the letter out. After reading a few lines of the same feminine script, he was left in no doubt it was from Lady Felicienne.

> *Dear Caldan,*
>
> *Forgive my familiarity, but after the other night, I feel we already know each other well. Not as well as we could have, had you taken up my offer to escort me home, but I understand your reluctance.*
>
> *We need to meet to discuss Avigdor's findings on your trinket. Please come to my offices in the keep at your earliest convenience. And by that I mean as soon as you receive this letter. Don't keep me waiting.*
>
> *I should inform you that this doesn't discharge my debt to you. In ordinary circumstances, I would count it as paid, but . . . there is one reservation, which I will detail later.*
>
> *—Felice*

Caldan glanced out the window at the darkening sky. Sunset was close, but Felicienne did say as soon as he received her letter. What had she uncovered that was so urgent? Could it be related to his family's murder? No, he thought it unlikely that whatever was in the trinket records could have led to her finding anything on that. But something had Felicienne intrigued, at least.

And that worried him.

He stood and paced his room for a while but couldn't pull away from the fact that he wanted to see Felicienne and find out what she now knew. Any danger he envisioned was probably in his imagination.

AT THE KEEP, Lady Felicienne's letter drove away any reluctance the guards showed him, and he was passed swiftly along through various functionaries until one deposited him in a room with instructions to wait. A short time later, Lady Felicienne walked in. She looked as he remembered, slender, with plain but expensive shirt and pants, though now her hair hung loose, making her face softer, less serious.

Felicienne gestured for Caldan to take a seat, then gathered up a few sheets of paper before she spoke. "I'm a bit pressed for time, I'm afraid. I've been receiving reports of some strange goings-on. I only wish I had more solid information." She shook her head as if to clear it. "Now, to your problem. Our people are very efficient, otherwise I wouldn't employ them. It didn't take long to find what they were after; the empire's records on trinkets are quite thorough."

At her mention of trinkets Caldan had to stop his hand from reaching up to touch his ring, which hung from its chain around his neck, along with the bone ring. Without a shield crafting he couldn't risk wearing the trinket on his finger. "Forgive me, Lady Felicienne, but this was all I was after. The information, I mean. Anything you found will be enough."

"Please, call me Felice. And I have quite a bit of information on your trinket. It makes for a fascinating story."

Caldan's heart thumped in his chest, and he hardly dared breathe. "Is that it?" he asked softly, nodding at the paper she held. Would the page reveal the answers he'd been looking for? After all this time, would it be so easy?

"Yes. Your trinket's history is quite interesting, especially since the last known entry on it was over a hundred years old. Purchased by the emperor's procurers, no less, from a bankrupt noble family, then it was presented as a reward a few years later for 'unspecified services' to one Karrin Wraythe." She looked Caldan in the eye. "Does the name mean anything to you?"

Caldan shook his head. "No, I've never heard it before."

"Well, it's all very innocuous, unless you dig a little further, which Avigdor did. It seems that Karrin was in the emperor's employ, but strangely enough, there were no records as to what her function was. I've come across this before, though, as the emperor likes to keep the functions of certain individuals and groups secret from all but his closest advisors. Those with unique talents and those whose aptitude eclipses others in their professions, usually sorcerers and those versed in the more arcane arts. To say any more would be speculation." She paused to read the next sheet of paper.

"How would it have come to be in my parents' possession?"

Felice snorted. "I'm hardly in a position to guess. Can you tell me more about them?"

Reluctant to do so, no matter how helpful Felice had been so far, Caldan decided to be cautious. "Not really. They died when I was very young. I scarcely remember them." Though the day they died was burned into his memory. "I'm sorry."

"No matter. A little more digging, and I'm sure we will find something." Felice gave him a smile. He wasn't sure whether it was friendly or knowing, or both. "What Avigdor did find was that the function of the ring is unclear, though the amount paid for the trinket, a rather hefty sum, indicates a certain efficacy. We can infer from this that the 'unspecified services' were quite important and substantial. Notes on the sale indicate the trinket has warding and focusing properties, but there were no specifics. Does that sound correct? What can it do?"

"Nothing yet, so far as I can tell. I haven't been able to wear it for any length of time, I'm afraid, only since learning how to use a shielding amulet."

"Ah . . . that's . . . a skill usually for journeymen and above, is it not?"

"With the trinket, I felt I needed to concentrate on that skill. I eventually worked it out."

"I'm impressed. Though I wouldn't rely on it. People can be creative when it comes to stealing trinkets, or anything of value, for that matter."

Caldan nodded, grateful for her concern. "I keep it in a safe place." No need to tell her it was on his person.

"Hmm . . . There was another note appended to the trinket record." Felice kept her eyes averted from his and brushed at some dust on her sleeve. "Was there a bone ring along with the trinket?" she asked casually.

Far too casually.

Hanging from around his neck, the bone ring suddenly felt like it had gained a few pounds. He froze for a moment before managing to smile weakly and shake his head.

"The trinket is all I have. There was a fire . . . our house . . . If there was a bone ring, it would have burned." He hoped that would stop her questions, but from the look in her eye there was more to this. For Felice to be interested in it was a bad sign.

"Probably. Anyway, it's not important."

Then why ask about it? No matter—just mentioning it means that it's something far more important than I would have thought. And that makes all this incredibly valuable information.

"Alas," said Felice, "we come finally to the bad news. An addendum added to the entry almost forty years ago stipulates that anyone with information regarding the trinket must inform the emperor's advisors at once, more specifically the First Adjudicators. I felt I should tell you this, and that's the reason I consider my debt to you not fully reckoned. Because the addendum was so old, and because you intrigue me, I haven't yet decided whether to dispatch a missive to the First Adjudicators. No—that's not quite true. Actually, I *have* to . . . but I can delay doing so for a while."

Caldan groaned audibly. His heart felt fit to burst. "But why, if it was so old? Who cares anymore?"

"Because that's what I was asked to do."

"I mean, why do they need to be informed?"

Felice shrugged. "It doesn't say, which is a pity. If I knew why, I could decide whether to arrest you or not. Sit down! I'm not going to!"

Having leaped to his feet, Caldan stood poised between making a break for the door and subduing Felice. Both very bad options. Taking a few deep breaths, he calmed slightly when no guards came bursting in.

Felice's laughter brought him to his senses. She seemed genuinely amused at his reaction. "Please sit down," she repeated between chuckles. "If I wanted to arrest you, you would have been taken as soon as you walked into the keep. And why bother sending a note to summon you?"

"You're right, of course. I just . . ." The weight of the bone ring pressing into his chest made him feel guilty.

With a wave of her hand, Felice dismissed his embarrassment. "The addendum was very specific, but I like you, so here's what I am going to do. You"—she pointed a finger at Caldan—"are going to sit tight. Don't leave Anasoma while I make further inquiries. A few weeks' delay informing the First Adjudicators won't matter after all this time. And if there is anything you're not telling me, you would be wise to rethink your reluctance and be forthright. Am I clear?"

By the ancestors, she knows! No, how could she? She suspects. It is one of the possibilities, and she has to cover them all, as any good Dominion player would.

Palms sweaty and heart racing, Caldan replied as calmly as he could. "I've told you everything I know. It all happened when I was young. I wish I did know more—but that's why I asked you in the first place."

Felice stared at him a few moments, then nodded. "Very well. Once I have gathered as much information as I can, I'll send the missive. If I were you, I'd wait for their response. It will come to me, and we can decide what to do. Agreed?"

Not seeing any other option at the moment, Caldan nodded.

"Good," Felice said. "Now, another thing. I've arranged it so we're on opposite ends of the Dominion draw for the Autumn Festival tournament. I assume you'll be entering?"

The festival had slipped Caldan's mind. He was so busy these days. "Yes, I want to. A lot has happened since I arrived. I'd almost forgotten about it. But—you rigged the draw?"

"Don't look so surprised. It's part of what I do. I'd have hated for us to have met in the earlier games. Now I think we'll both be in the final four." She grinned. "I'm looking forward to it."

AS SOON AS he arrived back in his room, Caldan drew out the bone ring. It looked exactly as it always had, just bone with runes carved into the surface. A fake trinket without any of the usual properties or powers. Such a cheap copy, it wasn't even made of metal. What was special about it?

Caldan sat on his bed and put his head in his hands. At least he had gained some information from Felice, which was a start. But it looked like, instead of him having to venture out and find more information, it was going to come straight to him. A few weeks for Felice to research what she could, then a few months for a messenger to reach the capital and return with a response. He didn't care to think of what would happen then.

Nothing good, he was certain.

CHAPTER 27

Barrows lay to the east of the Sorcerers' Guild, bordered by the river Modder. A less well-to-do district than West Barrows, Parkside, or Five Flowers, it was conveniently close to the major guilds without being too expensive. It had become an area where a great many businesses set up shop, as those that provided materials and equipment to the guilds found it ideal due to its close proximity. The river Modder and North Road were perfect for resupplying stocks as the voracious appetites of the guilds ate them up.

Discreet inquiries among the apprentices and a few journeymen had directed Caldan here. It was obvious, once he thought of it; there had to be merchants close to the guilds, and where there were large merchant businesses, there were also small ones. The merchants who dealt with the guilds were contracted to abide by certain rules to keep their business. It hadn't taken Caldan long to learn that all rare earths the merchants acquired were to be sold exclusively to the Sorcerers' Guild, with their reputation and the guaranteed flow of ducats more than enough to prevent the merchants from gouging prices. Still, materials entered the city through other avenues, and the merchants were by no means the only sources of the metals Caldan needed.

He found himself in the streets of Barrows, first stop a jewelry supplier, for the majority of the metal and some beeswax. After some tough negotiating, the shopkeeper thumbed the ducats Caldan handed over. Caldan tucked the pouch of white gold he'd bought deep into a pants pocket, then put his purse on top, lighter by a fair amount. With luck, he would still have enough left for some rare earths, depending on what price the merchant wanted and his own bargaining skills. He carried a lump of beeswax the size of his fist wrapped in cloth and made his way to a general store he'd heard had what he needed.

Caldan crossed through an intersection and made his way up another street, passing a butcher's shop and a merchant selling uncommon liquors and ales from around the empire. Soon he stood in front of a chandler's, and according to his information, across from this was the general store that stocked a supply of rare earths.

As he pushed through a beaded curtain and entered the store, a tinkling came from some bells. Inside, the air was fragrant with the merchandise stored in barrels and crates, and on the shelves around the walls were wood and iron, oils and leather. Hardly any dust, though, and the floor and surfaces looked as clean and polished as any he had seen in the city. And yet, something was off. Caldan sniffed the air again. Underlying it all was the scent of something . . . rancid.

Behind a counter at the back, the shopkeeper stepped through a dark doorway. Tall, with close-cropped hair, he moved fluidly, gliding around the end of the counter. Caldan started. The man had a faint reddish glow to his skin.

Caldan blinked and the glow was gone.

"Why, hello there," the shopkeeper said as he rubbed his eyes. A startled look on the man's face was replaced by a frown of annoyance, which just as quickly disappeared when he smiled affably.

Caldan breathed in to reply and choked, his nose filled with a stench akin to rotting meat. He coughed and blew out through his nose to clear it.

"Oh dear, are you all right, good sir?"

Caldan shook his head and tentatively took a short breath. Nothing. The reek had cleared. *Strange.* It felt similar to the time he met Quiss.

"Sorry, just a dizzy spell. Perhaps I have been working too hard." Caldan wiped a hand across his brow.

The shopkeeper gave him a concerned look. "And what work would that be, young sir? I would normally place a muscular lad like yourself as a guard recruit or apprentice blacksmith, but I can sense something else about you. Something that sets you apart, an . . . intelligence."

Caldan shook his head, bemused. "I'm apprenticed to the Sorcerers' Guild."

"Apprenticed? Aren't you a little . . . old?"

"I only recently arrived here and was lucky enough to find a position with them."

"Indeed you were. No doubt you have family in the city?"

"No, no family to speak of."

The shopkeeper smiled. "A shame. Forgive me." He held out a hand. "My name is Amerdan."

Caldan eyed him suspiciously, wishing he knew why he had seen a faint glow over the man's skin. He clasped the hand in his own and shook. No sensation, other than the man's viselike grip.

"Caldan," he replied, squeezing back for a moment before they both released. He thought he had been assessed in some way.

"So, young Caldan, an apprentice of the sorcerers. Why, I imagine you must learn all sorts of things up there with those powerful men and women. And I must say, you aren't like any sorcerer I've ever met. Aren't they all . . . bookish, pale from studying by candlelight?"

"Most are like that, I have to admit. From what I've seen so far, there are different talents there. I may be more inclined to physical skills, but I guess I'll find out if I have a talent for the rest."

Amerdan looked disappointed, but Caldan couldn't figure out what he had said to upset the man. Before he could think on it further, the shopkeeper asked, "Well, what brings you to my shop? Ink, pens, paper? Perhaps a lamp?" He touched a finely worked lamp atop a crate.

"I heard you might have some rare earth metals. I'd be interested in having a look, and if they're what I require, purchasing some."

"Ah." Amerdan moved back behind the counter and retrieved a wooden box two hands square and one high. He placed it carefully on the counter and opened the lid. "I do happen to have a few ingots left, as well as some crystals."

The box was divided into eight compartments, each holding ingots or crystal chunks on rough pieces of hessian. Caldan recognized all the crystals but was only interested in two. He sighed under his breath with relief. They were what he needed.

Glancing at Amerdan for permission, he picked up a yellow, translucent, sharp-edged crystal. There was more than enough here for his needs, and he selected another crystal, placing both on the counter next to the box, each the size of his thumbnail. Next, he selected a similar-sized piece of a reddish hexagonal crystal.

"Vanadis, and good quality, too." He placed it with the yellow crystals. "I'm afraid that's all I need. Do you have a set price for them? I'm only an apprentice, so my funds are limited." He looked at Amerdan, who was frowning at the crystals on the counter.

"One moment." Amerdan removed a handkerchief from his pocket and settled it on the counter before placing the three crystals on top. "There. Ah, well . . . truth be told, I have had the minerals for a while, and they aren't selling as quickly as I'd like."

Caldan blinked. A very strange shopkeeper. *First the glow, and now he's not haggling . . . or he's doing a bad job at it.* He felt like washing his hands of the whole thing, but if he could get these materials cheaply, he could put up with some peculiarities. He decided to take the initiative.

"I would expect to pay, say, two silver ducats for each of the yellow, and three and a half silvers for the vanadis." He fetched his purse out and started counting coins. He had a mix of five silvers and the rest copper and had to count enough copper to cover the difference.

"That seems fair enough. Perhaps you could spread word among your colleagues about my shop? And that I have some rare earths for sale?" He wrapped the three crystals in the handkerchief and slid the bundle across the counter.

"And that sounds fair to me," Caldan said. *More than fair.*

"So, tell me, Caldan," Amerdan said, "what exactly do you do as an apprentice?"

"Mostly crafting, metallurgy, and alchemy."

"Crafting? And do you have a talent for . . . that sort of thing?"

Caldan double-checked his coins. "I like to think I do."

Amerdan gave a pleased smile. "Excellent. The world needs people with talent. Be sure to learn all you can, to stretch yourself." He paused. "If I might be so bold, I do have another question for you."

Caldan shrugged, itching to be off and working on his crafting design but not wanting to appear rude. After all, he might have to come back here if he needed more rare earths—especially at these prices. "By all means," he said.

"A . . . friend of mine, who is the shy sort, needs some crafting done. He values his privacy and has a need for the type of locks more complex than a blacksmith can make. Truth to tell, he is paranoid about his security and is reluctant to go to the Sorcerers' Guild for what he needs. He fears thieves would make use of the information, if they knew, so would prefer a—how do you say?—quieter solution."

"I'm not sure. I mean, if the man has something to hide—"

"No, no, nothing of the sort. Or, well, yes, he does, but not of an illicit sort. He just has certain valuables that he would like to keep secure, as well as his personal safety. Same as any man of means. If you play your cards right, maybe you could have a nice little earner on the side. It would bring some ducats in and help you with your studies."

"Well, if it's all aboveboard, then I might be able to assist." He could definitely use the ducats.

"Totally legitimate. Probably one door lock and a chest lock. Though I would have to confirm the details, but that won't take long. How can I contact you? A message to the guild?"

"It would be better if I came back here when I have some free time. It won't be too long."

"Excellent. Then I'll expect to see you in the next few days?"

Caldan's pressing need at the moment was the work he needed to do to complete his crafting. After that, he could see to his purse. His name was becoming known around the Yawning Rabbit Inn, and his Dominion winnings dwindled as the odds against him decreased. This sounded like a good way to earn some ducats to tide him over in the short term.

"Perhaps a week," he began, and he saw Amerdan stiffen. "I have a lot of work to complete. I'm afraid I won't have time earlier."

"Well," said Amerdan, "these things can't be helped. Best you be off to start your work. The sooner you are finished, the sooner you can make it back here."

Amerdan held his hand out, palm up.

Caldan handed him the coins and scooped up the handkerchief with his crystals inside. "Thank you," he said. "I'll be sure to mention your shop to other apprentices. I wasn't expecting to find the minerals I needed all in one place."

"It seems this has been a good day for both of us."

Caldan nodded. "Thank you again, sir. I'll see you in a week."

AMERDAN WATCHED THE young man's back as he left. A callow youth, but from what he said, talented. But there was something about him, a feeling Amerdan had when they were close, a niggling in his mind he had never felt before. Almost . . . an affinity.

The shopkeeper scoffed at the thought. He had been experiencing strange sensations in his mind since disposing of the apprentice to the sorcerers. Such a pathetic thing, it had been. Unworthy to survive.

He frowned at the itch in his mind, which had started only recently. His thoughts probed at it, like a tongue at a chipped tooth.

Never mind. The youth, Caldan, would be back before long, which gave Amerdan time for research, to find out whether he was worthy before taking things further. He opened his hand to count the coins.

Seven and a half silver ducats in total. Five silver coins and five sets of five coppers. Amerdan laughed. Of course.

CHAPTER 28

A mouse scuttled along the wall and disappeared through a crack. Caldan's lamp, the flame as low as he could manage, stirred shadows across the room. He carried a satchel, which he placed on the workbench—the same one he'd burned a hole into. It seemed fitting as he worked to replace what he'd foolishly lost.

The hour was late, and all the other apprentices had been asleep for some time. It had been no trouble to sneak through the buildings and into the apprentices' workshop. Hardly anyone was awake—a master or two, the ones known to keep odd hours, but that was it. All he had to do was be about his work quickly and quietly, and no one would be the wiser.

Deciding on what type of crafting was important, and he had spent hours during the day thinking about the issue, to the point where his distracted thoughts had earned him a reprimand in one class and extra work in another.

With all the glyphs required for a shield, anything too small was out of the question, which discounted an earring or ring. If he started wearing a large crafted brooch or medallion, though, people might ask questions. In the end, he decided to construct a flat wristband two inches wide. Wearing it on his forearm, he could cover it with his shirtsleeve to hide it from plain sight.

From his satchel Caldan drew out a copy of Jevons's *Commentary on Shaping Gold,* a beeswax blank of the wristband he'd prepared earlier, his handkerchief, the pouch of white gold ingots, and his scribing tools.

He walked to the furnace in the middle of the room, which had been set for the night, and added more coal, pumping the bellows to get it burning.

Humming to himself, he made a short trip to a storeroom and returned with a bucket of fine alchemical powder and a mixing spoon.

Opening the book, he removed two sheets of paper. Both were covered in his designs and working for the crafting, along with notations on different alloys and their properties. He'd circled one formula, his final choice.

Selecting a carving tool, he set to scraping the wax, trimming off the seam, and smoothing the inner and outer surfaces. Switching tools often, he started to carve the inside surface with one half of his pattern, slicing runes and symbols deep into the wax band. If all went well, his crafting should be strong, ten times better than the piece of shoddy workmanship he'd accidentally melted.

The added complexity had been a challenge, to work out how the anchors, controls, links, and buffers should act to strengthen the overall crafting, but he'd had a few days to figure it out. His finished design covered both surfaces of the wristband.

An hour later, Caldan finished carving both the inside and outside surfaces. He stopped to massage his aching fingers, pleased the fiddly part of the process was over.

He turned his attention to the crystals, or what was left of them. Unwrapping the handkerchief, he revealed two cloth pouches tied with string. Over the last few days, he'd used his spare time to grind the crystals to a coarse powder and refine the ores to allow him to weigh out the proper ratio of metals for the alloy.

Using a scale, he weighed enough white gold for the bracelet, then added portions of the rare earths until he had the percentages correct. He poured the metals into a crucible and placed it carefully into the furnace.

Back at his workbench, he prepared the wax casting with flues and encased it within a layer of alchemical plaster, which would set hard in a short span of time. Within minutes, the mixture gave off heat, a result of the alchemical reaction beginning to take place.

There was nothing left to do but wait for the mold to fully dry and the wax to liquefy, for the metals in his crucible to melt and combine.

The nervous energy bottled inside him for the last few days dissipated. The warmth of the furnace was comforting, and he lay his head on his arms to rest.

He woke with a start, fuzzy eyed and blinking. For a moment, he wasn't sure where he was, then it came back to him. By the ancestors, how long had he nodded off? He stumbled to the furnace.

Thankfully, his mold looked to be dry and hard, and no cracks were visible on the outside.

Caldan smiled.

Taking a pair of long-handled tongs, he carefully lifted the mold and tipped the molten wax onto the coals of the furnace to be consumed. Now that the mold was hollow, the inside contained only the shape of his wristband and the fine lines of the glyphs he had carved.

Again using the tongs, he reached into the fire and removed the crucible. Inside, the metal glowed molten white, the air shimmering violently with the heat.

Caldan rested the crucible on the furnace bricks for a moment, one hand wiping his brow. With much trepidation, he began to pour the liquid gold into the mold, the stream of metal glowing bright as it filled the hollow space inside, flowing into the glyphs and patterns.

As he poured, he sensed the metal as it filled his carvings, gently testing the link, buffer, anchor, and control glyphs in the overall pattern. He connected to the links, and power flowed through the metal as it formed a complete crafting. This was the essential stage. He had to maintain the flow through the object until it solidified.

Concentrating to maintain his well and its link to the metal, he took the mold from the furnace and placed it on an anvil, where it began to cool, then gently tapped it to remove any air bubbles trapped in the delicate details.

Now all he had to do was to stay linked while it cooled enough to handle. By then, both the metal and the paths of energy would be set.

As the minutes passed, Caldan's trepidation grew. What he attempted was more complex than most journeymen could craft. Casting was the easy part; any jewelry smith could do that. What took talent and skill were the glyphs, the raw materials, and finally the imbuement. All three had to be in harmony to create a crafting without the forces destroying it in the process or when it was activated.

Rousing himself from his thoughts, he dropped the rag he was using to wipe the workbench and looked at his mold. It was plain and dull, yet contained within would be the finest piece he had crafted, full of potential. It would be like opening a present, removing the covering to reveal the gift inside, only better.

Smiling, he used the tongs to plunge the mold into a barrel of water. Steam hissed out in a cloud, and he waved it away to see bubbles rising to the surface. He thrust an arm to the bottom of the barrel and retrieved the mold. He tapped the tongs against the cast until it cracked and fell apart in his hands.

Firelight reflected from the white metal, flickering over the patterns. Caldan took his time and gazed at his creation long and reverently.

To him, the object was the culmination of all his years of hard work and sacrifice, made possible only because he had ended up here in Anasoma and had been fortunate enough to have the means to purchase the raw materials. If he'd stayed at the monastery, it was unlikely he would ever have made such a piece. He certainly wouldn't have been able to afford the gold and crystals. Maybe injuring Marlon had been a blessing in disguise, or maybe it was fate. Whatever the reason, he felt elated at having given his talent free rein to create such a crafting. All he had to do now was trim, clean, and polish the wristband, but he could do that in his room.

Caldan clutched his crafting in one hand and gave the apprentices' workshop a final look over. The place looked untouched. *Good.* He blew out his lantern and left, tracing his steps back to his room.

RAIN PATTERED ON his shutters. The storm had come from the sea with remarkable speed. Clammy and cold, it made Caldan's room feel damp and uninviting. This night, he didn't care, as his mind was on other matters.

He sat on his bed, newly crafted wristband in hand, and stared at the bright white gold object, unmoving. He remained in this pose for over an hour, the only light in the room his lantern burning a small flame. As a precaution, he checked and rechecked his creation for any flaw in the casting and in the pattern. The last thing he wanted was for it to melt or crack under the strain of his well. Especially if it was on his arm at the time.

Finally satisfied, he opened his eyes and took a breath, then slipped the crafting over his wrist.

Opening his well, he linked it to the wristband, and a shield sprang up around him. His skin tightened, and his vision blurred. Following the flow of his well through the wristband, he sensed all was working as it should, though he couldn't test it properly on his own. That would have to come later.

Sighing with relief, Caldan broke the links and closed his well. A great weariness came over him as the stress and pressure of the day weighed him down. Only now did he realize how tired he was.

CHAPTER 29

Mist flowed through the streets. Soon the rising sun would burn off what haze remained, but while it was around, Vasile used it to cover his movements as much as he could.

As far as he could tell, one or more of his inquiries into the dealings of the Five Oceans Mercantile Concern had tipped someone off. And that someone was not pleased.

While visiting the magistrates' court to see some friends and call in a few favors, he'd been told by Japir, an informant of his, about people asking after him. Vasile knew of no one who would want to see him that didn't already know how to contact him, and he hadn't had much contact with women since his wife . . . for a number of years.

Yesterday, Vasile had waited for Japir in the usual spot by a fountain in the Deadhorse district, to no avail. When he'd failed to appear, Vasile went to visit Japir's home with all possible haste. The door swung open at his touch, but only echoes answered his queries. Japir lay on the bed, throat slashed to the bone. Vasile covered his body with blood-soaked sheets before taking one last glance around the room, then scurried out the door in a rush.

Last night, he drank deeply before going to sleep—water, of course—then packed what few belongings he thought necessary for a short stay away from home. He slept badly, waking well before dawn with a full bladder—which had been his plan. He relieved himself, gathered his belongings into a leather pack, and slipped out the back door. The streets were empty, save for the rats and roaches. Crouching low, he slithered along and kept against the buildings.

He pressed himself to a brick wall and stopped, breathing heavily. *Did that shadow move?* Peering into the mist, he squinted. *No. Must be my imagination.* But they *were* out there. He knew it.

His purse contained only a few ducats, enough for him to lay low for a while until the heat subsided. If he disappeared long enough, they would think he had left the city or met some unfortunate end, and perhaps they would stop looking for him. During his time working for the chancellors, and through them the emperor, he'd had cause to visit some unsavory areas of the city. They were populated by citizens who skirted the edge of the law, people who'd sell their own mother for a copper ducat. It was to one of these people he was headed, Luduss, who had a reputation not quite as bad as the rest of his fellows. Hopefully, he wasn't dead or out of business by now.

Eyes darting back and forth, Vasile peered into the evaporating mist, back against the wall of a butcher's shop. His problem was that Luduss was known to sleep late and wouldn't look kindly upon being dragged out of bed at such an hour. Luckily, plenty of eating houses were scattered about the industrial areas and opened early to cater to workers on a morning shift. As long as his ducats lasted, Vasile would be free to secrete himself in one of these establishments among nondescript workers and while away the hours until midmorning, when he could appeal to Luduss for a secure bolt-hole.

Vasile glanced left and right down the street, then darted across the cobbles and into a long alley. A few turns later, he entered a modest eating house through a doorway, the likeness of a knife and a spoon scratched into the bricks above it.

Like many such places at this time, it bustled with the morning trade, and he had to squeeze past two workers in the corridor, on the way to start whatever job they had after their morning meal. Judging from the white dust on their clothes, and the smell as they passed, he guessed they were millers.

Aromas from fresh-baked bread and tea drew Vasile farther in. He took possession of half a loaf, a platter of salted butter, and a mug of tea, handing over the required ducats as payment. Looking around the windowless room lit by a few lamps, he found an out-of-the-way booth. He stirred a spoonful of honey into his tea and tore off a chunk of bread. It tasted as it smelled: hot, fresh, and delicious. He chewed with satisfaction.

A man slid into the other side of the booth. Sharing was common, so Vasile kept his head down, not in the mood for conversation. The man coughed politely and cleared his throat. Vasile pretended to ignore him and slurped his tea, softening the bread in his mouth.

"Ahem," the man said. "Vasile."

Vasile jerked his head up. Across from him sat Luphildern Quiss, a smile plastered on his thin face. Vasile almost soiled himself. *Ancestors! How did he find me?*

"Easy," said Quiss. "You look like you've seen a ghost. How's the bread?"

Vasile tongued the mash of bread and tea in his mouth, which no longer tasted as appealing as it had a moment ago. He glanced around the room but couldn't see anyone who might be associated with the merchant. *But then again, how would I know?*

"Good," he mumbled, swallowing the now tasteless pulp. With a shaking hand, he placed his mug of tea back on the table.

"I must remember to come back here. One rarely gets the opportunity to mingle with such hardworking folk over a good meal," remarked Quiss.

Vasile eyed the dirty, hollow-eyed men around him gulping down porridge, bread, and tea, mostly silently, fueling up for another day's hard labor. "Yes," he said hesitantly, and slid toward the edge of the booth.

Quiss shook his head slowly, obviously amused. "Anyway, enough pleasantries. I need to tell you you're in great danger."

"You don't say."

"Indeed, there are those who want you . . . silenced. Don't move!" Quiss whispered sharply.

Vasile stopped moving, terrified. These people hadn't hesitated in killing before, and he was sure they wouldn't hesitate this time. Inwardly, he cursed himself for the last few years of wasted life. The man he was before wouldn't have quivered like a child in front of an angry adult.

Bad time to stop drinking.

"Good. I'm not here to threaten you, Vasile. No, it's not me you have to worry about," said Quiss, in a matter-of-fact tone. "Actually, I'm here to *help* you. If you'd run into the others first, well . . . let's just say you would be floating in one of the canals right now." He smiled grimly.

Vasile's eyes flicked again to the door.

"Not a good idea," said Quiss.

He's telling the truth . . . and that's what scaring me so much. What's waiting for me out there?

"What's going on? What do you mean, 'the others'?"

"There are people who want you dead, and I don't—that's all you need to know right now. Ultimately, they will fail and have to answer to the First Deliverer, but they have a number of followers. Until their threat has passed, we do what we can to contain them and thwart their plans. And that's where you come in. They've discovered your attempts to find out more about us and want to stop you."

"Us?" queried Vasile. "I thought you said you weren't one of them."

"We are all part of a . . . shall we say 'family'? But like any family, we don't always get along. In your case, we have opposing views about our . . . impact here." Quiss frowned. "Forgive my pauses, but I have to choose my words carefully."

"So you aren't here to kill me?"

"Goodness, no! Far from it. I already told you: I'm here to *save* you. Without me, I fear your life would be . . . short."

Vasile swallowed. He doubted it'd be much longer with this man, but so far everything Quiss had said was the truth.

Quiss stood and straightened his jacket. "Come. You'll have to trust me. That I haven't harmed you yet should go some way to persuading you of our good intentions." He tilted his head, as if listening to something. "The coast is clear, as they say. I can explain more when you're in a safer place. Let's get out of here, before something dreadful happens."

VASILE FOLLOWED THE mysterious Quiss to Dockside, where they entered the main office of the Five Oceans Mercantile Concern. The place was swarming with people rushing about, packing crates, filling bags and sacks with records and large lockboxes with ducats. Quiss appeared unconcerned by the activity. Teams of burly laborers carried the goods to the back of the building, where they were loaded onto carts and driven away with armed escorts. Quiss excused himself for a few moments to consult with a number of his colleagues, then approached Vasile.

"Why are we here?" asked Vasile.

"I offer you a choice. The city is about to be invaded, and we have to leave. I will not go into the reasons why, but I am authorized to tell you a few facts. I gather you will be able to determine whether I'm being truthful with you." He gave Vasile an appraising look.

How he had come to know of Vasile's ability didn't matter. A number of people knew, and it wouldn't have surprised him if one of them had sold the information for a few ducats. Human nature never surprised him anymore.

Vasile sighed heavily. "Yes," he agreed. "I will."

Quiss nodded. "Confirmation, then. Interesting." He glanced around at the disarray of the offices.

He looks resigned, thought Vasile. *Why?*

"Very well," continued Quiss in his strange accent. "I'll tell you a number of facts." He paused. "As I believe them to be, that is. If at the end you think I have lied or tried to deceive you, then you are free to go."

"I thought I was already free to go. Am I a prisoner? You promised safety from your other faction. The ones who are after me."

"I do. But there's more to the story than opposing factions of a mercantile concern. Much more." Quiss's face remained expressionless. "We have to leave. My whole . . . company. The people who are coming to invade are after us. But capturing us is merely one of their goals. Anasoma, indeed their dissatisfaction with the empire, is simply a cover for their true purpose."

"I . . . I don't understand. Surely the Quivers could deal with an invading force?"

Quiss's face turned grim. "The Quivers are overmatched. Sorcery not seen before in this land has been and will be used against them. Once we escape, we'll need your services to help us in the future."

"Go on."

"As I said, the invaders are after us, and unless we leave, they'll find us and we will be destroyed. Their sorcery is more powerful than that practiced here in the empire. They will be able to conquer this city, root us out like rats in a barn, and kill us all."

Vasile was shocked. Quiss was telling the truth so far, despite how far-fetched this all sounded. "Why are they after you? Are you the reason they're invading Anasoma?"

"We're not their main objective, just something to be tidied up as their other plans unfold. Tying up loose ends, you could say. As you've probably guessed, we're not just a mercantile company. That is a pretense, albeit a profitable one, to be sure."

"Then who are you? What's your purpose?"

"All you need to know is that we're willing to help you, to shelter you from those who wish you harm. In this, our goals align. Those who want you dead are those we are opposed to. In return, we might need your help from time to time."

Though Quiss was still being truthful, he was holding something back. *But doesn't everyone? Nobody likes someone else knowing the truth about them, being privy to their innermost thoughts.* Vasile had learned that the hard way.

"Accept your protection and help you, or be left for the wolves," said Vasile.

"That's about the sum of it. I promise you won't be asked to do anything beyond your ability or morals. And your unique gifts would be invaluable to us. There are projects we're working on that could use good men."

"Good men," scoffed Vasile. "They're in short supply."

"Indeed, but we believe you're one."

Vasile frowned. "Most don't want to know the truth."

"I agree. Believe me when I say we've examined ourselves and been found wanting. Part of our plan is to correct the ills we've done."

Despite the heat in the room, Vasile shivered. "Which are?"

"Some truths are too big, even for you. Suffice it to say, no one will work harder to make amends for our mistakes than we will. We've been exploring alternatives to our dilemma, but so far none have proven viable." He shook his head. "But no matter; that's not for you to worry about."

I think I might have cause to be a little worried. But again, nothing Quiss was saying was an outright lie.

"What now, then? Why do you need me? What help could I possibly give you?"

"The invaders are driven by an evil that hides among them. This we know for truth, through our own sorcery. Now, after gathering its strength, it has come here. Sorcery the likes of which the empire has never seen will be unleashed. Perhaps another Shattering." Quiss dropped his head in dismay. "It cannot be allowed to happen again. The First Deliverer has determined we must show ourselves in order to gather help. We need your help to convince others of our truthfulness. You're uniquely positioned to do this, are you not?"

"I . . . I guess so."

"I know so," Quiss said.

"The First Deliverer . . . you mentioned him before. Who is he?"

"Our leader. He saved us all. It was he who guided our sorcerers and delivered us to salvation. Without him, we would all be dead."

Thoughts churned through Vasile's head. It was almost too much to take in all at once. His legs felt weak, and he lowered himself to the polished stone floor. Quiss stood quietly beside him, waiting expectantly. Vasile chewed on a thumbnail.

What should I do? I'm free to go—or so Quiss said. But go where?

In the end, Vasile knew he couldn't take any other path. He knew he needed a purpose to his life, one that justified all the hardships he'd endured in the past. Redemption was a strong motive. His talent had propelled him to great heights only to cause him to be cast down. He couldn't dispose of it, though. It was part of him. It made him who he was. He too craved salvation.

"I need time to decide. And if I find out you are not telling me the whole story . . ." He left his words hanging.

Beside him, Quiss raised his head, eyes moist. "Of course. Come, there is much to show you that may help convince you of our cause."

CHAPTER 30

The storm had broken early in the morning, before dawn. It was the last day of the week, and all apprentices and journeymen had the day off. Apprentices from wealthy families in the city usually went home, while everyone else relaxed.

Caldan slept well into midmorning. Laughter woke him as a group of apprentices passed his room, chatting loudly on their way out of the building. His mouth felt dry as he sat up, retrieved his waterskin, and drank deeply.

Though it was a rest day, he had much to do. Since his smith-crafting hadn't failed, he planned to work on another project, and to visit Miranda later.

But first he needed breakfast. As usual, he was starving. He dressed quickly, the long sleeves of his shirt covering his wristband. He hesitated for a second, then slipped his trinket onto his finger, confident that no one would suspect what it was. His bone ring he left around his neck, hidden under his shirt. Considering Felicienne's interest in it, he had to be careful.

At about midday, fed and ready to go, he walked out of the Sorcerers' Guild and headed toward Five Flowers in search of a clockmaker.

The overnight storm had left the streets relatively clean, though that meant the rivers would be dirtier until the runoff dispersed. As Caldan crossed a wide canal that fed into the river Stock, the stench assaulted his nostrils, and he covered his nose and mouth with a hand. Both the Stock and Modder were rivers in name only, having been turned from sources of freshwater hundreds of years ago, when Anasoma was sparsely populated, into brown murky sludge filled with all the detritus of a city so large. By themselves, the rivers weren't bad; it was the canals around the city that fed into them that were disgusting. Some flowed swiftly, while in others, the water lay motionless and viscid. Poor scavengers from the slums regularly poled makeshift rafts over their surface, trolling for anything of value floating in the garbage. Human remains were not uncommon, and Caldan had heard certain individuals paid a handsome amount for corpses, fresh or otherwise. Only to the west of the city, where the wealthy made their homes, were the rivers and canals a semblance of their original selves. Luckily, a past emperor had decreed that aqueducts be built to draw water from dams to the far west of the city. Without them, Anasoma would have decayed long ago, from diseases of the body and of the spirit.

Passing over a bridge into Five Flowers, Caldan paused to find his bearings. The wooden walkover was crowded with people going about their business, including the odd beggar ever alert for Quivers.

Days ago, having failed in his attempts at crafting a working simulacrum that lasted more than a week, Caldan had spent long hours mulling over his problem. Eventually, though it galled him to admit it, he'd decided he needed help. Crafting his wristband had been hard enough, and it was one solid piece of metal. Now that it was accomplished, though, he had refocused his energy on creating moving simulacra—such as his paper animals—which he had been fascinated by since his time at the monastery. The idea had come to him of visiting a clockmaker to see how their creations functioned, and after inquiring at the Yawning Rabbit, he had learned of a decent clockmaker, one who happened to be in a wealthier part of the city.

Shielding his eyes from the sun, Caldan took in this side of the river. The change was evident. Buildings were well kept, and some even had gardens behind walls, others flower beds outside their doors. On the side of the river he had left, the buildings looked rotten in comparison, ill kept and decaying.

Caldan shook his head and turned back to Five Flowers. People on the other side had better things to worry about than how their houses looked, he supposed, like providing enough food for their families or having a roof over their head at all.

Which is probably why I'm on that side, he thought ruefully.

He continued south. After polite questions to a few of the passersby, who were always polite in return and glad to assist, he found himself outside the clockmaker's shop he had been looking for. Pausing to straighten his shirt and run a hand over his short hair, Caldan turned the knob on the freshly painted door and entered.

Inside, he stopped and stared, mouth open. Three bright sorcerous globes illuminated the shop. All four walls were covered in gleaming clocks of different shapes and sizes, as well as boxes and strangely shaped objects he couldn't begin to guess the function of. All were made from polished wood and burnished metal, shining under the light of the globes. The atmosphere inside was redolent with wood, wax, and an alchemical polishing solution.

A workmanlike crafter approached, dressed in sturdy clothes protected by a leather apron. A graying beard covered his face, and he wore a pair of spectacles on the end of his nose. Both the spectacles and the sorcerous globes revealed to anyone that the owner was exceedingly prosperous.

"Ah, young sir, a fine day it is now, is it not? Please"—he waved a hand—"look around and see what you fancy. A timepiece as a present? We have many large ones, as well as pocket watches for those whose time is valuable . . ." He trailed off. "Though you don't look like my regular customers. Are you here to pick something up for your master?"

"Pardon? No, I'm here on my own behalf."

"Well, I daresay you have wandered into the wrong shop." The man looked Caldan up and down. "What were you looking for? Perhaps I can help you on your way."

Undeterred, Caldan smiled. No, this shop was exactly what he was looking for. "I was hoping I might look around."

The clerk sighed. "If you're wasting my time . . ."

"Not at all! I'm fascinated by clockwork and wanted to see the best the city had to offer. I asked around, and everyone pointed me here."

"Oh . . . well," the man said, puffing up a bit. "They sent you to the right place!"

Caldan simply smiled and started wandering the shop.

Everything was indeed wonderful, but he was particularly drawn to a shelf covered in brightly polished wooden boxes.

"If I may: What's in the boxes?"

Rubbing his hands, the clockmaker stepped to a shelf and opened a dark wooden box. Immediately, tinkling notes of music drifted into the air, although the box was empty.

"One of my designs for ladies' jewelry: a box that plays music. It's my best seller," he said with pride. "A mechanical music device is hidden under a false bottom."

The clockmaker closed the lid and the music cut off. He moved to another shelf, gesturing at a brass bird perched on a branch. "The same design led me to more ornamental objects for a lady of means." Taking what looked like a key from his pocket, he inserted it into a hole in the wood and gave a few turns. "Watch," he said, and stood back.

Once again, music flowed from the object, though this time the bird's beak opened and closed while its wings flapped up and down. Caldan thought he recognized the tune, a song sung between lovers, a romantic melody. This tune was more complex than the one in the music box, the chiming notes overlaid with deeper tones. The music sounded as if it were played by a skilled harpist. He was entranced.

"Such an object wouldn't be possible without the assistance of the Sorcerers' Guild, of course," the man said. "But the mechanism is my own devising, and I have sold many, even one as a present for the emperor's sixth wife."

Caldan hadn't known such complexity was possible for a mechanical device. The workmanship opened his eyes to possibilities he hadn't dreamed of before, for his own smith-crafting, and for his desire to craft a simulacrum.

These devices were exactly what he was looking for, though he hadn't realized it. He turned his gaze from the mechanical bird to the clockmaker and bowed. He could learn much from this man. Caldan's flimsy paper animal craftings were interesting, but if they could be transformed into metal creatures . . . His mind swam with the possibilities.

"I must admit to being impressed. I'd thought clocks to be simple things." At the clockmaker's frown he continued quickly. "But I see I was very much mistaken, and your work has made me reassess my own desires."

"And what desires would those be?"

"As I mentioned, I'm interested in clocks and their movements. Well, the internal workings, that is." Caldan pointed to the musical bird, whose song had trailed off while he spoke.

"Lad, I am sorry to say I can't help you, unless you are a member of the Clockmakers' Guild—which I don't think you are."

"Good sir," Caldan began, "you misunderstand, though that is probably my fault. Let me introduce myself first. I'm an apprentice in the Sorcerers' Guild, and—"

The clockmaker coughed disbelievingly. "Young sir, that statement would be more convincing from someone of a few less years than yourself."

Caldan sighed. One day someone was going to believe him when he told them that.

"It assure you that it is true," he said. "I have only been in Anasoma a few months. I was lucky enough for the sorcerers to accept me based on my talent, and I can say your reaction to this isn't the first I have encountered."

The clockmaker frowned. "It's possible, I suppose, though what does this have to do with your presence here? Are you interested in purchasing a clock or one of my mechanical marvels?"

"No, I'm afraid not. I find myself short of ducats at this time."

"And I find myself short of patience. I knew you were going to waste my time. Please, off with you, sir. I have work to do."

Not put off, Caldan continued. "Again, I apologize for any misunderstanding. You see, I'm interested in mechanical workings, not so I can make a clock or any other device, but for an idea I have. I may not have ducats to pay for a device to study or for some of your time, though I fear I will need both. But what I do have to trade is my own skill, my own talent in crafting, which is not inconsiderable."

With a sigh, the clockmaker said nothing for a few moments, giving Caldan another inspection over his spectacles. "Perhaps I believe your story and you're an apprentice sorcerer, but what could you possibly offer? Some work I have done by sorcerers, craftings so complex and expensive an apprentice couldn't possibly help. They charge a pretty ducat, too, for such work, though I don't begrudge them that. They can do things I can only . . ." He shook his head. "I'll say again: I don't see how you can help me."

"And I'll say again: what I have is talent and access to resources where I can devise craftings and no one asks questions as to what I am doing. I can smith-craft better than most journeymen." He raised his hand to hold off the man's imminent protest. "That's no idle boast. I may be an apprentice, but I'm *not* new to crafting."

He rolled his left sleeve up to reveal his wristband. Light from the three sorcerous globes reflected off the burnished gold, complex patterns and glyphs visible on its surface. The clockmaker leaned forward, curiosity evident on his face.

"This is my work. Recently smith-crafted by me alone, according to my own design and resources, from start to finish. The metallurgy, the design, the crafting—all my own."

"It looks pretty," the man said with a shrug, "but any goldsmith could make something similar." He looked again at the wristband. "Almost any," he added. "I'll admit, you may have a talent for making pretty jewelry."

Caldan opened his well and linked to the wristband. His skin tightened and his vision blurred as the shield flowed around him.

With a gasp of surprise, the clockmaker took a step back, hands raised.

"What?" he exclaimed. "I've heard of such craftings but never seen one before." He reached a hand out, then looked at Caldan for permission. "May I?"

Caldan nodded, and the clockmaker extended his arm to touch two fingertips to the shield. Where they touched it, tiny motes of purple light spread from the contact, fading to nothing a few inches from their origin.

"I'm impressed," the clockmaker said, nodding. "And that means I think we can do business."

AFTER A LONG discussion, Caldan and the clockmaker shook hands on an agreement. In exchange for limited knowledge on the internal workings of his devices, answers to any questions Caldan could think of, and assistance with a simulacrum design, the clockmaker would receive from Caldan pieces of smith-crafting he usually paid a high price for from the Sorcerers' Guild, as well as knowledge of how the basics of crafting worked.

Both were pleased with the final bargain, and Caldan left the shop in good spirits, promising to return in three days with the craftings the clockmaker required—relatively easy pieces for him, once he located designs in the library.

CHAPTER 31

Sunset bled through the streets and alleyways of Anasoma, filtering through the small window into Caldan's room. Through the thin clouds on the horizon, and the dust and pollution of the city itself, red light filled rivers and canals. Looking up, above the city, smoke from countless fires across the districts obscured the sky, and the smell of burning wood and coke pervaded the evening air, mixing with the usual rank stench of overpopulation.

Master Simmon rousted Caldan from his room as he rushed past, explaining hurriedly that he should join him, as the experience would show him what the Protectors were really about. Puzzled, Caldan scrambled after the master down a few corridors.

All eyes turned to Caldan as he entered a secluded courtyard. Gathered around Simmon were seven fully armed Protector journeymen, and Master Jazintha, a woman Caldan had only seen fleetingly. All of them were bristling with crafted amulets and rings, the masters also sporting trinkets. Two journeymen carried large shields, the outside surfaces covered in a thin sheet of crafted steel.

Master Simmon spoke, raising his voice to address them all. "He's coming with us. He needs to see what we have to deal with."

"A bit early, isn't it?" protested an older journeyman, one of the two carrying the strange shields.

"Maybe in terms of his training, but he's old enough, and from what I've seen, he can handle himself well."

The older journeyman shrugged, and they all returned to their tasks. With a nod, one of them handed Caldan a sword with a worn leather scabbard and belt. He checked it quickly before buckling the belt around his waist. It was serviceable, but hardly a quality blade. He noted that the journeyman who had given it to him gave a small nod of approval for the fact that he had checked at all.

I can handle myself well, Caldan thought. *Now I just wish I knew what I was handling myself against.*

Gear was inspected, blades eyed for rust and given a quick wipe with oil. Both masters examined each journeyman before nodding and moving to the next.

Soon both Master Simmon and Master Jazintha stood before Caldan, eyeing him critically. He'd seen Jazintha only in passing as she walked the halls. She was the master in charge of all the Protectors who traveled outside of Anasoma. She made sure they left well equipped, kept tabs on where they were and their status, and debriefed them after they arrived back in the city. Slender and wiry, she carried herself with assurance and exuded a presence of stillness similar to Simmon's. A thin sword with a crafted hilt was buckled to her belt.

"Leave him," she said to Simmon after a cursory glance. "We can't afford to babysit someone tonight."

Simmon grunted, eyes still on Caldan. "We also don't have time to argue. I think he needs to come with us. I'll take responsibility for him. He needs to see what we do firsthand."

"Ancestors willing, there won't be any excitement. Make sure he knows his place and doesn't bugger this up for us." With one last frown directed at Caldan, she turned to berate a journeyman who hadn't polished his leather belt and scabbard to her liking.

"Don't mind her," said Simmon quietly. "We're all edgy tonight.

A lot of things could go wrong, and that wouldn't be good, for us or for you." He looked around to make sure no one was close. "Show me your ring," he said firmly.

Nothing much escapes Simmon. *He knows.*

Warily, Caldan raised his hand. Simmon ran a critical eye over the trinket before touching it lightly with a finger. Caldan sensed him access his well, and a faint hum combined with the scent of lemons filled the air around him. After a moment, the vibration faded, along with the smell.

Caldan started. Was that what the lemons signified? Casting his thoughts back, he remembered smelling lemons before, when the master teaching them about shielding had disarmed the wards on the box containing the crafted amulets. Curious.

Simmon's voice brought him back to the present. He sounded puzzled. "I can't tell what it does. Perhaps you can enlighten me?"

"I'm afraid I can't. Not that I don't want to," he added when Simmon frowned at him. "I just don't know. It was handed down to me, but I can't figure it out. I was told it was my family's, an heirloom." Caldan swallowed, his throat thick with sudden emotion.

"It's good I haven't seen you wearing it. Without proper protection, you might find yourself in some trouble from people who wouldn't hesitate to murder to get their hands on a trinket. Wear it tonight. You might find out something about it, if you're lucky, but don't wear it any other time until you can protect yourself properly."

With a nonchalant shrug, Caldan rolled up his left sleeve to reveal his crafted wristband. "I made something that might be helpful."

Simmon's eyes widened. "You made this?" Again, Caldan felt the air hum and caught a faint hint of lemons before both faded.

"Yes. I needed one so I could start wearing my . . . ring." Caldan was hesitant to say trinket with so many people around. In the darkness, no one would notice it on his finger, he hoped.

"It feels sound, but without proper testing, I wouldn't rely on it."

"I tested it—it works."

"That's all well and good, Caldan, but *all* craftings are tested before earning the guild's approval for sale or for individual use. We can't sanction faulty goods being sold in our name or allow unsafe craftings to be used by guild members. The quality looks good—better than good, in fact—but I still wouldn't rely on it. Come to me tomorrow, and we'll see about having it certified. If it doesn't pass, you'll have to melt it down, you know."

Caldan scowled. The medallion he had purchased was probably a reject, a crafting that hadn't passed the tests, and he had paid well over what such a crafting was worth. If his wristband was to be melted down, its only value was in the cost of the metals. Besides that, it sounded like the bracelet would have to go through a rigorous process to determine if it passed the guild's assessment, and that meant he'd be without the protection during that time. Though a part of him knew his crafting was good, he couldn't help but feel trepidation at having his work judged by masters he scarcely knew.

"Wipe that expression off your face," Simmon said.

Caldan quickly composed himself.

"That's better. Like it or not, you're a member of this guild, and you're subject to its rules like everyone else. You may not be an ordinary apprentice, but that doesn't make you *extraordinary*. Don't make me regret inviting you tonight."

"No, sir."

"Good. Listen carefully," said Simmon. "Despite what Jazintha says, I think it's important you come with us tonight, if only to see how we operate. So far, all you have to go on is what I've told you."

Or not told me, as it were.

"I want you to remember," continued Simmon, "that what we do is for the good of all. There are reasons for keeping secrets, and there won't be parades in the street for us. What we do is best done with as few people knowing as possible. I can't repeat this enough: stay back and keep your head down. If all goes well, there won't be any drama. If it doesn't, well . . . we might be glad you're along." He gave Caldan a pat on the shoulder and moved on, leaving him to his thoughts.

They're preparing as if for battle, but what could they be fighting in Anasoma?

It wasn't long before the group formed up and moved out of the guild headquarters and into the city proper. Simmon headed the group, leaving Caldan at the rear with Master Jazintha. Caldan could feel her eyes on his back.

They followed Simmon without a word, booted feet against the pavement and the creak of leather the only sounds of their passage. Deep into Deadhorse they went, a district Caldan hadn't yet had occasion to visit. They avoided larger groups when they could, and major intersections along the way that were lit by sorcerous globes, one of the many services the Sorcerers' Guild provided for the city. When they passed squads of Quivers, Simmon paused to make his presence known, and they continued without fuss.

Simmon gave a signal to halt as they approached a well-lit intersection from a dark alley. Glowing a muted yellow, two sorcerous globes bathed the junction with light. Across the street was a large three-story stone building with double doors, above which was the sign of a bank, three golden ducats arranged in a triangle.

Without a word spoken, one of the two shield bearers quickly crossed through the light and positioned himself to the side of the door. Two journeymen moved behind him. The other shield bearer disappeared into the shadows at the side of the building and headed toward the back, with another two journeymen following.

Simmon motioned Jazintha and the last journeyman forward. Caldan moved up behind them.

"What's the plan?" Jazintha asked.

"You know the drill," Simmon said. "Shield bearers lead the way with support. They'll flush him out. If he heads for the front door, you take him out. Same for us if he moves toward the back. If he goes up, we'll have him cornered and he shouldn't be any trouble. My guess is he'll try to move past one of the shield bearers and head for the nearest door out to the street. That's what I'd do, and that's where we'll be waiting for him. One journeyman stays outside as a runner in case things go wrong."

Jazintha glanced at Caldan. "Sure he won't hamper you any?"

Simmon shrugged. "I wanted him here, so I'll handle it. Nothing flashy, if you can avoid it. We need to find out how much he knows and whether he's acting alone. I don't have to tell you what's at stake here."

Jazintha nodded curtly, and they moved across the intersection to the other side of the door.

"Caldan," said Simmon. "Stay behind me. Our role is to stop anyone coming our way and to provide assistance to the others if they need it. Understood?"

Caldan nodded, biting his lower lip. *What could put up enough of a fight to get past seven journeymen sorcerers and two master sorcerers with crafted shields and weapons?* His throat tightened. He didn't want to think about it, but soon he would see what the Protectors feared. *No, they don't look fearful. Wary, maybe.* He wiped damp hands on his pants.

I'm the only one who's fearful. He straightened up a bit, knowing he was being observed.

"Let's move," whispered Simmon, and he took off down the side of the building. Caldan followed in his wake.

As they passed the double doors, he saw Jazintha press a flat stone crafting against the lock. A flash of light and a sizzling sound filled the street. Door hinges creaked, and Jazintha shouted, "Go, go."

Moments later, he and Simmon arrived at the rear of the building. A smaller access door stood open. The smell of burnt wood and hot iron pervaded the air.

"Inside," Simmon said to the Protectors. The shield bearer disappeared through the dark opening followed by two others, then Simmon. Caldan stood alone in the street.

"By the ancestors," he said, plunging inside after them.

A muffled explosion came from the front of the building. A blinding flash erupted, and sparkles filled Caldan's sight. He raised an arm to cover his eyes as the shield bearer stumbled forward, closely followed by the two journeymen. Thunder rippled through the air and prickled his skin.

With watering eyes, he followed close behind Simmon, who shimmered as a shield engulfed him. Following the master's lead, Caldan opened his well and linked to his wristband. His skin tightened and his vision blurred.

Ahead of them, the shield bearer and journeymen were on their knees. Smoke drifted up from their torn and bloody clothes. One clasped a hand to his side. Blood spattered the floor and flowed through his fingers.

Simmon cursed. He dragged the shield bearer out of the line of sight through the doorway. All three journeymen wore dazed expressions and red faces, as if exposed too long to the sun. Small pieces of shattered stone littered the floor.

"Stay here," Simmon ordered the men. "Stop the bleeding, and wait for us. If you feel well enough to assist, follow us when you can."

Despite their shocked state, all three nodded. One fingered a hole in his pants. His finger came out red.

Another reverberation shook the air, again from the front of the building. Simmon turned to Caldan and nodded, obviously seeing he had his shield up.

"They won't be able to move for a while. Come, it looks like our man left a surprise to stun us and enable him to escape."

"Shouldn't we take the crafted shield?" asked Caldan. It lay next to the injured journeyman.

Simmon shook his head. "You have your own and I have my bracelet. We need speed now. Leave it."

Caldan was aware that two of Simmon's trinkets had been linked to his open well. The rings he had sensed when he first met the master.

Simmon looked around the room, searching for something. He frowned and motioned for Caldan to follow, moving carefully into the next room.

Caldan wiped his still sweaty palms on his pants, took a breath, and followed into a large sitting room with open doorways on the left and right sides, and a door ahead.

Simmon quickly poked his head into the two side openings.

Caldan nervously eyed the room for anything that looked like it could cause an explosion. Not that he knew what that would look like. It seemed the more he learned, the more there was to know. His hand gripped his sword hilt so tight it ached. With a conscious effort, he released his hold.

"Hallways," said Simmon, disappointed. "I thought there would be a back stairway somewhere, for servants and the like. We'll have to join up with the other team. Let's hope there are no more surprises on the way."

Simmon stood near the door in front of them, hand on the knob. With a twist of his wrist, he jerked the door open, rushing into the room ahead.

Another spacious room, this one with a marble floor and a wide staircase leading up. Lying amid scattered stone fragments were the other three journeymen and Master Jazintha, their clothing in tatters, covered in blood. A twisted metal shield lay on the floor, bent and rent. Jagged holes pierced the crafted metal.

Between Simmon and the bodies, the floor was clear, save for fragments of stone. With a growl, Simmon rushed forward and skidded to a stop over Jazintha. He felt her neck for a pulse and motioned for Caldan to check the journeymen.

With a sigh of relief, Simmon pulled his hand away. "Alive. She's been knocked unconscious. Looks like they ran into the same thing we did, only stronger."

"The others are alive, too," Caldan said. "But they need aid. Should I get help?"

"There isn't time. They'll have to wait. We can't let this man escape. This sorcery—destructive, so strong—I have not seen its like since—" He broke off. "We have to stop him."

Simmon looked Caldan in the eye. "You are bound to us now. No one except a select few know what some people are capable of perverting sorcery into. I told you this before, but now you've seen it." A steely look came into his eyes. He stood and peered up the staircase. "Come."

Simmon set off at a run, bounding up the stairs three at a time with Caldan racing after him. At the top, a large landing opened onto a hallway, with more stairs continuing up.

Simmon stopped abruptly at the landing, eyes closed. Caldan sensed he drew from his well, focusing his talent to search for something. On his hand, one of his rings pulsed with power.

For a full minute, both stood there, Simmon with eyes closed, Caldan too nervous to close his own. Blocking external stimuli always helped, but he was too scared. He sensed nothing on this level, though below them he felt pulses of power from Jazintha and the journeymen, and an . . . absence, the size of which led him to believe it had to be the shield. Still functioning, whatever its use was, despite the damage it had sustained.

Nothing else. "I can't sense anything," said Caldan.

"Me either. The two of us can't search the entire building. He's bound to escape." He took a step across the landing toward the hallway.

A faint draft of air brought the scent of lemons from above them.

"Wait," Caldan hissed.

Simmon stopped.

"Upstairs. I . . . I can smell it. It's like lemons."

Simmon looked at him disbelievingly. "You smell it?"

"Yes, sir."

"Like lemons?"

Caldan nodded. "Yes. I smell lemons, I think whenever someone close by opens their well or is linked to it. Someone is linked to their well. A sorcerer. I couldn't sense anything else. No craftings, no trinkets."

Master Simmon looked intently at Caldan. "I knew someone once who could do something similar, though it wasn't lemons. And he wasn't a sorcerer. His talent lay in other areas." He glanced back at Jazintha and the injured journeymen. "I guess we'll find out." He turned and, with a brief nod to Caldan, rushed up the staircase.

At the top, the stairs narrowed further until they were barely shoulder width before ending at a thick door, secured with a solid iron lock.

"Stand back," ordered Simmon. He removed a fingernail-sized piece of crystal from a belt pouch. Etched into its faceted surfaces were tiny glyphs. Simmon wedged it into the keyhole, then stepped back.

Caldan sensed Simmon draw from his well and link to the gem. Simmon looked at him. "Too late now," he muttered. "Doubly bound."

Caldan looked questioningly, but Simmon only shook his head.

As each moment passed, Caldan could sense the power building in the gem. There must have been powerful buffers built into the crafting to handle that much, and still it absorbed more. *What is it for? Could it unlock the door?*

A sharp retort emanated from the lock. Caldan ducked his head.

Simmon raced back up the stairs and pushed the door open. Heat radiated from the broken, twisted mess of the lock.

Through the doorway, they entered a rooftop garden. A low wall surrounded the edge of the building. A lily pond stood in one corner, the water's surface reflecting the moonlight. All around the garden, stone and metal sculptures were placed, some knee-high, while a few were man-sized. Shadows stretched across the roof, and the plants were composed of shades of gray in the washed-out light.

The garden was empty.

"By the ancestors," cursed Simmon.

Yet a strong smell of lemons hung in the night air. A gentle breeze blew the scent away, but moments later it returned.

The sorcerer was still here.

Caldan grasped Simmon's arm and squeezed, sniffing pointedly. His gaze roamed around the garden. Simmon stiffened in his grasp.

In the shadows, one of the statues moved. Moonlight shone on a short man in a fine coat and shirt.

"Ah, well," he said, voice filled with mock sorrow. "I guess it was too much to hope you wouldn't get this far. A pity. I do hate to kill unnecessarily. Such a waste."

Simmon stood straight, hands by his sides. "By the power invested in me as a Protector, I am arresting you for the use of destructive and coercive sorcery. You will be given a fair trial, and you had best come quietly."

Coercive sorcery? wondered Caldan.

"Tsk, tsk. A fair trial? A quick death is what I'll have at your hands. No, I think not."

Caldan fingered his wristband nervously. Both he and Simmon had their shields up, but what had happened below had him worried his crafting wouldn't be able to withstand such forces.

"Whatever your crimes," continued Simmon, "you'll receive a fair trial. We aren't monsters."

"Again, I think not. There is more at stake here than you realize." He tossed something in front of them that spun in the moonlight.

There was a crackling sound and a solid wall slammed into Caldan and Simmon, knocking them backward. Caldan's entire shield turned purple, totally obscuring his vision. His wristband whined under the strain, becoming hot on his skin. Lying on his back, he groaned. Simmon lay motionless beside him, without a shield protecting him. Blood trickled from his ear. Blackened and twisted, the master's thin bracelet lay next to him. They'd been lucky it hadn't been destroyed.

Caldan rolled over and levered himself to his knees. His shield had held and was still linked to his well. He felt the strain decreasing as it strove to reach equilibrium. Grunting, he dragged himself to his feet. His body felt bruised all over. Pieces of shredded leaves and branches covered the ground. He stumbled a step forward, fumbling with his sword hilt, and managed to draw his blade. The tip hit the ground. Its weight seemed to have doubled.

A voice reached him through the ringing in his ears. "My, my—your shield held."

Sweat dripped from his every pore. His skin burned hot. Ancestors, he felt like he was burning up. Caldan raised his eyes and saw the man surrounded by his own shield, this one shimmering with multicolored tones. He stood twenty paces away. Too far.

"Urgh," Caldan croaked.

"Well said. That pretty much sums up your predicament. I don't know what you're planning to do, but unless that's a trinket or a supremely smith-crafted blade, it won't be of much use. And if it is a trinket, well, that would be a blade worth dying for—which I'm afraid you're about to do. Alas, you'll find my shield far superior to yours, with your rudimentary knowledge of crafting." He shook his head. "Why you limit yourselves, I'll never understand. Crafting devices to keep the nobles and emperor happy, scrabbling in the dirt for their approval and ducats when you could have much, much more."

Caldan staggered forward another step, watching as the man drew something out of his pants pocket. He needed to act, to try something.

His skin grew hotter. Strength filled him. Aches and pains flowed away like water. He lifted his sword. This was how he had felt before the accident with Marlon, when he had driven the practice sword with strength he never knew he had.

There will be no accidents this night.

Without hesitation, he ran at the sorcerer, crossing the distance between them in the blink of an eye, faster than he had ever moved before. As he thrust with his sword, the man's confident smirk changed to a gape of surprise through the wavering air around both shields.

The tip of his blade penetrated the sorcerer's shield, cracking ribs and burying deep into his chest. For an instant Caldan saw Marlon's face overlaid on the sorcerer's and he gasped with shock.

With a pop, the sorcerer's shield winked out, and he grabbed at Caldan, lips moving but no sound coming out. The light drained from his eyes. He slumped to the ground, sword sticking from his chest. From his right hand, a crafted metal ball rolled free.

Caldan sank to his knees, trembling, exhausted. As powerful as he'd felt just moments ago, he felt equally weak now. He sucked in lungfuls of chill night air.

A boot scraped on stone behind him. He turned to see Jazintha in the doorway, leaning on a side wall. Her clothes were torn and bloody, but she was moving.

"How did you do that?" she exclaimed.

Caldan shook his head, too tired to speak.

"You must be one tough bastard. Stay there. Help is on the way." She staggered over to Simmon and knelt next to him, placing a hand on his neck. "This one's a tough bugger, too. Takes a lot to put him out of action." She glanced at Caldan. "Looks like he was right to bring you along tonight." She laughed loudly. A surprisingly warm and mellow sound.

Jazintha sat next to Simmon and used a rag to wipe his face, chuckling all the while. "For a moment there, I thought we were in trouble. But . . . we're alive," she said cheerfully.

Caldan groaned and lay back on the chill ground, looking up at the moon, letting the night air cool his hot, sweaty skin.

It wasn't long before he heard boot treads rushing up the stairs. Two masters and six journeymen surged onto the rooftop, spreading themselves as if prepared for action. Probably not a bad precaution, considering what they must have been told, and what they must have seen downstairs.

Seeing nothing dangerous in the roof garden, they relaxed. Most gathered around Simmon and Jazintha, while two journeymen hurried to where Caldan lay. They stopped short when they saw the corpse.

Jazintha spoke in hushed tones to the Protectors around her, frequently glancing in Caldan's direction. They all turned to look at him. Jazintha continued and drew their attention back to her. Two journeymen near Caldan rifled through the clothes of the rogue sorcerer, retrieving items from his pockets, removing his rings and a pendant from around his neck, and gathering up the metal ball. All went into a cloth sack, which they tied securely and handed to one of the masters.

Caldan sighed. He didn't understand what had happened himself, and no doubt they would question him for hours on his version of events. Right now, he could do with a hot bath and a good meal.

And a few strong ciders.

CHAPTER 32

Aidan was drunk off his ass. What remained of Caitlyn's company—now *his* ragtag troop—had set a blistering pace after he'd killed her. They were heading for Anasoma as fast as they dared. The wounded men and women in the wagons were slowing them down, but he had ordered everyone to maintain a fierce pace. Two wagons lay abandoned in their wake, axles broken, occupants squeezed into the remaining wagons, horses laden with as much as they could bear.

They'd been on the road for weeks, the injured slowly recovering, physically if not mentally. Aidan had become increasingly withdrawn, taking to his bedroll early, more often than not carrying a jug of spirits to console himself. The consequences of his actions and Caitlyn's death haunted his dreams and his waking thoughts. Though he'd saved the women in the barn, he knew the damage to his psyche would take a long time to heal, if it ever did.

He was shaken awake by Tully, a soldier who'd traveled with them for years, when they were a few days out from Anasoma.

"Piss off," Aidan cursed at Tully in a slurred, stumbling voice. He turned into his bedroll, away from Tully. "A little while longer," he mumbled.

"Sir . . . Aidan . . . it's well past dawn. We should break camp and get going." He hesitated. "If you don't mind me saying, sir, you shouldn't be drinking so much. It won't make things any better."

Aidan turned to face him. "It's none of your bloody business! Leave me alone."

Tully backed away and stood by the fire, now no more than glowing coals. From the look of things, everyone had been fed and water had been boiled for tea. One of the women approached, her belly swollen with child. She looked wan and tired but much better than the condition they'd found her in. Food and rest had done her good.

She looked around nervously. "Sir," she said and waited. Aidan made no reply. "Please, sir. You mustn't blame yourself."

Only the crackling of the fire and the background noise of the camp permeated the silence. She knelt next to Aidan, hands resting on her thighs, eyes downcast. "You and your men saved us. We'd still be in that place if it wasn't for you." Her hands gripped her skirt tightly. The bulge in her stomach pressed against the material. "Your leader . . . the lady . . . she thought we carried them inside us, thought our babies would be like them, but they aren't. They chose the strongest men from the villages around, the smartest, and brought them to us. We don't know why, but we talked among ourselves, reasoned a few things out. They raised the children well, fed them, clothed them, made sure they exercised and didn't hurt themselves. But they never taught them anything, save for what they could to make things easier so they didn't have to look after them all the time. It was like . . . they didn't need them to grow, you know, in their minds." She reached out and touched him gently on the shoulder. "I hadn't been there long . . ." She touched her stomach. "Long enough, I suppose. But others were there years. They saw their children grow to a certain age before they were taken away. Sometimes one would come back, later. They were one of them then, changed somehow, as if their minds were taken over. But we knew our children were normal until then.

They were normal," she repeated fiercely. "Your leader, the lady, would have killed us all. Slaughtered all of us and all our babies for no reason. You did the right thing."

Aidan blinked through tears then reached up and clasped her hand. "Thank you," he said.

She nodded.

He watched her leave, then stood, brushing dust from his pants. He rubbed sleep from his eyes and looked around for a waterskin. He drained one dry.

"Tully," he called. "Is there any breakfast left?"

"Some porridge. Cold, though."

"Dish me up some. I'm hungry."

"Right you are, sir." Tully scraped cold porridge into a bowl and handed it to Aidan.

Looking at the gluggy mess, Aidan sighed and spooned in a mouthful, chewing methodically.

"Good to have you back, sir."

Aidan grunted in reply and set to devouring his breakfast.

"The tea's bitter by now. Do you want any?"

Aidan shook his head, swallowing the last spoonful of porridge. "Gather the men. We can't handle all of this ourselves. The women need somewhere to stay, to settle down, and we need to let people know what we found."

"Lady Caitlyn was trained by the Protectors," said Tully. "She always said if things went bad we should get word to them."

Aidan pondered this for a moment and then nodded in agreement. "That's what I was thinking. Though how am I going to tell them I killed her?"

Glancing toward the rescued women bustling around the camp, Tully shrugged. "Tell them the truth."

CHAPTER 33

Caldan's fingers traced the runes cast into his wristband. It had performed remarkably well last night, its strength keeping him conscious long enough to give them a chance.

After arriving back at the guild, he'd waved away questions directed at him and fallen into an exhausted sleep until midday. When he managed to rouse himself, his first thought was of Simmon.

He trudged to the infirmary, where the master rested. Apparently, Simmon had woken earlier in the morning, and they'd managed to get some broth into him before he slept again. Caldan had sat on a couch beside his bed since arriving hours ago, waiting for him to wake.

When he did, Simmon's eyes were clear, and judging from his protests at drinking another bowl of broth, he suffered no long-term effects from his hard knock. He waved away those fussing around him but asked Caldan to stay and go over what happened after he lost consciousness.

Simmon lay half-awake in bed, covered by two blankets despite the warm afternoon air. He was still groggy from the bump to his head. The prognosis was that he would have a headache for a few days but would otherwise recover with no ill effects.

Caldan's own body ached, as if after a particularly strenuous day of exercises followed by being beaten with sticks, though the long sleep had done wonders for his spirit.

He recounted his version of the raid to Simmon a few times. Each time, the master picked at his observations with probing questions on what he'd seen and felt. He was especially interested in the events directly after his shield had failed and he lost consciousness, making Caldan go over every second of the encounter, every word said, every action taken, everything Caldan had sensed and experienced.

Caldan sighed and rubbed the back of his sore neck. His head ached. "Then I said, 'Urgh,' or maybe it was 'Argh.' I can't be sure."

"Don't be flippant, lad. The smallest thing could prove useful in the future." Simmon had by this stage thrown off his blankets and sat cross-legged on the bed. He rubbed both eyes vigorously. "So then he spoke about how we only have a basic knowledge of crafting and his shield was superior to ours."

"Yes. And how sorcerers sold themselves to the nobles and emperor for their approval and ducats."

"And then you ran him through." Simmon looked pointedly at Caldan. "As he drew out another crafting, one similar to what laid us both out and destroyed my shield. What I can't figure out is that he must have been fifteen yards away or more. How did you get to him before he could use his sorcery . . . and how did you pierce his shield?"

Caldan could only shrug.

"Pass me your wristband," said Simmon suddenly.

With feigned nonchalance, Caldan pushed his sleeve up and drew off his crafting, placing it in Simmon's waiting hand.

The master looked it over critically, and Caldan felt the hum as he opened his well. Simmon stared intently at the wristband for a few minutes before nodding in approval.

"Well, lad, it's a fine piece of work. I wish all journeymen could craft such a lovely piece. And a few masters could take note, too. A good alloy—you'll have to tell its composition. A fine casting. The overall aesthetics are pleasing, as well."

He weighed the wristband in his hand before returning it. Caldan grasped the metal, but Simmon didn't let go.

He looked Caldan in the eye. "It weathered much last night, better than my own crafting did." Caldan remembered Simmon's bracelet lying blackened and twisted at his side. "There's true virtue in it. It seems you've found another of your talents, one that will set you up nicely here. There's high demand for crafting of such quality, and I fear the standards of the sorcerers have . . . diminished over the centuries. Those with such a talent are well regarded and can charge a high price for their work."

"I hadn't thought . . . that is, I hadn't given much thought as to what I would end up doing once I became a journeyman."

Simmon let go of the wristband. "I'll give my approval of this piece," he said, to Caldan's surprise. "Normally, it would be tested by a few masters, but it's already proven itself by surviving when mine didn't. And we're lucky it did. I'm glad I asked you along. Furthermore, I'd have you submit the piece as proof of your mastery of the intermediary principles of crafting, for your admittance to the rank of journeyman."

Caldan was stunned for a few moments. "That's . . . really good. Thank you."

Yet even as he said it, he realized what that could mean. Smith-crafting day after day for other people held no appeal for him. Still, the rank and access to better resources, including the libraries, was invaluable. Chances were, he would make better progress researching his trinket, as well as smith-crafting a simulacrum.

"If your crafting is all like that, you deserve it. Show the lazy journeymen and masters a thing or two. But it isn't just for your own benefit I'm doing this. Many masters—and journeymen, if rumors are to be believed—thought I was wrong in admitting an apprentice as old as you, despite the talent I saw in you. Old habits die hard, I suppose, but when you're raised to journeyman rank so soon, it'll silence their talk. And it may get them thinking. They're too set in their ways. Anyway, enough of my rambling. Back to last night."

Simmon shifted his weight on the bed to a more comfortable position, obviously organizing his thoughts before addressing Caldan again.

"Jazintha was here earlier this morning, when I first woke. She . . . detailed what she saw of the encounter, and it corresponds closely with your version."

Caldan opened his mouth to object that he wouldn't have lied to the master, but Simmon held up a hand to forestall his protest. "I trust you, lad, but it's always better to have multiple views of events. People sense and feel differently. What seemed like a moment to you could actually have been longer. It's important we find out all we can about the encounter. From what the sorcerer said, he wasn't acting alone, and we need to know how you managed to overcome him." He gave Caldan a sidelong look. "More than that, though, I have to ask: Are you all right?" he said softly. "Have you killed anyone before?"

Caldan shook his head. "No. Almost, once. But . . . no, I haven't."

Simmon nodded grimly. "It affects everyone differently, and it isn't something you get used to. I would say it's not something you *should* get used to. Some try not to think about it, to push it to one side, imagine it's either him or them, and that's the end of it. Others feel it deeply, the taking of a life, and it weighs on them forever."

"I . . ." Caldan swallowed. "It was him or me, but . . . I don't think I will get used to it, and I hope I won't have to do it again."

As he spoke, he saw Simmon eyeing him, gauging his response.

"Good. If you need to talk about it, come to me. Now, Jazintha confirmed you crossed the distance between you and the sorcerer in a heartbeat. To quote her, 'I wouldn't have believed it if I hadn't seen it myself.' Her exact words." He looked at Caldan expectantly.

Not knowing what to say, Caldan shrugged again and spread his hands in uncertainty.

"You don't know how you did it?"

"No. I remember feeling hot. My skin felt like it was burning, as if I had a bad sunburn. It was like . . . like with Marlon."

"Who's Marlon?"

"Jemma's . . . my friend's brother, at the monastery. He was the reason I had to leave. He didn't like his sister hanging around with me, thought their family was too good."

"And what happened?"

"It all came to a head one day, and we dueled with wooden practice swords. The monks didn't let us use anything else, except on certain occasions. And while I'm a competent swordsman, Marlon was a great deal better."

"I think you sell yourself short. You defeated me."

"That was another strange moment," he admitted. "But trust me: before that night, I had never bested Marlon—never even come close. I don't know—maybe stressful situations change something. I just don't know." Frustration tinged his words.

"Maybe. I have heard . . . No matter. Go on."

"Marlon was . . . is . . . a master swordsman. Even the monks at the monastery were impressed. He had a rare skill and liked showing off. It was one of the things I didn't like about him." Caldan gazed out the window into the windy courtyard. "We fought, and it was the first time something like this happened, these 'strange moments.' I thrust at his chest, but . . . I had a speed, a strength I didn't know. My sword cracked; the broken half pierced his chest. I blacked out after that. All I know is that he survived, and because of what I'd done to him, the monastery wouldn't have me there. They feared Marlon's family would make trouble if I remained."

"They did you a kindness."

Caldan looked up sharply. "How so?"

"Sounds like Marlon's the type to make trouble, and not just for the monastery, but for you as well. I'm sure he hasn't forgotten, and if he has the resources is probably looking for you."

Caldan shook his head in denial, then stopped. Simmon was probably right. Why hadn't he thought of that before?

"Don't worry," the master continued. "As a journeyman Protector, you won't have anything to worry about. We have a lot of weight with the nobles and with the emperor. He knows how important we are.

Let me think about this for a while—although I do wish you would have told me all of this before." He gave Caldan a steady look before saying, "What about the sorcerer's shield? Any thoughts on how you managed to pierce it?"

"Excuse me, Master Simmon, but *was* he a sorcerer? I mean, aren't all the sorcerers known by the guild? Should we be calling him one?"

"Technically, he's a rogue, not a member of the guild. But there was no doubting his skill. Talented and well trained, more so than many of us, apparently. And in forbidden knowledge, destructive sorcery."

"I don't know if I'm ready for this. Last night was . . . like something I've never seen. The power in the sorcerer, the confidence in his ability. I can't help but think I'm not ready."

"It doesn't matter. You've seen and you know too much. The choice is no longer yours."

"The choice was never mine—I only know about all this because you told me and took me along last night!" protested Caldan.

"I did what I thought I had to do. This isn't a game we play. The very empire is at stake. I saw something in you, and after last night, I'm sure I was right to bring you in, to make you one of us."

"But I'm not one of you—"

"There is no stopping it now. It's done."

"And what if I don't want to be a Protector?" demanded Caldan.

Simmon smiled. "The emperor is harsh with those who want to leave the Protectors. I'm sorry. Usually, we give people time to decide if they want to spend the rest of their life with us. With you . . . well, I don't think we could afford to pass up someone with such talent. More than talent, perhaps."

"What do you mean?"

"I'll need to consult a few other masters, and maybe a few texts in our library. Suffice it to say, I've heard of someone with some of the abilities you've shown—smelling sorcery, the flashes of speed and strength. Someone who was more dedicated to the cause than the Protectors, if that's possible. But that's all I'm willing to say until I'm sure."

Caldan stood and paced the room. He *did* want to know more.

More about the Protectors, more about sorcery, more about his own supposed talents. Most of all, he wanted to continue learning and smith-crafting his own creations. His visit to the clockmaker had opened up areas of possibility he hadn't thought achievable before. Becoming a Protector would offer all this. But the strings attached . . . He snorted.

Strings or chains, depending on how you view the situation.

He sighed deeply. He knew Simmon watched him, expecting a reaction, but what could he do? It didn't sound like he had any choice in the matter anymore. The last time he had been exiled, he had landed on his feet, lucky to have found himself at first apprenticed and now raised to journeyman rank so soon. Now he couldn't think of anywhere else he could go, and being hunted by other Protectors or the Quivers didn't hold any appeal. And what happened to Protectors who knew too much and wanted to leave? He pushed that thought to the back of his mind to go over later. He didn't think it would be pleasant.

"All right," he found himself saying to Simmon's visible relief. "I still have much to learn, and that's why I joined the guild. As long as there aren't any repeats of last night anytime soon."

Simmon laughed. "Last night was an exception in more ways than one." His tone grew serious. "You saved everyone, Caldan. If you hadn't been there, we'd all be dead. I won't sugarcoat it; being a Protector is a hard life. But it's important work and very rewarding. Not only do we defend others from harm, we are caretakers of knowledge thought to have been lost during the Shattering." He gestured toward the door. "Go. Think about what I've said. Rest if you can. I'll find you tomorrow. We need to go over the process of having you raised. Don't worry, it's not overly complicated."

CALDAN STRODE THROUGH the darkening streets of Five Flowers. He walked briskly along the paved main road, shops on both sides closing their doors while others put out lanterns or sorcerous globes for the night's custom.

Clutched in one hand was a bag filled with craftings the clock-maker required.

Caldan was relieved the shop door stood open. Inside, the clock-maker rubbed his hands and smiled, seeing the bag Caldan carried.

A short while later, Caldan left, the bag bulging in different places as the contents had been replaced.

CHAPTER 34

Demons came in many forms, Amerdan knew. Mostly sorcerers. But they could be found among the lowliest vagrants and the highest nobles. Never children. Most of those he walked among had no inkling of what he was, what he was becoming. They were vessels that served only to be drained of their talents, if he judged them worthy. But this Caldan . . . this sorcerer . . . was not like the others.

This Amerdan knew with certainty. He sensed something in him. A potential.

He looked up at the wall of the Sorcerers' Guild. Caldan could be in there, somewhere. But so could many other sorcerers—with their powers and their malevolence. He felt the urge to go in, to find Caldan, to question him.

Though that would end up bloody. It always did. And sorcerers had their tricks. They might discover him.

Amerdan shook his head to clear it. There was something binding Caldan to him. A likeness. A kinship.

Amerdan savored the word. It contained both weakness and strength. And as such, what he felt was . . . untrustworthy. The simplest solution was to take his essence, like he had so many others. But if Caldan was indeed like him, then were there others? Or was Caldan the only one? This thought both disturbed and excited him. What would he become if they merged? A thrill passed through him.

Risky. Too risky. For now. He nodded to himself. *I'll find out more.* To be sure.

He turned his back and strolled down a busy road, with barely a thought to where he was going. It didn't matter. Opportunities would present themselves. They always did.

He'd come across one on his way to Anasoma. He'd joined a merchant train along with a few other travelers, led by an affable trader with three guards and their wagon full of goods. They thought their journey would be an easy one. Amerdan knew that sometimes there was no safety in numbers. Two other travelers came along on that trip: a quiet serving girl, who was on her way back from visiting relatives, and a coarse barbarian sell-sword, who stank like he hadn't bathed in months. The trader's hand had been shifting his plums constantly, with no thought that people might see, and in front of the girl, too. Bloody savage.

And a bloody journey that had been, the road not as safe as everyone had hoped.

Amerdan gave a quiet snort of amusement at that, then realized he was entering Gallows, one of the poorest districts in the city, just north of Cabbage Town. He scowled, moving to the side of the road. Shops lined the street, and barrels were stored against the wall closest to him.

The street shifted under his feet, like the deck of a ship in a storm. His hands gripped the edge of a barrel, his back against a wall for stability. The feeling would pass.

A shopkeeper in an apron approached cautiously. It was his barrel.

"Sorry, good sir," Amerdan mumbled. "A slight . . . dizzy spell. I'm sure it'll pass soon." He wiped a forearm across his sweaty brow.

The shopkeeper nodded curtly and went back behind his stall, keeping an eye on him.

Amerdan sucked in deep breaths. The world swam again before righting itself. A gentle breeze blew over his damp skin, cooling it and raising bumps. His strength returned in a rush, as it always did. Blood pumping hard, he stood up straight. He had no idea what caused these weak episodes, but he wished they would stop. They were more frequent after he absorbed someone; they tailed off but never went away totally.

His hands brushed his vest and tugged at the hem, straightening his shirt. He bent his neck to one side, then the other, stretching tightened muscles. The shopkeeper had finished with his customer and was staring at him. Amerdan ignored him and strode off into the crowd.

The stench of this part of the city assailed his nostrils. Forgotten in his rare moment of weakness, the stink came back multiplied. He fished about in a pocket for a perfumed kerchief, which he held to his nose. A plain-looking woman sneered at him.

If only she knew, he thought. Sneers came cheap. She wouldn't be sneering under his knife.

He looked away. She wasn't worth it. A no-talent peasant. A nobody, destined to mediocrity and a squalid life. The thought cheered him greatly.

He liked to come here, despite the smells, the seediness, the nastiness that was the slums. Every city had them, these pits of foulness where people of no consequence lived until they did the only useful thing of their miserable existence and died, usually young, before they could add too much misery to an already miserable world. Anyone worthy lifted themselves above such a place, as he had long ago.

Dust stirred, dirtying the bottoms of his pants. Paint on buildings was cracked and flaky. Threadbare washing hung on lines crossing the street, strung from windows. Drops of water fell into the crowd.

It was good to remind yourself of your origins, lest you lost sight of how far you'd come.

Twenty yards in front of him, a head peeked out from an alley. Tangled blond hair framed a dirty face. A young girl. His breath caught in his throat. She looked so like Teresia, his youngest sister.

Amerdan moved to the side of the street and pretended to examine the clumsy pottery wares of a street vendor. He waved the vendor's offers of assistance away with a frown and picked up a teapot.

Out of the corner of his eye, he saw the thin waif sidle around the corner and look about the street with trepidation. Her gaze kept returning to the stall next to the pottery, where Amerdan stood. An herbalist. Bunches of herbs with various medicinal properties lined the table, as well as glass jars filled with ground powders and a weighing scale. The fat woman behind the stall stood chatting to another woman.

Really, this teapot was shoddily made. The spout and the handle didn't line up.

The girl glanced warily around her, then weaved through the crowd. Not much of a challenge for one as small as she was. Hands moved to secure purses as she stepped past. Amerdan could tell that wasn't what she was after.

And the glaze, who would choose brown for a pot they planned to sell?

The girl's shoulders hunched in her baggy gray smock as she tried to make herself look smaller, less noticeable.

Ah, little one, haven't you realized no one notices those less fortunate than themselves? No one cares.

Inept, too, the streaky brown glaze. Patches of fired clay poked through gaps.

The girl approached the herbalist's stall. A few paces away, she stopped, hesitant. Her grubby face was tear streaked, and she bit her bottom lip. Her hands clenched into fists. She stepped forward.

A price was written on the glaze of the teapot in black chalk. *A whole silver ducat, for this piece of crap?* Perhaps the pottery vendor was trying to pass it off as the work of a known local artist. The vendor edged closer, warming to the idea that Amerdan was interested in the teapot. Amerdan caught his eye.

The girl furtively snatched some herbs and a glass jar. A bunch of mint and . . . chamomile tea in the jar, unless he missed his guess. Unlikely. Strange herbs for a girl to be stealing, unless she had an upset stomach, but that's not an ailment worth risking the labor camps for. The herbalist paused in her conversation and turned toward her table.

Amerdan dropped the teapot, which smashed on the cobbles. Broken shards struck his shin. Heads turned at the sound. The pottery vendor's face went dark. The herbalist frowned in his direction. The blond-haired girl disappeared into the crowd.

"Oops," said Amerdan.

Muttering rose around him as the pottery vendor approached, his face angry. Amerdan pulled out a silver ducat and held it up. The man smiled, and all was forgiven, as it was with these types of people and coins. The shopkeeper reeked of days-old sweat and onions. Amerdan resisted the urge to smash his head into the wall. He handed the ducat over and walked off without a word. Twenty paces up the street, he turned into the alley the girl had disappeared down. Racing up a rickety staircase attached to the side of a building, Amerdan reached the top and scrambled onto the roof.

It didn't take long before he caught up with her. She scurried quickly down alleys and lanes, not bothering to lay a false trail or double back, making a beeline for somewhere. She cast a furtive look behind her now and again to confirm she wasn't being followed. Her bare feet slapped on the cobbles.

She disappeared inside the entrance to a wooden tenement, the type Amerdan knew well. It was falling apart, probably abandoned by its owners as a derelict and taken over by local toughs, who rented cheap rooms to the desperate and needy. From his vantage on the rooftops, Amerdan could see through some of the windows. There was barely any furniture in sight, mostly scraps of rags, rickety cots, and one chair.

The girl hadn't thought to look up, though if she had, she wouldn't have seen him stalking her. He was too good to get caught.

He looked down into the street. Empty. He stepped off the roof and plummeted the three floors to the cobbles, landing on his feet. He grinned. His new self always kept him impressed.

He stepped inside the dark doorway, eyes adjusting instantly to the lack of light. He took the steps three at a time, following the scent of mint the girl carried to the first floor and down a corridor.

A door opened, and a burly man stepped out. Half a head taller than Amerdan, with skin like tanned leather and a graying beard, he looked surprised to see him, and his dark eyes narrowed.

"Ain't seen you around here afore," his gravelly voice rasped. He took in Amerdan's fine clothes and trimmed hair. "Best you be leaving, 'less you want a beating."

He folded muscular arms across his chest as his eyes moved to the purse attached to Amerdan's belt. Through the open door to the apartment, empty bottles of cheap liquor littered the floor.

Amerdan smiled. "I'm looking for a little girl around so high." He held a hand at waist height. "Blond hair, thin. Seen her?"

The man stroked his beard, and a cunning look came into his eyes. "Maybe I have, and maybe I ain't. What's it worth to ya?"

"A ducat. Silver, of course," replied Amerdan.

The man grunted, scratching an armpit. "For a silver, I know where she is; for two, you can spend a little time with her. Been keepin' an eye on the lass. She'll be a beauty, that's for sure." He leered at Amerdan.

He doesn't know me at all, but how could he? I barely recognize myself.

Amerdan's hand shot up and clamped around the big man's throat. He squeezed as the man struggled, cutting off his breath. Amerdan ignored the man's futile attempts to break his grasp. He lifted the man's feet off the floor, pushed him into his room, and kicked the door shut behind him.

With a crash, he slammed the man against a wall, which shook with the force. Old timbers groaned, dust drifting down from ceiling beams. Amerdan pressed hard against him, stopping the man's legs from flailing out. His face turned an ugly shade of red. His stench was an assault on Amerdan's senses.

"You think you know me?" hissed Amerdan as he squeezed tighter. The man whimpered, his pounding fists grew weaker, and his heels scraped futilely against the wall.

Amerdan punched him twice in the chest above his heart with the force of a hammer striking an anvil. Ribs cracked, blood dribbled from the man's mouth; his heart beat once, twice, then stopped.

Amerdan released his grip, and the corpse slid to the floor in a crumpled heap. Five red finger marks lay deeply gouged in the man's neck, already purpling to bruises.

He left the room without a backward glance.

Stopping at the door across the corridor, he sniffed. No. A few steps to the neighboring door and he stopped again, sniffed. He rested his forehead on the rough door. This one.

He tested the doorknob. Locked. He twisted, and with a shriek of metal, the lock broke. He pushed the door open and strode into the gloomy interior.

There were no windows, and the only light filtered in through cracks in the old timber walls. A few larger cracks were stuffed with rags, presumably to keep the wind out. He could hear breathing from two different sources, through a doorway to the right.

At the doorway, he stopped. The little girl knelt next to a bed, on which lay a boy breathing in shallow, hurried gasps. Sweat poured from his skin.

Both were filthy and clad in rags. A cockroach ran across the floor into the corner.

The girl didn't look up at Amerdan as she busily shredded mint leaves into a cup. She stopped tearing the mint, then opened the jar of chamomile tea, pouring a teaspoon's worth into the cup. From a clay jug beside her, she filled the cup with cold water, then gave the mixture a stir with her finger.

"There," she whispered. "I got you some medicine, Pieter. You'll get better soon." She lifted the cup to the boy's lips and poured. Most of the mixture dribbled down the side of his face. "Drink, please," she said between quiet sobs.

Amerdan knelt beside her on the dirty floor. He removed the cup from her hand.

"Little miss," he said gently, "I don't think those are the right herbs to make Pieter better."

He felt the boy's brow. He was burning up, and Amerdan judged he had damp lung. Nothing to worry about if you were rich, had a nice place to live and plenty of ducats for a physiker. But here, with the cold, the malnutrition, the lack of medicine to ease the symptoms, it would be fatal.

The girl ran the back of a hand across her face. "He's my brother. I . . . I don't know what to do."

"Shh, there, there." Amerdan patted her shoulder. "Don't be sad. I'm here now." He looked around the room. As bare as a larder at the end of winter. "We have to take him to . . . get some real medicine."

"We can't leave. We have to wait for Da."

From the look of the place—and the smell of their clothes—Amerdan guessed they'd been waiting for some time. No chance they would be missed for a while, if at all. He turned the girl to face him. Tears ran through the dirt on her face, leaving trails of cleaner skin. "I'll make sure your da knows where you are when he gets back, I promise. What's your name?"

She tilted her head and stared at the floor. "Annie."

"Listen, Annie, we're going to take Pieter somewhere where he can get better. Soon he won't suffer anymore, but I need you to be strong for him. Can you do that?"

Annie nodded once, hands clenched tightly in front of her dress.

"Good. Now, I need you to gather up what belongings you have." She frowned and looked puzzled. "Your . . . stuff," he added. "Clothes, whatever you have of value."

Annie nodded. Patting Pieter on the hand, she shuffled off to a table.

Amerdan slid an arm under the sick boy and lifted him off the bed. Pieter moaned, though his eyes remained closed. Amerdan cradled him against his chest with one arm. Annie returned carrying a comb made from bone. She looked at him expectantly.

"That's all?" he asked.

She looked around the bare room for a few moments, then nodded.

Amerdan placed a hand on her back and gave a gentle push. "Good. Let's go."

AMERDAN LAID PIETER gently down onto the clean sheets. There was a tart alchemical scent in the air, and a child coughed in the next room. The boy groaned and writhed, skin slick with sweat, and the physiker moved in to calm him. Annie had a firm grip of Pieter's hand, and Amerdan didn't think he'd be able to pry her loose for some time. Annie watched the physiker timidly and with curiosity as the woman peered into Pieter's ears and throat, using a strange instrument with a tiny sorcerous globe to create a beam of light.

Amerdan patted Annie on the head and left her clinging to Pieter. Outside, the head physiker, Zakarius, a bald man with skin as dark as midnight, waited patiently. Amerdan handed him a purse heavy with ducats.

"Make sure the boy is taken care of. And the girl. Is there anywhere she can stay?"

"It's unusual," Zakarius said, "but she can stay in the dormitory with the children who have almost recovered. Though, if she isn't sick herself, she can't stay long."

Amerdan nodded. "Just until the boy recovers, then they can both be moved. Their parents won't be coming for them, so I'll have to arrange for accommodation after that."

Zakarius shook his head sadly. "Ah, perhaps I can ask around. A good number of wealthy families pass through here; a place could be found with one of them."

"I don't think they should be split up; they should remain together as a family."

"I agree. I will see what I can do." Zakarius coughed discreetly into a hand. "There is one more thing." He hesitated. "I hate to bring this up, but your sister's treatment needs to be continued, and the ducats you provided last time have almost run out. You need to decide whether to continue or—"

"No. You must keep going; she will recover."

"I'm afraid her illness is as much of the spirit as it is physical; perhaps if—"

Amerdan silenced him with a glare. "Here." He handed over another purse. "That should last a few more months." It was all the ducats he had left, apart from a few remaining in the shop. He needed to obtain more, and soon. Luckily, with his talents, it wasn't hard to take all he needed from those beneath him.

"As you wish, sir." Zakarius gestured down the hall. "Would you like to visit her? Although there hasn't been any measurable progress, the physikers believe your presence could help to bring about some change."

Amerdan shook his head. "I . . . can't. Not yet. Not until I atone."

Zakarius nodded thoughtfully, and his eyes wrinkled in sympathy. "I won't ask, we all have demons. Very well. I will make arrangements for her and for the two children. Annie and Pieter, isn't it?"

"Yes."

Zakarius held out a hand for Amerdan to shake. "I must say, it's always a pleasure to know there are people like you out there. So noble and selfless."

Amerdan ignored the proffered hand. He didn't want to help the children; it was a weakness he hadn't been able to rid himself of. But they were innocent, as he and his sisters had been before the sorcerer . . . Amerdan squeezed his eyes shut and clenched his jaw. The sorcerer deserved his anger and contempt . . . and if he was truthful, perhaps some gratitude as well for what Amerdan was becoming.

CHAPTER 35

Caldan woke to scuffling outside his room. Rubbing his eyes, he glanced out the window into the pale light of dawn. Who would be making a ruckus at this time?

He opened his door and poked his head out. At the end of the corridor, two men dragged an unconscious master, while more men came toward him clad in smith-crafted armor and carrying naked blades.

He didn't recognize them . . . and he knew something was very, very wrong.

Stifling a gasp, he retreated into his room, locking the door. Thinking frantically, he scrambled for a blank piece of paper, drew the stopper from a bottle of ink, and madly scribed glyphs. As he had done in his room at the inn when he first arrived, he fixed the still wet crafting to the door and opened his well, sealing the entrance against all but the most determined assault.

Sounds of struggle reached his ears, punctuated by claps of muted thunder.

Moments later, the latch jiggled. A fist banged on the wood.

"Open up!" a voice commanded.

Caldan sunk back against the far wall, away from the door. Muffled voices sounded in a strange accent he hadn't heard before.

" . . . doesn't matter; we need to clear every room . . ."

" . . . you go. I'll deal with this . . . No . . . We don't have time."

By the ancestors! If he hadn't been so worn out or had woken earlier. Although, if the masters were taken, would that have mattered? Even now, "safe" in his room, he wasn't sure what he could do. Should he fight? Should he go quietly? Or should he continue to cower behind his door like a frightened child?

Definitely not a child.

Creeping to the door, Caldan listened intently as footsteps faded. They were gone. But then he could hear clothing rustle, and there was a scratch at his door.

The scent of lemons reached his nostrils, faint at first, then steadily stronger.

Caldan grabbed his wristband and purse of ducats, shoving them into the sack he had brought back from the clockmaker's. He yanked his trinket off his finger, the bone ring from around his neck, and added them to the sack. He opened his window. Two floors below in the garden, a row of shrubs ran along the wall. He dropped the sack, praying it would remain hidden until he could retrieve it.

A flash of light blinded him, and an invisible force knocked him back against the wall. His ears rang like a bell. Smoke filled the room, and his door fell toward him onto the floor, hinges and lock melted into misshapen lumps of glowing iron.

He coughed and raised an arm to protect himself, his eyes watering as he saw a blurry figure approach.

"You bugger. Made me waste a flash."

A hand cuffed Caldan roughly around the head, then grasped his shirt, dragging him across the floor on his knees.

Not quietly either, then.

Caldan drove a fist into the man's groin, dropping him like a stone. The man wheezed and clutched his plums. Pain exploded in Caldan's head, and he fell to the floor. He blinked and shook his head to clear it. Above him stood another man, a club raised to strike.

"I wouldn't do that again," he said. "We've orders not to harm anyone . . . too seriously." He nudged his comrade with a toe. "Get up, Castens, you lazy bastard."

"Piss off, Mosey," Castens moaned. "You take a punch to the plums and see how you feel."

Mosey laughed. "That's something I don't plan on doing." He watched, amused, as Castens levered himself to his knees, breathing deeply and wincing. "Come on, we don't got all day."

With short, shallow breaths Castens gingerly rose to his feet, hunched over, hands on knees. He muttered something under his breath. Turning to Caldan, he drew a dagger.

"Now, now," Castens said. "Don't do anything stupid. Keys will kill you; and Bells . . . well, she don't need to kill you."

Keys? Bells? Were those people?

Castens gave Caldan a hateful look, then drove the knife deep into Caldan's thigh and twisted. Caldan screamed, burning pain shooting up his leg.

"Castens, you stupid bastard! How's he going to walk now?"

"He punched me in the plums. He deserved it."

"He's bleeding everywhere."

"So?"

"You're an idiot. Here, help me bandage him up."

"I ain't helping."

"You're going to help, and then you're going to help me carry him."

Caldan clutched his leg. Warm blood leaked through his fingers. Suddenly, a foot pressed Caldan's hands into his wound. Pain flared.

"Stop that. We need to get him locked up as soon as possible. Time's a-wastin'."

Castens cursed, then wiped his blade on Caldan's pants. The other one removed a rolled bandage from a bulging pouch attached to his belt and wrapped it tightly around Caldan's leg. Even in his pain, Caldan realized they were professionals, despite their roughness— prepared for contingencies, and organized.

They dragged him to his feet. "Oof! You're a heavy one, aren't you?" One hand held his shoulder tightly while another frisked his clothes, searching for something. Caldan wiped his eyes, blinking to clear them.

"No mark of rank," said Castens. "No craftings and no trinkets. Bugger, why do I get all the duds?"

His companion laughed. Neither wore the smith-crafted armor he had glimpsed in the corridor, but each sported a number of crafted items—rings, medallions, and an earring.

"Apprentice, are you?"

Caldan nodded, leg throbbing. *Who are these men? Where are the Protectors and sorcerers?*

"Bit old, aren't you? Slow learner?"

Both men laughed.

Caldan remained silent.

"And dumb as well. Curse this, let's get him locked up and keep searching."

"Mostly done by now. I think their higher-up *sorcerers*"—he sneered the word—"have been taken."

"Best we get this lump stored, then find their workshops and libraries. Should be some good loot there."

They marched him limping along the hall and down a flight of stairs to the main building, then along a corridor Caldan had not yet explored. They passed through a heavy door bound with steel bands, then down another three flights of stairs. The air grew cold and damp. They entered a cellblock, one Caldan had no idea existed. Why would it be needed? Maybe the Protectors used it for captured rogue sorcerers.

Stone cells lined both sides of the room. Each had a moldy wooden door with a window, the opening blocked by two thick, rusty metal bars.

Caldan strained his neck as he was marched past closed doors but couldn't catch a glimpse of the occupants, if there were any. Without a word, he was thrown into one of the empty cells, falling to his knees. Once again pain flared from his leg. With a thud, the door slammed shut behind him. He heard a key slide into the keyhole, and the lock clicked into place.

Damp and musty, the cell was barely six paces on each side, the floor covered in dust and dirt. Moldy straw littered one corner, along with a scrap of what looked like a dirty rag. The bed, he assumed. A puddle of water pooled in a back corner. Through the window in the door leaked a faint yellow light, which Caldan recognized as characteristic of a sorcerous globe, though a weak or old one.

He stood and wiped his hands on his pants, though some grime from the floor remained. He shivered and rubbed his arms. It was cold but not too bad, as long as he wasn't here indefinitely. *Of course, I have no idea how I'll get out,* he thought. A rescue seemed unlikely, for even though he didn't know what had become of the masters, journeymen, and apprentices, it was safe to assume—based on Castens and Mosey's chatter—that most, if not all, had been taken prisoner. Caldan couldn't imagine any going without a fight, and the commotion he'd heard earlier meant there had been some resistance, but he hadn't heard much of anything when he had been dragged to his cell. If there had been a defense mounted, it was over now.

Which means there's probably no one out there that even knows I'm down here.

He grasped the two bars covering the window in his door and looked outside, seeing no one around. Taking a deep breath, he strained against them, grunting with effort. After a few moments, he released his hold, then strained again, to no avail. Cursing and clenching his teeth against the pain in his injured thigh, he backed up and kicked the door with a solid thump, hurting his foot.

"By the ancestors!"

Caldan clenched his fists in anger.

What was going on? Why would anyone attack the Sorcerers' Guild? Were they only after the Protectors—some sort of retaliation for the sorcerer I killed? But surely Simmon would have anticipated such a response and had the masters and journeymen on alert. Caldan thought about the crafted armor, the soldiers' casual expertise, and the way they had searched his body for craftings and trinkets.

Maybe the Protectors had been ready and it hadn't mattered. These men knew what they were doing. They were well informed and drilled. This wasn't simply a raid for loot and murder. No, imprisoning the sorcerers meant a longer-term plan, one that included keeping them alive for a purpose.

He eyed the door again. Despite its age, the timbers were solid and the rusted bars still effective. They must have known the cells were down here, which meant excellent knowledge of the building . . . which probably meant a spy. Or someone high up was working with them.

The thought was disturbing.

Caldan stood quietly at the door, listening. Silence, except for the drip, drip, drip of water somewhere behind him.

"Hello?" he whispered into the gloom, pitching his voice loud enough to be heard in the other cells. "Is anyone there?" He waited a few moments. "Hello. If you can hear me, say something, or make a noise."

"Hello back," came a woman's voice. "Who are you?"

"Caldan," he replied. "An apprentice. What . . . what's happening?"

"There's been an invasion! Soldiers and sorcerers from Indryalla, following someone they call the God-Emperor."

"Who's that? What's happened to the masters and the other students?"

"I don't know, about either. I heard there was fighting in the streets, with the Quivers always coming off second best. I was going back to my room when some men jumped me. Roughed me up and stole my craftings. The ones I had on me, anyway."

Caldan heard the woman cough before continuing.

"Sorry," she said. "My name's Senira. I'm a journeyman. I've heard of you, but you probably haven't heard of me."

"No, I haven't. Sorry." He was surprised she'd heard of him.

"No need to apologize. It's a big place. Anyway, what have you seen? Do you know what's going on?"

Caldan shook his head before realizing she couldn't see him. "No," he said. "I was in my room but managed to craft a lock on the door when I heard fighting outside. They . . ." Caldan thought about the crafting they'd used on his door. Senira wouldn't know about destructive sorcery, unless she was a Protector.

"They disabled my crafting with sorcery," he half lied.

"They must be sorcerers themselves, then. If they can open your lock, they're at least journeyman level."

"Do you know what's happened to the masters? Did they fight? Were any wounded . . . killed?"

"I didn't see anything, though I heard sounds of fighting in the garden."

Caldan frowned. The invaders meant business and, from the look of things, knew the layout of the place and had potent craftings to help them. He would bet the crafted armor was at least as good as that the Sorcerers' Guild could make. He thought of the rogue sorcerer the other night.

Maybe better.

If Simmon and the other Protectors were going up against them, he wished them luck. He sighed.

"Are you there?" Senira called.

"Yes."

"Sorry. I got . . . scared. It's cold down here. Is it just us?"

"Some of the other doors were locked, but no one's said anything yet. Well, it can't hurt to try. Hello?" he called. "Anyone else there?"

They listened in silence for a few moments. No one replied.

"Hello?" called Caldan again, to be answered with more silence. "Maybe they're unconscious or . . ." His voice trailed off. *They could be seriously hurt. An assault like this wouldn't end without some bloodshed.* His leg pulsed with pain, almost as a punctuation to his thoughts. He sucked in a breath, anticipating more.

"Do you think they're . . . alive?"

"Yes," replied Caldan with as much conviction as he could muster. "Maybe just knocked out or tied up. There wouldn't be any reason to have them here otherwise."

"Oh. Of course."

"Listen, did you manage to hide anything on you, a crafting or anything like that?"

"No," she replied hesitantly. "I didn't think to hide anything. And what I have . . . had . . . wouldn't be of any use." She began to weep.

"Shhh. Don't worry. If they were going to hurt us, they would've done so already. I can't think why, but maybe they were only after masters."

Senira continued to cry, muffling her sobs.

Caldan closed his eyes. *She isn't going to be much help. It's up to me to protect her.*

But what can I do? I have no craftings or means to make anything. A quick search of his cell revealed nothing useful. Not that he was expecting anything, but even a nail or a leftover spoon would be better than nothing. He shook his head at the idea of overcoming a guard with a spoon.

At that moment, a light appeared at the top of the stairs, sending long shadows down to the cells. Three more men appeared, dragging an unconscious figure—a man, head lolling.

"Hey!" yelled Caldan. "What are you doing? His injuries need to be looked at."

"Shut up, or I'll come in and shut you up myself."

"Why are we here? We haven't done anything."

"I told you to shut up!" The voice changed tone, murmuring to another person. Footsteps approached, followed by a tinkling. A pale-skinned woman, tall and slender with long dark hair falling to her waist, came into Caldan's limited view through the barred window. Woven into her hair were tiny silver bells of different sizes, the biggest no larger than a thumbnail. On her hand she wore a number of crafted rings. She tilted her head and gazed at Caldan. Black eyes pierced his.

"Mistress," a voice behind the woman called. "This one's locked up. We should get back now."

"In a moment," she replied, warm voice carrying in the quiet of the cells.

"Mistress, please . . ." Caldan could hear pleading in the man's voice. "The others will be—"

She turned to glare at the man, who trailed off into silence. For a few moments she stared at him before turning back to Caldan.

"I thought we were only bringing the apprentices and journeymen down here," she said.

Caldan frowned at her, puzzled. *What does she think I am?*

"We are, Mistress. All the masters are accounted for, the ones we managed to capture and those still on the run."

She tapped a cheek with one hand and pursed her lips. "What's your name?" she asked Caldan.

He clamped his lips together firmly and shook his head.

"Mute, are you? Or just stupid?" She waited a moment for his response, then breathed out a long sigh. "And yet your well is remarkable, so smooth and stable."

Caldan blinked in surprise. Of all the masters in the guild, only a few had the talent to see others' wells so clearly.

"Nothing to say?" she said with a smile. "Pity. I don't have time for niceties."

Hot needles of pain dug into Caldan's skull. His knees buckled, and he cried out wordlessly. As suddenly as it appeared, the pain receded, leaving behind a dull ache. He rolled onto his side on the floor. He didn't remember falling. Must have blacked out.

"Caldan," the lady stated. "An apprentice. There, that wasn't hard, was it? You weren't on the list. Curious."

He pushed himself to his knees, tasting blood. His nose felt hot and sticky. He wiped it, and his hand came away red.

"How . . . ?" he said shakily, and the lady laughed.

"So primitive here, so limited. Allowing such talent to go to waste." She tutted in disappointment. "We have to leave, so don't go anywhere." She chuckled at that. "My name is Bells, and I'll be back for another chat soon."

Bells. Mosey talked of her.

He heard scuffling from the cell her two men had entered. There was the sound of a fist hitting flesh. Then again, followed by a gurgling moan. Caldan strained against the opening.

The woman's footsteps echoed down the corridor to be joined by the men as they climbed the stairs. The gentle tinkling of bells receded into the distance.

Caldan rubbed his head. He lurched to his feet, weak at the knees, and clutched the bars of the door for support.

"Senira," he called. "What happened?"

"She asked you your name, then you yelled in pain. What did she do to you?"

"I don't know. Something . . . painful."

"After that, you went quiet for a bit, and then she asked you again. You told her your name and that you were an apprentice."

Caldan shook his head. "No, I didn't say anything."

"You did. You said, 'My name is Caldan, and I'm an apprentice Protector.' You sounded strange, distant."

"I don't remember anything after she first asked. I thought I blacked out."

"Well, whatever she did, you told her," Senira said. "Though I don't suppose it makes any difference. From the sound of it, they're more interested in the masters."

Caldan rubbed at the drying blood under his nose and on his hand, then knelt by the puddle in the corner, using the water to wash his hands and face.

With a grunt, he sat on the floor, back against the wall. Without the materials to craft anything, he wasn't going anywhere. The best he could hope for was to survive long enough to come up with an escape plan. Whatever these people wanted, it wasn't for the good of the Sorcerers' Guild or the Protectors.

Now there's an understatement, he thought, almost smiling. It quickly turned to a frown again.

They know destructive sorcery and . . . something else. Something that compelled my answers. The only thing that made any sense was that they were rogue sorcerers who didn't want the Protectors coming after them to bring them to justice.

For now, all he could do was wait. Once the Quivers found out what was happening, he was sure they would come to the rescue.

I hope.

Caldan rested his aching head on the cold wall and closed his eyes.

CHAPTER 36

Sweat covered his skin. Caldan blinked a few times and opened his eyes wide, trying to clear the blurriness in his sight. He shivered as his perspiration evaporated in the cold damp air of the cell. With one hand, he tried to massage the stiffness in his neck. His mouth felt dry. He needed water and hoped they wouldn't be forgotten about and left to die. Though, from what the lady with the bells in her hair had said, she would be back.

Sooner rather than later would be good, though.

He had no idea how much time had passed. At a guess, he judged a few hours, though with no window to see the sun or stars, it was impossible to tell. Shifting his weight, he knelt, trying not to put pressure on his leg wound. Not feeling any pain, he rose slowly, hands on the wall to steady himself, then paused to take a few breaths. His leg didn't feel too bad, considering it had been stabbed—a slight stiffness but that was all. Little by little he put more weight on the injured leg, testing it. The blood-soaked bandage had dried, crusting up and darkening to black in the dim light. He took a step forward, then another.

Stiff, which wasn't surprising, but he managed to hobble to the other side of the cell and back. He frowned. At the very least there should still be some pain.

He slid to the floor and removed the bandage, tearing the layers apart, as his dried blood had glued them together. Underneath the cloth, his pants were stuck to his leg. Gingerly, he pried apart the gash in the material the dagger had torn. He couldn't see much of the wound, but at least it looked closed and hadn't reopened during his exertions. He stood and walked to the shallow pool of water in the corner. He scooped up a handful and dribbled it onto his wound. It was probably all right to wash with the water, but he wasn't going to drink it . . . not yet, at least.

Gently, he rubbed his hand over the wound, washing away a layer of dried blood. Another handful of water, then another. He squinted at his leg, frowning. The wound had started to close. He traced the line with a finger, then probed cautiously. There was no mistaking it, the wound looked days old, or more. He rubbed tired eyes, bewildered. This wasn't natural. Shaking his head, Caldan scrunched the bandage up and threw it at the wall. This didn't make sense. How could a deep knife wound heal so fast? Sorcery was out of the question. He didn't know of any sorcery that could speed healing and had never heard it was likely.

His hand reached up and fingers traced the thin scar on his cheek. That had healed quickly. Nowhere near as quickly as his leg, but he remembered both Miranda and Elpidia commenting on how fast he had mended. Could this and his sudden surges of strength and speed be related? There was no way to tell, and as confusing as it was, he needed to think about escaping this cell. He realized his hopes of the Quivers rescuing them were but a dream, so if he was going to leave this cell, it was going to be of his own volition. Between him and freedom was the door with a solid iron lock. It looked far too strong for him to break through. He'd likely injure his foot if he tried to kick it down.

He racked his brain for a solution. The obvious area to focus on was the lock. Before coming to Anasoma he hadn't thought breaking a lock was possible. Master Simmon had shown him differently, though Caldan didn't have a gemstone like the one the master had used. Thinking of that remarkable piece of sorcery now, Caldan pondered a few explanations that came to mind. All required a crafting strong enough to hold the forces in check until you released them. This, he had surmised, was the gemstone's function. It was not a crafted object with a reusable purpose, but a storage device.

Such a crafting was uncomfortably close to destructive sorcery. *And that is why no one leaves the Protectors,* he thought as it finally dawned on him. *In order to prosecute their campaign against destructive sorcery, the Protectors have to be proficient at it themselves. How else could you fight such power and hope to prevail? You have to fight fire with fire.* It made a perverse sense. And yet, in using such sorceries, the Protectors damned themselves, became the very thing they were fighting against.

Caldan sighed. Unless he got out of here, he might not have the luxury of confirming his insights. Still, at least he knew *why* he was bound to the Protectors.

Fat lot of good that does me, now. Or maybe this insight is *of use . . .*

The iron lock stared at him silently. If only he had a piece of paper, he might be able to replicate what he had seen Simmon do with the gemstone.

Calculating the forces needed to destroy iron wasn't easy, but he knew a fair bit about metals from his metallurgical studies. A few moments later he came up with a theoretical crafting and whistled slowly. The power required was large, and it still left him needing iron to make it efficient enough to work.

Anything made of iron or with iron in it. He clutched his short hair despairingly. *There must be something here I can use. What has iron in it?* And then it came to him.

My blood.

The answer was both obvious and nauseating.

He sat back, taking a few moments to organize his thoughts and imagine a schematic of what the crafting should look like. Placement of the anchors and runes to shape the forces was crucial. He left out any buffers; they wouldn't be needed. The crafting only had to work for a second or two, long enough to draw from his well, then . . . break. He couldn't think of another way of describing it. The crafting was designed to destroy itself, quickly and efficiently. Now that he knew it could be done, and how it worked, it was straightforward. And that, he realized, was the danger Simmon had tried to press upon him so many weeks ago.

Destruction is always easier than creation.

He looked at the ball of his thumb, then at the lock.

With something like this it was best you didn't think too much about it. He rose and walked to the door, kneeling in front of it, eyes level with the lock. Taking a breath, he bit down hard on his thumb, deep into the flesh. He tasted blood, spat, and then clamped his index finger over the wound to stem the flow. His thumb felt like it had once years ago when he accidentally hit it with a hammer during a forging lesson.

Working quickly, he released the gash and using a finger as a crude quill, traced his design on the lock.

Clamping his finger over his thumb, he stood back and surveyed his work. Crude, with lines too thick and inelegant.

It should be sufficient, though.

Caldan closed his eyes and opened his well, joining it to the links he had crafted onto the lock. *A few moments is all I need . . .* He cut the flow of power and ruptured his makeshift crafting.

Light flashed through his closed eyelids, and the stench of hot metal filled the room, overlaid with lemons.

Caldan opened his eyes. The lock had been transformed into a molten mess. Red-hot iron dribbled like wax from a candle.

He let out a relieved laugh.

Drops splattered to the floor and hissed, rapidly cooling to solidity. *Ancestors!* He ran to the door and shoved it open so the cooling molten metal didn't weld the door shut.

He crouched in the opening, still, listening. His breath echoed in his ears. He counted to twenty. There was no outcry, no rushing of footsteps, no guards coming to investigate the noise. He breathed a sigh of relief.

"Senira? Which cell are you in?" He heard movement, though he couldn't pinpoint which cell it came from.

"Here," her muffled voice came from down the corridor. Hands clutched the bars of a cell door; a face framed by long blond hair pressed between them. He scurried to her.

"How did you get out? Never mind. Get me out, please."

"Just a moment," Caldan replied. He passed her cell and started toward the stairs.

"Hey! Where are you going?" Senira shouted.

"Be quiet!"

"Don't leave me here!" she said, a bit softer.

"I *won't*. I'm looking for the keys. Now, please . . ." *There, on a hook in the wall.* Caldan grabbed the key ring, which held only one key. He presumed it opened all the cells. He backtracked to Senira's cell and opened her lock with a twist.

"Thank you!" she gushed and hugged him tightly. She was slim, almost too thin, and looked younger than her journeyman status indicated. "Now what do we do?"

"We check the other cells and let everyone else out."

"Oh . . . of course."

Senira ran sprightly from cell to cell, peeking into each as Caldan looked into a few on the other side. They found all were unoccupied save one, which held the person who had been dragged in after they had been locked up. A forlorn figure lay on the cell's stone floor, curled up and hunched against a wall. Dried blood caked his hair and pooled under his body.

"Is he . . . dead?" Senira asked.

"I don't know."

Caldan opened the door. Inside, he crouched over the body and felt at the neck for a pulse. Nothing. He grabbed a shoulder and turned the man onto his back. Caldan didn't know him. It looked like the blood had leaked from two puncture wounds in his chest.

"Do you recognize him?" he asked Senira.

She edged into the cell. "He's dead, isn't he?"

"Yes," he replied gently. "Do you know who he is?"

She nodded. "A journeyman. I've seen him around, carrying messages. I think he was assigned to assist one of the masters. I don't know why they would have killed him."

Probably for the same reason we were imprisoned: he was in the way of whatever they had planned. But a look at Senira was all he needed to see she wasn't interested in reasons right now. He moved to comfort her. Tears streaked her face. He gave her arm a reassuring squeeze.

"We're alive and unhurt. All we have to do is get out of here and find where the sorcerers and Protectors are. Then we'll be safe."

Senira nodded numbly, staring at the dead journeyman. Caldan placed a hand on her cheek and turned her head away from the sight. "Come on. We have to get out of here before someone comes back."

They exited the cell, leaving the dead body behind.

"We have to be quiet," said Caldan, "in case they have men patrolling the corridors or we run into trouble. Can you do that?"

Senira licked her lips, then nodded once. "I'll stay behind you, if that's all right." Her voice quivered.

"Of course it is. If we run into trouble, do as I say."

She followed closely behind as he moved to the stairs. The short flight ended at another door, this one unlocked. He supposed there was no need for it to be locked if the cells were. He placed an ear to its surface, listening for noises on the other side.

All was silent. Taking a breath, he lifted the latch and opened the door a crack, enough to see into the corridor beyond. It was clear.

Gesturing for Senira to follow, Caldan slid along the wall and headed to where he knew there were stairs. They were on the level below ground, and he wanted to try to recover the belongings he'd dropped out the window. A shield would be extremely useful and might make the difference between their being captured again and reaching safety.

And he couldn't abandon his trinket.

"Where are we going?" whispered Senira, tugging at his arm. "Where do you think the masters will be? We should find them, if they're alive."

"Of course they are. But there's something I need to retrieve. We'll be safer with it."

Senira looked unimpressed. "How can you worry about getting your own things back at a time like this?"

"Trust me. I don't have time to explain. I hid something—a crafting. It will help us."

"You're only an apprentice. What could you possibly hope to do that would help? We need to get to where the masters are. They'll know what to do."

"Please, we shouldn't argue. I need . . . we need to get to where I hid it."

"Did you steal it?"

"What? No. I made it."

Senira scoffed disbelievingly. "Sure you did."

"I'm sorry—did *you* get us out of the cells?"

Ignoring that, she said, "Listen, if we don't get to where the masters are as soon as possible, we are in big trouble. I don't intend to spend more time in a cell."

"If we are caught, I think cells will be the least of our worries. Besides, wherever the masters are, they're almost certainly heavily guarded. At least with my gear, we'll have a chance. I don't suppose *you* stashed any craftings that might be useful?"

Voices echoed along the corridor from behind them, accompanied by heavy footfalls. A wall lit up as the steady glow from a sorcerous globe approached.

"Quick," Caldan said. "This way." He grabbed Senira and dragged her along. They rushed down the corridor and around a corner.

"What if they were on our side?" whispered Senira.

"We can't take that chance, and I'm guessing the only people down here with a sorcerous light wouldn't be. At least I know Master Simmon wouldn't be so stupid."

Senira swallowed and glanced fleetingly over her shoulder, then looked at Caldan and nodded. Taking her hand, he edged along the hall until they came to another set of stairs. Here they crept upward one step at a time, pausing now and again to listen. No stray noises reached their ears—no coughing, no tread of boots.

They reached one end of a wide corridor paved with dark stone.

Caldan recognized it as a main thoroughfare in one of the wings of the building taken up by the Sorcerers' Guild. The gardens were only a short distance away, and he was confident that once they got there the bushes and shrubs around the perimeter would hide them until he retrieved his belongings.

They headed off to the left and peeked around the corner in case someone was there. Again, their luck held and the hallway was empty. Ahead, a wide open doorway led out into the gardens.

Next to him, Senira breathed heavily. She clutched his arm in a tight grip.

They passed into the garden and pressed against the wall, kneeling behind a bush. Caldan looked up at the night sky. Moonlight bathed the garden. He half stood and looked around.

"What are you looking for? We need to find somewhere safe."

How many times did he have to explain it to her? And she questioned *him* on *his* skill?

"I know," he said, the impatience creeping into his voice. "But as I said, I need to retrieve my crafting. I threw it out my window."

Senira wrung her hands, eyes darting around the garden. "They could be anywhere."

"It'll be all right," Caldan reassured her. "Follow me."

Senira just sat there, eyes downcast, teeth worrying her bottom lip. She looked scared, anxious, and sad at the same time. Caldan knew this was a traumatic experience for her.

It wasn't easy for him, either. But he did take a moment to see it from her perspective. She'd clearly never known such hardship, having been at the guild for years, progressing in the relative safety and comfort of these halls. Her whole life had been thrown upside down.

I, at least, have been through that once or twice. Gently, he raised her to her feet.

"It *will* be all right." Nodding, she followed behind him.

Crouching low, they traversed the wall surrounding the garden. The edge was darker than the middle, so they had good cover among the bushes and shrubs. His boots made hardly a sound as they trod on sodden leaves.

A cloud passed over the moon and the garden went dark. Lights shone from a few windows but far fewer than would normally be occupied at this time of the evening.

They scurried behind the bushes and he half expected to hear the shout of a sentry spotting them and raising the alarm. His breath came in short gasps, and his hands were clammy with sweat. Remaining still for a few moments, he listened. Still nothing.

Caldan ran his hands along the ground, through the dead leaves, searching for the sack. *By the ancestors, where is it?* Finally his hand bumped into something. *Ah, there.* He grabbed the sack and pulled it close.

He rifled around inside—everything was there. He drew out his purse, which he stuffed in a pocket; his crafted wristband, which he slid onto his left forearm; his trinket, which he slipped on a finger; and the bone ring on the chain, which he placed around his neck. Everything else he left in the sack. At the moment they were only components, a jumbled mess of metal rods and plates with a few semiprecious stones. He was glad he had managed to save these as well, though they were useless to him right now. Perhaps, if they had time, they could find a way to make use of them. He threw the sack over his shoulder.

The wristband gave him a degree of confidence, though from what he had seen and experienced of the invaders, they had their own craftings as well, and high-quality ones, too.

Senira touched his arm.

"I should have asked earlier, but what is it?"

Caldan hesitated, for no reason he could fathom. There wasn't any harm in telling her, and she deserved to know. "It's a shield."

"And you made it?" She was still skeptical.

"Yes—and it was approved by the masters."

At that Senira smiled and fixed her eyes on him, as if evaluating him in a new light. Caldan cleared his throat.

"We should get going," he said.

"To where, though? Do we even know which areas might be safe?"

"I think the apprentices' smith-crafting area would be a good place to hole up, and we could do some scouting from there. Plenty of rooms to hide in. And nothing much of value for the invaders to bother searching the place more than once. Too, there's water to drink, although finding food will be harder."

"But then what? How are we going to find the masters and the other sorcerers who managed not to get caught?"

"I don't know . . . yet. Let's go before the moon comes out from behind the cloud. We can discuss it more once we're at the smith-crafting area. Luckily there's a door that opens onto the garden."

"Which way is it?"

"This way." Caldan pointed toward the door. It was a fair way across the garden. He was glad the night had been still so far. They hadn't heard sounds of fighting or much of anything since escaping the cells. He wondered if that was a good or a bad sign.

He went first, pushing his way through the bushes, trying to make as little noise as possible. Branches scraped against his body and arm, but he ignored them. After a few moments, they were clear of the bushes and moved from tree to tree across the lawn, pausing at each to listen until they reached the door. Satisfied there was no one behind it, he pushed the door open.

Except it didn't budge.

He cursed under his breath.

"It's locked, isn't it?" said Senira.

"Yes." Caldan thought furiously. *Can I open the door from the out-side?* There was no lock. It was likely barred from the inside. He doubted his crafting could open it.

"Maybe I should hop in through that window there and open it from the other side," suggested Senira.

"What?" Caldan looked to where Senira pointed. An open window a few yards away. "That's . . . a good idea," he said.

Without waiting, Senira stuck her head through the opening.

"A storeroom," he heard her say. "Empty. Do you mind?" She lifted a foot and raised an eyebrow.

Caldan clasped both hands together and held them out for her to use. Senira stepped into the makeshift stirrup and dragged herself onto the window ledge, swung her legs inside, and dropped out of sight. A few moments later, the door leading onto the garden opened and Caldan slipped inside.

The familiar forge room was empty. All the tools and materials were stowed in their proper places, tidied up for the night. It didn't look like the place had been ransacked, and he doubted a workshop used by apprentices was high on the list of priorities for the invaders. Light from banked coals gave the room a soft orange glow.

They closed the door and rebarred it. Senira approached the forge and held her hands to the heat.

"Stay here and get warm," he said. "I'll go and find some water."

"Thank you," said Senira, brushing hair from her face. "I could use a drink."

Caldan nodded and left her by the forge. He still carried his sack in one hand, reluctant to let it out of his grasp. He moved among the rooms, at one point finding something interesting. Smiling, he put it in his sack. It wasn't much, but it might brighten Senira's spirits.

Eventually he found water. He filled a wooden jug and drank deep, slaking his thirst. He refilled it, as well as another, before returning to the forge.

"Here," he said, offering Senira a jug, from which she drank deeply.

With a grin, Caldan pulled a metal pot and a cotton bag from his sack. Senira frowned but didn't say anything. Placing the pot next to the hot coals, he poured in water until it was full, then opened the cloth bag and threw in a handful of black leaves.

"Tea?" asked Senira.

"Yes. The master in charge here had it in his room. We can replace it later."

"If he . . . if we get out of here."

"*When* we get out of here."

Senira sighed.

At a loss for what else to say, Caldan busied himself at a bench. From his sack he withdrew all the metal parts and the stones.

"Oh! You're hurt!" exclaimed Senira. "I didn't see before."

Caldan followed her gaze to the tear in his pants, his thigh covered in dried blood. Unable to explain it himself, he simply said. "It's all right. One of the invaders did it. They bound it before I was taken to my cell. It wasn't deep."

"It certainly looks bad. Do you want me to take a look?"

"No," he replied quickly. "It's fine. It didn't hamper me on our way here, did it?"

"Sorry. I feel like I'm useless. I need something to do." Her gaze returned to the coals, hands extended.

"You have helped." When she looked at him quizzically, he pointed to the window. "You got us in, remember?"

She seemed to sit up a bit straighter with that.

Caldan looked around the room, thinking. He wanted to get to work on his jumble of metal and see if he could cobble together enough to get the simulacra he had in mind working, and in the meantime they could use some paper and ink for emergencies. "I don't think we should go too far from here. But we do need a few things, and it would go quicker if we both searched for them."

Senira looked at him brightly. "Of course. We need something for tonight—blankets, any food we can find, possibly a lantern or crafted globe." She scratched her head. "And mugs to drink the tea from."

"Ah . . . yes." He hadn't thought about tonight. His focus on his crafting had blinded him to the obvious. "Then we'll do it this way: you gather what you can and I'll work on some craftings, in case we need them."

Ancestors be praised, Senira didn't ask any questions. *Happy to have a task*, he supposed. She left through a doorway, and he heard her rattling around a storeroom. Abandoning the workbench, Caldan went straight to another storeroom, one he knew held general supplies for sketching schematics. Rifling through the supplies, he took a stack of paper and ink and pens.

When he returned, a pile of rags was lying next to the forge along with two metal cups. Senira was nowhere to be seen, but she had obviously been busy.

Sitting at the workbench, he laid out a sheet of paper and opened a bottle of ink. Taking one of the pens, he dipped it into the ink, but paused. *Where to start?* With his experimentation in opening the cell lock, he knew he had stumbled upon a secret. Possibly one the Protectors would have revealed to him soon, but it was hard to say. Did they condone the use of destructive sorcery if it was for the greater good? Master Simmon had used it on a lock, but what was permissible and what wasn't?

His biggest problem was Senira. He had a shield but she didn't, which meant he needed to keep her out of any confrontations, if possible. There wasn't time to make her one, and she probably couldn't use it anyway. He guessed her talents didn't run to complex sorcery, since he hadn't heard of her before this.

So he needed to protect them both. He stretched his neck and massaged his writing hand. *Best to get to work, then.* He started scribing.

CLUNK. A METAL mug filled with hot tea thumped down next to Caldan and he jumped. Senira's tinkling laugh filled his ears.

She waved at the workbench. "You were so engrossed, anyone could have come in without you hearing. I've made a few trips for supplies, and the tea has oversteeped while you sat here drawing." She jumped up and sat on the workbench next to him. "Sorry—I couldn't find any honey." She shrugged.

"Thank you." Caldan lifted the mug with both hands and sipped. He welcomed the warmth on his hands and throat, despite the bitterness. "I lost track of time."

Around him lay scattered pages filled with patterns of runes. A few had been folded into quarters, and three he'd scrunched up into balls.

Senira examined the paper with an interested eye. "I don't recognize some of the runes, let alone the purpose of the patterning. Care to explain?"

Caldan laid the pen down and recapped the ink bottle. His rubbed his fingers to ease the ache. He had finished the destructive sorcery craftings first and secreted some in his pockets and some in his sack. One he folded a few times and slipped into his boot in case of emergencies. What remained on the table were craftings designed to keep them safe tonight and warn them if anyone approached. There were a few entrances into this section of the building and he wanted to seal them off, leaving them the run of the place without fear of discovery. Once secure, they could try to relax for the rest of the night.

"These craftings"—he took hold of a piece of paper and started a pile, moving others to join it—"will block doors. Place one on either side of the door and the jamb, activate them, and they should hold against all but the most determined sorcerer."

"Should?"

"Will," Caldan replied firmly. *These are expertly crafted, not hastily cobbled together.*

Senira nodded. "A neat trick. I don't remember the class on that one . . ."

He coughed into his hand. "It's not taught here. I learned it before I came."

Senira raised her eyebrows but didn't comment.

"The other ones"—he began to separate the other pages into piles—"all have a different purpose. One can be activated close to the doors we will block, and it can tell us if anyone nearby has craftings or trinkets on them." He gestured to another pile. "Those I need to fold later. They'll help us in the morning, when we get out of here and try to find the masters putting up resistance."

"If any are. I mean, I hope they are, but . . ." She shrugged and folded her arms tight around her chest.

Caldan rose on stiff legs and gave her shoulder a squeeze. "Don't worry. I'm sure everything will be all right. A good night's sleep here, safe, and everything will look better in the morning."

With a sad smile, Senira nodded, then hopped off the workbench and began arranging the pile of rags near the forge, which had grown while Caldan was preoccupied with scribing.

"It's not much," she said. "But it's better than sleeping on the floor." She gestured at the rags spread around her, barely big enough for one person, let alone two. "And keep your hands to yourself," she added.

Caldan smiled. "Don't worry. You take them all. I still have a lot to do and don't think I could sleep now anyway."

"Oh. Thank you." She stood and looked around uncertainly. "Do you think . . . maybe we shouldn't spend the night here? I mean, if it's quiet out there, wouldn't we have a better chance of moving around unseen now?"

"I think it's a few hours before dawn now, and maybe we should move before daybreak. That would be best. Whatever's happened, it's likely everyone is resting up. There's probably been some heavy fighting. When it's time, we can sneak out. We know the layout better than the invaders, so we shouldn't need luck to avoid anyone. What do you think?"

"Sounds good to me. I could use a few hours of sleep." She brought a hand to her mouth and stifled a yawn.

Caldan felt himself start to yawn in response and suppressed it with an effort.

"You get some sleep. It's been a rough day. I'll place these craftings and make sure the doors are secure."

Senira gave him a grateful smile, then settled herself onto the pile of rags. Her breathing steadied almost immediately.

Caldan gathered the paper craftings and busied himself locking the three doors leading into the apprentices' workshop. He resolved in the future to secure his own doors, no matter how safe he felt.

With barely a thought, he reached for his well and activated the craftings, one for each door along with the one that would detect the presence of other craftings and trinkets close by. Splitting his well into separate strings felt easier than it had before.

Well, he'd had enough practice the last few days.

Returning, Caldan poured more water into the teapot next to the coals. It would help him stay awake to finish the paper craftings before working on his major crafting: another simulacrum. Small chance he could finish it tonight, but the more he assembled now, the less he would have to do later. It would be a big help to them if he could get it right: a far sturdier scout than a paper bird, and a second shield if he required one. He had a feeling they would need all their talents to get through the next few days. And besides, if his simulacrum worked, it would be like nothing he had ever seen crafted before, something new. His craftings were growing in complexity—who knew where it might end? A metal bird that behaved just like a bird? A person, even. Caldan scoffed at the idea: he might manage the form, but never the mind, the soul. People were far more than that.

And yet, the possibilities . . .

Caldan spent the night fussing over the many pieces of metal provided to him by the clockmaker, muttering to himself or sitting motionless for a few minutes staring at one piece or another. None of the pieces were marked as yet with runes. He had planned to etch or stamp them in later, but barricaded in the apprentices' workshop as they were, he couldn't risk making any noise for fear that someone would hear.

Rummaging around another storeroom, he found a few different types of ink, one of which suited his purpose for the time being. Usually used for marking stone or metal, it was thicker and stickier than normal. The larger metal pieces and rods could wait, but the smaller ones he would start marking tonight. The clockmaker's idea was that Caldan should create a smaller model first, a prototype so he could see if his theories worked and he didn't waste materials refining his craftings. A good idea, he admitted. He had never experimented much before, and it was likely the construct would need many variations before he came up with one that worked as he wanted.

Sitting back at the workbench, Caldan folded his remaining sheets of paper into small, easy animals. He knew he might have to leave them behind, which was fine, since they wouldn't last long. He poured himself some tea and began the laborious process of marking the metal pieces and rods with crafting runes.

CHAPTER 37

W e've been turned away from the gates," Aidan said. "There's no choice but to find another way into the city."

Chalayan nodded at his statement, while Anshul cel Rau merely grunted.

Aidan used a leather-gloved hand to lift a battered kettle that sat on the edge of their cooking fire. He could feel the heat of the handle through his glove as he poured tea into his own mug, then refilled Chalayan's. Both the sorcerer and Anshul had kept their distance from him since the . . . incident with Lady Caitlyn. Over the last few days, though, they had made a point of reporting to him and deferring to his leadership. His moment of weakness with the bottle had put them off, shown them he was fragile.

Well, let them have to kill the leader they loved, and see how they fare afterward.

"Those sorcerers were ahead of us all the way?" he asked for the second time that morning.

"Yes," replied Chalayan, licking his lips. His fingers strayed to the trinket he always wore around his neck. Aidan suspected its power was in detecting sorcery, but he couldn't be sure. There was a great deal he didn't know about sorcerers, but he now knew they were far more dangerous than anyone believed.

A few days ago, Chalayan had woken Aidan in the middle of the night. He had felt a massive flow of energy flare up, he said. A sorcery like he'd never encountered before. The initial surge had died down, but he could still sense power flowing from the direction of Anasoma. Eventually, he had calmed enough to settle back in his blankets, but Aidan was sure he hadn't slept the rest of the night.

Aidan had expected to head straight in and to ask the Protectors for assistance with looking after the women they had rescued, as well as hunting the rogue sorcerers. He was stunned to see the city's walls aflame with a pale blue fire, crowds milling outside the barred gates. From what they could gather from the people, either the city was quarantined due to disease, a civil war had broken out among the guilds, an army had invaded and enslaved everyone, or an old evil had risen from a graveyard and was killing people at night.

Aidan didn't put much stock in any of these rumors and wondered whether the flames on the wall were to keep people out or to keep them in. Chalayan almost had an apoplexy when he saw them, and he wandered back and forth in front of the wall, constantly looking to the barrier and to the sky. All the while clutching his trinket and repeating that they were impossible.

Which they clearly weren't.

Aidan took a step away from the crackling cooking fire and crouched on his heels, gazing at the flames. "So they either entered the city or weren't able to get in, same as us."

"I don't think they could enter. The sorcery I felt the other night had to have been the creation of this barrier and would have been up before they reached the city."

"Are you sure?" asked Aidan. "We ran into unknown sorcerers with unknown powers, chased them to Anasoma, where we find the people locked out by more unknown sorcery. I'd think they're related, wouldn't you?"

Anshul cel Rau spat into the fire, saliva sizzling in the coals. "I don't like it," he said flatly.

On that, we can agree.

Chalayan studied the walls. "While I would normally agree with your logic, the sorcery is different. I believe they're from diverse schools of knowledge. The ones we ran into and have been following have a strange feel." He spread his hands apologetically. "I can't put it any more precisely than that, but take my word for it. I've never encountered their like before, and I've studied under many masters."

Aidan cleared his throat. "So there are two groups of sorcerers running around unleashing power for no reason we can fathom?"

Cel Rau grunted and spat into the fire again. Chalayan simply kept his eyes on the blue flames.

"Whatever is happening, our first priority is to get these people to safety." Aidan gestured at the wagons and women around the camp. "Then we can worry about the sorcerers."

"What will the sorcerers be doing while we waste time with the women?" asked cel Rau.

Aidan fixed him with a firm stare. "We cannot abandon them. We need to make sure they will be looked after." He left unsaid *I didn't kill Caitlyn to just leave them to die somewhere else.*

The swordsman looked away.

Chalayan nodded reluctantly.

With a flick of his wrist, Aidan sent the dregs of his tea splashing into the fire. "Let's get packed up." He stood. "I want everyone ready to move in half an hour. There are a few towns close by, and we can see the women safely settled at one. They'll be out of harm's way, and then we can do something about these sorcerers."

AIDAN HAD THEM approach the town cautiously, reluctant to head straight in after all they had seen. As towns go, it was large, probably due to its proximity to Anasoma. It was considered an outlying district of the city, although it was an hour's ride to the west.

Their wagons rolled down the dusty main street, with only the occasional resident showing an interest in their group. Most ignored them as they rushed about, too busy and important to be bothered with strangers. The place had a soulless feel to it, but there wasn't much they could do at the moment except find somewhere to drop off the women and babies.

On the outskirts of the town, a tent city had sprung up with more temporary residents pouring in even as they passed close by. People turned away from the gates of Anasoma were looking for somewhere to stay. Circles of wagons covered with canvas formed enclaves, while horses cropped grass around their tents. In a few days, the place would be a breeding ground for trouble. Aidan didn't want to leave the women there.

The only logical place was the town's hospice, and Aidan was relieved when they readily agreed to take on the group of rescued women who, once they had recovered, were willing to work in exchange for their food and a place to stay. The place was understaffed, as there had been an influx of extra patients since the gates of Anasoma closed. Wealthy people who couldn't enter Anasoma had no alternative but to forgo the expensive city treatments and turn to the hospice instead.

It didn't take them long to get the women and their babies settled into quarters. With grateful hugs and smiles, Aidan left them to their new life. As soon as possible, he gathered his men and left without a backward look.

ANSHUL CEL RAU grabbed Aidan's arm and dragged him up out of the long dry grass. "No need to hide," the swordsman said gruffly. "There aren't any sentries on the wall."

It was a long speech for the man. Aidan nodded.

He'd been lying in the grass all day, keeping an eye on the walls of Anasoma close to one of the gates. Travelers and traders still approached without knowing, or perhaps without believing, the city was locked down, only to mill uncertainly in front of the closed gate before wandering off, taking themselves and their wares elsewhere.

Aidan trudged back to their makeshift camp with cel Rau. Their band, what was left of it, had chosen a clearing next to a copse of trees as their campsite. A brook flowed nearby toward the sea, and the ground was rocky and hard.

He surveyed the greatly reduced numbers of their group. With Lady Caitlyn's death, and the losses they experienced during that battle, some of their men had chosen to stay with the women at the hospice. Aidan didn't blame them, since most were only in it for the ducats, and such heavy losses dented their desire to stay on, no matter what the pay. Truth was that only a few of them had followed Lady Caitlyn because they believed in her cause, and over the last few days, men had deserted the band with infuriating regularity. He would rather they followed him not for the ducats but because they believed. Lady Caitlyn's cause was as strong in him as it had been in her.

Their fire had burned down to black coals and ash. Aidan crouched and poked at it with a stick. After a few minutes, Chalayan knelt on his left, then cel Rau on the right.

Both men fixed their eyes on him.

"What's the plan now, Aidan?" asked the sorcerer.

Cel Rau spat into the fire again, as if the sorcery left a bad taste in his mouth. "That city is bad. We aren't likely to get inside."

Aidan scratched his arm. "We still need to find the sorcerers we've been following."

Chalayan looked pleased at his words.

He will need watching, thought Aidan. The lure of power for his kind was strong.

"They're a danger," Aidan continued. "You saw what they did. They are evil." He looked at the sorcerer and the swordsman in turn, meeting their eyes. Both nodded in agreement.

"Getting inside is impossible," said Chalayan. "But . . . I don't think they went inside. The barrier went up before they got here, and as I said before, it feels different." He shifted his weight and shrugged.

"Which means they either backtracked or turned north or south?"

"I'm pretty sure they didn't backtrack and pass us. I would have felt them." Chalayan's hand strayed to touch his trinket.

"So north or south."

"Send some scouts each way," said cel Rau gruffly.

Aidan nodded. "Yes. See to it."

Cel Rau stood and left without a word.

"Chalayan?" said Aidan.

"Yes?"

"Can you match them?"

The sorcerer stood and stretched his legs, grimacing at the stiffness. "I would have thought it was obvious I can't," he admitted. "In a pure power against power fight, they are far above me. They do things I would never have thought possible. But I have a few tricks."

"Think of a few more. I have a feeling we're going to need them."

Chalayan gave a nervous laugh. "Believe me, I've been thinking of little else since we found them, but . . . if Caitlyn were here . . . Sorry . . ."

"No. It's all right. Go ahead."

"If she were here, we would probably go charging after them . . . and would die." He shrugged. "We need help. Maybe from the Sorcerers' Guild; that's if they're still alive."

Aidan thought for a few moments. "I agree. The Quivers—"

"I don't think soldiers would do much good," interrupted Chalayan. "You saw what happened to ours. I fear we are overmatched. That way would mean our deaths."

"And we won't do any good dead." Aidan smiled grimly and gave the ash another poke.

A boot scuffed, and a shadow fell across the fire. Aidan looked up, squinting into the evening sun. A large, middle-aged man stood between him and Chalayan. The man cleared his throat.

Aidan stood. To his eyes, the man appeared unarmed, though looks were deceiving, as they all knew. He had his hands spread in a nonthreatening gesture.

Aidan assessed the stranger for any menace. Though overweight, he wore a fine dark shirt with silver buttons down the front and pants tucked into polished leather boots.

Both Aidan and Chalayan glanced around the camp. Their men hadn't alerted them to the stranger's presence, which meant they hadn't seen him approach.

"Who are you? How did you get into our camp?" demanded Aidan. His hand strayed to the hilt of his sword. Chalayan took a step backward, increasing the distance between him and the stranger.

"My apologies for the abrupt appearance." The man's voice rang through the clearing, though his accent was strange to Aidan's ears. "But I couldn't help overhearing your conversation."

Aidan and Chalayan exchanged a quick look. There was no way someone could have overheard them, not without being close enough to be seen.

Aidan took a step toward the man. If he was a sorcerer, then Aidan wouldn't have a chance unless he was closer. "Who are you?" he demanded.

"You may call me Mazoet." He bowed from the waist. "Mazoet Miangline, at your service."

Chalayan took another step back and flicked Aidan a warning look. Sweat spotted the sorcerer's face, and he clutched at his trinket.

Aidan spoke. "You're a sorcerer."

Mazoet Miangline frowned, then tilted his head in acknowledgment of the statement. "That's what you would call me, yes. Though I must say, it's not what we call ourselves."

"You're one of them, the sorcerers?"

Mazoet shook his head. "No. Well, yes, but no." He waved a hand in dismissal. "They have strayed."

Strayed? What does that mean? Aidan noted all his men had stopped whatever they were doing and were staring at the three of them.

The stranger noticed him noticing.

"He's opened his well," Chalayan said quietly.

"My . . . well?" Mazoet said, puzzled, then realization came to his face. "Oh, of course. A mere precaution only. You can understand my provisions to safeguard myself."

Aidan held a hand up to his men, gesturing them not to approach. "What do you know of the sorcerers we've been following, and what they did to the women they captured?"

Frowning, Mazoet ran a hand through his graying hair. "What women?" he said. "What use would they have for . . ." He broke off, and a horrified look came across his face. He hissed under his breath. "What happened? Tell me everything," he demanded.

"Wait a moment. We don't know who you are and—"

"Listen to me," interrupted Mazoet, voice commanding. "You will tell me. Now. I need to make a decision quickly."

Chalayan and Aidan exchanged looks. Chalayan gave a short nod.

Aidan wasn't sure what the man's business was, but he seemed to have an interest in them and the sorcerers they were following. He made his mind up. "We were following some men who we suspected of . . . something. They killed a number of men with sorcery. They led us to a town, where we were attacked by sorcery."

"Quickly, boy," said Mazoet. His eyes scanned the grass to the west.

Aidan bristled at his tone but continued. "We found a building near the center of the town. There were women inside, tied to beds. They were breeding them against their will."

A hard look came over Mazoet's face.

Chalayan gasped. "What are you?" he whispered.

"Do you swear this is true?" Mazoet said, the calm of his words belying the storm in his eyes.

"I do."

Mazoet turned to Chalayan. "And you?"

The sorcerer only nodded.

Mazoet shook his head, jowls wobbling, his shoulders slumped, deflated. "Fools," he said softly, so quietly Aidan almost didn't hear him. He pointed at Chalayan. "You, you're what they call a sorcerer?"

"Yes."

"Stay well out of the way, please."

"Out of what?" asked Aidan.

"The sorcerers you were following are on their way here. They knew you were trailing them. I wasn't sure what they were up to, but now I know. You're in danger." He gestured to the whole camp. "All of you. And I need you as witnesses. You have to tell the First Deliverer what you saw."

"We aren't defenseless—" began Aidan.

"You are. I'm going to have to reveal myself. This could get . . . troublesome."

"I can help," offered Chalayan, oddly subdued.

Mazoet looked at the sorcerer for a few moments. "Ah . . . Perhaps you should stay out of this. If it comes down to fighting, and I hope it doesn't, then you can make sure no one gets hurt. I'll be fine. Look to your men."

Chalayan nodded.

"They'll be here soon," continued Mazoet. "Round up your men, and make sure they stay behind me. It'll be easier if everyone is clustered together."

Cel Rau stood with a few men, hands on swords, ready for trouble. Aidan took a step toward him, then stopped.

"What decision did you need to make?" he asked Mazoet, recalling the man's earlier words.

"Whether you lived."

AIDAN GATHERED THE men together, while Chalayan drew a circle around them, using a spade to scribe a line in the hard earth. Mazoet raised his eyebrows at this, then stepped outside the ring. He turned his back on them and fixed his gaze to the west, where the sun dipped toward the hills in the distance.

Aidan, Chalayan, and cel Rau had engaged in a heated argument in front of the men, something Aidan disliked intensely, but there was no helping it. They needed to discuss what was going on, and the men needed to know. In the end, they reluctantly agreed, if not to trust this strange man, then to see if he was right about the sorcerers coming after them.

Chalayan kept glancing at Mazoet.

"What is it?" Aidan asked.

"It's . . . him. He feels like one of the sorcerers we were following. He did say he was one of them, then changed to say he wasn't."

Cel Rau spoke. "From what I heard, I think they are at odds. The ones we're chasing are bad apples. And this guy is here to clean up the mess."

"It certainly looks that way," Aidan said. "Chalayan, what do you think?"

"I think we're in over our heads. This . . . Mazoet . . . his well is powerful. I've never felt the like before. I need to keep preparing if we're to get through this alive. If I had their knowledge . . ." Chalayan glanced toward Mazoet, then busied himself with his circle, taking four flat stones from his pack and placing them around the edge at even intervals. Each bore runes etched into its hard surface.

Cel Rau eyed Chalayan warily. "He's spooked," he said to Aidan. "He has seen what they are capable of and knows his sorcery can't stand against it."

No—it's more than fear. It's almost like there's longing in Chalayan's words. But Aidan kept that to himself, making note to keep a close eye on the sorcerer.

"Yes. So we are to rely on this stranger. Can't say I'm happy about it."

Cel Rau shrugged. "Unless we run, there isn't much we can do. This way, we see if he can be trusted. If we survive."

With a grimace, Aidan eyed Chalayan, who sat inside his circle facing Mazoet. "Let's hope he can shield all of us."

"Let's hope he doesn't have to."

A murmur rose from the men surrounding them, and they both turned to see two shapes standing at the edge of the clearing. Mazoet and Chalayan were staring at the figures. Mazoet stood relaxed, but Chalayan's hands clenched into fists, and his face glowed with a sweaty sheen.

Both of the newcomers were thin, unlike Mazoet, and they stood a good foot shorter than him. With a start, Aidan realized they were young, barely out of childhood, and one was a girl.

She called out in a high-pitched voice. "Mazoet. Leave here."

Wind blew through the leaves of the trees and the grasses surrounding them as Mazoet remained unmoving. "I will not. The First Deliverer will hear of this, and of what has been uncovered."

Holding a hand over her mouth, the girl tittered. For such a young girl, she had an odd bearing. She held herself with a confidence only age could bring. She turned to her companion, and words were whispered between them.

The girl raised her arms high in the air. Aidan heard Chalayan take a hissing breath through clenched teeth. Pale blue light sprang up around Mazoet, covering him like a second skin.

"Do not do this," he boomed. "You will be excised."

The girl smiled and laughed again. "Join us. Come, we offer more than that fool Gazija could ever imagine."

"We cannot travel down that path."

"We can. We will."

They both quieted, and the girl, arms still raised, clenched her fists. Air crackled, and a vibration filled the space around them. Two blue glows joined Mazoet's as shields surrounded the girl and her companion. A dark cloud formed and enveloped them.

"Oh, crap," breathed Chalayan as he thrust a hand out to touch one of the stones.

Lightning arced from the girl's fists, slamming into Mazoet. Strands weaved around him toward Aidan and his men. They stopped suddenly as they crashed into a barrier surrounding them, revealing a transparent dome. Thunder roared. Aidan's hands clamped over his ears in a vain attempt to block the deafening noise.

Chalayan keeled over in a faint, and the stone he touched cracked in two. With a faint popping sound, the dome surrounding them winked out. Filaments of lightning streaked into two men, igniting them like torches. Screams of agony pierced the night. As they rolled in the dirt, others attempted to smother the flames with their coats.

"Do not leave the circle!" boomed Mazoet. "On your life!" His shield glowed brightly as strand after strand of lightning arced from the girl into him. He stepped back to the edge of the circle.

As the girl's attacks continued, her companion remained motionless.

Another dome appeared around Aidan and his men, this one glowing a pale red. Steam rose from the bodies of the two men who had been hit by lightning. Aidan stared in horror at the corpses.

Mazoet grunted with effort. Glowing red balls trailing sparks sprang up around him and shot toward the girl. Corkscrewing through the air, they slammed into her from all directions, and she fell back on her ass. The look on her face was pure fury.

Her companion picked her up; her clothes were smoking even through her shield. He kept hold of her hand. She drew herself straight. Lightning flashed from her free hand, redoubled in ferocity. Around Mazoet, his shield grew brighter as it absorbed the lightning. Soon he glowed brilliantly, white light hurting Aidan's eyes, a keening sound filling the air.

Aidan clamped his hands over his ears. Around him, most of his men were on their knees with their eyes closed. Some were praying. *This is where we all die,* he thought. *I'm sorry, Caitlyn.*

Mazoet knelt and thumped a fist into the ground. A wave of dirt rose up and burst out. It hit the girl and her companion like a runaway horse, sending them both tumbling back, but they regained their feet in moments.

Mazoet struck the ground again, sending one more wave. The girl stood firm, only to be met with another volley of the glowing red balls, appearing out of nowhere above her and slamming down.

Some red balls broke through.

She gave an inhuman shriek.

Aidan collapsed as the sound penetrated his skull.

Another wave sent the girl and boy flying backward into the dark. Her clothes burst into flame, and her companion threw himself on her to smother them. Wrapped around each other, they rolled in the dirt.

With the flames extinguished, the girl and the boy recovered and backed away, glaring at Mazoet. After a few paces, they turned and ran.

Mazoet's shoulders slumped.

Cel Rau staggered to his feet, reaching for Chalayan and checking him for signs of life. The swordsman met Aidan's eye and nodded.

Aidan's head pounded. He wiped his ear, his hand coming away red with blood. Steam rose from the ground outside the circle.

Mazoet turned to face them. "That went well, don't you think?" he said with a weary grin.

CHAPTER 38

A rattle of metal woke Caldan. Blurry eyed, he raised his head from the workbench where he had fallen asleep. Senira groaned as she levered herself to a sitting position. He raised a finger to his lips. Metal rattled as the door latch was tried again, and voices murmured on the other side. Footsteps retreated.

Caldan crept to the door the sound had come from and peered through the keyhole. There was a flicker of movement down the hall-way. Caldan kept his eye there, watching for further indications they had been discovered. He saw movement but couldn't identify who had been there. Senira came up behind him.

"I think we've been discovered," he whispered.

Senira immediately looked frightened.

"It was bound to happen," he said, "but I didn't think it would be so soon."

"What are we going to do? We should get out of here."

Caldan pulled her away from the door and into the workshop area.

She's right. We should avoid fighting, if we can. "If they look through the keyhole, they'll see us in here. We need to pack up and leave before they come back."

Senira nodded and busied herself gathering the food and bits and pieces they thought would be useful. Caldan went to the workbench and hurriedly stuffed the pieces of metal and paper into his sack.

"Leave the pile of rags and the teapot," he said. "They know some-one's been here, so don't waste time hiding them."

"If you say so. What are you doing?"

Caldan reached up and placed one of his paper figures into a nook in the brick wall. He glanced around, then placed another figure above the main door, sitting on the lintel. Opening his well, he linked to both of the craftings. Keeping two strings going for any amount of time was still difficult, but he was managing better and better.

"They look creepy." Senira eyed the figures with suspicion, then went back to gathering their scavenged supplies.

"They're just craftings. Weak ones at that. They'll be able to sense who comes in here and relay that back to me."

"Why do you have to make them look like people?"

"Because . . . one day I hope to be able to make them move," Caldan replied with a shrug.

Senira shuddered. "That's definitely creepy."

"No, it's not. I can get paper animals to move, but it's harder with stronger materials."

Senira shook her head. "Come on. You can experiment all you like once we get out of here and we're safe with the masters."

She sounded confident they would reach safety without any prob-lems. Caldan wished he was as sure.

Muffled voices reached their ears.

"Quickly," hissed Caldan, grabbing Senira's shoulder and propel-ling her toward another door. He opened his well and disengaged the crafting lock he had placed on it.

Senira poked her head outside. "All clear . . . I think."

Caldan stood close behind her and pushed his head through the gap above her blond hair. It looked clear, but he wanted to be certain.

He reached into a pocket and drew out a paper shape covered in runes. Unfolding its wings, he frowned in concentration, linking it to his well, and then gently tossed the crafting into the corridor. Pressure built in his head as he maintained the three strings.

Wings flapped, and the bird rose close to the ceiling, then glided down the corridor. The runes adorning its surface glowed faintly in the dark.

"Oh," gasped Senira. "That's . . . beautiful."

Caldan grinned. "Still think they're creepy?"

"The bird isn't. Those other things were." She looked up at him. "What's it doing?"

"Scouting. It's crafted to tell me if there's anyone around, like the figures I left in the workroom. Though it won't last long." He paused for a moment. "All clear. Let's go."

Senira stepped into the corridor, followed closely by Caldan. He closed the door behind them and re-fused his crafted lock. Whoever tried to follow them would have a hard time opening it. Too, it would hopefully make anyone think they were still inside. If nothing else, it would delay them for a while, and that's all Caldan needed.

He took hold of Senira's hand.

"What are you doing?" she asked.

"Sorry. It's so I can shield you, if it comes to that. I need to maintain contact with you."

"Oh. That's all right, then." She gave him curious look. "You can shield two people?"

"I'm fairly sure I can."

Senira looked doubtful but gripped his hand tighter.

They crept along the dim corridor, feet scuffing on the flagstones. Ahead of them came a pale orange light, where Caldan knew the corridor split to the left and right. Left would lead to the gardens, and right to a courtyard frequently used by the apprentices when they tested their smith-crafting.

They stopped short of the intersection, hugging the walls. "It's clear," whispered Caldan.

Senira frowned at him.

"The bird," he reminded her, pointing at the paper crafting sitting in the middle of the intersection. A wisp of smoke drifted up from it.

"You first," she said, waving him ahead.

Caldan knew two other doorways entered the area from the courtyard to the right. He was confident they could make their way outside the guild buildings from either of the two.

One of the crafted figures in the workshop alerted him to a presence entering the room, though he couldn't tell who or how many. A faint tug on his awareness from the other crafting above the door told him they were moving swiftly. If they had broken through his crafting lock on the first door, it wouldn't be long before they broke through the second.

He grabbed Senira's hand more firmly and rushed ahead.

Both his links with the crafted figures in the workshop shattered simultaneously. A crackling sound filled the corridor, and behind them, the door to the workshop swung open.

Caldan activated his shield, and his skin tightened. With a thought, he extended it around Senira.

Through the doorway strode the tall, pale-skinned woman from the cells, followed by two men. The bells in her dark hair tinkled as she stepped forward.

"Hello," she called. "I see you." She laughed warmly.

"Run!" yelled Caldan. He sprinted toward the corner, dragging Senira with him.

A violent force hit them from behind, lifting them off their feet. Senira screamed. They tumbled to the ground just shy of the intersection. Caldan strained to hold on to Senira's hand. His shield withstood the barrage, though it keened with the strain. Sparks flew as globes of yellow light sizzled past them and struck the walls.

A strong scent of lemons reached him.

Another cluster of yellow lights flew at them, spread wide to cover the width of the corridor, striking Caldan and Senira. The force pushed him back, and he lost his grip on Senira's hand. With a faint pop, the shield around her vanished.

A third cluster followed behind the second. Caldan watched helplessly as two globes slammed into Senira, and she staggered, screaming. Her knees buckled, and she collapsed in a heap. Smoke billowed from two charred circles on her body.

Her eyes glazed over, and she grew still.

"No!" he cried. "I had you!" *You should have been safe.*

"Take him alive!" he heard Bells yell behind him. "I don't care about the girl."

Caldan grabbed his sack and scrabbled around the corner on hands and knees. He glanced back at Senira lying on the cold stone floor. His face burned, and he dripped sweat. He should have kept her safe. She had relied on him. And now she was dead.

And if he didn't keep going, that could be him, too.

As it was, Caldan's body ached from where the lights had hit his shield. It had protected him from the energy they emitted but not from the physical force.

He lurched to his feet and stumbled into the courtyard, straight for the opening ahead. At the opening, he paused and thrust his hands into his pockets, dragging out fistfuls of paper. He crushed the shapes he had painstakingly folded that night, but he didn't care. It didn't matter now. All that mattered was escaping alive.

He scattered the paper to the ground and disappeared through the doorway.

With a wrench, his link to the bird shattered, so he knew they had reached the spot where Senira lay. He needed to hurry.

In front of him, the corridor headed straight. Doors studded the walls on either side, but he knew they led only to classrooms and offices, dead ends. At the end of the corridor stood another door with bound metal edges. This one opened onto a side road next to the guild buildings.

He ran along the corridor, not caring if he made any noise. At the door, he fumbled with the latch, clicked it open. Turning, he glanced behind him. No one. They probably didn't know which way he'd gone. He drew out another piece of paper.

A shadow moved in the courtyard. He guessed they should be standing among his discarded paper shapes.

Caldan opened his well and linked to one of them, then another, then another. Gritting his teeth, he linked to a fourth. His head felt ready to explode. He linked to a fifth. Panting, he filled all five with power but didn't activate them. He reached into his well and pushed as much as he could . . . and then ruptured their anchors.

All five shapes were consumed in an instant as he unleashed the power flowing through them. It had no focus, no purpose. He simply set it loose.

A painful light erupted in the courtyard. Air shook around him. A hot wind rushed down the corridor into his face.

Caldan held his breath and waited. One moment. Two.

A figure appeared from the courtyard. A silvery tinkle echoed.

The lady, Bells, stood there, clothes steaming. Spots of blood spattered her face. There was no sign of the two men who had been with her.

"Naughty," she said, and stepped forward.

Caldan dragged himself through the door and slammed it shut behind him. The narrow alleyway was empty. As fast as he could, he folded a paper into a square and wedged it between the door and the frame.

He reached for his well, but in his panicked state, it slipped from his mind's grasp. *Have to focus!* He dragged in a deep breath and reached again, fumbling like it was his first time. There. He linked to two different craftings on the paper, filled them with force from his well. Again he ruptured one of the anchors.

Around the paper, the metal glowed orange, then red, then white. Caldan struggled to hold on to his shaping. Metal liquefied and dripped between the door and the frame. He closed his well. In the cold air, the metal solidified, welding the door shut.

He grabbed his sack and ran, never looking back.

WHAT FELT LIKE hours later, Caldan stopped running. He bent over, hands on knees, and sucked in huge breaths. People he had passed looked at him like he was a madman, and he thought for a while he might be. He hadn't stopped taking random turns, ducking into the narrowest back lanes and alleys he could see. Soldiers were patrolling the streets, clad in armor and wearing craftings similar to those Mosey and Castens had worn. He'd managed to avoid them so far.

He looked around, having no idea where he was. Somewhere between Barrows and Dockside, he guessed. He remembered crossing a bridge over the river Modder some time ago, though with the twists and turns he had taken, he probably hadn't covered that much distance.

He'd made it out with his trinket, bone ring, ducats, wristband, and crafted metal, but he had lost Senira, a thought that almost brought him to his knees. He took a deep breath and wiped his eyes. *Think.* He needed to think.

Miranda. I need to find her, make sure she's safe. But it was only a matter of time until he was caught if he stayed in the streets. He had to find somewhere nearby to hide. His pants were also covered in dried blood. He desperately needed somewhere to clean up and change. *But where?* He looked around, getting his bearings. He thought he recognized—yes. He was near the store where he'd bought his ore crystals, the one with the odd shopkeeper. What was his name . . . Amerdan? Yes, that was it. He could ask him for shelter until he could figure out his next move.

He remembered the first time he'd met the man. The fleeting reddish glow of his skin and the strange smell had stuck in his mind. He didn't know what it meant—and he was pretty sure he didn't like it—but he had to take a chance; he had no other choices. He wiped sweaty palms on his pants and ran a hand across his head.

Caldan trudged toward a main road, keeping an eye out for the invaders. It had been a while since he'd seen one, but it wouldn't pay to let his guard down now, when he was so close to Amerdan's shop. Once there, he could find his bearings.

He made his way cautiously to Amerdan's street. With a plan in mind, his thoughts wandered back to the door he had welded shut. He bet Bells was surprised it wasn't crafted shut. The fused metal would be hard to break through without destroying the entire door. He chuckled grimly. It wasn't enough to pay her back for what she'd done to Senira, but he would work on that.

Caldan stopped. He'd held on to his well and shaped the forces after his paper crafting must have burned to nothing. If he didn't have a crafting, with its links, shaping runes, and anchors to shape the forces from his well, then . . . how had he kept crafting the molten metal? Sorcery needed physical links and shapes to mold the forces, didn't it?

"No. That's not possible," he muttered. *But I did it.* He thought the destructive sorcery he'd seen used the same principles as well, except you unleashed the pent-up forces all at once. Yet the lights the lady had sent at them were focused, not chaotic at all. Which meant they had to have been shaped.

Caldan shook his head, then winced at the pain. Drawing on his well so much had drained him, and the intense headache he could feel coming on was the least of his worries. He could think later. He hurried off toward Amerdan's.

CHAPTER 39

Caldan pushed through the beaded curtain hanging across the doorway. Silver bells tinkled overhead.

Amerdan stood behind his polished counter. He rubbed his hands together as Caldan came in. "This is unexpected," he said. "Welcome. I wouldn't have thought with the invasion you would . . . but wait . . . you look a little—"

"I'm sorry, Amerdan," Caldan said, "but I'm in trouble. I was close by, and your shop seemed like the only safe—"

"Yes! Safe. Come in. Don't just stand near the door. There's blood on your pants."

"I had to be sure you were in. The blood's dry; there won't be any mess. Wait a few moments, please, and I'll come back. There's a girl waiting for me."

Caldan quickly exited the shop and scanned the street. There, in the shadows of an alley across the way, stood a ragged little girl with brown hair hacked off at uneven lengths. She'd waited, as he'd asked. *So maybe she's dependable and will get the message to Miranda.* He approached her and held out a coin.

"Here you go. Can you take that message for me now?"

She nodded eagerly, eyes all the while on the silver coin out of her reach.

"Good. Remember, Miranda will give you another one of these when you give her the message." He handed her the coin, wishing there was a more reliable way, but he was pretty confident the promise of a second silver ducat would ensure delivery—and he was sure Miranda wouldn't balk at paying it.

The little girl scurried off.

Caldan breathed a sigh of relief. With any luck, the girl would find Miranda at her warehouse and let her know he was all right, and likely to hunker down for the time being at Amerdan's shop. He turned and found Amerdan staring at him.

Inside, the shopkeeper ushered him through a back room, past stairs down, and out the back door into a courtyard with a well and some pigs in a sty. He kept up a smooth patter of words along the way and handed Caldan a tin mug, pointing to a bucket by the well.

"Drink," Amerdan said. "You look parched. Then you can tell me what's happened. How did you injure your leg?"

"One of the invaders—"

"Here. Let me take a look at it."

"No! Thank you, but no. It's fine. A shallow cut." Caldan filled the mug from the bucket and drank deeply. He drained it along with another, then splashed water on his face, neck, and arms. He sighed and removed his shirt, pouring cold water from the bucket over himself and rubbing his skin. He worked swiftly to remove the grime and sweat of the last few days, then tipped the bucket over his head. The water felt refreshing, and for a few moments, he pushed the stress of his capture and escape out of his mind. Only, some things refused to go: Senira shouldn't have died. He should have been able to look after her. He cursed under his breath and opened his eyes to find Amerdan had left and returned carrying a pair of pants. They looked similar to those he wore at the guild, and they seemed to be the right size.

"Here," Amerdan said. "I was waiting until you finished. I think these should fit."

"Thank you. I'll change inside."

"Of course." Amerdan glanced toward the pigs, then back to Caldan. "Did you use sorcery to kill them? The Indryallans."

"What? No. That's not possible." *Except I now know it is. But if the invaders are so open with their use of destructive sorcery, soon everyone will know. And they are from Indryalla. That ship in the harbor—I knew it felt wrong.* "Sorcery . . . doesn't work like that," he finished lamely.

"Then I guess you haven't heard. The city walls are awash with blue flames that give off no heat. They sizzle and crackle, though. I went to see them. Anasoma is sealed up so tight, a rat couldn't get out. Though a few have died trying." Amerdan chuckled at his own wit, then his face grew serious. "I saw a drunken young fool try to run through the flames. He caught fire and died horribly. So, you can see, sorcery does work like that. There's no point lying about it. Come, now—it must be incredible to have such powers."

What should he say? He couldn't just blurt out the truth—especially since he wasn't exactly sure what the truth was himself. Until he figured it out, Caldan felt it better to keep whatever information he had private. "I'm only an apprentice, but the masters I knew didn't think sorcery like this was possible. I certainly can't perform it."

"Then they lied to you."

The implication was clear: *Or you're lying to me.*

Caldan shrugged, unsure of why it mattered to the shopkeeper so much. "Maybe," he said. "I can't worry about that now. I need to wait here until nightfall, then find a friend of mine. Is that all right?" He cupped his hands and rinsed his face again. When he looked up, Amerdan was a step closer.

"That is . . . fine. Yes. Stay here."

"Thank you. Is there somewhere I can lie down to rest? A spare bed?"

"Of course. In one of the back rooms there's a bed. I'm afraid it's a bit narrow, though." Amerdan gave Caldan an appraising look.

"I'll manage. It's just for a short time. Until it's night."

"Oh dear. The Indryallans announced a curfew starting at sunset, and they've posted notices in the streets to that effect."

Caldan thought for a while. If he left before sunset, then the streets should be busy with people rushing, before curfew. It would be an ideal time to mingle with the crowds, all hurrying, to help him go unnoticed.

"I'll leave an hour before sunset then."

Amerdan stared at Caldan intensely, almost scrutinizing him. "As you wish," was all he said.

He'd found safe haven here, for a short time anyway. And despite Amerdan's odd behavior, Caldan owed him for that. But he needed to remember these were troubled times, and he had to be careful.

CALDAN CHECKED TO be sure his craftings were still safely tucked away in his sack, and both his rings were still around his neck. He hadn't been able to sleep; his thoughts kept drifting to Miranda, and he worried if he slept, he'd wake after the curfew cutoff. A vague feeling of being watched had stayed with him. The room had a small barred window, and when the overcast clouds began to tinge with orange, he rose from the bed.

After changing into his new pants, he made his way to the shop proper and found Amerdan with a bucket and cloth, scrubbing the already gleaming counter. He smiled at Caldan when he entered, and wrung out the wet cloth.

"I hope you're feeling better, young Caldan."

Caldan wished everyone would stop calling him young. He was bigger than most people he ran across. "Yes. Much better. Thank you."

Amerdan looked toward the shelves behind the counter, and Caldan noticed a tired-looking rag doll sitting in the corner of one. It seemed oddly out of place in the spotless store.

"So where is this friend you're looking for?" Amerdan asked, pulling his eyes from the doll.

"She owns a warehouse in Dockside. She'll be there, if she has any sense—and she has."

"The docks will be teeming with the invaders. You'd better be careful."

"She's a short distance from the wharves, so hopefully it's far enough away from the docks that it will be clearer. I'll find it."

"Dockside, you say? That's got to be Cockle Street."

"Houndshark," Caldan said, then winced as Amerdan gave a satisfied nod. He didn't entirely trust Amerdan and shouldn't have given so much information away.

"As you say, far enough from the docks proper," Amerdan said. "Should be safe."

"Excuse me."

Both Caldan and Amerdan turned at the girl's voice. The street urchin—she was back. She stood in the doorway, arms folded tightly across her stomach. Her eyes darted around, as if she expected trouble at any moment.

Caldan rushed over to her and knelt to bring his head level with hers. "Did you find her? Is she all right?"

The girl's head bobbed. "Yes. Gave me a message for you. That'll be another coin." She held her hand out confidently.

Caldan fished out another silver ducat and pressed it into her palm. "She was at the warehouse, I assume? What did she say?"

The girl screwed up her face, thinking hard. "'Come here. It's safe. We need to get out of the city.' That's it."

Caldan handed her another ducat, which disappeared somewhere under her dirty clothes along with the first. "Thank you. Stay off the streets, if you can. There are bad men about."

The girl frowned, like he'd asked her to fetch him a piece of the moon. "There are always bad men."

All Caldan could do was nod in agreement. "Would you like something to eat?"

She glanced at Amerdan, then shook her head, something wild in her eyes as she did so. "No. I should go." With that, she turned and left the shop.

"So that's settled then," Amerdan said. "With this invasion, I feel like I should be doing more to help. I know I'm only a shopkeeper, but it would be good to stay together. You'll never make it to Dockside without being picked up, but I know some back ways."

Caldan shook his head. There was something about Amerdan that made him wary. But maybe it was the city rubbing off on him. "The Indryallans will be looking for me. You'll be in more danger, if you're with me." He held out a few ducats. "How much do I owe you for the pants?"

"Nothing! It's the least I can do for you. Someone has to resist these terrible invaders."

"Then I'll let you get back to your business. I've troubled you enough already."

"Not at all. It's been my pleasure to assist you."

Caldan gave him a smile and a nod. He exited the shop and headed toward Dockside.

CALDAN HURRIED ALONG the Highroad toward Dockside. He was reluctant to use such a major thoroughfare, but it would take too much time to go through back alleys. Worse than that, he'd already experienced firsthand what could happen if you ran into shady types. He wasn't taking his chances again.

He kept his head down, keeping his eyes as best he could on who was around him. When he saw Indryallan patrols ahead, he ducked down streets and circled around them.

He was avoiding one group when he passed through a square with a fountain in the center. A lean man sat on a short stool next to it, a basket of oranges at his feet. Men and women were filling containers with water at the fountain, which must have been supplied through the aqueducts under the city.

Caldan crossed the square and was about to leave it behind him when a woman rushed toward him—Elpidia.

She uttered a yelp of relief and clasped him in a brief hug. "Caldan! You're safe," she gushed. She pulled back a step. With a glance down at her hand, she hastily shoved a metal disc into her pocket. But he had caught enough of a glimpse.

That's a crafting. Where would she have gotten that? And why did she try so hard to hide it? "And you, Elpidia. What are you doing on the streets? It's not safe."

"I needed to find you. It's important."

"And we just happened to run into each other?" As his suspicions flared further, he grabbed her arm. He'd had enough of being pushed around. "Show me the crafting you just put in your pocket."

Elpidia's mouth opened in shock. "Ah . . . it's just . . ."

"Show me, or leave me alone."

With a great display of reluctance, Elpidia drew the crafting out. She clutched it tightly in one hand.

"What is it?" Caldan insisted.

"It's . . . a compass . . . of a sort." She stretched out her hand, slowly.

It took only a glance for Caldan to determine what its function was. He'd read about them but had never seen one. The only drawback was, you needed the blood of a person for it to work. Most masters frowned on such sorcery, and the details of the crafting he'd seen were sketchy.

This one clearly worked, though . . . which meant she had *his* blood. "You saved some of my blood," he accused.

"I . . . I didn't throw the rag away when I took the stitches out."

Elpidia had the grace to look embarrassed. Her cheeks reddened, and she wrung her hands. "Caldan, listen, please. You heal unnaturally quickly. I've seen it. My research, it's important. I need a favor of you."

"This is about your rash, isn't it? You're sick. Really sick."

Her arms dropped to her sides and her shoulders slumped. "Yes. I'm dying. I woke one morning and found a few red spots on my neck. A mild irritation, I thought. I couldn't have been more wrong. Nine years of marriage, and what do I get for it? The Great Pox, that's what. My bastard husband left me and gave me a disease as a parting gift."

Caldan hissed under his breath. No cure was known, and sufferers ended their days in pain, sometimes months, sometimes years after the first symptoms showed. His heart clenched, and he cringed inside. He hesitated, not knowing what to say, and knowing nothing he did say would be of comfort to Elpidia.

"The gash to your face healed quickly," Elpidia continued. "*Too* quickly. Sorcery can sometimes be used to speed the healing process, though it takes an extremely skilled master. But this . . . I've read of a few cases where a person has healed themselves, much like what's happened to you."

Caldan grunted. "And now you think my blood holds some kind of secret. I can assure you, it doesn't." But as he spoke the words, he realized he *wasn't* so sure. His leg had started healing while he'd been passed out. A few hours, at most. It wasn't natural.

"Don't brush me off!" Elpidia said, as if confirming his own doubts. "I've been looking for someone like you! If what I suspect is true, I want to be able to use it. And if I find out how it works, I'm sure I could figure out a way for other people to benefit, not just me."

Caldan shook his head. He didn't have time for this. "This is going to have to wait. I need to find out what's happened to the Protectors, and to the others in the Sorcerers' Guild. If you haven't noticed, the city has been invaded."

"Please," begged Elpidia. "I need more of your blood—just a vial."

"What? No!" This woman was insane.

Elpidia clutched Caldan's arm. Her eyes welled with tears. "It's a small amount—little more than a few drops to experiment with. Anything to give me hope. You won't miss it. Please."

"Won't miss my own blood? No," Caldan said firmly. It was too much. He couldn't even think about it right now. "I won't be used as an experiment. This scheme of yours is mad. I don't want to argue about this anymore. I've made up my mind."

"But—"

"I said no, Elpidia. I'm going now, and I don't want you following me again. Is that clear?"

Caldan turned his back on the physiker and hurried toward the docks. He'd lost valuable time arguing with Elpidia. He just hoped he'd make it to Miranda's before curfew.

CHAPTER 40

Caldan stood back as Miranda unlocked the heavy door of her warehouse. When she'd opened it wide enough, he slipped inside and was immediately enfolded in a hug. Miranda squeezed him so hard, he worried she'd never let go. Her head rested against his chest, and her hair brushed his chin, smelling of lavender and almond.

He let out a sigh and wriggled an arm free so he could return the hug. "It's all right," he said softly. "I'm all right. I made it through uninjured . . . Well, almost."

Abruptly, she let go and pushed him away. "Almost? Are you hurt? Where?" She looked him up and down.

"It's nothing." He hesitated, but realized it made no sense. If there was one person in the world he trusted, it was Miranda. *Besides, Elpidia already knows about my healing, and Miranda will guess soon anyway. I may as well tell her now.*

"I was stabbed in the thigh."

"Oh! How bad is it? You walked here, though. It's bandaged?"

"No. Something strange happened. One of the Indryallans stabbed me with his dagger when I tried to resist. It was pretty bad. He wasn't trying to kill me, though, just hurt me."

Miranda covered her mouth in shock.

"When they threw me in a cell," continued Caldan. "I passed out. When I came to, the wound had healed. I don't know what happened."

"Someone healed you? With sorcery? Why would they do that?"

With a shake of his head, Caldan touched the spot on his leg where he'd been injured. "It wasn't sorcery. It was me. You saw how fast my cheek healed. I don't know what it is. Elpidia thinks it's in my blood—"

Miranda looked at him sharply. "Elpidia? The healer? How does she know?"

"I ran into her on the way here. That's another story. I'll tell you later."

"Fine. I'm just glad you're safe." She hugged him again.

"Me, too. I was lucky to get out alive. The Sorcerers' Guild, I mean. Others weren't so lucky. The Indryallans rounded up all the sorcerers, I think. They locked me in a cell, but I managed to escape."

"I heard there was fighting at the Sorcerers' Guild. There have been clashes between the Quivers and the Indryallans, but there's hardly any real resistance. It's a worry. Something's wrong. I would have thought the Quivers would have reacted quickly to the threat, but . . . there are now dozens of Indryallan ships in the harbor. Where is the emperor? Why isn't he doing anything?"

"I don't know, but I wonder if the wall of blue fire around the city has anything to do with why there hasn't been more resistance."

"I guess," she said. "It's strange, though—this isn't even the capital. I wonder what they want."

"I got the feeling they were after something."

She pulled away, looking up to meet his eyes. "What did you see? Did they say anything to you?"

Caldan shook his head. "They didn't say much in front of me. All I know is they're using alchemy. They must want something, but I don't know what it is." He couldn't bring himself to tell Miranda about the destructive and coercive sorcery, at least not yet. She had enough worries.

Miranda stared at him for a long moment. "Well, whatever it is, it's not here. This close to the harbor, they would have come by now if it were."

He looked around the warehouse, nodding.

"Anyway, there's plenty of room," continued Miranda. She ran a hand through her dark hair, and Caldan remembered how soft it had felt. "I retrieved some clothes and other things from my rooms, and some food, water, and a flask of cider. I guess we can stretch it for a few days. Four or five, at the most."

"I'll need a few crafting materials as well. There should be somewhere close I can buy some." He realized he could have just bought them from Amerdan, but in his rush he hadn't thought about it. To be fair, he'd also wanted to get away from the shopkeeper as quickly as possible.

"Well, take a look around. I wasn't supposed to own this place for very long. But who knows what'll happen now?"

The door opened into a large foyer with a scuffed floor covered in a thin layer of dust, except for a trail leading to a doorway ahead. The air inside was stale and overlaid with decay and old spices.

"I haven't had time to clean up," Miranda said, gesturing at the floor. "I wasn't really expecting to ever use this place."

To the left were three areas partitioned with cheaply constructed thin wooden walls, meant to be used as offices.

"Sorry about the accommodation, but this is what the warehouse came with. We'll have to make it comfortable enough while we hide out here."

"It's fine." Caldan poked his head into each of the three rooms, sneezed at the dust, and rubbed his nose with the back of his hand. "It won't take much to clean them up, and we won't be here long anyway."

"We won't? Where are we . . . you don't mean to go back to the Sorcerers' Guild, do you? You can't!"

"I have to. I need to find out what's going on." The thought of returning to where he'd been stabbed and imprisoned filled him with unease. And if everyone else in the Sorcerers' Guild had been captured or even killed . . . His unease turned to dread.

"The Indryallans have taken over the entire city," Miranda said. "And the Quivers are nowhere to be seen, probably completely overwhelmed. These people are serious. Their whole operation was well planned and executed. What could you possibly hope to accomplish by going back to the guild?"

"I don't know what I can do . . . but I need to try."

Miranda approached him and placed her hands on his shoulders. She looked at him until he met her eyes. "Try what? At best, what can you do? And at worst, you will be killed. They stabbed you!"

Caldan's heart thumped in his chest at her closeness, her touch, the scent of her. He wanted to draw her in closer. Instead, he dropped his gaze. *That's what the monastery will do to you.* Even with Jemma he'd been a dolt. "Yes, they stabbed me. But I healed. Besides, they weren't going to kill me. From what they said, they were capturing all the apprentices, maybe to get them out of the way. They're up to something, and I have to know what. I have to learn what's happened to the Protectors."

Miranda was quiet for a moment. Her mouth was stretched into a thin line, and he could tell she was fuming.

"You're risking your life," she said. "And for what? You've no idea what you'll find there."

"I . . . have to. Can't you see? When I was young, I lost my parents. Then, a few months ago, I lost the only life I knew at the monastery; and now . . . They took me in. I found a place with them. I took an oath. I can't lose this, too."

She laid a hand on his cheek. "Caldan, I'm sorry. I can see what this means to you, I truly can. But we *need* to get out of the city."

He shook his head with stubborn resolve. "The Protectors . . . they're important. They can help."

Miranda blew out a breath and paced the room, her footsteps stirring up low clouds of dust. "If they could help, they would have by now, Caldan. The Indryallans are imprisoning or killing sorcerers.

They had to have done something to the Quivers, too, or there would have been more resistance. They know you now and are probably looking for you. We should leave . . . We have to get out of here."

"Listen to me. People I know—I respect—are missing and in trouble. I can't leave them. I have no choice."

"Of course you do! We can leave the city."

"How? The walls are barricaded, the city gates are closed and barred."

"There are always ways out of any city. Smugglers' tunnels and the like, if you can contact the right people."

"For a price."

Miranda shrugged. "Of course for a price. But what price wouldn't be worth it? It won't be easy, but I can make some inquiries."

"Some prices *are* too high," he said, thinking of Senira. "No, I have to find out what happened to the Protectors, or at least Master Simmon." Caldan grasped both her shoulders and looked into her eyes.

She met his gaze, then turned away. *Does she know how I feel about her?* The hugs, the concern . . . they all seemed to indicate she did, but he couldn't tell.

Maybe she was just trying to find a way not to embarrass him.

"Give me a few days," Caldan said. "If I can't find out what's happened to them, we can leave. I promise."

Miranda nodded. "We can't just ride out this storm and come out the other side, like I've done on the open sea. Two days. Then we get out of here. Agreed?"

"Agreed." Caldan dropped his arms to his sides and took a step back. He looked around the dusty room. "We'll need somewhere to sleep, and I need somewhere to work. We can use one of these partitioned areas."

Miranda nodded. "Sounds good. I'll use this front room to work in."

She looked into the warehouse proper, which was empty except for a mass of crates and barrels close by the main doors to the street. "Do you need any more supplies? I have food, but it's only enough to last a few days."

"Two days is all we have to last. But we should buy more, just in case, and some bedding." A rickety table and chair stood in a corner. Caldan dumped his sack on the table. "There's only one chair."

"I didn't think I'd be having guests."

"Funny."

"I thought so. There's a broom inside somewhere, and a chair in the other room. You tidy up, and I'll go out and get some blankets for tonight. With the Indryallans patrolling the streets, probably with a description of you, I don't like the thought of you being out there in harm's way."

The logic made sense, but it was the sentiment that lifted his heart—there was something about the way she looked at him when she said she was worried about him that made him think she was saying something deeper than just mere practicalities. He wanted to say something back, something to confirm this—both for her and for him—but all he could do was nod. "Sure."

"I shouldn't be long. If I'm not back soon, send out a search party."

"Don't joke about it. Please."

"I'll try to be as quick as possible." She hesitated, then continued. "Don't open the door for anyone you don't know."

CALDAN HAD JUST finished when Miranda returned carrying a bundle of blankets. She relocked the door and gestured for him to take them into the freshly swept back rooms. A faint peppermint aroma pervaded the air from the fired clay stove in a corner, on which he'd placed a kettle above glowing coals. On the floor next to the stove were two enameled clay cups he'd found in a dusty cupboard.

"You've been busy," she remarked.

"I wouldn't dare slack off with you around. You might curse at me and my tender ears couldn't take it."

Miranda gave him a weak smile.

Caldan couldn't blame her for her lack of amusement. Their situation was dire.

"I heard something while I was outside," said Miranda hesitantly.

"It's not good news, I take it?"

"No, it's not."

Caldan poured peppermint tea into the two cups and handed one to Miranda. "What happened? What did you hear?"

"A few . . . quite a few of the nobles and some of the most powerful merchants are dead."

Caldan gasped. "The Indryallans killed them? Why? The nobles I can understand, but why the merchants?"

"That's the strange thing—the Indryallans didn't kill them; they killed themselves. From what I heard, the count is around thirty and rising."

"Suicide? That doesn't make sense."

"Yes. Some slashed their wrists, hanged themselves, poison. What is even stranger is they all did it at the same time, or close enough."

"Weird. Who were they? Anyone important?"

"Most were. High-ranking nobles, commanders of the Quivers in the city and the surrounding districts, some of the chancellors. Of the merchants, I'm not sure. I don't know any of them. I didn't hear mention of Izak, Lady Felicienne, or Sir Avigdor, which I hope means they've also escaped capture."

That gave Caldan a moment's pause. "You know, Felicienne would have some idea what to do, and I think we could trust her." He frowned. "Of course, I don't know how we can possibly find out where she is or contact her."

"If they haven't been named, then we have to assume they're alive. From what you told me of the Lady Felicienne, I doubt she'd be one to take her own life. The emperor would have punished the nobles for what's happened here—their lack of resistance and the loss of the city. There would have been demotions and possibly banishment, so that might explain it. But I don't think suicide would be preferable."

"I agree. I think that . . ." Caldan stopped. A sudden thought came to him. Bells had used sorcery to control his mind. He remembered the man he'd killed, that Simmon had tried to arrest: *for the use of destructive and coercive sorcery.*

They didn't have to kill them—they could make the nobles and mer-chants kill themselves.

But why?

He thought on it a moment more and realized Miranda had given him the answer. She had said that someone would have to be blamed for what happened here, but what if they *were* to blame—albeit, because they were coerced into their actions. It would then stand to reason, after their usefulness was over, that the Indryallans would dispose of them. And while he had no doubt some of the nobles were corrupt, no one deserved to have their mind used, then have their body disposed of like garbage.

Miranda gave him a concerned look. "What is it?"

Again, he didn't feel it was worth worrying Miranda about the possibilities of coercive magic right now. There wasn't anything they could do to defend against it, so why add to her problems? Caldan placed his mug on the table and kept his eyes averted. "Nothing. Maybe . . . they might have been dealing with the Indryallans and decided they didn't want to face the emperor after this. We will probably never know, though the Protectors might. This makes it more urgent I find them." He couldn't look Miranda in the eye. Lying to her felt wrong, but coercive sorcery was knowledge the Protectors kept secret, and he didn't know what they'd do to her if they found out she knew.

"Do you need help with anything?"

"No, thank you. With the materials I have, I won't be able to craft much, but I should be able to put a few things together, and I want to try and finish my project as well."

"Do you think this is the time for projects?"

"It'll help us, so if I have a chance, I want to finish it. It'll be . . . bet-ter than anything I've crafted before. Paper is too flimsy, and with this we have an extra shield that might come in useful." Caldan looked out through the doorway to the barrels and crates of goods Miranda had stockpiled. "If you have coffee somewhere in there, I could use some; it's going to be a long night."

Miranda nodded and went to rummage through the crates.

Caldan turned to the rickety table and his sack of crafting materials. He upended the sack and spread the materials across the table—paper, ink, pens, a few scraps of wood, two wire spools, and the metal pieces he'd acquired from the clockmaker. It wasn't much to work with.

CHAPTER 41

Surprisingly, the streets appeared normal. The lack of Quivers had led to an increase in crime the last few days, but most of the population continued on as if nothing much had happened.

Caldan gave Miranda an annoyed look. After working through the night, he was tired and not in any mood to be arguing.

"You said I have two days," he said. "You don't have to come. Actually, it would comfort me greatly if you didn't."

She narrowed her eyes. "Really?"

"For your own safety, I mean. I can't bear the thought of you being injured." Senira's blood was on his hands, and if Miranda was hurt . . . he didn't think he could forgive himself for dragging her into this.

"Well, if that isn't the sweetest brush-off I've ever received, I don't know what is."

"It's not that," Caldan said. "I don't want you to be in danger—ever—and it's going to be dangerous." He looked at her intently, and her eyes widened. He wished he could tell her how he felt. He was brave—or stupid—enough to go back to the Sorcerers' Guild, but he couldn't seem to talk to Miranda. For now, his protection would have to be enough.

"It's my decision. And two are always better than one. I'm not entirely defenseless. You don't survive long on a ship if you can't take care of yourself." She patted her loose pants. A while ago, before they left the warehouse, Caldan had seen her strap a dagger to her leg.

Again he found himself wishing for a sword. It wasn't like there were any Quivers to object to it now. One of his priorities had to be to acquire a blade of some sort.

He pulled on a wide-brimmed hat and tugged it low over his eyes to hide his face as best he could—Miranda's idea and one easily purchased from a market—in case the Indryallans had soldiers out looking for him. It wouldn't stop someone recognizing him up close if they had a description, but it would serve to screen him from casual observers.

"Nothing much has changed," Miranda said. "For normal people it hasn't. So what if the emperor loses power here and is replaced by someone else? Life goes on. And it might be a better life for a lot of people. The only thing that will upset the stability now is the city being closed to supplies. Shortages will begin to bite soon."

She's wrong. For me, everything has changed.

Caldan grunted noncommittally, then waved toward the west. "Let's go along the river."

Already, this early in the morning, the sun had warmed the river Modder's scummy surface enough to make it reek and sting their nostrils and eyes. The thought of what it would smell like in high summer made him gag.

"Good idea. It stinks, but fewer people will walk this way," said Miranda as if reading his thoughts.

They continued in silence. Roaches scuttled away from their movement into nearby buildings and down the bank along the water. Rats stopped and stared as they passed. After discussing their options last night, they'd decided to approach the Sorcerers' Guild in daylight, to blend in with the general populace. It would be too risky moving about at night now that the Indryallans had imposed a curfew. This way, they'd look less suspicious.

"Just make sure," Caldan said, "if there's any sign of sorcerers, hang on to me. I can protect you." He wouldn't let what happened to Senira happen to Miranda.

Miranda nodded and chewed her bottom lip.

They passed children on the other bank, dressed in filthy rags and dragging sticks through the shallow water. Two old men sat farther along, smoking pipes and gossiping.

"I can't show you here, and I didn't think to before we left"— Caldan rubbed his weary eyes—"too much to think about, but once we get to the guild and find a safe place, I can show you my shield."

"Sorcery?"

"Yes. I need you to believe me when I say I can protect you." The fact was, though, that if they ran into heavy sorcery, he wasn't so sure he could. He thrust the thought to the back of his mind.

Miranda nodded. "Let's get going, then!"

Caldan smiled and shook his head at her enthusiasm. They continued walking, the morning sun warming their backs. On the way from the river, they had to avoid two patrols of Indryallans by ducking down side streets. As they approached the Sorcerers' Guild, Caldan led Miranda into a deserted lane running along the south wall. They crouched behind a rain barrel, directly opposite a locked door.

"I want you to keep close."

"I get it. You've said it three times since we left the river." Irritation tinged Miranda's voice.

Caldan gritted his teeth, more in frustration at himself than at Miranda. He clenched and unclenched his fists. If only he'd said it four times to Senira . . .

He figured they should try to get the door open as quickly as possible, then leave it open in case they needed to escape.

He nibbled a thumbnail as he thought about the problem and weighed his options. Using destructive sorcery would open the door, but the unleashing of so much power might alert anyone who had their well open. He had an idea, though, one that stemmed from his experiments with moving craftings.

Searching through the contents of a pocket, he drew out a piece of white chalk.

"Let's go," he said, grabbing his sack and taking off across the street for the door.

Miranda hesitated a moment, then followed.

Caldan knelt on one knee, eyes level with the lock.

Miranda hurried up beside him. "Whatever you're doing, do it fast," she hissed. "We're exposed here."

Caldan nodded, and with swift, sure strokes, drew two patterns on the lock with the chalk, one on the left side and one on the right. He closed his eyes and opened his well. Visualizing the internal workings of the mechanism, he linked his two patterns. With a shriek of grinding metal, it twisted and broke.

Miranda gasped. "It's open?"

"Yes." He felt a bit sheepish, though. "I just wanted it to open; didn't mean for it to break. I think I know what I did wrong, though."

"That's great. The next time we break into a defended guild hall, you can do it right."

They slipped through, and once inside, he closed the door behind them.

Miranda breathed a sigh of relief. "That was easier than I thought."

They found themselves in a dimly lit corridor, the only light coming from the far end, where it opened onto the central garden. Apart from their own breathing, not a sound reached their ears. Gone was the usual background noise of a busy guild going about its day-to-day activities. There was no sign of life at all.

Moving as quietly as they could, they passed doors on both sides. Outside, the garden remained green and lush, unchanged, though conflict had raged around it.

"Wait a moment," Caldan whispered, waving Miranda to a halt. He pulled the rune-covered bird he'd made from folded paper out of his pocket and placed it on the ground. Opening his sack, he drew out a fist-sized cluster of metal rods.

Satisfied, he turned to Miranda. "I said I'd show you how I can protect you." He held his other hand out to her. Miranda hesitated, then reached out to grasp it.

Caldan gave her a reassuring smile. "Don't be alarmed with what you see. Trust me."

A pale blue light enveloped Caldan. Miranda gasped and pulled back, and she would have lost her grip if not for Caldan's firm hold. "See, there's nothing to be afraid of."

She swallowed. "It's a shield, isn't it?"

"Yes. It can stop a sword thrust or a knife, even protect from sorcery. It's withstood a lot already, and I'm confident it will guard us from most things." He gave her a reassuring smile.

"But this is only good to shield one person. How are you going to protect me?"

Caldan squeezed her hand harder, so she wouldn't pull away. "With the runes I put in the crafting, and more concentration, I can shape the forces like this . . ." In the blink of an eye, the shield enfolded Miranda.

She let out a strangled yelp and tried to pull her hand away. "It's squeezing me," she hissed.

"It's all right," Caldan said. "It's only a little and you'll get used to it. Stop squirming."

Miranda had squeezed her eyes shut and was breathing rapidly. After a few moments, she opened one eye. "I can see." She opened her other eye.

With a faint popping sound, the shield blinked out of existence as Caldan closed his well. "If I'm using sorcery all the time, someone is bound to sense it. We have to keep it in reserve, in case we run into trouble."

"And we would be much more noticeable and suspicious."

"Yes, anyone who saw us wandering around shielded would want to find out what we were up to."

Caldan became conscious they were still holding hands. Her skin felt warm and soft. His cheeks grew hot, and he released his grip. Miranda gave an impudent grin, cheeks dimpling as she smiled, and looked away.

He turned toward the opening to the garden, heart pounding. "Now you know why you have to stay close to me, close enough to grab me if there is any danger. If I think we're in trouble, I'll grab you."

"Grab. Yes, I will do that." She sounded amused.

Caldan gestured at the paper bird and the pile of metal rods held together with wire. "These will be our scouts. They can move ahead and let us know if anyone's around. We should be able to keep moving quickly, as long as we don't encounter someone."

"A paper bird and a pile of . . . metal sticks?" Miranda said, disbelief tingeing her words.

"Trust me."

"Of course. I'm just not used to sorcery."

Sometimes I'm still not used to it, he thought.

He reached out to touch the bird and opened his well, linking to the crafting. The runes covering the bird shimmered in the dim light, and it flapped its wings, rising from the floor. With a thought, he sent it through the doorway and into the garden. Out of the corner of his eye, he saw Miranda watching it fly away, a look of wonder on her face.

"I'm going to perch it high up in one of the trees so it can cover as much of the garden as possible. Its range and view is small, but it should guide us to a safe path. And it won't last long, so we should hurry."

"How long will it last?"

"A few minutes. I have more, anyway."

"It's sad to know something beautiful will be destroyed so quickly, once its usefulness is over. What does the metal do?"

"It's probably better if I show you." He opened his well and linked to the crafting he had spent hours perfecting with the clockmaker's help.

Giving a shiver, the metal rods started to slowly rearrange them-selves, forming a squat animal. With jerky movements, it rose up on four metal legs. Atop an egg-shaped solid metal head sat two tiny yellow stones acting as eyes. Miniature claws studded the ends of metal paws.

"Oh!" exclaimed Miranda. "It's a dog."

"Well . . . not really. I wanted something that could move and sense better than the paper animals. Four legs for speed, and a head was all I needed."

"It's a dog," Miranda said firmly.

Caldan shrugged, then glanced out at the garden again. "Come on, we shouldn't waste the paper bird." With a thought, he sent his construct skittering ahead, metal claws clicking on the stone pavers before it moved onto the gravel path in the garden. In moments it crossed half the garden, veered off the path onto the grass, and disappeared behind a hedge.

"It's fast." Miranda squinted after it.

Caldan nodded. "I wanted it to be. There are still improvements to make, but I'm pleased with this prototype. Since it's made out of metal, it'll last a long time." He grasped Miranda's hand. "Come on."

They ducked through the opening into the garden and veered left, taking advantage of a row of bushes to screen their movement. They stopped for a moment under the tree in which the paper bird perched. Caldan used his link to the crafting to sense if the coast was clear. He tugged Miranda's arm, and they crossed an open grassy space, then dove between two thick bushes.

"Almost there," whispered Caldan.

Miranda bent over, hands on her knees, gasping for breath. "Almost . . . where . . . ?"

Caldan found he was breathing normally, showing no signs of exertion after their weaving run. "We're almost to the Protectors' training square, where we're taught sword work. There's an armory. I want a sword, in case we need it, and then we can search for the Protectors."

"Any ideas where to start looking?"

"Probably the cells. I hadn't realized there were any until I was thrown into one. Now I think . . . there are a few stairs going down that could lead to more. The cells in the room I was in were relatively empty, so there have to be others."

"In other words, you have no idea where to go."

"No, I do. Down to the underground level. I don't think it's as extensive as this level, so there can't be too many ways down." Caldan turned back to face the tree where he had left the bird. "Ah. It's fading."

"Is that going to be okay?"

"Yes. The . . . dog . . . should be enough for now." He froze. His construct had sensed something . . . a tingling life force that came closer. "Someone's coming," he whispered. He concentrated. "More than one."

"It can see through the door?" asked Miranda in a hushed voice.

"Not exactly. It can sense people, their life force, and can tell if they have a well. It's a variation on how the Sorcerers' Guild detects talented youngsters."

They waited in silence for a few minutes. The strength of the tingling sensation leveled off, then faded as whoever it was moved farther away.

"They're gone," said Caldan. He took a moment to send his awareness into the dog to check for further danger. Nothing. "It's all clear. Let's go."

They moved along the wall behind the hedges until they reached another door. Caldan lifted the latch, ushering Miranda through. The metal construct skittered in front of her.

Ahead extended another corridor, twenty yards in length, opening at the end onto a courtyard of packed earth. To the left and right of them were more doors, two on each side.

"This one." Caldan twisted the knob of the closest door on the right. It was locked.

Miranda came up behind him. "Try your trick again."

He fished around in his pocket for the chalk and scribed patterns on the lock. Moments later, it clicked open. Much smoother this time; he was getting better with practice. He winked at Miranda, who frowned in disapproval.

"You'd make a good thief," she said.

"I wouldn't do that."

"I know. It's one thing I like about you."

Inside, blades of all sizes hung from wooden pegs on the walls, each with a leather scabbard and belt. Three large chests presumably held weapons of other kinds. Miranda tried to open one.

"Locked," she said, disappointed.

"Let's not take too long. Anything serviceable will do."

Caldan scanned the walls and took the first sword that looked suitable for his height and lifted it down. Plain and unadorned, it was good enough for now. He strapped the belt around his waist and adjusted its position until it was comfortable. He turned to find Miranda staring at him.

"You look . . . deadly," she said matter-of-factly. "With your build, the sword, the sorcery . . ." She shook her head.

"Let's hope it doesn't come down to that." If it did, though, he'd be ready. He might not be deadly, but he'd do whatever it took, especially if it meant protecting Miranda.

They left the armory and stepped quietly along the corridor, then stopped before the courtyard. Ahead of them, the sparring circles were covered in leaves blown by the wind.

In the center of one of the circles lay a thin body, facedown with limbs twisted. One hand clutched a slender sword. Around the figure, dark stains stood out from the lighter dirt of the courtyard. A larger stain spread from under the body. Though the clothes were covered in dust, Caldan recognized them as the cut and color most masters preferred. And that sword . . . He drew in a breath. *Jazintha . . . ?*

With a glance at Miranda, he motioned her to follow and approached the body with hesitant steps. The master had been dead a day or two. The head and neck were a greenish-blue color. Caldan and Miranda held their noses as the stench of rotting meat was almost overwhelming. Miranda backed away, waving at Caldan to continue. He took another step forward, drew in a deep breath, then crouched over the corpse briefly before he staggered back to Miranda and gasped in fresh air.

"I wouldn't believe she could be bested," Caldan said.

Miranda, hand still covering her mouth and nose, turned away from the body. "You know her?"

"Yes. Jazintha, a master in the Protectors. She was very good with a blade."

"But it looks like she died in a sword fight. If she was good, then who could do that?"

"Exactly. Someone better than she was . . . and that scares me." Caldan blew air hard out of his nose to try and clear the lingering smell. "She's been slashed pretty badly, and her sword doesn't have any blood on it. It looks like whoever killed her was more than a match."

Miranda shivered and rubbed her arms. "Caldan, if she was a master and was beaten so easily . . ."

"No," he said firmly, reading into her silence. "It doesn't matter how powerful these Indryallans are—we have to keep fighting them. I have to keep fighting." He lingered, his eyes drawn to the mutilated body before him.

"I . . . know," she said. "But we should get out of here."

"We should do something for her. Bury her or . . ."

"Or what?" asked Miranda sharply. "We need to get away from here. We can't spend the time to do anything for her." She took Caldan by the arm. "Come on."

He hesitated a moment longer, but he knew Miranda was right. Taking a deep breath, he turned away from Jazintha. "That way." Caldan pointed across the courtyard to another corridor.

With a thought through his link to the construct, he sent it ahead, where it vanished around the corner into the corridor.

"It's not very stealthy," said Miranda. "What if someone sees or hears it?"

"It should sense them before they see it, and I'm keeping it to the shadows and behind benches, anything I can find to hide it. But you're right, I need to make some improvements."

"Think about that later. Worry about finding the Protectors."

"We will."

Caldan walked across the courtyard, one hand resting on the pommel of his new sword. Without hesitation, he entered the hallway, followed by Miranda, who flicked a nervous glance behind her to make sure the courtyard was still clear.

To their left lay two more corpses, one on top of the other. Swords lay next to the bodies. Both had their throats sliced, and slashes of crimson painted the wall above them. Wordlessly, Caldan ushered Miranda around them.

After a few turns into dim hallways, they found themselves at the top of a set of stone stairs leading down into semidarkness.

"Here's one," whispered Caldan. He took a few steps, then paused. A moment later, his metal construct crept past their legs and made its way fluidly down the stairs. When it reached the bottom, Caldan sent it farther ahead into the gloom. Within moments, he confirmed there was no one close.

"It's all clear. Let's go."

He quickly descended the steps and found himself exactly where he had expected: a room with cell doors on either side.

"Wait," hissed Miranda. "It's dark. How can you see down there?"

He turned to see her edging along a wall guided by her hand, descending the steps one at a time, making sure both feet stood on a step before taking another. Caldan could see her clearly, despite the apparent darkness. Strange. He'd always thought he had good night vision and had often been able to read well past the time when others would need a light to see by, but this was a surprise. Was his sight that much better than Miranda's?

"Is it too dark for you?" he ventured.

"Yes. Don't you have a light?"

"Of course." He opened his sack and pulled out a candle along with his alchemical sticks. He scratched a stick across the wall, and it burst into flame. He lit the candle and blew out the stick. Miranda hastened down the remaining steps.

Caldan gestured at the cell doors. "These are like the ones I was held in, though there's no one here."

"Are you certain?"

"Yes. But let's check anyway, to be sure. Quickly, though."

They went to each cell door and looked through the bars to confirm none were occupied.

"This place is empty. Let's find another."

This proved to be easy, though the next room they found at the bottom of the stairs was only a cellar storing cheeses and jugs of cheap wine. Soon, though, they found yet another set of stairs and another block of cells.

Despite the distance they had covered inside the Sorcerers' Guild, they hadn't encountered anyone. Caldan worried over this. *This is all too easy. Where is everyone? The Indryallans should be patrolling the building or using the place as a base for their operation, whatever that entails. And where are the sorcerers?* The corridors were as silent as a tomb. Caldan shuddered at the association the thought brought to him. Perhaps the Indryallans had found what they were looking for and moved on.

Clinking on the stone steps, his construct swiftly descended into the room below. This time, it sensed one of the cells was occupied.

Caldan brought a finger to his lips, gesturing for Miranda to be quiet. She froze in place.

He whispered in her ear. "There's someone in one of the cells. Move a few steps down, so you can't be seen from the hallway, then stay there. As far as I can tell, there isn't a guard, but I want to make sure."

Miranda nodded her assent. "I'll be fine," she whispered back.

Caldan gave her as reassuring a smile as he could muster, then descended the steps slowly. He gripped his sword and drew a hand-span of the blade out of the scabbard.

Like in the cells where he had been kept, the air reeked of decay and urine. Taking care to be quiet, he crept forward one step at a time. His construct stood before one of the doors, and he moved toward it.

Metal clinked against metal. Chains scraped over the stone floor. A sob came from the cell.

Caldan stood still, heart thumping, breathing as quietly as he could.

Chains clinked again. Someone cursed. A voice rang out.

"Who's there?" a man croaked, the sound echoing loudly after the silence.

Caldan hesitated. He thought he recognized the voice.

"I know someone's there." The man gave a ragged cough. "Show yourself . . . or not . . . It doesn't matter."

Through the barred window, Caldan saw a man on the floor, curled into a ball. His clothes were torn and bloody, face smeared with dirt. Chains led from fastenings in the wall to manacles around his wrists.

"Master Simmon? Is that you?"

Simmon flinched. He drew himself in tighter, as if trying to close out the world around him.

"Go away. Get out of here."

Caldan fumbled in his pocket for the chalk and hastily scribed patterns on the lock. "I've come to rescue you. We can get you out of here. Do you know what's happened to the other masters?" He accessed his well, and the lock opened with a sharp click.

Simmon grimaced. "I know." His voice barely carried to Caldan. "I know what happened to them all." He turned his head away.

Caldan drew open the door and knelt over the master. Simmon reeked. He had soiled himself and lay in his own filth. What could have left him like this?

"It's all right. We can get you out of here."

Simmon laughed, weakly at first, then stronger as it went on. After a few moments, his laughter dissipated into a coughing fit. He levered himself up to a sitting position, blank eyes staring through Caldan. "No," he croaked. "I don't want to leave."

Caldan frowned, confused. "I've opened the door. We can get you somewhere safe, away from here."

Simmon shook his head. "No. I can't. I don't deserve to."

"What do you mean?"

"I should stay here."

From behind Caldan, Miranda spoke. She must have come down the steps when she heard their voices. So much for staying put.

"Master Simmon," she said softly, all calm and reason. "What happened to the other masters? You said you knew."

Simmon let out a despairing groan and squeezed his eyes shut.

"I . . ." he gasped. "I couldn't help it. I didn't mean to." He screamed, "I *watched*."

Caldan and Miranda exchanged a worried glance. She stepped over to the master, who flinched at her approach, and knelt beside him.

"What do you mean?" she asked. "Did they have you bound and force you to watch?"

Master Simmon moaned, breath ragged. "No," he whimpered.

Caldan turned his gaze away; he couldn't bear to see what this man he respected had become.

Miranda put a hand on Simmon's shoulder. "But you watched . . . I don't understand."

Simmon met her gaze. His eyes were dull and devoid of reason. His tongue flicked over his lips. "They made me do it. I was here." He punched the side of his head. "But I couldn't stop myself. I killed them. The masters. Me but not me. I couldn't stop myself. I had to watch." He slumped to the floor and curled up into a ball, weeping.

Caldan couldn't believe what he'd heard. It didn't make sense. How could Master Simmon kill all the people he respected, worked with, fought for as a Protector? Part of him thought he'd heard wrong, that Simmon couldn't have done those things. Then he remembered the body of Jazintha in the circle—killed by someone much more skilled with the sword and able to overcome a master with potent craftings.

Still, it didn't make sense. Unless . . . Simmon had been controlled by the Indryallans, like Bells had done with him. *Is that even possible?*

Caldan looked again at Simmon lying helpless on the dirty stone floor. Broken. His mind shattered. It seemed all too possible. What better way to infiltrate the Protectors than to control one of the masters, then use him to dispose of the others when you needed to?

It would explain, too, how they knew the guild so well. They didn't need a spy . . . they *created* one. And the nobles and merchants that Miranda said had committed suicide . . . perhaps they'd been corrupted in some way as well?

Caldan took Miranda by the arm and pulled her away from Simmon, whom she was vainly trying to console. If Simmon had been controlled using sorcery and forced to do horrific acts, then he would take a long time to recover, if he ever did.

"Listen to me—we have to leave. If what he says is true, then all the masters are dead."

"But . . . but why?" whispered Miranda.

"I think I know. It's part of what the Protectors are. Explanations will have to wait." He ran a hand through his short hair. "We won't find anyone left who can help us. There's no one, unless they escaped, in which case they'll be hiding somewhere in the city. There's no point searching here any longer."

Miranda nodded her agreement and wiped her eyes. "We free Simmon and get out of here."

"Yes."

He examined the manacles around Simmon's wrists. They had been riveted closed, no lock, as if his captors would have no reason to release him. "I should be able to get them off. The hinge on the other side is the weak point."

"Do it," said Miranda.

Crouching over the master, Caldan spoke softly to him. "Master Simmon, can you hear me? We're going to get you out of here. Free you from the chains. Do you think you can walk?"

Simmon moaned incoherently, then stiffened. His hands covered his face. "I can't. Leave me here. I deserve it."

"We can't. You will recover. We need to get you out of here."

"No. You don't understand. Leave me here. And leave me a blade."

Caldan swallowed and looked at Miranda.

Her face screwed up in anguish. "We . . . can't do that. Don't ask me to go along with this."

"You're right," Caldan said to her. "We can't, and I won't ask that of you." He turned to Simmon. "I can free you, and together we'll make it out of here. We'll need your help."

Simmon grasped Caldan's arm. His eyes shone with determination. "Help with what? Betraying you and everything I've ever believed in? No—leave me a blade and run. Get away from here. Someone must survive." He released his grip and sank back to the floor. "Get to the capital. The other Protectors must know."

For a long time, Caldan stared at Simmon lying there, chained to the wall. Simmon had given up. He was . . . broken. They couldn't drag him unwillingly through the Sorcerers' Guild and the streets of Anasoma.

A faint scent of lemons reached him. Caldan jerked his head to the right and slightly upward. He probed—someone had accessed their well close by. And they didn't care to hide their strength. *Indryallans.* He thought of the long-haired pale-skinned woman, Bells.

Simmon was staring at him. "You sense it, too," he said. "She's coming. You can't hope to resist her; you must flee!"

Caldan glanced at Miranda, then back to Simmon. How close was the sorcerer's well? Did they have enough time?

"Go!" shouted Simmon. "You can't do anything against her coercive sorcery." Simmon licked his lips. "Leave me your sword, I can defend myself. Maybe I could kill her, if I'm lucky."

"Luck's been in short supply lately," Miranda said. She tugged on Caldan's shirt. "Free him and let's go. He isn't going to defend himself. He'll—"

"I will," said Simmon wryly. "I promise. Leave me your sword. It's the only way you'll have the time to escape. Quickly now, she's coming!"

Caldan didn't believe Simmon for an instant. But he was right. There was no time if he wanted to avoid capture and get Miranda out alive. He unbuckled his sword belt and laid the blade at the master's feet.

Simmon opened his eyes for a second, then closed them. "Thank you," he murmured.

Caldan took a step back. For a few moments he stood there, silent.

"I . . ." He broke off, shaking his head. "Good-bye," he said.

"Caldan, you've given me your only weapon. I can't let you go without a replacement." Simmon struggled to his knees, hands groping for the sword Caldan had left. "It was mine, passed to me from a long line of Protectors. I used it to . . . to betray them. I know it wasn't me . . .

Still . . . it was. I didn't deserve it anymore. Unworthy. In the training yard. The well. After I . . . Jazintha . . . I hid it there. They took everything else. I couldn't let them have it."

"A sword?"

"Take it. Return it to the Protectors. Warn them about what happened here. You must get word to them, and the empire." Simmon's eyes grew distant. He drew the blade and stared blankly at the bare steel. The belt and scabbard, he tossed toward Caldan. "Go," he said.

With a final nod, Caldan picked up the belt and scabbard and they left the master in the cell. Chained. Alone. Shattered.

Like a crafting that had finally burned out.

THEY LEANED OVER the well in the training courtyard, looking into the depths. A wooden bucket tied to a length of rope sat beside a half-full barrel next to the well. Behind them was Jazintha's corpse, and Caldan's construct stood near a door, waiting and watching.

Caldan grimaced at the smooth stones in the wall of the well. They looked to offer no purchase whatsoever for climbing down. He peered closer, his eyes adjusting to the darkness of the well.

"Oh, wait," he exclaimed. "Here, under us. We couldn't see them because they were directly below us. Some of the stones have slots carved into them. Whoever built it must have realized one day someone might want an easy way down, for repairs, I would guess."

"The reservoir at the bottom is probably fed from the aqueducts, so it makes sense." Miranda looked around the courtyard, avoiding the master's corpse, which kept drawing her focus. "Can you hurry up, please?" she pleaded.

"Hopefully, this won't take long."

Caldan removed his boots, decided to leave his wristband and trinket on, then tugged off his shirt. He sat on the lip of the well and swung his legs over the side.

"Wait here, and if you see anyone, yell. I'll come up as fast as I can."

"Don't worry, I'm not going anywhere." She crouched behind the well, making herself as inconspicuous as possible.

Caldan descended into the darkness. Close to the top of the well, the stones and air were dry, but the farther he descended, the colder and damper they became. The slots in the stone made the going quick and painless, and soon he saw a glimmer of water below him.

Under the water, one side of the wall opened up into a tunnel, which had to lead to an aqueduct, but directly below him, he spotted what he was looking for. Metal gleamed in the pale light, and he made out the shape of a sword.

He drew a breath, let go, and plunged into the cold water. A few strokes, and he had the sword hilt in his grasp, then he turned and pushed off the bottom. With the blade in one hand, the ascent was harder, but before long his head poked over the top of the well and into the sunlight.

He wiped his face with his spare hand and levered himself over the well and onto the hard-packed dirt.

Miranda stood and stared.

Caldan held the sword up and let out a low whistle of appreciation. The blade was a ribbon of silver in the moonlight. It was perfectly straight, a handspan shorter than the standard swords he was used to practicing with. The hilt looked plain, scratched in places with a few spots of rust, leather grip worn, but the blade . . . smooth and even, as if forged and polished yesterday. Engraved along the first half of the blade were runes. Some were filled with a reddish metal Caldan didn't recognize. He traced a finger over one of the patterns, having no idea of their function. The end of the blade, which was without crafting runes, was covered in random minute patterns of banding and mottling reminiscent of flowing water.

Miranda's eyes traveled along the blade. "It's crafted, isn't it? Someone spent a long time working on that sword."

Caldan nodded. He wiped a drop of water from his nose and opened his well, attempting to link to the blade. He frowned. He couldn't connect to anything. There was nothing to attach to.

"I can't link to it. And the metal of the blade . . . I couldn't begin to understand how it's been forged. It isn't smith-crafted, at least not in any way I know." *Could it be . . . ?*

"I think it's a trinket."

Miranda's mouth opened in surprise, and she covered it with her hand. "That's incredible," she gasped. "I've never even heard of a sword as a trinket before."

Neither had he. He could have bought a small city with the price it would have fetched. No wonder Simmon had hidden it. How the master had broken free of the coercive sorcery was beyond Caldan, but he could imagine that for something this important to the Protectors, even he would have done everything in his power to keep it out of an enemy's hands.

"It's incredible."

Miranda met Caldan's eyes. "And now we have it."

He held the sword out for her to hold so he could put his shirt and boots back on. She grabbed it, and the instant he let go, the blade dropped from her hands, hitting the dirt with a thud. Miranda cursed, struggling with the sword's hilt.

"It's heavy. Why didn't you warn me?" She lifted the blade a hands-breadth above the ground, then dropped it back down, cursing again. "You must be stronger than you look," she muttered.

Caldan drew on his shirt and boots and picked up the leather scabbard and belt. "Here," he said, and grasped the sword hilt. With relief, she let go, and he slid the blade into the scabbard. "Not a good fit, but it works."

With the blade concealed by the scabbard, the hilt looked unremarkable, battered and plain. Perhaps that was the point. Hands working swiftly, he buckled the belt around his waist and gathered up his sack.

"Wearing a sword in the city is prohibited, remember?" said Miranda.

"I don't think the laws mean too much right now, do you?"

They retraced their steps back to the garden. Sending his construct ahead, they safely crossed the space and found themselves back at the door to the outside.

Moments later, they were heading straight for Dockside.

CHAPTER 42

Under the cover of night, Quiss and two other employees of the Five Oceans Mercantile Concern, a young man and woman, ushered Vasile down to the docks and into a rowboat. Vasile sat at the bow, while Quiss took up a position at the stern. The young man and woman seated themselves at the oars to row out into the harbor.

Despite his nervousness in their company, Vasile's apprehension regarding being caught at night, on open water, in such a small boat, overrode his reluctance to speak. When he queried whether it was wise to row out in the dark, the young woman giggled and kept rowing. Quiss replied he needn't worry, as their passage would be veiled. Vasile sat back, the truth in Quiss's statement enough to assure him.

The docks receded swiftly as the young man and woman kept up their strokes on the oars with remarkable adeptness and strength.

Anasoma burned in the distance. Not literally, but from Vasile's vantage point, the blue flames erupting atop the city walls lent an eerie glow to the scene, as if the city had caught fire. Up ahead of them, the flames extended across the harbor, a daunting and perhaps deadly barrier to anyone thinking of trying to escape by water. As they approached the obstruction, his jaw dropped in astonishment as a hole opened up to the outside sea, just wide enough for them to fit through. The others in the boat laughed quietly at his puzzlement.

He shook his head and watched the lights of Anasoma fade as the boat rounded the southern breakwater and continued south, ultimately tying up to a large merchant ship anchored in a secluded bay.

Quiss directed Vasile to wait on deck as arrangements were made for his accommodation, and assigned a short swarthy man to watch over him before disappearing below.

The ship looked as unassuming as any Vasile had come across in his work, and there had been many a time he'd had to board a ship where a murder or theft had occurred. Crew members busied themselves with various tasks despite the late hour, their labor lit by sorcerous globes, which they each carried. An expensive luxury, Vasile noted.

His guard offered him an apple, which he accepted and bit into. The man was no sailor, dressed in expensive city clothes as he was. And his manicured nails and neatly trimmed hair showed he wasn't used to rough work.

Vasile sat on a cold bench at the aft of the ship, close to the steering wheel, left to his own devices. He finished the apple and, with a flick of his wrist, he tossed the remains of the core over the side, where it landed with a faint splash.

"Fish," his guard said abruptly.

Vasile frowned. "What?"

"Fish. I heard a fish."

"No, it was my apple."

The guard tilted his head, eyes fixed on Vasile. "No, the fish ate your apple."

"What? Oh, never mind." Vasile rubbed tired eyes and yawned. "Tell me, why are you guarding me? Who is the First Deliverer?"

"That would be me."

Vasile turned to see a frail old man stepping gingerly toward him, using two canes to support his weight. His stubble and hair were gray, and the clothes he wore, pants and shirt, were plain.

The First Deliverer stopped to hunch over and let out a hacking cough, waving away Vasile's guard when he stepped forward to assist.

Vasile could see the effort moving cost the old man, the sheen of sweat on his face, the grimaces of pain at each step. He couldn't help but stand and move to assist him, taking hold of an elbow and lending himself as support.

They made it to the bench, and the old man sat delicately with a sigh of relief.

Vasile stood above him awkwardly.

With a glance, the old man gestured for him to take a seat beside him. The First Deliverer breathed heavily for a while. He cleared his throat, then turned piercing eyes on Vasile.

"Quiss has told you about us?" he asked, obviously knowing the answer already.

Vasile nodded warily in reply. If this was Quiss's master, then he must be the one who'd ordered the murders. All was not as it seemed.

"And has he answered any questions you may have had?" continued the First Deliverer.

"I . . . yes. It was much to take in, in such a short time."

"I can imagine."

"I do have more questions, but I am sure some answers will become clear in the next few days."

"I'd prefer if you asked them of me, or Quiss, and not bother anyone else."

Vasile said nothing. He shifted his weight on the bench and gazed out at the moonlit sea.

"But I'm remiss in my manners," said the First Deliverer, holding out his hand. "I'm Gazija. First Deliverer, they call me now, though what I have delivered my people to is a question I ponder daily."

Despite his reservations, Vasile took the offered hand, releasing it after a moment. "And I'm Vasile, once head investigator for the Chancellor's Guard, once the chancellor's advisor. How did you know about me?"

"We have many friends. Word of your skills came to me a while ago, though I must confess, it wasn't I who thought of how you could benefit us. In truth, we were not expecting events to unravel this far. It was Quiss who saw your true potential when he observed you acting as a magistrate. We knew at the time drastic measures were needed, and . . . well, there you were."

They sat in silence. Waves lapped against the ship.

"We need you," said Gazija. "The invasion has forced our hand. Their leaders are well versed in sorcery your empire cannot hope to match."

"That might be a good thing," Vasile replied, sharper than he'd intended. "The Mahruse Empire is . . . well, I've seen some things. The invaders can't be any worse."

Gazija shook his head. "I disagree. Their leader is dangerous beyond imagining."

"I should just take your word for it? But you can match them, can't you? No, that's not quite right . . . most of them."

"You are correct. I see Quiss was right about you. You see deeply. We might have to put you to work quicker than we'd like. There are people in power who have to be convinced of the truth."

"The chancellors don't see me anymore. Well, one does. I can convince him of your sincerity, but I don't know how much good it'll do you."

"Forget about Anasoma. No one will be entering or leaving for some time. No, we need you to contact someone else: the emperor."

"What? That's your plan? I barely know him . . . I met him a few times, but that's all."

Gazija waved away his complaints. "But you do know him. And he knows of you and your talent. That will suffice for introductions and for proof, will it not?"

Frowning, Vasile scratched his head. "Possibly. More than likely."

If he will see me at all, that is. It was hard to fight down the bitterness of having been virtually exiled from the emperor's presence all those years ago.

"Then we are agreed," Gazija said with finality. "I'm afraid Anasoma is lost, though there is hope yet for your empire—if the emperor sides with us, of course. If he doesn't . . . well . . . there are other options. Anything to avoid another Shattering. Let's hope the evil that followed us has learned from its mistakes. After all, a dead world is of no use to anyone."

They were followed by an evil? An evil what? From where? Vasile let out a deep breath. He turned his gaze to Gazija. "It's not an easy task you have set me."

"It's not an easy course we've plotted. We do what we must. Our hand has been forced."

Gazija coughed. He looked weak, sick, emaciated. He wouldn't be long for this world.

"We must try to settle this peacefully," continued Gazija. "My people . . . what there are of us, are the last."

The last of what? wondered Vasile. *Who are these people, really?*

Quiss stepped across the deck to join them at the bench, looking gaunter than usual in the dim light. He bowed respectfully before Gazija.

"Mazoet is on his way. He picked up a few stragglers," Quiss informed Gazija with a disapproving look. He drew out a brass time-piece from a pocket. "He should be here soon."

Gazija hissed. "He should know better. The fewer we have to deal with, the better."

"He'll have his reasons, as he usually does."

With a groan, Gazija rose to his feet. "Come. Let us greet him."

The First Deliverer gestured for Vasile to follow, then made his way unsteadily to the main deck, stopping to rest once. They took up positions near the side of the ship facing toward the shore. A light glimmered in the distance, slowly closing on them. They waited in silence as it approached, Gazija with an ill-concealed impatience, Quiss stolidly and still, Vasile fidgeting with nervous energy.

The light came from another rowboat. Wood bumped against wood with a thud.

Vasile identified a lean-looking woman as probably one of Gazija's people, though she was chatting amiably with a tall, middle-aged gentleman with an obvious weakness for food. The man stood proudly at the head of the craft, shirt closed tight over his large stomach with silver buttons.

A rope ladder was lowered for the boat's occupants, and soon the lean woman and pudgy man came aboard, followed by a few others: a young man with an air of command, a sorcerer wearing a number of crafted items, and a swarthy, rough-looking tribesman wearing two swords, who examined each of them in turn, then relaxed, as if weighing their measure and finding them wanting.

Self-consciously, Vasile drew himself up straighter.

With a bow from the waist, the man with the silver buttons addressed Gazija.

"First Deliverer, I had not expected to find you here." He took a step back and gestured at the people accompanying him. "I have some news. Perhaps . . ." He broke off with a sidelong glance at Vasile.

"He's with us, Mazoet," said Gazija. "What news do you bring?"

"Your will," replied Mazoet, bowing again, this time more perfunctorily, though still respectful. "These men have been chasing a group of . . . renegade sorcerers, who had set themselves up in a town some weeks' travel from here. I was fortunate to contact them and their men before the sorcerers they were following turned on them." His eyes kept flicking from Gazija to Quiss and back.

Vasile could sense he was telling the truth, though holding something back.

"I was able to see off the sorcerers," Mazoet continued, "but I felt it was my duty to bring the men here to tell their story, firsthand, as it were."

With a solemn expression, Mazoet clasped the young man by the shoulder and pushed him forward a step.

With an encouraging smile from Mazoet, he began to speak. "First Deliverer," he said in a calm, even voice, bowing as Mazoet had done from the waist.

Vasile thought he saw Gazija's mouth flicker with the ghost of a smile.

"Though I have never heard that particular title before, and I am quite learned in all the titles of the empire and surrounding king-doms."

"Obviously you are not as learned as you think. Go on. I'm not get-ting any younger standing here."

The young man raised his eyebrows and smiled. "As you wish. My name is Aidan. I'm the leader of a band of men and women oath-bound to seek out evil and wrongdoings in the empire and bring the perpetrators to justice. We have a commission from the emperor him-self, though it is under our previous leader's name."

"You bring this justice by the sword, unless I miss my guess," said Gazija.

"If necessary."

Vasile had the impression he'd had to justify their actions before.

"Evil takes many forms and seldom submits itself without a strug-gle. By its very nature, it resists righteousness."

Gazija coughed into his hand. "Indeed. Please continue."

"I was leading my band on the trail of a few sorcerers . . ." He broke off as Vasile cleared his throat loudly.

Gazija gave Vasile a sharp look, eyes narrowed, then turned back to Aidan. "Excuse me, but did you say you were leading them?"

"Ah. Well . . . at that stage I wasn't." Aidan stared at Vasile. "Cir-cumstances later led me to take over the leadership."

"I see," said Gazija without inflection, face expressionless. "Con-tinue."

Aidan hesitated, frowning at them both before restarting his story. "We followed them to a town, where we found they had imprisoned some women . . ." His voice grew colder, and his face turned grim. "They were not just prisoners. They . . . were being forced to breed, to have babies." His voice broke on the last word, and he looked away, distressed. Both the sorcerer and the swordsman with him shifted their weight and looked down at the deck.

"We don't know their purpose and don't care to. We rescued the women, but the sorcerers escaped. We were still tracking them when Mazoet here appeared and they turned on us. A young boy and girl. We're in his debt. Without his sorcery to counter theirs, we would surely have perished and wouldn't be able to bring you this news."

"Ah. A bleak tale, indeed," said Gazija tonelessly, in the manner of someone trying hard to keep himself under control. "They have strayed farther than I imagined."

Quiss's jaw worked silently, clenching and unclenching. Mazoet stood still and unblinking, staring.

Gazija rubbed both hands together, warming them against the chill night air. "Vasile, is what they say true?"

All eyes turned to him. Under their stares, he nodded confirmation.

"That settles it, then. We have much to discuss and plans to make." Gazija turned to Mazoet. "Please get these gentlemen comfortable and assign them quarters. We should have enough to spare. Let's meet again early in the morning, once we have a good night's sleep. It's late. Oh, and Mazoet . . . you did well."

The three men followed Mazoet and left the deck reluctantly, inundating him with questions, casting frequent glances back toward Vasile, Gazija, and Quiss. Once they were out of sight and their voices had receded, Gazija coughed yet again and shook his head.

"It's worse than I feared," he said. His face creased in pain.

Quiss gripped the rail with both hands until his knuckles went white.

Vasile shivered, not from the cold. "These men, Aidan and his companions, what are you going to do with them?"

"Aidan and the others are with us now, whether they know it or not. They'll eventually be drawn into this conflict, with or without our help. And I, for one, don't spurn gifts when they appear before me."

CHAPTER 43

Since they had found Simmon imprisoned, Caldan's mood had been dark, and he didn't feel like talking, speaking only when Miranda asked a direct question. She looked similarly despondent.

And Caldan's construct was failing. It wobbled as it moved and couldn't maintain a walk for more than a few moments without falling over. One leg moved a half beat behind the others. On the surface, the rods were mottled with different colors—yellows, blues, and purples, as if returned to a furnace and heated to different temperatures.

"Caldan," Miranda called. "I think you should do something about it. It's no good to us anymore and . . . I hate to see it like this."

"I know. But I can't bring myself to . . . destroy it."

"The way it looks now is depressing. There isn't any reason for us to use it . . . is there?"

"No," said Caldan with a sigh. "I guess you're right."

He accessed his well and linked to the construct for the final time. He could sense the damage the forces flowing through it had caused—fractured metal inside the rods, varying temperatures as different sections wore out faster than others. Once the slide into degradation started, it accelerated swiftly. With a thought, he closed the smith-crafted links, and the simulacrum clattered to the floor in a jumble of rods and wire.

"Oh!" Miranda exclaimed with a sad smile. "It's almost as if it died."

"It was never alive, at least not in any real sense. It was imbued with a rudimentary intelligence, but what it could do was limited. With what I learned from crafting that one, though, I can greatly improve the next."

Over the last few hours, he'd been toying with more of his metal rods, and inking runes and patterns on them. Longer and thicker, the parts were connected with actual joints rather than wire fastenings. On the whole, the new construct was larger and heavier, thicker of limb and body.

"Do you need the metal for anything?" Miranda pointed at the pile on the floor.

"Yes. I can always sell the parts or melt it down and reuse it." He picked up the now limp construct and tossed it into his open sack. Miranda winced as it landed with a clatter.

She approached him from behind as he returned to studying the parts for his new construct and placed both hands on his shoulders. He trembled at her touch, then went still.

She squeezed lightly. "It's not your fault, you know. There wasn't anything you could have done to save them. The Indryallans planned this well."

Caldan's head dropped. He wanted revenge on them for Simmon, for the Protectors, for Senira as well . . . but there was nothing he could do here with their tight grip on the city. And Simmon had set him a task. "I know . . . but I keep thinking there was something I could have done." He tilted his head back to look at Miranda, who was looking at him with concern . . . and something else. His words caught in his throat, but he finally managed to get out, "Thank you."

"You've lost a lot in only a few days—the new home you made

for yourself, the friends, the place you had found, somewhere you fit in, where your talents would be appreciated." Miranda let go of his shoulders, walked to the stove, and poured herself another cup of tea. "I haven't done much, but I can still remind you that there are people who care for you. I know you haven't had people like that for a long time."

"Who?"

"Me, for one, silly." Miranda took a sip of her tea. "I'm just saying it's all right to care yourself. For others."

"I do," Caldan began, then hesitated. He'd spent so long without many friends at the monastery, he still found it hard to express his feelings. And Miranda had a knack for making him feel especially awkward. Her closeness and her touch were arousing and terrifying at the same time. "I'm . . . not used to it, that's all." He toyed with a piece of smith-crafted metal.

"Caldan, I—" Miranda broke off with an irritated frown as a loud banging came from the door.

Caldan leaped to his feet with one hand on the sword grip, ready to draw the blade.

Miranda placed her cup on the table and crossed the room. "Who's there?"

"Elpidia," replied a muffled voice.

Miranda sighed in relief, while Caldan remained still, alert. She unbarred the door and clicked the lock open.

Elpidia's face shone with sweat, and she was breathing heavily. She looked harried. She raised an eyebrow at Caldan and his readiness. He relaxed and released his grip on the sword. He noted she wore travel clothes, a heavy skirt, and a shirt under a thick jacket. She carried a backpack and a leather satchel.

"There's a commotion in the streets," Elpidia said. "The Indryallan soldiers are all over the place, searching for someone."

Caldan and Miranda exchanged glances. "What are you doing here?" Caldan said to Elpidia. Though he knew why she was there, and how she'd found him. The sorcerous compass he should have taken from her.

Elpidia gingerly lowered her satchel to the ground and shrugged off her backpack, dropping it with a thud. "Remember our talk?" she said pointedly to Caldan. "Did you think I wasn't serious? My research is critical." She looked at the stove. "Is that tea, my dear?" she said, addressing Miranda, who nodded. "Lovely. I'll fix myself a cup." She crossed the room and peeked into the teapot.

Caldan stomped over to her and was about to give her a piece of his mind when there was another knock on the door. He whirled and grabbed the sword again.

"Were you followed?" he whispered to Elpidia.

She shook her head. "No. I don't think so. I . . . I didn't look."

Caldan nodded at Miranda to open the door while he stood in front of it, ready to fight.

Amerdan stood in the doorway, a panicked expression on his face. He was also dressed for travel, but wasn't carrying anything other than a few belt pouches and two sheathed knives. He ignored Caldan's readiness and took a step into the warehouse.

"They came to my shop looking for you, started smashing the place up."

Did they? wondered Caldan.

"I escaped out the back way and hid. By the time I got back they'd set fire to my shop. There was nothing I could do. You mentioned Houndshark Street, so I came here. I didn't know where else to go. Though I admit I thought you two would be long gone." He looked at them expectantly.

Left in a hurry and happened to be dressed for traveling? wondered Caldan. Amerdan must have had time to prepare . . . more than his story would suggest.

"Who are you?" Miranda asked.

"I'm sorry—I'm Amerdan. Caldan's friend."

"So we're friends, are we?" Caldan asked.

"Of course. I just gave you refuge! I was hoping to find the same here. I figured it'd be abandoned and I'd be safe. Like I said, I'm surprised you are both still here."

"We haven't left, as we had some things to do," replied Miranda. "We plan on leaving the city as soon as we can."

"Wait—what? No!" burst out Elpidia. She looked pleadingly at Caldan. "My . . . research."

Caldan held up a hand. "Not now, Elpidia. It's enough you show up here uninvited. You don't have a say in what we do." He looked at Amerdan, who appeared unconcerned. Whatever panic had gripped him had quickly evaporated.

Amerdan leaned against a wall, giving each of them a measured glance before he spoke. "I will be coming with you," he said flatly. "If that is acceptable." His tone implied it should be.

"And me as well!" exclaimed Elpidia.

Miranda cursed. "Four! I told my contact there would only be two of us. He's not going to be pleased. With four, the danger goes up ten times, as will the price." She ran a hand through her hair and rubbed the back of her neck. "How are you expecting to pay for it?" she asked, as if that would end the conversation.

Amerdan smiled and reached into a pouch at his waist. He placed a stack of coins on the table. *Gold* coins. "That should be sufficient for my passage, I assume."

Elpidia rustled around in her backpack and produced some ducats of her own. "And this is for me. There isn't anything for me here . . . not anymore."

Caldan sighed. Even though their reasons for turning up were dubious, and they'd complicated matters, he couldn't abandon them. He'd already let Senira die—he wouldn't let it happen to these two if he had the power to prevent it.

"If he can take two out," Caldan said, "he should easily be able to take four."

Miranda shot him a furious look.

He really didn't need this, but he didn't know how to refuse them. It was too dangerous to stay in the city, and besides, Simmon had given him a task, and he'd vowed to see it through. And he had a feeling Elpidia, with her damned compass, would follow him whatever happened. Which reminded him . . . He held out a hand. "Give me the compass."

"What's that?" asked Miranda.

"A crafting," replied Caldan. "Designed to find someone. In this case, it was me."

Miranda fixed Elpidia with a level stare.

The physiker's face went red. "You know why I needed it." Her mouth tightened into a thin line.

"Oh, I know, and now it's served its purpose. You've found me, and you're coming along. But now that you have, I don't like the idea of someone being able to find me like that. Especially not with what's happened."

Looking distinctly unhappy, Elpidia pressed the crafted item into his palm with a sour look.

Caldan slipped it into his pocket. "You've just been on the streets," he said. "What's the situation now? Is it worse? Are we more likely to run into trouble?"

"The Indryallans are taking people off the street and holding them for questioning," Elpidia said. "Or so I heard. Somewhere in West Barrows, but where in that district, I didn't hear."

"Probably the keep, then," said Amerdan. "It makes sense for the Indryallans to set up their headquarters there. Especially since it looks like they want to keep everyone content and have a smooth change of power. They've also set up kitchens along the docks and are feeding the poor."

"They're letting people go, though?" Miranda asked.

"From what I heard, yes. After questioning, they're released." Elpidia hesitated, frowning into her teacup. "They look like they're trying to keep the city running as if nothing has happened. In fact, with all the good projects they've implemented, most people have welcomed the change."

"They don't mean well," growled Caldan.

Elpidia turned to look at him. "How can you know?"

"I know," he said flatly, feeling a chill. *Because they force people to kill against their will*, he wanted to say. "We need to leave as soon as possible. You can come, if you want. Miranda, when did your contact say he could get us out?"

Miranda shrugged. "He said he would bring word sometime today. That's the best he could do at short notice. I think they're taking advantage of the blockade and using their tunnels to make a lot of ducats. I suspect we're in a queue."

"So nothing we can do but wait."

"I'm afraid so."

Caldan nodded. "Make yourselves comfortable, then. We have to wait, and I have work to do." He turned back to his smith-crafted metal pieces.

Miranda took Elpidia's hand and drew her into the other room, where they began a conversation about what to take with them.

Caldan felt Amerdan's eyes on him as he returned to work. He attached metal rods to each other, tapping the ends with a hammer until they clicked in place. The rods were as long as his arm from elbow to wrist and thicker than his thumb. He tested the joints, easing the rods back and forth to check that they moved smoothly. Four of these joints lay in front of him as he began assembling a fifth, this one made up of shorter rods, five in total, each rod thinner than the last.

"Why five in that one?" asked Amerdan suddenly.

Caldan spared him a glance as the last rod clicked into place. He laid it next to the others. "It's a tail. When it runs, a tail is essential for equilibrium."

"It . . . runs?" Amerdan stared at him curiously.

With a shrug, Caldan drew out more metal pieces from his sack and piled them next to the legs and tail. "It should, if I get everything right." He turned to Amerdan. "Are you hungry? I'm starving." He stood and rummaged through their food supplies, and began preparing a meal of crusty bread and cheese. Inviting the women to sit down, they all dug in with gusto—Caldan, as usual, eating twice as much as anyone else.

"I thought Amerdan here did well, but you . . ." Miranda trailed off and shook her head. "I don't know where you put it."

Elpidia grinned, then covered her mouth with a hand.

"I'm still growing," protested Caldan.

"I doubt it."

Caldan was opening his mouth to reply when there was a knock at the door. All of them froze and looked at each other.

Miranda rose and wiped her hands on her pants. "It's probably my contact," she said, and strode to the door. "Who's there?"

"Rennen," came the reply through the thick timber.

Elpidia looked up at the name.

Miranda opened the door, and a dark-haired man entered. He looked at each of them in turn, raising an eyebrow at Elpidia, who returned his stare with a steady look of her own.

"I take it you two know each other?" asked Amerdan, echoing Caldan's thought.

"We have had occasion to do some business," replied the man called Rennen.

"He's one of the best sources of information in the city," said Elpidia. "And the most resourceful when it comes to finding things."

Rennen gave a short bow in her direction.

"Rennen, glad you finally arrived," Miranda said sharply. "When can we go?"

"Always business first with you, Miranda. You should learn to relax." Rennen smiled to take the edge off his words. "I had a hard time avoiding the patrols the Indryallans have out looking for certain people. Luckily, they've not issued a reward for these fugitives, who might otherwise have been delivered into their hands quick smart."

"Is that a threat?" asked Miranda.

Rennen clasped both hands to his chest over his heart. "Goodness, no! I wouldn't stay in business long if I made threats to my clients, would I?" His tone was half-serious, half-mocking.

"Do we have a way out?" continued Miranda. "I assume that's why you're here?"

Rennen frowned. "You told me there would be two of you, and yet here I see four."

"Circumstances have changed."

"Still, it'll be riskier. And taking such a risk will cost." He rubbed his finger and thumb together.

"How much more? And don't try to cheat me, mind!"

"I wouldn't dream of it." Rennen made a show of thinking for a few moments.

Caldan was sure he had calculated a new price the moment he saw there were four people in the room instead of two and was dragging the negotiation out.

Rennen gave Miranda a sly look. "I heard the invaders are searching houses and warehouses around the docks . . . Indeed, they're not too far from here."

Caldan and Miranda exchanged glances again. If this was true, it meant the invaders knew their general whereabouts. It was only a matter of time until they were found, if they stayed put.

"My thought is that the risk has increased since we last spoke. The new price is eight."

"Eight!" exclaimed Miranda. "It was two for two, and now it's eight for four?"

Rennen spread his hands in a helpless gesture. "More risk, more bribes, more people need wages. I'm giving you a discount because I know Elpidia. Though I wouldn't have thought she would leave the city. Perhaps there is a story there?" He gave Elpidia an inquiring look.

She shook her head but refrained from replying.

"Ah. Saying nothing is still saying something, is it not?"

Miranda counted out six gold ducats. She held the coins up in a stack between forefinger and thumb. "Six and we have a deal."

Rennen turned a glum look on her. He flicked a glance at Elpidia, hesitated, then slowly shook his head. "No. I cannot agree. It's said they are looking for someone, a young sorcerer with short hair." He looked pointedly at Caldan.

Caldan hissed through his teeth, and Miranda cursed under her breath.

The Indryallans who'd imprisoned him, and Bells, had gotten a good look at him. It was likely he wouldn't be able to roam the streets without being spotted. His chest tightened in fear. He was the only one in danger, but he couldn't abandon Miranda. As selfish as it was, he didn't want to leave her.

"Pay him," Caldan said. "We need to get out before they find us. And the longer we delay, the higher the price will go."

"Smart man," said Rennen, holding out his hand.

Miranda reluctantly handed over eight gold ducats, which Rennen accepted with a grateful nod. "We have a deal, then?"

"Certainly. Are you ready to leave now?"

"It won't take more than a few moments to have our gear organized." Miranda looked at Elpidia and Amerdan. "Do you have everything you need?"

Elpidia gestured to her belongings. "I'm sure if I require anything for my research, I can find a substitute, depending on where we are."

Amerdan patted the belt that held his pouches and knives. "Ready," he said.

Caldan noticed the shopkeeper also had a bundle inside his shirt and wondered what it could be. He shook his head. *Probably something valuable he wants to keep protected.*

"All right," Miranda said. "Caldan, are you ready?"

"Yes, it won't take long to pack up." He shoved the metal rods back into his sack and accepted the blanket Miranda handed him.

Miranda disappeared into the next room, returning shortly with two sets of bulging saddlebags, one of which she handed to Caldan.

"May I inquire as to where you are going?" Rennen asked.

"You may," said Miranda. "But we aren't sure ourselves. Away from here, until things settle down. It's only going to get worse."

"On the contrary, I find it to be very good."

"Depends on what you deal in."

Rennen narrowed his eyes and nodded, as if Miranda had stated something wise. "Indeed it does."

Miranda gave one last glance around the room, her expression resolved. "It's time to go."

AFTER A NERVOUS walk uphill through the southern area of Cabbage Town, Rennen led Caldan and the others to the back of a nondescript building. A squat, heavyset man opened a gate in response to Rennen's coded knock, whispered words, and ducats. They entered an overgrown yard, then passed into a stone building.

Caldan looked around at the bare room that greeted them, unimpressed. Two large windows high in the walls provided light, and the room was empty except for an open trapdoor in the center. Beside the opening sat an oil lamp burning with a flame.

Rennen rubbed his hands together in the cold air. "I hope you don't mind the dark." He picked up the lamp.

"I thought we might need something," said Caldan, drawing some glass balls from his pocket and handing one to each of them. In the center of each he'd placed a stone covered in tiny patterns. They were the first sorcerous globes he'd ever crafted, but he found they came easily to him.

Rennen gave a low whistle. "Expensive," he remarked. "Better not lose them."

Caldan shrugged. "These won't last long, but I can always make more."

Rennen clapped him on the shoulder. "We should talk when you come back."

Elpidia examined hers and gave it a shake. "It's not working. Is it broken?"

They looked to Caldan.

"No," he said. What people didn't know about sorcery still surprised him. "They wear out, so there's no point having them working all the time when light isn't needed. Here." He accessed his well and linked to all four globes, connecting the anchors in the gems. The way they were constructed, he needed only one string as they were fed from one primary globe, Miranda's. Each one began to glow faintly, a clean white light.

Rennen stepped to the edge of the hole. "I'm to be your escort. There's a ladder down to a room."

"What is this place?" asked Miranda. "The building, the quality of the stonework—this wasn't made to smuggle goods in and out of the city."

"Goodness, no," laughed Rennen. "It's part of the aqueducts. An access hole for repairs, to clear blockages. No need to dig a tunnel when the emperor provided plenty for us to use."

"Makes sense."

Caldan knelt above the shaft, saddlebags over one shoulder and sack in his left hand. His sword made it awkward, but he swiftly descended into the gloom.

"Er," said Rennen loudly. "Didn't you make a globe for yourself?"

Caldan cursed himself for being stupid. He could see well in the darkness, but it wasn't a talent he wanted known. He would have to watch himself. "No need," he replied calmly. "There's enough light to see by . . . and once everyone else is down, their globes will be sufficient." He reached a room, from which led two open doorways, one at either end.

Miranda followed him down, and soon they were all huddled together, holding their globes up for light while Rennen held up his lamp.

"This way." Rennen hunched over and set off along a narrow tunnel, head brushing the ceiling.

Caldan ushered the others through before following. Though damp and cold, the walls of the tunnel were mostly free from mold or mildew. They had traveled only ten yards into the tunnel when the scent of lemons reached him. He stopped, lifting his head. There was a tickle across his well that almost immediately strengthened to a gentle tug.

"What is it?" whispered Miranda.

"There's . . . something . . ." he began.

Thunder sounded, echoing deafeningly down the tunnel. The air shook as a strong blast crushed them to the ground. Another immense boom sounded, reverberating inside Caldan's head.

Screams came from above, along with a tearing, grating noise as stone cracked. Sunlight streamed down the shaft, illuminating the room behind them and the clouds of dust filling the space.

Miranda tugged at his arm. He turned to find her eyes red and watery. A trickle of blood ran from her nose. Elpidia lay curled into a ball. Amerdan crouched, appearing unharmed and alert. Rennen staggered to his knees, a vacant expression on his face.

"Go!" roared Caldan.

"What?" said Miranda in a daze.

He pushed her toward the others. "Run!" He turned and rifled through his gear. Behind him, they staggered away as fast as they could.

He had to do something, but what? Caldan reached into his pocket, and the answer came to him. He drew out four stone cubes, each the size of the dice used in taverns, surfaces covered in etched runes. He hadn't thought to be using these, but there wasn't time to make anything else, and he needed something stronger than paper.

He placed two cubes against the walls, one on either side of the passageway. The others he slipped into a pocket in reserve. Accessing his well, he activated the craftings. A barrier of light sprang up, blocking the passageway. It glowed a soft blue and sparkled where dust hit it.

On the other side of the shield, two figures dropped into view from the trapdoor. Caldan recognized the woman who'd visited him in his cell, Bells. Beside her was a man with a jumble of crafted keys hanging around his neck. So this was Keys.

Both were surrounded by their own shields. Their eyes locked onto his. He snatched up his gear, turned his back to them, and ran.

When Caldan caught up, Miranda and Rennen were arguing heatedly.

"Up, down, twists and turns—do you know where you're going?" Miranda asked.

"Of course I do!" Rennen shouted back.

"I've blocked the tunnel," Caldan said. "But I think they might be able to get through. I've only bought us a little time."

That ended any further arguments.

They scampered down another ladder, along a tunnel, then up yet another ladder to emerge into a wide corridor split down the middle. The side they were on was a stone walkway. The other dropped into a swift flowing stream, which disappeared into a black hole in the wall. If any of them fell into the water, there would be no hope of rescuing them, and who knew where the stream emerged, or if there was any airspace through the hole. Along the stone walkway, a slimy gray mold flourished, making the footing treacherous.

With nervous glances over their shoulders, the group hurried along the path. Ahead, in the darkness, another ladder led up to a hole in the wall.

At one point Elpidia fell to one knee as she slipped on the slimy stone, but Miranda helped her regain her feet, and they hurried along the ledge.

At the ladder, they stopped as Rennen raced up the rungs as fast as he could. All of them, except Caldan—and to his surprise, Amerdan—were breathing heavily and sweating.

"Who were they?" asked the shopkeeper as Rennen reached the top of the ladder and beckoned to Elpidia.

"The invaders . . . Indryallans," replied Caldan blandly. "They must have known about the tunnels and want to stop people escaping the city."

Amerdan looked at his face for a moment, unblinking. "Indeed. Let's hope whatever you did to stop them holds for a while."

The shopkeeper knew they'd followed him somehow, and yet he said nothing. Caldan still wasn't sure what to make of Amerdan.

"It should," Caldan said, but he admitted to himself that these Indryallans might be even more powerful than he thought. He glanced up the ladder at Elpidia making slow progress on the slippery rungs. "Can you hurry, please!"

"I'm going as fast as I can," said Elpidia.

A sharp crack sounded over the rush of water, and Caldan sensed his wards fail. Much more *powerful*. "By the ancestors," he cursed under his breath.

"What is it?" Miranda asked in alarm.

Caldan grabbed her arm and pushed her toward the ladder. "Go. As fast as you can." He looked at Amerdan. "You too. I'm relying on you to look after them."

The shopkeeper smiled briefly. "I will."

Caldan nodded. "They broke through my wards. I can make another, but it probably won't stop them for long, seeing how easily they got through the first one." He glanced at the fast-flowing, deep water in the trough beside them. An idea began forming.

"What are you going to do?" asked Miranda.

"I'm not sure just yet," he said with a tight grin, "but I think it will work." He dropped his sack to the ground and drew out the jumble of metal rods that made up his new construct.

"I hope you know what you're doing."

"Trust me."

Miranda grabbed the ladder and prepared to climb. "Caldan . . . Don't take any risks. Please. I'm sure we can lose them in here, since Rennen knows the way and they don't."

Caldan gave her a wry smile. "Don't worry. I'm not going to wait around until they come." He waved her away. "Now go—we don't have much time. I'll be right behind you."

As if punctuating his words, a number of sorcerous globes floated out of the opening at the end of the tunnel behind them. Two rose to the ceiling and stuck there, illuminating the area, while another continued slowly toward them.

Miranda shot one last worried look at Caldan and started climbing the ladder.

Caldan began assembling his new construct. He accessed his well and slotted the four legs onto the body, joints clicking into place, while simultaneously linking the pieces. Metal vibrated in his hands as the anchors, buffers, transference, and shaping runes activated. He caught a glimpse as Amerdan swiftly ascended the ladder, following Miranda and the others.

He just needed a little more time . . .

Movement caught his eye as two figures emerged into the tunnel, both covered with the telltale glow of shields. Though they were distant, Caldan recognized them as soldiers rather than the sorcerers by the strength of their wells. They moved cautiously along the slippery ledge. In their wake, two more figures appeared, stepping onto the ledge with a confidence bordering on arrogance.

Caldan firmly slotted the head into place, and with a minute fizz of energy, the two metal parts fused. It was sleeker than the original dog—catlike if anything. The new automaton rose to its feet. Standing, it reached to his knee. Blue stone eyes emitted a faint glow as the smith-crafting hummed with energy, almost inaudible to his ear. The tail extended behind the body and twitched.

Despite the situation, Caldan laid a hand on his creation and gazed at it with admiration. Compared to this automaton, the first had been a hack job of ideas without grace. This new one was refined in both the metalwork and smith-crafting, an order of magnitude more polished and complex.

And more powerful.

With a thought, he sent it slinking toward the Indryallans, then gathered up his sack and climbed the ladder. At the top, he turned to gauge how much time he had. The Indryallans were moving swiftly, since they hadn't been assailed, sending their sorcerous globes drifting up the tunnel. *Not much, then.*

He crouched in the hole in the wall at the top of the ladder. Behind him, he heard boots scuffling on stone and murmurs as Miranda and the others scurried away.

Caldan closed his eyes, awareness flowing through the link to his automaton. His sight lurched as he saw from the viewpoint of his creation, and he held a hand against the wall to steady himself. From his new knee-high viewpoint close to the ground, the tunnel looked bigger and wider.

Ahead, the two soldiers approached. He sent the automaton dashing forward. He couldn't possibly draw enough from his well to overload four shields or defeat two men and two sorcerers. But that had never been his plan.

It was time for the Indryallans to get a surprise.

In front of the soldiers his automaton broke through the darkness. Shouts of surprise greeted its sudden appearance.

"What is it?" Caldan heard one ask, through his automaton.

He sent the smith-crafting to the left, close to the wall, and made it continue ahead, as if angling to pass the men.

"No idea," replied the other. "Bells or Keys should know. By the God-Emperor, I ain't going near it."

Bells he knew, but now he was certain of the other sorcerer following them. The same one mentioned along with Bells when he'd been captured. For all the good it did him at the moment.

Caldan stopped the automaton as it reached a point on the wall where the two men lay between it and the water. He linked to another crafting in the runes of the animal's body. Light erupted around the automaton—its own shield.

"Crap! Where *are* Bells and Keys?" one squawked, stepping back and glancing down the tunnel toward the two sorcerers. "Hey!" he yelled.

He flicked the automaton a command. Around its body, the shield flashed and expanded, one side pushing against the wall, the other extending toward the two men.

"What the . . ."

Sparks crackled as the edges of the shields made contact. Designed to keep things out, to be as impenetrable as possible, the forces pressed against each other. Caldan drew from his well and pushed, hard and fast. The automaton's shield expanded, using the wall to brace against, and the two men had nothing to support them. Boots scrabbled for purchase on the slick stone. Failing to find traction, they slid toward the water. Crying out for help—but getting none—they slipped over the edge and into the swift torrent. Dragged by the irresistible current, they barreled away from Caldan toward Bells and Keys, arms flailing.

Their shouts caught the sorcerers' attention, and both stopped. Caldan sent the automaton darting at them. If he could use the soldiers as a distraction, he might be able to get close enough to use the same trick.

Bells stepped to the edge and watched the men as they passed, thrashing and yelling in the water. Simultaneously, both Bells and Keys froze, turning toward the approaching automaton. They reached out and clasped hands. Their shields merged and spread to a flat barrier across the walkway. There was no way to slip between them and the water.

Caldan felt a scrabbling, a scratching at his linkage to the automaton. Shocked, he drew deeper from his well in an effort to cement his link. Panicked, he pulled the smith-crafting toward him, and it scurried back along the path, wobbling unsteadily as Caldan drew even further from his well. The closer it came to him, the weaker the assault became. Sweat dripped from his face, and he gulped in air. His head ached. Abruptly, the forces assailing the automaton ceased.

In the distance, the sorcerers stood as still as statues. Alongside them swept their two men, ignored. They cried out as the water dragged them relentlessly through the hole in the wall and into darkness.

At the base of the ladder, his automaton leaped, using its momentum to propel itself up the rungs, metal claws scrabbling. It landed at Caldan's feet as the smell of lemons reached him, and he sensed a buildup from the sorcerers.

Snatching at his well, he shielded himself as three red balls blasted toward him. He dropped to the floor, making himself as small as possible.

Blinding red light exploded. Pressure ground against him, crushing him into the floor.

His wristband whined under the strain. His skin felt hot through the shield. He could feel his crafting begin to fail. Grunting with effort, he drew further from his well, striving to bolster his crafting, pushing himself to his limits. A searing pain filled his head.

I can't . . . keep . . . this . . . up . . .

After a few moments, though, he managed to restore balance to his shield. Whatever the sorcerers had sent, it had almost finished him. If he was unsure before, he was certain now: he was outmatched.

On hands and knees, he scrabbled away from the ladder, down the tunnel, and out of the sorcerers' line of sight. Clutching his head, he rose and hurried after the others, hunched and weary beyond belief. Ahead of him loped the automaton.

CALDAN APPROACHED THE group from the darkness behind them at a run. He skidded to a walk, and Miranda looked him over, concern on her face. He brushed away her fussing and motioned for them to keep moving. Ahead, man-made walls and floor gave way to natural stone opening out into a cavern.

"You weren't able to stop them?" asked Miranda, loud enough for the others to hear.

Caldan shook his head in defeat. "No. I . . . got rid of two men with them, but the sorcerers . . . they're too powerful."

Amerdan stared at him curiously. "What did you do?"

"I knocked them into the water."

Rennen looked horrified. "Are they . . ." he said. "Did they drown?"

"I don't know," replied Caldan. "Probably."

Elpidia's face was miserable, wide-eyed and trembling.

"It was them or us, Elpidia. It couldn't be helped. Look," he said, indicating with a thrust of his chin, "there's light ahead. We're almost out."

"Yes," confirmed Amerdan, with a probing look at Caldan. "There is." The shopkeeper looked at the automaton as it weaved through the group and continued ahead. "Interesting," he said, eyeing Caldan with respect.

They stepped onto the rough natural stone. For a few minutes, they trudged in silence, walking steadily farther into the cavern. The air was filled with the scent of dirt and a faint musky smell. *Bats, probably*, thought Caldan. It made sense. The engineers who constructed the aqueducts would make use of any caves in the surrounding countryside. Why dig, when it was much easier to use natural formations?

Behind them, the sound of rushing water faded the farther they walked. Caldan remained at the rear of the group, constantly glancing behind, trying to spot movement in the dark, though he thought it more likely the sorcerers would come shielded and he would see the telltale glow.

He maintained his well as they walked, both to keep contact with the automaton as he sent it to scout ahead, and to extend his senses behind the group.

The ground began sloping upward, gently at first, almost imperceptibly, then with an ever-increasing incline.

A tickle touched the edge of Caldan's mind from behind him. He stopped abruptly and turned, scanning the darkness. There had been something . . . a presence . . . but now there was nothing.

The others stopped one by one as they realized he no longer followed.

Caldan prepared to split his well into multiple strings. He reached into his pocket and then flung his hand into the air, releasing a flock of paper birds. Though only narrow strings from his well were required for the birds, his head ached with the strain. A sharp pain stabbed into his mind, and his forehead broke into a sweat. Flashing past his legs, the metal automaton shot back down the cavern.

Flapping their wings in the stale air, the birds flew around him. With a thought, he pushed them out in ever-expanding circles, flying at different levels from low to the floor to head height. He peered into the darkness.

"Keep going," he said to the others. "I'll catch up when I can." He turned to face Miranda as she hesitated. "Go," he commanded once again.

Miranda's mouth narrowed, and she frowned in worry. She turned to usher Elpidia and Rennen toward the light ahead. "Hurry," she said.

Caldan could hear Amerdan's breathing over the faint flapping of wings, he was so close. The shopkeeper had drawn both his knives and held them casually, giving Caldan the strong impression he knew how to use them. Caldan considered drawing the trinket sword but thought better of it. If he needed to run, it would only slow him down.

"They won't be any use," he explained quietly to Amerdan. "Their shields will block our blades."

Looking at his knives for a moment, Amerdan slid them back into the sheaths on his belt. He backed away a few steps, licking his lips. With a shrug, he turned and followed Rennen and Elpidia, passing Miranda, who was heading back toward Caldan.

As she approached, Caldan gave her a disapproving look. "Why aren't you with the others?" he hissed.

"I can take care of myself."

"Normally I would agree—you're one of the strongest people I know, Miranda. But I've no idea what these sorcerers can do. I wish you would stay with the others."

"Oh, for goodness' sake. How far do you think you'd have gotten without me? I handled myself on board the ship, didn't I? What makes you think I can't now?"

Caldan locked eyes with her, dumbfounded, knowing she was right and admiring her courage. He softened, wanting to touch her but not daring to do so. "I just don't want anything to happen to you."

Miranda reached up and touched his face, running her fingers across his scar. "You can't protect me from everything." She sighed and dropped her hand. "Do you think they can mask themselves somehow?"

"I don't know, but I would rather be sure than captured again . . . or dead."

Light flashed briefly in the darkness as one of the paper birds hit a solid surface. Sparkles glittered from the impact and spread across a shield outlining a figure, then flickered out.

Caldan cursed and immediately sent the automaton toward the spot along with the birds. A pulse of force erupted, and all his birds burst into flames. His automaton tumbled backward, metal limbs splayed as it lay in a heap. Strings from his well whiplashed back as they were severed, and his mind exploded with pain.

There was moment of stillness. Paper birds turned to ash, falling to the ground.

Two distinct glows broke through the darkness. Bells and Keys.

With sluggish thoughts, Caldan's mind groped for his wristband and linked to shield himself. He reached for Miranda's hand.

A massive burst of raw energy snapped into him. He tumbled backward onto the ground. Around him, his shield wavered. His wristband vibrated unsteadily and grew hot. It was all he could do to stop the energy penetrating his shield, but after a moment, the brutal initial force diminished, allowing him to draw breath.

Another wave of energy assaulted his shield, pinning him to the ground. His wristband keened under the strain and began to burn his skin.

Caldan cursed and cut his well from his crafting before it failed. Around him, the shield dissolved.

He looked around for Miranda, to warn her to flee. He met her eyes.

She shuddered, stumbled forward onto hands and knees. Her body jerked violently. She stood slowly, blank eyes staring from her face.

Caldan was transfixed with horror. What looked out at him wasn't Miranda. He gave an anguished cry.

In the distance, he heard Bells laugh.

Miranda rose and began to walk toward him, at first unsteadily, then with increasing control.

Caldan couldn't move. Immense pressure crushed him to the ground. He gave Miranda a pleading look, but still she came on. Desperately, he reached for the link to his automaton and found it, infusing the creature with power and sending it toward the sorcerers.

Miranda drew her knife. She knelt beside Caldan and lifted the blade with both hands.

"No," Caldan managed to croak. There was nothing he could do; he was paralyzed, utterly helpless.

She plunged the knife down, stabbing him in the side. Pain enveloped him, and his vision went white. His mind conjured an image of Simmon, controlled by coercive sorcery, hacking Jazintha to bloody ribbons. This is what it must have felt like for the poor woman.

Summoning what strength he could, Caldan pressed a hand to the wound. Once again, his awareness flew through the link to his automaton.

Bells and Keys stood together, shields glowing and arms raised. Around them, the air crackled with gathering force.

Caldan urged his crafting at them.

Out of the corner of his eye, he saw Miranda raise the knife for another thrust.

The automaton reached Bells and Keys. Grunting with exertion, Caldan ruptured the anchor. The forces from his well destroyed it

utterly. A thunderous reverberation echoed in the cavern, and filaments of lightning surged around Bells and Keys. Under the strain,
their shields sparkled blue, then a deep purple as they strove to absorb
the forces assailing them. One of the crafted keys around Keys's neck
melted, and his shield went red. He threw a despairing look at Bells,
then his shield winked out. His skin instantly blackened and smoked.
His body went limp.

Miranda's eyes rolled back into her head, and she collapsed, slumping senseless to the ground. Blood dribbled from her nose.

Bells let loose a wailing cry.

And another cluster of deadly sorcery.

"By the ancestors," groaned Caldan as he opened his well and
scrabbled to link to his wristband. Despite the crafting being hot
and close to failing, it was all he had left. Light sprang up around
him, and he clutched Miranda, covering her with his shield.

The air shook, and flashes of light cascaded as bright as the sun.
Caldan squeezed his eyes shut. Beneath him, the ground rumbled
with violence.

Under his crafted wristband, his skin sizzled . . . He couldn't hold it
any longer. If he did, it would fail, and they would be destroyed in the
process. He felt his wristband begin to fracture. With no choice, he
clutched Miranda to him and cut the link to his well.

His mind writhed with agony, and then, in a blink, it stopped, even
though the assault continued. Not daring to open his eyes, he knew
he was being shielded somehow.

The onslaught lasted longer than he thought possible. Eventually,
the flashes through his eyelids ceased. An overpowering odor of dirt,
molten metal, and above all, lemons filled his nostrils.

He prized an eye open. Around him, the air shimmered with dissipating heat.

Bells scrabbled toward Keys's charred body, whimpering wordlessly.

A glow emanated from under Caldan's shirt. He pulled on his
chain, and the bone ring spilled out, cryptic runes shining with an
inner light. The trinket on his finger lay inert and cold.

The bone ring shielded me? he thought incredulously. *That would mean . . . it's a trinket, too.* Never had he heard of one not made of metal, an alloy sorcerers for generations had tried without success to replicate, the supposed secret of crafting trinkets. Hundreds of years of failed experiments and theories, all based on a false assumption. This was why his family had been murdered, he was sure of it—for *both* his trinkets.

Amerdan walked out of the darkness toward Caldan, clothes singed, hair covered in dust. He held a hand out. "I think I have much to learn," he said cryptically, face expressionless.

"You . . . you came back." Amerdan said nothing, but reached out his hand, and Caldan allowed the shopkeeper to drag him to his knees, hand clutched to his stomach. Blood oozed through his fingers. Miranda lay on the ground unmoving. He kept a hand pressed into his wound to stop the bleeding as best he could. His head, arm, and stomach throbbed with pain. Gingerly, he struggled to his feet, staggering toward Bells. Miranda was injured, but she would have to wait. Bells was his priority. The sorcerer cradled Keys in her arms, fingers entwined in his hair. She sobbed the same words over and over: "Keys, my love, stay with me." Caldan motioned for Amerdan to see to Miranda and moved toward Bells.

She paid no attention to Caldan's approach. He stood behind her, bent over in pain. Slowly, he drew his sword, the trinket entrusted to him by Master Simmon. He raised it high, then brought it down, twisting at the last moment to strike Bells in the head with the flat of the blade.

With a sickening thud, she crumpled unconscious, silver bells tinkling.

Grabbing her by one arm, he dragged her over to Miranda, who still lay in the dirt, Amerdan hovering next to her.

He shuffled to Miranda's side, knelt, and gathered her to him. She stared at him blankly and then blinked. A trickle of saliva ran from the corner of her mouth.

"Wha . . ." she began, then swallowed. "Wha . . ." she tried again, then frowned. She looked down at her trembling hands.

Physically, she seemed whole, but mentally . . . whatever sorcery they used must have been wrenched out when Keys died. Her mind lay in disarray.

Caldan began to weep. First Senira had been killed, then Master Simmon. He'd seen so much death. More, he'd lost everything he'd gained since coming to Anasoma.

And now Miranda . . .

A hand clasped his shoulder, and he looked up into Amerdan's face. "She has been damaged. We should leave her."

Caldan couldn't believe his ears. He shook his head vehemently. "No. I can heal her. I . . ." With rising dread, he realized he *couldn't* heal Miranda. Nothing he'd learned or read talked about healing sorcery. The only thing that made any kind of sense would be for someone versed in coercive sorcery to figure out what was wrong with her mind and how to restore it.

With a deep breath, Caldan wiped his eyes, though they refused to obey him and leaked tears. He stood numbly, helping Miranda regain her feet. She stumbled. He picked her up in his arms.

"Bells," he grated to Amerdan through the pain. "Get her."

The shopkeeper nodded and lifted the limp sorcerer with seeming ease.

Caldan held on to Miranda, and he couldn't think of a reason he'd ever let her go.

THEY EMERGED FROM the cave, scrambling over loose stones scattered across the slight incline. A few bats flew around them, disturbed by their passage. The air changed from cool and damp to warm and dry almost instantly as they moved through the entrance.

Caldan's blood was soaking into Miranda's clothes, but he pushed himself to follow the others up the slope until the top, where everyone had paused to catch their breath. He placed Miranda gently on the ground. He tore off his shirt and tied it as best he could around his waist to stop the bleeding, then noticed it had already stopped.

Elpidia came over to him, concern showing on her face. "Here, let me take a look."

Caldan brushed away her hands and continued to tie the shirt over the wound. "No, it's all right. It's already healing." He saw a questioning—and somewhat hungry—look on her face, but didn't care. He had other things to worry about at the moment.

He looked back at Anasoma, blue flames still flickering atop the walls. They'd come a long way underground and were a fair distance from the city. He breathed a sigh of relief—his first since they'd left the warehouse. He knew that once the Indryallans realized both Bells and Keys were missing, they were bound to send soldiers to search for them, if they didn't already have people combing the tunnels after the commotion of the sorcerous battle.

"By the ancestors," cursed Caldan. Their smooth escape had turned to chaos, complication, and devastation.

He knelt in front of Miranda and touched her cheek. She didn't react, eyes staring dead ahead. Simmon's trinket sword pressed into his back.

Caldan stood and wiped his eyes. He now had two goals—return the sword to the Protectors and heal Miranda. The trouble was, he had no idea if he'd be able to do either. The capital was a long way off . . . and he wasn't sure if the Protectors could do anything against coercive magic.

Master Simmon certainly hadn't been able to.

He glanced at Rennen, whose face was somber, and Amerdan, who had Bells slung over one shoulder. Perhaps she could be persuaded to help. Forced, even.

Whatever it takes, he thought. *Whatever.*

"Rest time is over," he said as he bent to pick up Miranda. "They'll be after us soon, if they're not already."

Somewhere, he knew, was a way to make Miranda whole again. He could feel it in his bones.

AFTERMATH

To the south, in a sheltered cove along the coast, the ship dropped anchor in the shallows and awaited news from Anasoma.

Vasile had been tasked by Gazija with convincing Aidan to join with them, and he spent his time secluded in a cabin arguing with Aidan and his companions.

He expected objections, and he wasn't disappointed.

SAVINE KHEDEVIS APPROACHED the keep in Anasoma, surrounded by a dozen of his followers. Inside, within the cool stone walls, he was greeted briefly by a high-ranked Indryallan soldier, face haggard and marked by strain.

Savine motioned to his faction, and they knelt before the invaders' commander. *For the time being,* he thought to himself, hiding his grimace of distaste. Once Gazija was dead, he could lead his people along the righteous path.

FAR TO THE north, Kelhak, God-Emperor of Indryalla, received news that his forces had taken Anasoma, though at the cost of two of his children. Aboard his personal warship, he commanded the captain to urge the ship to greater speeds.

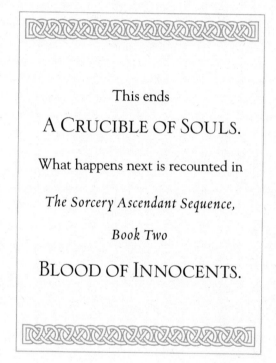

This ends

A CRUCIBLE OF SOULS.

What happens next is recounted in

The Sorcery Ascendant Sequence,

Book Two

BLOOD OF INNOCENTS.

To the Reader,

Having readers eager for the next installment of a series, or anticipating a new series, is the best motivation for a writer to create new stories.

New release sign-up. If you enjoy reading my novels as much as I enjoy writing them, then sign up to my mailing list at http://eepurl.com/BTefL. I promise to notify you only when a new novel is released, so no spam e-mails!

Share your opinion. If you would like to leave a review, it would be much appreciated! Reviews help new readers find my work and accurately decide if the book is for them as well as provide valuable feedback for my future writing.

You can return to where you purchased the novel or simply visit my website at http://www.mitchellhogan.com and follow the links.

There are also a number of websites like Goodreads where members discuss the books they've read, want to read, or want others to read.

Send me feedback. I love to hear from readers and try to answer every e-mail. If you would like to point out errors and typos or provide feedback on my novels, I urge you to send me an e-mail at: mitchhoganauthor@gmail.com.

Thank you for your support, and be sure to check out my other novels!

Kind regards,
Mitchell Hogan

ACKNOWLEDGMENTS

With love and thanks to my wife, Angela. Without her unfailing understanding and support this book wouldn't have been possible.

More love and thanks to my mother, Robyn, who introduced me to *The Hobbit* and the Lord of the Rings trilogy when I was eleven.

Much appreciation to those kind enough to provide feedback and advice on my early drafts, especially Barney Chambers and Valerie Combes.

There are a few people who have my humble heartfelt gratitude: Stephanie Smith, Deonie Fiford, and Kate Forsyth. Their words of encouragement, though they may not realize it, kept my dream alive for so many years.

Special thanks to the mentors and editors who helped sharpen both my story and my writing, Keith Stevenson, John Jarrold, and Derek Prior. Their positive advice and support meant a great deal to me.

ABOUT THE AUTHOR

When he was eleven, Mitchell Hogan was given *The Hobbit* and the Lord of the Rings trilogy to read, and a love of fantasy novels was born. He spent the next ten years reading, rolling dice, and playing computer games, with some school and university thrown in. Along the way he accumulated numerous bookcases' worth of fantasy and sci-fi novels, and he doesn't look to stop anytime soon. For a decade he put off his dream of writing, then he quit his job and wrote *A Crucible of Souls*. He now writes full-time and is eternally grateful to the readers who took a chance on an unknown self-published author. He lives in Sydney, Australia, with his wife, Angela, and daughter, Isabelle.